A Bargain So Bloody

Vasilisa Drake

Copyright © 2025 by Vasilisa Drake

All rights reserved.

No portion of this book may be reproduced in any form without written permission from the publisher or author, except as permitted by U.S. copyright law.

To anyone who has ever wanted a monster who would burn the world for them.

PART I

Chapter 1

I snatched a scrambling rat before it could retreat to its hiding hole, breaking its neck in one smooth motion.

Samara, a princess is not meant to hunt vermin.

That's what my mother would have said if she saw my dirty fingers grab the rat's matted fur, likely as her delicate fingers pinched her nose. I'd have meekly apologized for my unladylike behavior.

The dying squeak chased away the echoes of her imagined reprimand like smoke. It had been more than a decade since I'd last heard her voice, pained and pleading. Now, I went days, a week at a time, without uttering more than the occasional grunt. It was better that way. Safer. It was all too easy to remember I wasn't a lady, and despite my mother's wild wishes, I'd never been a princess.

The prison allowed no delusions.

I slid the carcass into the makeshift pouch in my skirts with the others, and hustled down the hall to check my traps, adding several more unlucky rats to my collection. My cloth-wrapped feet scraped over the rough stone as I worked systematically through the halls. Time. Somehow it passed too quickly in a day, and too slowly in a year.

A dozen rats weren't easy to catch, even with the traps I'd made.

Especially not today.

A new prisoner had come in. That wasn't so unusual. But whoever this prisoner was, he'd set off the rest of the inmates. The halls had echoed with screams for hours, the rough crack of the whip their metronome. The guards liked to have fun with the new ones. When the other prisoners cried out, they'd have the whip turned on them as well.

Catching rats was tricky at the best of times, but the yelling and carrying on had made my job all the harder. They hid in small corners and scratched and bit to try to escape the inevitable, even after they were caught.

Not that it ever worked. Something I knew all too well.

My mother would have thought it was horrific. Me? I was numb to the task after all these years. The disgust of being around dead vermin wears off pretty quickly once you realize it's keeping you away from the living ones.

A BARGAIN SO BLOODY

As I walked into the kitchen, Nelson was at his preferred post, the single half-functional chair in the main servants's chamber. It might as well have been a throne by the way he ordered everyone about. "Hurry up, you lazy shit!" he snapped with his scratchy voice. "Kitchen won't wait all day."

I picked up the pace, taking care not to drop my haul.

Nelson leered at me as I passed. I made a show of speeding up, hoping that would soothe his ego. He wasn't as highly ranked as a guard, but rather was a disgraced noble's son, which made him our superior. He lorded his status over us. He was constantly imagining infractions against him.

That was how you got sent to clean the toilets. It wouldn't have been quite so terrible if everyone took their turn. Instead, Nelson let his favored few skip their shifts, worsening the smell until some unlucky sap was sent to clean up. Unlike the rest of the Witch Kingdom, magic was inaccessible in Greymere, meaning the feces had to be scraped by hand instead of washed away with an enchanted card.

I eased through the doorway, trying to avoid the other servants. The kitchen was half the size it needed to be for the number of prisoners we had. It was the only warm room in the prison, except you couldn't enjoy it. The air was always sticky with sweat from the workers.

I deposited the rats near Cook, who was brewing the main course. He accepted them with a grunt, and I didn't bother to acknowledge him before starting on my next task.

There was always more to do, and if you looked like you didn't have enough for even a moment... *toilets*.

I'd delivered the rats just in time to be added to this supper's stew. Next on my rotation was washing the dishes from breakfast. Technically, Robbie was supposed to do that in the morning, but as Nelson's lone friend and co-bully, he got away with slacking off more than anyone else. Usually, he put the blame on me when the dishes weren't done by the evening.

Washing dishes had some advantages. It was the one place in the prison where we could actually use soap, even if it was the lousiest sliver of soap going. Baths were a thing of the past in Greymere. I got used to the smell after a while, sure. But inevitably, my fingers were plastered with blood after breaking the necks of the rats all day.

The blood was the worst part. It never really left, not completely, no matter how much I scrubbed.

The downside of washing dishes was that it left you exposed in the kitchen. Out of sight, out of Nelson's mind, meant you were safe. The kitchen, which Nelson peered in on with all the impudence of a cat surveying paralyzed mice, left you directly in his line of sight.

It took ages to clean the dishes. Long enough that Cook finished making his rat soup and supper had been dispersed to the prisoners. He poured one cup—a generous one, with big chunks of meat—and left it at my side without a word. I nodded my thanks, my stomach rumbling at the sight.

The nobles at the capital would've been repulsed. But when it's prison slop or starvation, you stop being picky in a hurry. I only got one meal a day, if that, and it was mostly due to Cook's charity.

I placed the last dish in the drying rack and reached for the cup. It was barely warm and would be cold by the time I scurried off somewhere safe to eat it, any heat sucked out by the prison's chill. But I'd be safe, and safety trumped comfort.

I reached for it, and readied to make my exit, when Nelson's nasally voice cut through.

"You've been slacking off," Nelson snapped, appearing so suddenly I just knew he'd been waiting for me to finish.

The kitchen was empty now. I just kept my eyes down. Cleaning the privy at this hour meant I wouldn't sleep until nearly dawn.

He lifted a bowl with an appraising eye, then another. "These are all still dirty."

They weren't, but I ground my teeth and didn't say a single word as he dumped a pile of bowls back into the sink.

"Do it again."

I said nothing, praying to any number of unspecified gods that Nelson would move along once I washed them again. Unfortunately, he wasn't satisfied.

He looked at the cup Cook had left me. It was small, a quarter of a normal portion the others got, even less compared to what Nelson claimed. I braced for him to dump it out and toss the dirty dish into my pile. My stomach clenched at the thought, even though I was no stranger to hunger. Not anymore.

Instead, he looked from the cup, to me, and back. And spat in it.

He didn't say another word, walking away with a spring in his step.

Whatever. I'd eaten worse.

Three years. Just three more years, and I'd be free of this place. Once my sentence was finished, I would go to the Monastery. They would take me in despite my criminal sentence. I'd finally have a place where I belonged. Where I was safe.

I just had to make it until then.

I continued on the dishes, my fingers pruned from the water. By the time I set the last one to dry, it was well past midnight. I stumbled out of the kitchen, the cup of soup clutched between my hands.

I just wanted to rest. Just a few hours.

But Nelson was still at his perch, a smirk on his lips. He slid a glass jar over to me. A healing balm, weak and non-magical.

This day just got better and better.

"You're to see to the new prisoner. Cell 48, Block D."

The one that had set off the other prisoners screaming.

A BARGAIN SO BLOODY

The balm wasn't a gift, not really. Sure, limbs rotting off from infection might sound unpleasant, but in Greymere, the only escape was death. The balm would take the latest captive that much farther from its clutches—though from the hours of whip-cracks I'd heard, it might not be enough.

I was so tired, I dared to ask, "Can this wait until tomorrow?"

Nelson shook his head, not dropping that infuriating smile. The fact he didn't slap me for insubordination was even more worrisome. "This fellow could use a woman's touch after the day he had. The guards were quite diligent with 'em. I heard they didn't leave the cell until after nightfall. Besides, I hear the new guy is a night owl."

His little joke barely registered. *All that whipping had been on one prisoner?*

I snatched the balm from the desk and left before Nelson could come up with some other task. Block D was on the opposite side of Greymere from the kitchens, where the most dangerous prisoners were kept. Not that it mattered. Even the strongest witches on the outside were powerless in Greymere. Cut off from magic, they invariably went mad.

I stuck to the shadows, clutching Nelson's skeleton key in my hand. Theoretically, it should've been safe to wander about the prison since all the inmates were locked up with no chance of escaping.

VASILISA DRAKE

Only a fool would think the worst part of the prison was the prisoners, though.

Three more years.

My footsteps were nearly silent as I approached the cell. The screams had quieted at least, the inmates asleep. I didn't relish waking this one up, but he'd be too weak to attack me if what Nelson said was true about what the guards had done.

I slid the key into the lock and opened the door, the metal letting out a loud, angry creak. A glint of red flared against the darkness. *A rat?* was my stupid thought. But those eyes were far too big for rats.

I dropped the key with a clang.

Nelson had sent me to tend to a vampire.

Chapter 2

I WANTED TO RUN screaming from the cell. If I disobeyed Nelson's order, he'd punish me. He might do something worse than simply sending me to the toilets.

But to have to touch a vampire...

Which was worse? His copper manacles glinted in the torchlight—copper instead of the normal thick iron shackles used on witches. He was bound, arms tied together in front of him, his legs tethered to a stake in the ground where he stood.

My stomach revolted. I swallowed down the bile and set my cup down, grateful I hadn't downed it on my way over.

"Is that supper I smell?"

VASILISA DRAKE

His voice was... unexpected. Stronger than it should have been after the beating he'd taken. Not an animalistic growl, but a silk-smooth voice that curled around me.

"It's not for you. You don't eat food, anyway." My voice was shaky.

"Oh, I can eat." It was almost a purr. "I just have other appetites."

His words made me flinch before I was able to hide it, and I didn't miss his eyes narrow on the movement. He was a predator. Any fear would be taken as a sign of weakness.

I squared my shoulders. Acting meek around Nelson might have helped me survive, but the bloodsucker would just see me as an easy meal.

"I've come to tend you," I said, making up my mind. He was bound. I could deal with this. "But I'll go if you give me a hard time."

It was an empty threat. I had no power here, but it'd be easier if he thought I did.

"Then by all means."

I stepped further into the cell, the door creaking behind me.

The space was dark, only the dim torchlight from the halls offering any guidance. The cells weren't large to begin with, but the presence of the vampire seemed to swallow more space than his build should've justified.

I clutched the jar of ointment like a talisman for protection, sticking close to the edge of the walls until I was behind him.

A sharp inhale through my nose was the only surprise I let myself show. Cruelty and violence had been constant companions in my time at Greymere. But this...

His back was flayed. I'd seen animal carcasses less mangled. I dipped two fingers into the salve, debating where to start. His right shoulder still had the most skin attached, so that was where I pressed. Part of me wanted to abandon the salve, to dig my nails in and finish the job the guards had started. Rip him apart. *Take revenge.*

The exposed flesh oozed blood, a dark red canvas. If he was a monster, what did that make the guards who'd done this?

I swallowed the thought. Of course he deserved it. Worse. Who cared if he looked no different from this angle, with his red eyes turned away from me, than any other male? He was an evil creature. I'd seen exactly the kind of cruelty vampires were capable of.

But I kept my press gentle. It must've been unfathomably painful. How was he even standing? The only hint of his discomfort was a single hiss, cut off with half a breath. Then, nothing. Did vampires even breathe? His chest moved under my touch, but they were the undead. It's not like they needed air.

No, just blood and blood and blood—

"Do you intend to continue, or just tempt me with the sound of your pulse all night?"

His words were unhurried and teasing, like a cat batting a mouse around. Totally belying the mangled state of his back. They snapped me from my dark thoughts. I resumed my movements, collecting more salve and covering his back in large swaths. I wanted to be done with this.

"You—you don't want my blood."

A soft snort. "I don't see why you'd be the authority on that. You're close, and your pulse is pounding like a filly's out on her first run."

"You don't," I insisted. He was in chains, but that did nothing to soothe my nerves. "The rats eat better than I do. The water I drink is half mud. My blood would taste awful."

"With the amount of blood I've lost, I suppose I wouldn't be too discerning," he said glibly. "Lean a little closer, and we can find out."

I pictured it, at his words. Tipping forward, his fangs sinking into me.

Blood and blood and—

I wanted to vomit. I slammed the salve's lid shut. I had mostly finished, but even if I'd barely started, I was at my limit. Let Nelson send me to the toilets for a month. It'd be better than spending another second in this cell.

I backed away, sticking as close to the wall as possible as I left.

"Before you go. Look at me."

A BARGAIN SO BLOODY

His words shouldn't have stopped me, but the vampire's voice was pure command. I obeyed before I even had a chance to think it through.

I hadn't let myself look into his eyes since I'd first walked into the cell. Despite the fact his back was ripped open, he stood tall, proud. His chest was bare, and though the front was bruised as well, it did nothing to hide the definition of his muscles. He had a warrior's body. Odd, for such a parasitic creature. His face, though. Even bloody and bruised it could only be called beautiful. It wasn't a gentle, regal beauty. It was a ruthless kind that, if anything, was enhanced by the cuts on it. His jawline was sharp, casting a shadow over his neck in the torchlight. His brows were stark white, matching his hair.

His red eyes snared me.

"Let me out of my chains."

Unlike his commanding tone, this he spoke in the same soothing tone he'd used before.

Did he think I was insane?

That's what I got for daring to speak with a vampire.

"No."

His brows rose, as if surprised.

"Unlock my chains." The commanding tone returned, promising violence if I didn't obey.

This time I didn't answer. I quickly gathered my supplies and turned towards the exit.

"Free me from my chains, and I'll let you escape with me," he hissed at my back.

VASILISA DRAKE

I slammed the cell door shut behind me.

CHAPTER 3

I BARELY SLEPT. By the time I got back to one of my sleeping spots—it wasn't good to stay in the same place too many nights in a row—it was hardly three hours until I needed to be awake. As usual, I fell asleep quickly. No matter what kind of day I had, I couldn't afford to skip a chance to sleep.

But my dreams were haunted by unnerving red eyes.

Greymere was quiet when I finally woke. My morning routine consisted of tucking away the one threadbare blanket I'd managed to keep from the others for the past year. It also meant I was nowhere near the warmth of the kitchen.

VASILISA DRAKE

The cold stone of the prison floor always left me sore, even after all these years. My back ached. My shoulders were tight. Grooming amounted to little more than cracking my neck and running my fingers through my hair to clear out some cobwebs.

The hollow hunger was a frequent companion. There was no point trekking over to the kitchen for breakfast. If I tried to get some when it was fresh, I inevitably got elbowed away, delayed from starting my chores—which got me in trouble—and usually didn't even succeed.

I was scrawny. I couldn't elbow back. It was better to keep my head down and stay away, so that's what I did.

I didn't have time to waste. At least the witch prisoners had the luxury of sleeping in. I wasn't so lucky. Voids convicted of crimes unlucky enough to be sent to Greymere didn't sit in cells—they served. Born without magic, we were the only ones who could physically tolerate working in Greymere. No void *volunteered* to live without the comforts magic offered. The witches weren't the only prisoners here.

I set off to check my rat traps.

I'd devised the traps from pieces of half-rotted wood, some spare twine, and metal scraps. They would've worked leagues better if I had any food to bait the rats with. Without, I caught at most three on a good day.

I'd gone to Nelson when I'd devised the first prototype. I was young then, maybe nine years old. I'd cast Nelson into the role of a guide, a leader. I'd thought he might be proud of me.

Instead, he snatched the prototype from my tiny hands and threw it on the floor, crushing it under his foot. Of course, that just set off the trap, catching his foot. He yowled, and I'd been so surprised I had actually laughed.

He beat me after that. And I learned not to ask Nelson—not to ask *anyone*—for anything.

Today, the first trap I checked actually had a rat. I made quick work of it, snapping its neck with practiced ease. It should've been a fortuitous start to the day.

I couldn't have been more wrong.

To start, aside from the first, the rats were harder to find than usual. The screams of the prisoners resumed, amplified when the whipping began. The halls of Greymere must've been engineered to carry sound especially easily, because no matter where I went, I couldn't escape it. It wasn't that the screaming was so unusual. After all these years, I could normally ignore it.

But not today. Instead, one question ricocheted back and forth over and over.

Was he screaming?

I couldn't picture it. Even when he tried to order me to release him, his voice had barely risen above its low purr.

Did he really think I would throw everything away to help him?

Perhaps he was simply desperate to escape his fate. They were whipping him. That, I didn't doubt. The wounds on his back would be barely sealed with the salve. A single stroke would tear apart any healing that had come from last night. Could you kill a vampire that way?

Why even capture a vampire? In all my years at the prison, I'd never seen one. All I had seen was every manner of witch be driven mad.

If he doesn't die, will he go mad too?

"Look who finally decided to show up."

I stiffened at Nelson's voice, cursing the vampire for dominating my thoughts so completely I'd failed in my main task.

My official job was to find the rats. The real one? To avoid Nelson by any means necessary.

I couldn't say what Nelson did during the day, except that it seemed to be the same thing he did during the evenings: make everyone around him miserable. The air soured from the scent of alcohol on his breath. Nelson had gotten his hands on some spirits. That *always* made for a worse encounter.

He saw the rat in my hands and snatched it from me. I forced my fingers to loosen, letting him take it.

He lifted it, testing the weight.

"Scrawny." He gave me a look. Did he want me to seem impressed at his powers of observation? We were coming out of winter. *All* of us were starving. "You'll need to find more. Fatter ones."

"There *aren't* any more. They're all scared of the damned bloodsucker!"

The words flew from my mouth before I could stop them. For a moment, we just stared at each other. When was the last time I'd talked back to Nelson?

"Oh yes, the bloodsucker you spent the evening with. The guards have been busy with him again today. Maybe you should pay another visit to him tonight." He gave me a meaningful look.

This time I said nothing. I forced myself to lower my eyes. I didn't need another sleepless night. Nothing could be worse than another evening in the cell with that awful creature.

He tightened his grip around the carcass. "I'll take this for my luncheon. Maybe it'll make you realize you can't slack off under my watch."

A whole rat for himself. My entire morning's work.

I bit down on my tongue so hard it bled. Nelson turned, and I should've been relieved it wasn't worse. Instead, anger rolled through me. Indignation. Feelings I'd do well to forget.

"It's not forever."

I meant the refrain to comfort myself, but Nelson heard it even over the choir of screams that rolled down the hall.

"What was that?"

Nothing. That's what I should have said.

But this time I raised my gaze, forcing myself to really take a look at my bully. I'd spent the night in a cell with a vampire, argued with him, *defied* him. Somehow, Nelson didn't seem quite as scary by comparison. Where the vampire was tall, Nelson's shoulders slouched like he was always falling towards you. His hair was matted, the same dark dirty brown like all of ours was, because even his elevated position among us didn't allow for bathing.

"It's not forever," I repeated. "My sentence. I only have three years left. Then I'll be released from this place. You'll still be here, still taking rats, but I'm going to be free."

I braced for the slap. For the fury. In that moment, I even convinced myself it would be worth it.

But Nelson didn't slap me. His face didn't contort with rage.

He laughed. He laughed so hard the rat he'd stolen dropped to the floor; he clutched his stomach, rolling his head back with laughter.

"Free?" he said between laughs. "You, free? That's the funniest thing I've heard in years."

"Fifteen years. That's my sentence. I've served twelve already." My words were clipped, quick arrows trying to cut through his laughter.

They bounced off Nelson's chuckles uselessly. If anything, they made him laugh harder and harder, until he coughed, and his spit flew at me.

Choke, I thought. I pictured it, wrapping my hands around his neck the way I did the rats. Pictured myself twisting.

"You're too funny. You *really* think they'll let you walk out of here? Caria's tits, that's a good one. I'll have to tell

Robbie. You're so simple, Sam." He loved the sound of his voice dearly. "There's no *end*."

"There is," I protested. "Three more years." *Just three more, and I could leave these dark, scream-filled halls behind and join the Monastery.*

He smirked. "Who d'you suppose is keeping count? Anyone who knew you has forgotten you exist. No one is going to come get you. Think, Sammy."

My normal revulsion to his assigned nickname was drowned out by the roar in my ears as the implication hit me.

Forgotten by everyone.

"Someone has to sign off on your release. And that someone is me. Your sentence is *done* when I write to the king and *say* it's done."

My gut twisted. Technically, Nelson wasn't a prisoner like the rest of us. He was a noble, and while in high society he would've been as valuable as a gutter rat, here he had absolute power.

He grinned at my obvious distress. "Who knows? In another ten, twenty years, Sammy, we could be friends, and you'll talk me into letting the royals know your sentence is finished. But mark my words, you will never leave without my blessing, and you're nowhere close to earning it."

Acid boiled in my stomach, a mix of fury and nausea.

"You can't do that," I protested, even though reality was forcing the walls to close in on all sides. Because yes, he could.

VASILISA DRAKE

My future hinged on Nelson's charity.

I was doomed.

"And who would stop me?" He shrugged, as if it was just a fact of life. "Besides, you're better off in here than out there. Even if ol' King Stormblood himself came down to pardon a gutter rat like you, do you know what kind of life you'd have? No one would hire a filthy thing like you. Even the brothels wouldn't take you, except to have something cheap on the menu. When they used you up, you'd be on the streets. See how much you make begging with your ugly face."

Nelson laughed again, then turned, collecting the rat once more.

This time, I didn't say anything.

His words played on a loop over and over. Twelve years I'd been here. I'd be here ten more. Twenty. Forever, if it was truly up to Nelson. Until either he grew so tired of me he killed me.

Or I killed myself to make it end.

I bent into a corner of the hall and heaved, vomiting up what bit of precious food my stomach had held. The smell, foul as it was, actually drew the rats forward. I killed them with only half a mind, still turning over Nelson's speech. Even as I killed their brethren, they came forward. They were starving, and any chance of food, at survival, however disgusting, was worth it to them.

Did they know they were doomed?

One came slower, dragging a trap half caught on its neck, squealing, squealing. I snapped its neck. Put it out of its misery.

I collected the last of them and brought them to Cook.

Nelson left me alone. Apparently, he'd had his fill of tormenting me today.

But there would be tomorrow.

And the day after. And the one after that.

He's lying. He has to be. I nearly vomited again in the sink, but there was nothing in me but the barest bit of water. The acidic taste clawed my throat while I forced myself to swallow it down. Now was not the time to show weakness.

Nelson's taunts played over and over in my head.

My life.

Forever.

If Nelson had his way, I'd never make it to the Monastery.

I'd never see the sun again.

I can't do this. I can't.

Death on my terms would be better than a life like this. A life of dark hallways, of killing rats, of Nelson's taunts.

I took my time with the dishes, my mind clouded and hot. Even when the kitchen emptied, I kept scrubbing dish after dish, my mind turning over what I'd learned. I'd thought about escaping before—it was impossible. Especially for someone like me.

But maybe not for everyone.

VASILISA DRAKE

Once everyone else had gone to sleep, I tip-toed behind Nelson's desk and slipped the skeleton key into my pocket. I hid in the shadows and kept my footsteps silent, counting the cells until I hit number 48.

The key slid into the oiled lock without a sound.

Red eyes flared open, meeting mine.

"I'm going to let you out."

Chapter 4

THE VAMPIRE'S WHITE BROWS drew together. "What changed?"

"I don't confide in vampires." I drew a breath. "But I'll make you a deal. I'll unlock your shackles. In exchange, you get me out of Greymere, unharmed."

The truth was, even if the bloodsucker agreed, I had no guarantee he'd follow through. But what choice did I have? Even if he killed me, he'd only be accelerating my fate.

"You have my word."

It should've been hard to make myself step into the room. To betray my country and every value I held dear. To willingly unleash this beast on Greymere. But like a cornered animal seeing a sliver of a chance at escape, I barreled forward.

This late at night, the cell was utterly dark. The faint torches from the hall barely reached the bars. The vampire's red eyes seemed to glow, tracking my steps into the cell.

The chains wrapped all around his legs, with locks on both feet and hands. I started with the feet. I didn't want to be kneeling before him when his hands were free, even if we theoretically had a temporary alliance.

I slid the skeleton key into the lock of one, then the other. The manacles snapped open, but the vampire didn't make a move to kick them away, even though the skin under them was covered in blisters. I tugged them away as quietly as I could to avoid the telltale sound of metal against stone. Next came the hands. I rose to my feet, adjusting my body so I wasn't directly facing the vampire. I'd been close to him last night, but being in front of someone was a different kind of closeness. Standing slightly to the side, I could see his back. If possible, it looked even worse than yesterday.

"I'm sorry to say they undid your efforts," he said, as if reading my thoughts.

Heat rushed across the back of my neck. Caught. I shouldn't care. He was just a vampire. But something like shame licked at me all the same.

"I'm not surprised." They only ever healed to inflict more pain.

A BARGAIN SO BLOODY

I slid the copper handcuffs off. I could've discarded them like the others. Instead, I slid them into my skirts, cushioning them as best I could.

The vampire slid his hands over his wrists. The only hint of discomfort.

"I suppose if you knew how to escape this prison, you'd have done it yourself," the vampire mused.

I exhaled through my nose. "Of course I know the way out. The trouble is there's only *one* way out, and it's manned with half a dozen guards at every hour of the day." Not to mention the patrols that went through the halls. But nothing ever happened at Greymere, so they were light, and I knew their assigned routes. "Can you handle them?"

Stupid. I should've asked *before* releasing the beast.

A sardonic twist of his lips. "Six mortal men? How will I ever survive?"

The movement revealed just a hint of canine, unnaturally long and sharp.

I stumbled back.

Blood and blood and—

He sighed, and the casual nature of it shook me from my panic. "So skittish. Relax, mortal. Six or sixty makes no difference."

I swallowed the bile in my throat, and with it any thoughts of guilt. It was too late to turn back now. "Follow me."

VASILISA DRAKE

A vampire at my back was unsettling at best, but I didn't trust him to not draw attention stumbling around Greymere. The last thing we needed was someone alerting the prison guards of an escape. The guard routes looped through the cell blocks, so I led us around towards the kitchens. It was a risk, but if we continued straight down, we'd definitely hit the patrol, and they'd raise the alarm.

After years of practice, my steps were silent. The vampire's were effortlessly silent. He was so quiet, I kept wanting to look back to confirm he was really there. Once was enough. My silent shadow was staying very, very close.

Halfway down—seventy-eight steps from the bottom, precisely—I paused. My plan for the vampire had been half-thought-out at best. But going down this particular staircase offered me another opportunity I hadn't explained to the vampire. I bent down to the loose stone I hadn't removed in years. My last connection to my family, hidden away. A necklace I'd been given as a child. I couldn't leave without it.

The vampire's gaze burned. My body blocked his view as I slid the contents of the hiding spot down the front of my shirt, tucking them between the band of fabric and my chest.

I stopped just before the last step and waited, listening.

I could barely hear anything over the roar of my own heart. I drew forward, slowly.

No one will be there.

A BARGAIN SO BLOODY

I forced myself forward. A glance out said the area was clear. The hallway had no shadows to hide in, no curves to hide behind. But it was late enough, everyone should be asleep, tucked away in different corners. Once we got past this long hall, we'd be just a few quick turns from the entrance.

"Who's there?" someone slurred.

Shit.

I should've bolted. But a decade of instinct made me stop and turn to the voice.

Nelson emerged from the kitchen, a bottle of spirits in his hand.

"You..." He braced on the doorway, rubbing a hand over his eyes. "You insane bitch! You set the vampire—"

Crack.

One second, the vampire had been by my side. Next thing I knew, he was in front of Nelson, twisting his head around.

Nelson collapsed with a *thud*, his neck at an unnatural angle.

"You... you killed him."

"How observant." His words were... bored. He'd just snapped Nelson's neck, the man who had made my life hell for a decade, and he was bored.

I could do nothing but blink. *Monster.* He was a monster.

"Tell me, mortal, what do you think I'm going to do when we reach the guards?"

He'd kill them. I knew it. I'd told myself I was okay with it—my freedom for their lives.

Maybe I'm a monster too. Especially because when I gave Nelson's body one last look, there was no grief, no regret. Just dark satisfaction.

Those next hallways were a haze. Our steps were silent; no one had heard Nelson's last words. My heartbeat crashed against my eardrums over and over, louder with every *thump*.

We rounded the final corner.

One spotted us. "Prisoners escaping!"

The other guards turned to us at once and began to move towards us.

The vampire stepped in front of me, blocking me from their view.

"Stay out of the way," he growled at me.

I had no delusions he was protecting me—only trying to make his battle easier. He'd hear no protests from me.

Then they collided. The clang of metal pierced the air. Even unarmed, the vampire made quick work of the king's soldiers. He snapped one's neck, same as Nelson. The next, he used as a shield while a third attacked. He tossed the body at the third, then moved to the fourth.

"He's got a thrall!" another shouted, leveling his sword at me.

I didn't know what a thrall was, but the guard charged at me, sword high.

I screamed.

A BARGAIN SO BLOODY

The vampire slipped from his fight in an instant. The guard never reached me. The vampire threw the guard against the door so hard the metal *dented*.

The remaining two didn't have a chance.

One, he killed with a dead guard's sword. The next, the vampire slipped behind and bent the man's neck sideways, killing him instantly. But he didn't drop the body. He bent his mouth over the man's neck and pressed against it.

I stood frozen, unable to look away. *I unleashed a monster*.

All the guards, dead. Because of me. Because of my choice.

He released the guard's pale corpse a moment later, letting it slide to the floor and stepping over it like it was nothing but trash. He wiped his lips with the back of his hand, smearing the remainder of the guard's blood. His ruby eyes glowed even brighter when he leveled his gaze at me.

My knees shook. *Was I next?*

"W-we had a deal," I stammered.

"Of course." Despite the violence, the words were the same hypnotic lull he'd used before. "Now, to leave."

The massive door stood before us, the floor slick with blood. I made myself ignore it and forced myself to believe that my heel nearly slipped in a puddle of water, nothing more. The vampire went to the door, testing the handles. It was locked, of course. I cursed. I hadn't seen this mechanism before. My skeleton key would be useless. I'd need time to figure out—

Boom!

The vampire had thrown one of the fallen guards past my head straight through the door.

Chapter 5

THE RUINED DOORS COLLAPSED with a thud, and I stumbled out of Greymere.

The sound barely registered. I could scarcely breathe, tipping my head back to take in the sky.

The three moons glowed overhead, almost painfully bright after a decade of waning torchlight. How could the sun be brighter than this? My dreams had lost the vividness, the way you could see the light radiate from each of them. Phrygia, the dancing moon, was nearly full. Caria, the walking moon, and Lagina, the running moon, were scarcely slivers. The taste of the night air was soft on my tongue, like an embrace. It was just newly spring, then, but unseasonably warm.

Or maybe that was from the sweat that coated my back after our frantic run to escape.

Our run.

My shoulders stiffened. I'd been so lost in the sight of the three moons that I'd noticed little else. But the area around me hadn't. The forest surrounding Greymere was eerily quiet. A great predator lay in their midst.

Right behind me.

I turned back to the vampire. I'd half-expected him to take off the moment he was out of the prison. There were no guards outside to stop us; no one ever tried to *enter* Greymere without invitation. His silver hair glinted in the moonlight. His red eyes were fixed on me, but for the first time, they lacked that raptorial glint.

I fought the urge to wipe a sweat-soaked lock of hair from my face. Now that I remembered his presence, I didn't dare take my gaze away from him.

How easily they could kill humans. Memories of blood, of flesh rending from bone as easily as one tore off a piece of bread, flashed in my mind. I swallowed.

The moment stretched on, and I felt the last thing I expected around a bloodsucker.

Awkward.

I shuffled on my feet, edging back. "Well. Thanks for helping me get out. You've held up your end of the bargain."

"I have."

His voice was different outside the walls of Greymere. Irrationally, it reminded me of the night breeze.

Then what are you waiting for? I thought irritably.

"The western border is closest." I pointed in the direction, which, naturally, was the opposite way I intended to go. True, we were several days's ride from vampire territory, but witches avoided settling near the borders. Greymere was the farthest outpost in the Witch Kingdom, and it was still nearly a respectful distance from vampire territory.

"I'm aware."

But still, he stood there, looking at me.

I was loath to turn my back on a vampire, but it seemed he wasn't leaving until I did. *He hasn't killed me yet.* It wasn't the most reassuring thought, but it was the best I could manage with my heart pounding so loudly I could barely hear myself think.

He'd just drained the guard. *He could drain you too*, my vicious mind hissed. But surely he wasn't hungry now. I just needed to escape before that fact changed.

"I'm... just going to head out, then." To find a Monastery outpost that would take me in before word spread, and I was hunted down.

One step back, still facing him. Then another. When he didn't move, I began to twist away in earnest, but his voice cut through as sharp as any of the guard's blades.

"No. You're not."

Chapter 6

My heartbeat accelerated, pounding so fast I could scarcely breathe. "Yes, I am." Mad. I had to be mad to argue with a vampire. *Be silent and survive*. Words I'd lived by my entire life, even longer than I'd been in Greymere. But this night was so far out of the realm of my reality, I could scarcely believe it wasn't one big hallucination. "We had a *deal*."

A deal I must have been a fool for believing would protect me. A desperate fool.

"And I upheld my end of the bargain, seeing you safely out of this wretched prison. However, you'll hardly survive on your own."

I stiffened, but the vampire gave no notice.

A BARGAIN SO BLOODY

"The guards will be found at the next shift change. This will hardly go unpunished."

"You're the one who killed them," I protested.

"You're the one who set me free, dove." He rolled his eyes and began to tick his observations on his fingers. "They'll have hounds on your scent, and tracking spells too, once they can convince a witch to come to this cursed place. You'll be executed for treason before the end of the week. And that's all assuming a troll or kobold doesn't get to you first. Your *only* chance to survive is through me protecting you."

I'd rather a kobold kill me than a vamp. I wanted to hurl the words as I fled, but if I ran, the vampire would catch me. He'd killed six guards like it was nothing.

If he wanted me dead, I'd already be in bloody pieces. My feet remained rooted in the ground. "Why would *you* want me to stay with you? I'll just slow you down."

The vampire canted his head to the side, studying me. Whether he'd expected me to immediately bow to his wishes or to stubbornly refuse, I wasn't sure—probably the former—he hadn't expected questions.

But he'd said the magic word: survive.

"Perhaps I'll want a snack."

Absolutely not. I'd rather die than let a vampire feed on me. There was nothing left in my stomach to vomit up, but if there had been, I'd have lost it all then. My fingers shook as I tried to reach for my skirt pocket, clasping for the cursed copper cuff like it might save me against this beast.

"Or perhaps not. You smell utterly repugnant. I'd likely get a tastier meal from a half-rotted animal carcass," he drawled, wrinkling his nose slightly.

I'd never been more grateful for the lack of hygiene at Greymere.

"Though it's true I'd move faster without you, you can still be useful to me. I need to pay a visit to Apante."

The City of Answers. "But you're a vampire." The oracle magic there would never serve him, never give him what he needed.

"How observant." A flash of teeth, this time almost mischievous. "But *you* are decidedly *not*."

That was true—I could get him the knowledge he craved, whatever it was. This definitely made more sense than him continuing to protect me out of the goodness of his unbeating heart. But it would be another betrayal of my kingdom. "What answers do you seek there?"

"Sorry, dove, I don't confide in smelly mortals." He took a step closer, sensing me wavering. "You don't trust me. That's wise. But you're safer with me than without, especially since I could use your assistance."

My stomach twisted. Above, the sky had already lightened from utter darkness to a deep mauve. The guard change would happen soon. I didn't want to be anywhere near the prison when the bodies were discovered. If I went with the vampire, I could still find refuge in the Monastery.

Apante would have a big outpost—big enough to protect me if any of the king's men came searching.

"Fine."

And with that, I gained a bloodsucker for a traveling companion.

Once I agreed, the vampire wasted no time setting off. We traveled three days with little rest. He didn't seem to care much for either of our comforts, but I wanted as much distance between us and Greymere as possible, so I didn't protest.

We mainly traveled during the night. I was so perpetually exhausted that switching to sleeping during the day wasn't a big adjustment. If anything, it was easier. After so many years of darkness, the sunlight was almost disturbing in its glory.

We did walk during the day as well, however. I'd thought vampires were unable to stand sunlight; my vampire apparently just found it irritating and stuck to the shade. In fact, there were a great many things about the vampire that didn't match what I'd thought. He didn't act anything like the uncontrollable fiend that haunted my memories. He moved fast, much faster than me, but whether that was because he was a vampire or simply that his legs were several inches longer than mine was hard to say. His eyes were the telltale red, but after a day or so, I found it less terrifying and more just a bit unsettling. He didn't bully or taunt me. In fact, he barely spoke at all, which was an improvement over my experiences with Nelson.

We slept on the forest floor; we'd need to find proper shelter eventually, but right now we were in silent agreement to rough it. The vampire slept on his stomach, his bare back exposed and still shredded. Once, as we settled to the ground, I saw him cover a wince—a reminder he was, if not a living creature, then a creature that could feel pain all the same.

Truthfully, the forest floor was soft compared to the places I'd slept during the past few years. As bad as traveling with a vampire was, there was one major benefit: Everything knew he was the most dangerous creature around and steered clear.

On the fourth day, I woke to him returning to the clearing we'd settled in from the thick of the forest.

Blood colored his lips. My own parted at the sight. Just when I was getting close to—not forgetting, exactly, or accepting, but at least adjusting to the vampire—

Blood and blood—

Those blood-red eyes rolled at my palpable horror. "Relax. It's not human, just a stray deer."

"You might have brought the deer back with you," I groused. I scavenged what I could of plants when we walked, but I wasn't confident I could tell nightshade berries from blueberries after all these years of rat soup, so my pickings were conservative. I'd never spent much time in the forest, and I didn't have any cards imbued with healing magic. I was used to eating little. It didn't stop my stomach from rumbling at the realization he'd had a deer, fresh meat, in his hands and just... left it wherever.

"Catch one yourself if you're hungry," was all he said.

But the next day, a rabbit, drained of blood, was by my head when I awoke.

I couldn't force the words, *Thank you*, out of my mouth. Not even when he said nothing as I took the time to dress and cook the rabbit, eating my first real warm meal in years. I had no utensils, so I ate with my hands, crouched over the small fire I'd made to cook it on.

It was *delicious*. Tender and juicy. I gripped the food closer to my mouth. My mother would've been horrified. My stomach could scarcely believe it was properly eating and threatened to cramp, but I refused to stop.

Only when I was nearly done with the rabbit did I catch the vampire watching me. He leaned back against a tree, arms crossed over his bare chest. His white hair fell forward over his eyes, but I felt them acutely.

"You'd be a wonder with fangs," he mused.

Was he mocking me? From a vampire, that was probably a compliment.

The thought of being turned into one of his kind made me lose the last remnants of my appetite. I buried the bones and covered the fire. The forest was colder at night, so it was good to move. We had no spare clothing, no layers. We were lucky we'd avoided any bad weather.

The food in my stomach put a spring in my step, even if the sensation of being full was disorienting. I wasn't exactly sure how far away Apante was. I hadn't seen so much as a map since I was a small child. The only thing I was confident in was that we were going north since Phrygia and Lagina were at our back.

The night we'd escaped had been a fever dream. The next few nights were, too, as if things were half-happening to another person while I watched. Now, the haze seemed to settle. I had escaped Greymere. I was traveling with a vampire. I had betrayed my country, resisted my sentence, and set free one of our mortal enemies. Even if I helped the vampire and then escaped to the farthest corner of the kingdom, I'd still be a criminal.

"Stop thinking so much. It's distracting."

I stumbled behind the vampire. I always walked two steps behind him. How could he tell what I was thinking?

"Can you read minds?" I asked.

He huffed. "I don't need to read your mind to feel the cogs turning between your ears. Spit it out."

I wasn't about to confide in the vampire. Instead, I asked the other question on my mind. "Why isn't your back healing?"

The skin was still ripped several days later. Scabs had started to form. There were blisters along his broad shoulders. Blood was caked around. It looked impossibly painful. And since it didn't feel right to walk side-by-side with the vampire, that had been my view for the past few days.

He turned back, an arched brow raised as if surprised this was my question.

"A few reasons. First, we've been walking during daylight hours to make up for the fact you're so slow. If we limited ourselves to the cover of darkness, the guards would catch up in a heartbeat—if they're foolish enough to pursue us, that is. It would take some horses soon to put proper distance between us and them. Even you must know the sun is no friend to vampires."

So the sun did do more than just make him irritable. Good to know.

"Then there's the animal blood." He grimaced. "It's not what we're meant to eat. It'll keep me alive, but little more."

Meant to eat. Like it was natural to feed on people.

Why didn't he try to bite me, then? There was nothing I could do to stop him.

That question, though, I kept to myself. I didn't need to be giving the vampire any ideas.

"Would the salve help?"

He paused in his step, just slightly. So slightly that anyone watching less closely would have missed the moment of hesitation. For once, I'd truly surprised him instead of the other way around. "The salve... of course the salve would help. I'm healing like a cursed mortal at the moment. But unless you know how to make more..." He stopped and turned to me, his lips thinned in annoyance. "You took some with you?"

He read the answer on my face.

"By the blood, why didn't you say something?"

I hadn't said anything because I'd planned to keep it for myself, either to use or barter with when I reached a nearby town. But seeing him suffer like that, knowing it was due to my slow speed that he had to face the sun, made me feel guilty. "Does it matter? The point is, I do."

"You should have told me," he snarled, his fangs catching the glint of the moonlight. "I can't protect you if I'm weak."

Did he really expect me to believe my safety was his biggest concern? Besides, I'd seen how he'd dealt with the guards—saw it every night when I closed my eyes. Even weakened, he was a monster.

"We'll stop here," he announced.

It was early, for our standards anyway. Dawn was nearly an hour off. "Shouldn't we keep going? You're the one who keeps mentioning how slow we're traveling. They'll have horses."

"Don't pretend like you aren't exhausted."

"I'd rather be tired than dead," I snapped. "Let's keep going."

The vampire sat on a fallen tree trunk, stretching his legs. From this angle, he was below me, tilting his head up to meet my gaze. Yet it still felt like he was looking down on a lowly human.

"I'm not going any farther until you put that salve on my back. And since you're so twitchy, it'll probably take you until dawn to work up the courage to do so, even though it's in your best interest."

Twitchy? Was that what he called having an extremely rational fear of creatures that could tear me limb from limb in a matter of seconds? I took the jar from my pocket and threw it right at his torso. He caught it instantly, not so much as flinching.

"Do it yourself." Let him tend to his own wounds.

"Or," he drawled, tossing the jar up and down as he considered me with those awful red eyes, "I could drink some of your blood and heal in an instant. Your choice."

Since I'd rather turn myself over to the Crown than let the vampire feed on me, I chose the other option.

I despised the shaking in my arm as I took the ointment back. The vampire turned wordlessly, point made. I settled behind him on the log. It was almost like the night I'd met him. Except this time, instead of obeying an order to deal with him while he was bound and powerless, I was choosing to heal him. And he was choosing to just... let me.

The copper cuffs I'd snagged sat heavy on my thigh. My one possible defense if he attacked me, though I was probably deluding myself in thinking I'd get a chance to use them. Maybe when he slept, if I needed to get away. But again, I was here by choice. I thought I'd fallen far when I was sentenced to serve at Greymere. Now, I was teamed up with the mortal enemy of all witchkind.

The antiseptic smell of the ointment tickled my nose as I opened the jar and dipped two fingers in. Once again, I started from the shoulder.

"Will we keep walking after I do this?" I was still anxious about the thought of the guards catching us. All it would take is one well-aimed arrow and I'd be dead. I didn't have so much as a fortifying card, let alone any proper defensive ones.

"You can rest easy. If they find me, I'll take care of them."

Then more people would die because of me. Because I'd traded their lives for my freedom. An immoral choice, but it was impossible for me to pick anything other than survival.

But they'd be chasing the vampire. They'd probably assume he had killed me by now, right? While there was magic that could find guilty parties in the kingdom, it wouldn't specifically seek me out if the vampire was the prize.

"If they're hunting you, then I'm not any better off than on my own." They had caught him before, but I didn't point that out, too eager for any justification to split up. "We could split up. You'll be faster without me."

"So quick to be rid of me, human?" His voice was low, teasing. "And how do you suppose you'll fare against the trolls?"

A BARGAIN SO BLOODY

"We haven't seen any trolls," I reminded him.

He chuckled, the large muscles on his back rippling with the movement. "Because you're with me, and even creatures as stupid as trolls know better than to mess with vampires. Besides, you forget we have a deal. You're going to help me in Apante. Then you'll be free to do as you wish. By blood, you could join that cult of a monastery. Even the king wouldn't come for you then."

Shock rippled through me and all I could do was stare. Was my plan so obvious? The Monastery was one of the few sanctuaries for voids like myself. Those with magic had all the power in the Witch Kingdom, but the Monastery would take in voids as disciples to serve in their ranks. It was my only chance to live a life after deserting my post.

I frowned. How did the vampire know all this though?

The silence stretched between us as I smoothed the salve over his rough skin. Seventh hell, they'd done a number on his back. Yet he just sat there, letting me apply the healing ointment without so much as fidgeting. I slid two fingers into the container again and targeted a particularly bad spot on his back. By mistake, I misjudged the depth of a wound and hit what was an especially sensitive part. Other prisoners had hit me, sometimes, for that kind of thing. Those in pain liked to inflict it on others, even if they were helping them.

The vampire didn't move at all. The only hint of pain was a barely audible hiss that could very well have been the leaves rustling.

Were vampires naturally so still? Or did he force himself to stay in one place because I was so "twitchy," and he worried I'd run off if he moved too quickly?

I can't protect you if I'm weak.

Laughable. As if anyone had ever been able to protect me. And yet, if I imagined anyone other than a vampire saying the words, I might have tucked them in my chest and held on to them, precious as gold coins.

"Thank you," I eventually said. "For the rabbit."

He waved it off. "Think of it no more."

The rabbit was more than I'd eaten most weeks. I *would* think of it. As I slept, when the gnawing pain I'd almost grown numb to was gone. When I woke, and my first thought wasn't of food.

Finally, his back was covered. The jar was two-thirds empty. Flecks of blood were interspersed in the ointment. Unlikely anyone but the most desperate would trade for it now. Then again, if I joined with the Monastery, I might not need to trade.

I moved back and stood from the log, adjusting the jar in my skirts as I scanned for which part of the ground I might like to sleep on tonight. I braced to take a step, then paused. "My name is Sam." I wasn't sure why I offered him my name. He'd likely never use it, continuing to call me *human* or *mortal*. "Samara."

"Samara," he repeated. "I'm known as Raphael."

Raphael. A monster with a name.

"You're quiet, for a human, Samara," the vampire murmured after a long moment.

Talking seldom got me anything but trouble.

"And you're sane, for a vampire, Raphael."

He chuckled, the sound like storm clouds over the moon. "Only sometimes."

We settled into our respective spaces, giving each other a wide berth. There wasn't much to our sleeping ritual beyond claiming our spaces and shutting our eyes.

Maybe because we'd stopped earlier than usual, though, I lay there awake. The three moons would soon be chased away by the sun.

And instead of waking with the hunger on my mind, I woke with a name on my lips.

Chapter 7

Learning the vampire's name shouldn't have changed anything.

In many ways, it didn't. No more than the rabbit I woke up to the next morning, neatly drained of blood. Or the way Raphael watched me eat, any semblance of my once fine manners long gone.

It was late in the night when we veered close to a lake. Excitement thrummed through me at the sight, at the thought of possibilities. Clean drinking water. Buckets and buckets of it. I hadn't submerged my body in water since I'd been a small child, oblivious to the luxury. Dirt caked my skin in layers upon layers. When I'd first arrived at Greymere, I'd done my best to maintain the fastidious habits my mother instilled in me. Of course, most of them involved someone doing everything for me, which had no longer been an option. Cleanliness was a losing battle, and my useless efforts cost me precious time I could've spent sleeping. My nose had gone blind to the stench in a matter of weeks; the men of Greymere certainly didn't waste any effort cleaning. Anyone who had leverage used it for extra food or alcohol rather than something as mundane as soap. And I never had anything to bargain with anyway. But there, glittering in the moonlight, was a lake.

"Your heart is racing. Why?"

"It's nothing," I mumbled.

We couldn't afford to waste time stopping at the lake. At best, when we got closer, I'd veer off long enough to take several long sips of water. That would be enough for me. It had to be.

He narrowed his gaze at me, brows furrowing. That was one thing that had changed since I'd learned his name. Now, instead of lingering two paces back, I walked shoulder to shoulder with the vampire.

"You want something."

"I don't." I did. Desperately.

His gaze flicked past me to the lake. His expression didn't change, but I sensed him putting the pieces together.

"We may as well stop here," he declared. "Besides, you reek. You can do something about it over there." He lifted a hand to the lake in a careless gesture.

I wrinkled my nose. "You're no fresh lilac yourself."

Raphael grinned. "Then perhaps I should bathe with you."

I stumbled at his words, and he chuckled. "Don't like the idea of bathing with a vampire? Then don't complain."

I huffed and broke his gaze. The trouble was, my shock wasn't from the thought of seeing the vampire naked. It was from the thought of bathing with any man at all. Or any man who looked the way Raphael did—broad-shouldered, towering over me, with a face that would have been arresting even without the red eyes and the elegant, savage panes nearly carved from marble.

"I'll leave you to it," Raphael declared when we reached the lake.

My neck snapped back. "You're leaving?"

"Did you want me to watch?"

My cheeks flushed. "I don't want to be eaten by a... a kobold!"

"Relax, dove. I don't scent any kobolds nearby. I'm going to get some dinner of my own and see what's ahead. I'll be back in an hour, two at most."

With that, he disappeared back into the woods.

I was alone for the first time in days. My shoulders relaxed immediately. There were knots in my back just from how I constantly tensed around the vampire, even though I was forced to admit he hadn't actually done anything to me—yet. But there wasn't long enough for me to lie about and massage them.

The first thing I did was fix a small fire. I wasn't sure when I'd get the chance to wash my clothes again, so I stripped and dunked them in the lake, then set them to dry by the fire. I unwrapped the band of fabric that pressed over my chest, slipping out the necklace I'd taken from Greymere. The fabric was thin, not really a proper undergarment, but it was the best I'd managed since clothing was hard to come by in the prison. Most of what I had worn through the years were hand-me-downs from dead prisoners.

With my clothing settled, I went to the lake. Phrygia's full glow lit the water around me, chasing away some of the darkness. The water was cool, bordering on cold, but I didn't care. The water wasn't deep, which was good since I wasn't the best swimmer.

I cupped my hands and splashed my face, clawing off the layers of dirt and grime with my nails. Then I gulped more water from my cupped hands, trying to take advantage of this chance. I had no soap, so I made up for it with hard scrubbing. Tall stalks grew at the edge of the lake, so I snapped one off and tested it, then used it to scrape at the years of filth that coated my body. My skin burned bright red under the harsh ministrations, but I savored the feeling of my clean skin. My hair, I rinsed as best I could, frowning at the color. It darkened as years of dirt and dust fell out, turning from a hazy brown-gray to sable black. Unrecognizable.

Just like my situation.

Free. I was free.

When tears pricked at my eyes, I splashed more water on my face to chase them away before they could fall. *I'm never going back there.* Twelve years, gone. But if I was smart, careful, I could have more than what they'd robbed me of.

More was a dangerous thought. But seeing the new color of my hair, feeling my skin without the weight of dirt and dust, it seemed almost possible.

A rustle in the forest snapped me from my thoughts. Raphael rounded the curve of the lake, coming into view past the border of stalks. I yelped and sank down to my neck, my hands crossed protectively.

"You said two hours!"

"At most. It's been over an hour, anyway," he said dismissively.

Had it really? First hell damn me, I'd lost track of time.

"Go away," I snapped. "I need to dress."

"But what if there's a kobold?" His tone was as innocent as a child's.

A mischievous child. I squeezed my arms tighter, hoping he couldn't see into the water. "Then it'll eat me. Now, go!"

He didn't reply, but he took loud, deliberate stomps, unlike his usual silent steps.

A BARGAIN SO BLOODY

I waited another beat, then exited the water, shivering as the night air surrounded me. The advantage of my clothing being threadbare was at least it didn't need much time to dry. The fire had only half dried my skirts, but I was so glad to have them clean that I didn't care. I tucked my few meager possessions back into their hiding spots.

Raphael stepped into view a moment later. He now wore a simple shirt and a cloak, hood down. A matching set was in his hands. Where had he gotten them? Stolen, certainly. From whom? I decided against asking—I didn't want an answer, and I wasn't too proud to reject stolen goods, so there was no point in posturing.

He froze several feet from me though. His jaw stiffened. The look he gave me had every nerve in my body screaming to run. Like I was looking at a barely restrained animal.

Like a cornered rat, I froze.

"What?" I asked when the silence stretched uncomfortably long. *Maybe he's not thinking of eating you. Maybe his leg had a cramp.*

He shook his head slightly, and the predatory aura around him faded away like smoke. "You smell... different... without the stench of that prison on you."

You'd be a wonder with fangs.
You smell different.
He was a wizard with compliments.

"Well, I didn't have any perfumes, so it'll have to do," I huffed.

He continued as if I hadn't spoken. "The clothes help mask it still, at least."

"Mask what?" I asked.

"No matter." He tossed the second cloak at me. "There's a village just a few miles away. We'll rest early tonight and reach there midday tomorrow."

Chapter 8

A village shouldn't have been scarier than a vampire.

But Raphael, whatever else he was, was only one person. The town was... so much more. Sounds and scents warred for my attention. The afternoon sun blazed overhead, warming the crown of my head. The cloak Raphael had gotten from who-knows-where was wrapped around my shoulders; Raphael wore a matching one, the hood drawn low to hide his red eyes and shield him from the sunshine.

My attention bounced between the different sights, my steps slow and unsure. When we'd finally broken through the forest onto the main path and the rooftops had come into view, I'd frozen in the spot. Raphael had reached for me, to urge me along. That had startled me enough that I kept moving, even though it felt like I'd spilled into another world.

A boy ran towards us, chasing a stray ball.

A child.

Gods, it had been so long since I'd seen one. My mind had convinced me the only other people who existed were men between fifteen and thirty-five, who served time in Greymere. But... here was a boy, with soft brown hair that stretched in every direction, and outstretched, unafraid hands that reached for the ball.

My throat tightened.

Raphael toed the ball with shoes he'd stolen from some poor fool, and it landed easily between the boy's hands. The boy giggled, clutched his prize to his chest, and ran off in another direction in search of fresh amusement.

"We'll get supplies while we're here," Raphael announced.

I eyed his stolen items. "We have no money."

He reached a palm out to me, a small leather pouch in it. I took it and startled at the sound of coins clinking together.

"Where'd you get this?"

His face was hidden by the cloak, but I knew he was judging me for my silly morals. "I found it with your cloak. Do you need more details than that?"

I didn't.

"Use that to buy what we'll need to make it to the City of Answers. Better shoes and clothes than what you have now. Some food staples, if they won't slow us down. And cards. I'm not sure what the peasants might have here but try to barter wisely."

I frowned. "Where will you be?"

"Concerned, dove?"

I scowled. "Hardly."

He chuckled, low and smooth. "I have other matters to attend to. There's a tavern at the edge of town. I'll meet you there after dusk."

Raphael disappeared with ease into the crowd. I headed for the market. A strange pit filled my stomach. People looked at me, curious who the new face was. A village this size surely got occasional visitors, but likely the same ones over and over. I was a new face.

I didn't dare become a memorable one. Not if the soldiers came looking for us after Nelson's murder.

The cards were the most daunting, so the first items I took care of were more mundane. A new blouse and skirt cost me a coin each, but I was ashamed to admit, after all my years of forced asceticism, I couldn't resist. Not when I'd finally washed away the grime on my skin. Wearing the worn, dirty clothes, the same ones I'd worn for several years, was like wearing a set of iron shackles.

Raphael's constant comments about my clothes smelling had *nothing* to do with my decision.

Food was... overwhelming. My memories of the palace lingered like hazy waypoints, telling me I shouldn't be impressed with the meager offerings from the baker, the hard cheeses and dried meats. But years of rat and stale, moldy crusts had turned those simple options into the most luxurious foods I'd ever seen. I wasn't sure exactly how long the rest of our trip would be, but I didn't let myself spend too much money. It was safe to say Raphael wouldn't take kindly to his "hard-earned" money disappearing into spoils he couldn't appreciate, and I didn't need a lecture from a vampire.

Or for him to bite me in retribution.

It was uncomfortable, walking between the stands, making small talk with the sellers and villagers. In Greymere, I would go weeks without speaking. With Raphael, our conversations were also brief. But this was my chance to gather information. I gave a fake name of course, and made vague allusions to the husband I was traveling with. As benign as the village appeared, I'd be foolish to let anyone think I was alone or unclaimed. We were two days's journey by horse from the City of Answers, closer than I would've guessed. That was likely closer to five days if we went on foot.

I asked in a roundabout way for gossip on the capital, but there was little that reached this village. King Vaughn the Storm-blooded still reigned; that was hardly surprising—if anything had happened to him, it would've reached even Greymere. *Prince Marcel the Bountiful is the*

A BARGAIN SO BLOODY

light of the kingdom, added a girl my age, winking as she told me of his latest feats in a tournament.

I gave her a tight smile and asked for directions to the enchanted card dealer. She shrugged and pointed me towards a shop a few doors down.

The door chimed as I walked in, though no bells hung from it. A sure sign I was in the right spot.

Witches each had their own specialty of magic, like King Vaughn, who commanded the weather, or Marcel, who created abundance as he wished. They could use their magic, or store it with intricate spells in the form of cards. If someone wanted to access magic from others, they could do so using the cards, which led to a thriving trade industry across the kingdom. A pyromancer might make cards for someone in the winter with enough heat to keep a fireplace burning without wood for several weeks, or just a few hours, depending on their strength. All witches paid a tithe of magic to the king through their cards.

As a void, I had no magic and had to rely on the cards of others to use magic. And since I had none to trade, my only choice was to buy it.

"Greetings, traveler," the shopkeeper said from behind the desk.

The woman was melting. That was my first thought upon seeing her. Every part of her body seemed to sag. Her ears dropped, her chin dipped towards me, highlighting the hanging skin on her neck. Her hair was silver, with dark strands interspersed, her mouth half open as she regarded me like she couldn't quite be bothered to close it.

My mother would've had a fit if she'd ever looked like that. She'd have used every beautifying card in the kingdom to avoid that.

But then, my mother would never grow to be that old.

"Hello," I said, rushing to get the word out before my memories took over. "I need some cards."

She snorted, gesturing to glass cases that lined the store which were filled with enchanted cards. "You and everyone else who walks into my shop."

Apparently, merchants's attitudes towards service had changed since I was a child.

I stepped closer and examined the cards. "I need travel staples, so some warmth, body enchantments, and protection. And two disguise cards."

We could wander around the village with just our cloaks hiding our identities, but in the city, it would take something stronger to hide Raphael's red eyes. Besides, I didn't know if the guards might come looking for me before I had a chance to get to the Monastery.

"Is that all?" A huff. "Let me see what I can do."

She eased off her stool and trudged to the back. The door chimed as someone else came in. I fingered the coins in the pouch, trying to figure out what would be reasonable to pay while scanning the cards. One was enchanted for clean drinking water, made by an aquamancer. Could be useful to have. It came in a variety of types, from little enough to sip from, to enough to enchant a never-emptying flask.

"Alright, I've got your cards." She slapped a small deck onto the glass desk and took her place back on her stool. The cards fanned out, and she pointed to them, one by one.

"Warmth for a cloak, to keep off the spring chill for a week. Bodily enchantments for your legs so they don't tire. A hunger spell to stall your body's needs for up to three days—if you want a card that will give you food, that's extra—this one will make you a tent, no muss, no fuss, and collapse when you're done. Two disguises." She gave me a judgmental look. "Will distort your face. Just picture how you want to look, and it'll work. These ones will let you start a fire, even if the wood is soaked through. And for protection, this is premium."

The icon on the card depicted a swarm of insects.

"Bees?" I asked.

"Hah!" She looked down her drooping nose at me. "Wasps. Much better."

"Do you have anything more powerful?" Wasps wouldn't be any good against ogres or trolls. I had the vampire for protection—for now. But counting on someone to keep me safe was asking to get hurt. "Like a fireball or... or an explosive?" I asked hopefully.

She snorted. "Bah! I'll be surprised if you can afford these. Fifteen gold pieces."

"Fifteen?" I clutched the coins in my fingers. It sounded high, but the truth was, I had no idea what a fair price was.

"Fifteen?" a voice echoed. "Now, Darlene, you and I both know this is nine, at best. Eight, if Brian made the tent one."

I blinked.

The other patron who had come in had wandered closer. He was a boy, or maybe more accurately a man close to my age, except he seemed so much softer than all the men I'd seen.

He eased closer, peering over my shoulder to look at the cards.

"Seriously, Darl?"

The shopkeeper—Darlene—frowned, clearly unhappy that he was negotiating on my behalf. "Don't you have your own business to ruin? And don't call me Darl, boy."

I peered up to see his reaction, my shoulder brushing against his. He gave her a stern look. My savior was blond like the sun itself loved him, with bright brown eyes that twinkled with mischief, and a mouth that even at its sternest with the dealer wanted to smile.

"I can't have you taking advantage of a pretty girl like this, now can I?"

Darlene glared at me, like this was my fault. "Twelve."

The boy put a hand on my shoulder, leaning in conspiratorially, "Honestly, it's probably only worth seven. She doesn't even carry the good stuff anymore."

I flushed at the easy contact, and the impish tone he had, whispering even though it was obviously said for Darlene's benefit. How long had it been since someone had just... touched me? Not to hurt me, not to threaten me. Touched me like I was just a village girl.

"Ten. Take it or get out."

I slid out a handful of coins and placed them on the counter before the boy could continue to argue on my behalf. "I'll take it."

I scooped the cards up and slid them into the pouch. I should get a proper deck holder for my belt; most people wore one. But that was an expense for another day. Still, I hesitated. "Do you have anything specifically for vampires?"

Darlene scowled. "Case to the left of the door. Back row."

I went to look while the boy spoke to Darlene. The back row had several cards that wouldn't fit my needs. Only one card could've been the one she meant. It wasn't one I'd ever seen before. The glass was enchanted so I couldn't actually take the card from it, so I went back to Darlene.

"Interested or not?"

"What does it do?"

She rolled her eyes, mumbling to herself. "The chit is asking for cards and doesn't even know what they do." Theatrics done, she fixed her frown on me. "It'll hold off a vampire's thrall for up to a week. Rare. Three gold pieces. *No haggling*."

The last part was directed at the boy.

Thrall. The guard at Greymere had used the term. "What does that mean?"

"If you don't even know what thrall is, you probably don't need the damn card," she huffed. "It's how the bloodsuckers get you. One look in their red eyes and they can make you do anything. They can enthrall any person, void or witch, with just a single glance unless you have an enchantment. They're rare too. *Three pieces*," she repeated.

Did Raphael have that ability? The first night... he'd told me to look at him and ordered me to untie him. But I hadn't felt compelled. Then again, Greymere blocked all witch magic. Perhaps it blocked the vampire's powers too.

I handed over the gold and added the card to my stash, then headed out.

The bells chimed behind me.

"Say, why's a pretty girl like you worried about vampires?"

The boy had followed me out.

I shrugged. "Um. Just paranoid."

"And after all that work I did to save your gold." He shook his head at me, but his smile said he was just teasing. "Name's Thomas, by the way. Go by Tom to my friends and pretty ladies Darlene tries to take advantage of."

Pretty. He'd called me that twice now.

He held his hand out to me, and I shook it, all the while my cheeks burned. His skin was warm, slightly callused but soft.

"I'm Sam," I blurted, before I remembered to give him the same fake name I'd given the others. "Short for Samantha," I added, trying to salvage it.

He eased in a bit closer. Not quite so close I felt like I needed to back up, but almost. "Sam. You blush real cute, Sam."

I wasn't sure what to say to that, so I stammered something that approximated words but meant nothing.

He grinned, like I hadn't just made a fool of myself. "Will I see you around here much in the future, Sam? I'm hoping you say yes."

For a moment, I let myself enjoy the conversation. Imagine a life where I could just meet a boy, flirt, and learn what kissing felt like.

A life where I wasn't on the run after betraying my kingdom and conspiring with one of our deadliest enemies to infiltrate the City of Answers.

"Probably not, Tom."

He reached for my hand. By reflex, I jerked back, but I was a bit too slow, and he caught my wrist.

"You and I could head out into the woods and have a little fun before you continue on your errands, then." A dimple appeared in his cheek as he beamed down at me.

I blinked up at him, surprised by his forwardness. "Oh. Um. That's okay."

He flashed me another smile, though it was a little disappointed, then fished out a card from his own deck.

Some kind of fast travel spell—likely not for big distances, though, because those were pricy.

"See you around then, Sam."

The writing on the card faded as he activated it, the magic emerging, eager to complete its task. It engulfed him in a small tornado, lifting him high as the sudden wind slammed against me. Once there was no sign of him, I went off to the tavern to find Raphael. Sunset had settled over the town, darkness looming at the edges. I drew my cloak tighter around me. There might not be any ogres in town, but I was a scrawny woman who didn't live around here, walking around in the dark.

With no small amount of self-loathing, I realized I actually missed having the vampire around. At least when he was nearby, he was the only thing I had to worry about.

Rowdy noises signaled the location of the tavern, light trickling from the frosted windows. I pushed the doors open, scanning for the vampire as I unhooked my cloak.

But it was Raphael who found me first. No sooner had I taken a few steps into the warm tavern than the vampire was at my side. His hood had fallen back just slightly so I could see his red eyes, blazing, even though they were hidden from onlookers.

"Why do you smell like a male?"

Chapter 9

I jerked back.

"None of your business." *Could he really smell Tom from that brief contact?*

The look Raphael gave me was chiding. "It is, since you're under my protection and the biggest threat to you at present is men of your own species."

No, the biggest threat to me was the bossy vampire. Who was he to chide me? He'd run off, and I'd navigated the village, getting us supplies on my own and avoiding any suspicions from the townspeople on my own.

I shoved past him to get to the counter. I had a little of the stolen gold left, and I'd be damned if I'd let an ornery vampire deny me a warm meal while he made a scene.

"I just met a nice boy," I grumbled, snagging a seat at a recently emptied table.

Raphael slid into the stool across from me, utterly casual. His back was to the room, his red eyes fixed on me. I glanced around to see if anyone realized a vampire was in their midst, but no one reacted. The thought of how easily he moved around among humans sent chills down my spine. And he could enthrall people with a single look?

I'd thought the scariest thing about vampires was their fangs. The violent animal their human-shaped bodies contained. But no. Their true gifts were apparently much worse.

"A nice boy," Raphael murmured. His tone was mocking, in that soft, sensual way that made it clear he was playing a game I didn't know the rules to. "Is that what you like?"

Where was the bartender? "It doesn't seem like any of your business."

My cheeks warmed, and I could feel Raphael's gaze fix on them. The blood rushing under them. Then his attention drifted lower, taking in my clothing. I regretted the indulgence. The clothes I'd been wearing had been threadbare and shapeless. Now, the blouse clung to my frame, cut a bit low. It might've been immodest except for the fact my body was nearly stick straight.

He didn't leer. I couldn't accuse him of that. But he saw me in a way that left me feeling utterly exposed.

"Is that what you want, Samara?" he goaded. "A simple village boy who will whisper sweet nothings in your ear?"

I wanted to snap back something clever. In truth, anything I said would've come out petulant and stammered. I was saved when the barmaid finally spotted us and strolled over, a sway in her hips I could never manage.

She sashayed over to the table, a pleasant smile to me before she turned to face Raphael.

Her eyes widened in shock, mouth quivering for a second before she opened it, about to yell. How had Raphael been so stupid to—

"You notice nothing unusual about me. I am just another man with plain blue eyes."

His tone was even, unhurried. From the moment he began to speak, the shaking stopped, and she stared deep into his eyes. Then, as if in a trance, she nodded.

Thrall.

My mouth went dry. So that was what it looked like. I fingered the card at my side. Would I use it on myself? Or to protect the barmaid?

"Well, what can I get you, sir?" Her words were unafraid. She really didn't realize she was talking to a vampire.

Actually... her gaze was no longer fixed on his eyes. Instead, it roamed around the angles of Raphael's face, his sharp jaw, full lips, and then dipped lower.

"Nothing for me."

"You sure?" Her voice dropped slightly. "I can't get you *anything* you might like?"

"How kind," he drawled. "But no. My companion, however, is hungry."

Actually, seeing him hypnotize the barmaid had knocked down my ever-present appetite. But it would be childish not to take advantage and force at least something down my throat. "A cup of soup, please."

She nodded and turned to go, but Raphael stopped her. "And of course, a full dinner. Roast chicken or whatever is cooking in the kitchen, vegetables, potatoes, and something sweet."

The nod Raphael got had a much brighter smile than she'd given me. That smile shouldn't have irritated me. It was just... she was smiling at a vampire. And she had no idea.

"I'm not that hungry," I snapped when she finally left.

"Your growling stomach says otherwise," came the easy reply. "It's... irritating to listen to. Consider quieting your hunger a personal favor to me."

"Watching you screw with the barmaid's mind ruined my appetite."

He arched a brow. "Would you have preferred I snapped her neck before she could scream? I could still do that, if you're so distressed. She'd be missed, eventually, but we could leave before anyone realizes."

My horrified expression was answer enough.

"That's what I thought. It's harmless. In this case, anyway."

"It's unnatural," I hissed.

He chuckled. "As if witches have any right to complain about what's natural."

I wasn't a witch, but I felt like I should defend my countrymen all the same. "Witch magic is a gift from the gods."

"Who's to say mine isn't as well?"

The barmaid came back, a spring in her step as she set several platters down on the table: a thick, creamy soup that smelled of herbs I hadn't seen since I was a child; a hefty chicken leg, surrounded by roasted potatoes and colorful vegetables; and a hefty slice of pie. My eyes fixed on it. The sugar of the crust sparkled in the dark light. To my mortification, my stomach did growl at the sight.

Raphael smirked. He didn't need to say anything to make his point.

"Anything else I can get you?" Once again, her attention was turned to Raphael, because of course it was.

"Nothing. We're to be left alone for the rest of the evening, unless I call you over." His red eyes lifted once more, and that same blank expression came over her face as she nodded. "My companion wants all my attention on her after all."

I ignored the last teasing comment. My gaze was directed at my soup while the barmaid walked away. I fingered the small deck of cards in my pockets. "Have you done that to me?"

"I've certainly tried." There was an unusual tinge of annoyance in Raphael's tone. "Don't look so shocked I'm admitting it. Whatever else I may be, I'm not a liar."

"What do you mean *tried*?"

"I mean," he drawled, "it seems my thrall doesn't work on you."

I looked up at him.

"But we were in Grey—" I bit my tongue to stop speaking. Just what I needed, to give him the idea. Puzzles were a problem for me. I always wanted to solve them, even if I was better off keeping my mouth shut.

His red eyes glowed as he looked at me. "Tell me about the nice boy you met, Samara."

He was being childish. Perhaps it was better than something more nefarious to prove his point, but I ground my teeth all the same. Still, no vampire thrall compelled me to tell Raphael a word about Thomas, which was good, because I wasn't sure what I would have been compelled to share. What he looked like? Or the fact he'd invited me off to the woods?

"See?" He shrugged. "Doesn't work."

"Is that common?" I asked. Maybe he was weak for a vampire. Because I certainly wasn't strong for a human—I hadn't even used the card yet. I didn't want to waste the temporary effects, not while we were still days from Apante.

His expression shuttered. "Your soup is getting cold."

So he wouldn't lie—if I was to take the vampire at his word—but he was in no rush to answer my questions.

Still, in a weird way, he'd answered the most pressing question—how the thrall worked and if he could use it on me. Why tip his hand? Because I was easier to travel with if I wasn't scared of his mind manipulation? But then, why not answer my other questions?

His pointed look at the soup had me lifting the spoon to my lips, as compelled as any thrall.

My questions fell away as creamy soup met my lips. By the third hell, it was so rich it was almost overpowering. Delicate layers of herbs rolled over my tongue in a symphony of flavor. Rosemary, thyme, garlic. I hadn't tasted any of them in years. Rat soup was seasoned with sweat and spit. I shut my eyes, swallowing the soup down with a slight groan.

When I opened them, Raphael's gaze was fixed on me. There was something new to his expression, something I had seen only a hint of once or twice, like when I ate the rabbit. I swallowed again, nothing but my own worries.

He parted his lips like he was considering saying something, but held back.

I certainly wasn't going to ask. The single morsel of food had awakened my hunger, and I had to fight the urge to tip the bowl to my lips and drink it down before someone could take it away.

My mother's many hours of training prevailed. I took another small sip to my lips. I was eating faster than she would've approved of, but, well, she wouldn't have approved of me breaking bread with a vampire. And she was dead, so she couldn't have an opinion.

VASILISA DRAKE

From the soup, I moved to the roast dinner. I'd insisted I'd lost my appetite, but I made quick work of the plate, polishing off even the vegetables I'd disdained as a child.

My stomach cramped from the sudden influx of food. But still I eyed the dessert.

It would be stupid to eat it. Dessert would hardly sustain me on the rest of our trip. I might well lose all the food if I ate it.

But it was hard to look away. The crust was golden, beckoning me. I put my fork down with a slight clang, pushing the plate away.

We sat for a while as the food settled in me. *We should leave*, I realized distantly. We had the essentials we'd come for.

Raphael rolled his eyes at me. "Oh, just eat it."

I flushed at the mocking gesture. "It's fine. I don't need it."

"No one *needs* pie. But you've been making eyes at it since the barmaid brought it over. You *want* it."

I did. I hated that Raphael saw it so easily.

"No. I don't." I pushed my palms onto the table and stood, leaving payment on the table. Raphael rose, and mercifully didn't say another comment about the slice of pie. Even though I was full, the gluttonous part of me wanted to turn back and eat it. Dessert wasn't a word that was even whispered in Greymere, the taste of sugar and sweets from childhood something found only in the cruelest dreams. How would reality compare? Was it as glorious as I remembered?

Raphael would know. And if there was anything worse than going without, it was others knowing that you wanted more.

"We're just a few days's walk from the city," I told him as we left the tavern. With the cards I'd secured, our trip would be a bit easier.

"Oh, we won't be walking."

I frowned. "We won't?"

"No. We're going to steal some horses."

CHAPTER 10

Raphael's plan was simple: Find a couple of horses and take them. Enthrall anyone who dared protest.

Or kill them, he offered. If I'd "prefer."

The tavern itself was our best bet, with a stable at the side. The town didn't have a wide array of horses to steal from. This late, most locals had left for home and taken their mounts with them. In the tavern stable, only two horses remained.

One was a fine black stallion with broad shoulders. His ears flicked forward and back as Raphael strolled into the barn. Me, I followed after, scanning for any stable hand. It was late enough that whoever worked here had likely gone to sleep.

A BARGAIN SO BLOODY

The other was an older horse. His eyes drooped, tail not so much as swishing as we walked by. It would be faster to walk than to ride the old mount.

"We should look for another," I said quietly.

"And hope the one good horse is still here when we return? No. The one will suffice," Raphael declared.

He moved into the stall like it was his own stable, drawing the tack from its resting spot and expertly strapping the gear to the horse. I watched awkwardly, shifting on my feet. He was so comfortable with it. Perhaps he'd been a stable hand before he turned vampire.

It doesn't matter what he was before. He's a monster now.

Proving my point, Raphael drew himself onto the horse with preternatural ease. He strode out of the stall and lowered a hand to me.

"Let's go."

My stomach twisted, this time not from the food. I braced my hands on the side of the horse, unsure how to lift myself. Fast as lightning, Raphael bent down, gripping me under the shoulders and hefting me in front of him.

And with that, we were off into the night.

It was impossible to settle into one spot. The fact there was only one horse meant I didn't have to admit that I didn't know how to ride. But it also meant we were so, so close.

A week ago, being so near to the vampire that my back hit his when I lost my balance would've had me in tears, vomiting. Now, I felt echoes of that fear, but I was forced to admit that the echoes were eased by the fact it was Raphael—the vampire who brought me breakfast, even if I had to cook it myself—and hadn't forced himself on me once, not for blood, not for anything else.

Some distance from the village, I leaned too far forward, trying to avoid contact. My balance shifted, the world spinning around me. My hands desperately reached for the horse's mane, but it was too late. I was falling—

A firm arm snapped around me, catching me before I could hit the ground. Raphael's hand clamped over my stomach, fingers spread he like he was locking me in place. The horse didn't miss so much as a step as the vampire deftly maneuvered the reins with just one hand.

My stomach flipped, and not from nearly falling.

"You can let me go," I said quickly. "I'm fine."

"You nearly cracked your head falling." He sighed. "Humans. So... breakable."

"I'd rather take my chances with the ground than a vampire." I should've insisted on taking the old horse. Though there was no way it could've managed even this pace.

"Good thing I'm not giving you the choice."

The horse's pace increased. I was jostled by the movement, landing even closer against Raphael. I tried to lean away, even if it made his hand press deeper into my stomach, the thin fabric of my cloak doing little to muffle the sensation. It was either feel him behind me or in front, and at least I could see his hand. Unfortunately, against an immortal vampire, I wasn't able to do much more than put an inch between us, and even that I lost and regained every other step.

"Stop writhing like that," Raphael said slowly, "or you're not going to like what happens."

"What?" I hissed, trying for anger that would mask my helplessness. "You'll toss the breakable human off the horse?"

"No." I could feel the grin at my back. "But you'll soon feel the effect of you rubbing your body against mine. And given the fact you blush like a maiden when I even mention that 'nice boy' you stink of, you're liable to burst into flames on the spot."

I immediately stilled as his implication settled over me. *Like a maiden*. There was no *like* about it. Greymere wasn't a place where one was courted. Though I had a sense of what bodily effect he was mentioning, given the crude nature of the other servants. His fingers flexed on my stomach like he was adjusting himself. No longer fighting him, I was forced to settle against his chest, keenly aware of the contours of his body against my back. And at my rear... was it his normal body? Or was he... aroused? It was hard to tell. Gods, it was impossible to even fathom. The idea *I* of all people could affect a vampire.

Mortifying.

But... perhaps just a little enchanting too.

VASILISA DRAKE

THE NEXT EVENING BROUGHT a chill with it. It was spring, and in Eurobis that was the most fickle season. We'd had fairly warm days so far, but our luck had run out. The horse meant we had moved to open roads, which made navigating easier but left us ready targets for the wind. The cold lanced through me, no matter how tightly I wrapped my cloak.

Raphael, of course, was unaffected. Perks of being a soulless monster instead of a "breakable human."

His arm was wrapped around me once more. It no longer felt as awkward as it had the day before—instead, it was a steady source of heat. I loathed myself for the fact I liked it. But in this weather, it was a matter of survival.

As the sun set, the last of the warmth was sapped from the air and replaced by an icy rain.

Of course. Because the cold wasn't bad enough.

The rain started slowly, but it was enough to freeze me to my core. There was no hiding my shivering. Raphael pulled me closer. *How was his undead chest warm?* I leaned back, desperate for the protection from the cold. I hated seeking comfort in the vampire, but I'd hate losing my limbs to the frost more.

"We should stop for the night," I said between clattering teeth. "There's a shelter card. With that and a fire one, we can get warm."

"No need."

This close to him, I could feel the rumble of his chest as he spoke.

"Maybe you don't need rest, but Alphonse and I do," I insisted.

"I'm aware of your needs. It's the smell of chimney smoke ahead that tells me we'll find proper shelter soon."

I should've apologized, but I was tired and weak. The soup from yesterday no longer warmed my bones, and the cold was taxing. We rode in silence for a moment, the sound of rain lulling me as my eyes began to shut.

"Alphonse is the horse?" Raphael prodded, not letting my earlier words drop.

I started to shrug against him, then forced my shoulders down. This close to the vampire, it was best to avoid any more movement than absolutely necessary, based on yesterday's comments. "I figured he could use a name."

"It's just a horse." His words weren't exactly judgmental. More puzzled.

"And I'm just a void." A void to a vampire was probably the same as a horse to a human: powerless, mortal, too quick to die. "But I have a name all the same. And so should Alphonse."

My head began to tip forward, but Raphael spoke again, jolting me from any sleep. I knew it wasn't good to sleep in these conditions, not when I was this cold, but it was difficult to keep myself awake.

"I take it names are important to you, Samara."

Samara. My lips twisted, repeating my own name. "You want to know something sad?"

"I wish to know all your thoughts," Raphael said quietly. Or at least, that's what I thought Raphael said. With the rain and the siren call of sleep beckoning me, who could be sure?

There was no reason to tell the vampire my private thoughts. If I'd been more aware, I wouldn't have. But something about being so close, his body sheltering me from the rain without seeing those unnerving eyes, made me feel almost safe. "You're the only one who's said my full name since I was a little girl." At Greymere, as the only female servant, my sex had become my name. *Girl. Lazy girl. Slow girl. Ugly girl.* I frowned. "In fact, everyone who knew me as a child... they've forgotten me by now, I'm sure."

Anyone who knew you's forgotten you exist. Even from beyond the grave, Nelson's words taunted me.

There was something almost gentle in the vampire's voice as he said, "Not your parents."

"My mother's dead." Frost followed the cold words from my mouth.

Wisely, Raphael didn't ask about my father.

"I'm sorry," he said. "No one deserves to be forgotten. If it's any reassurance, Samara, I intend to live a very long life. And I will not forget you for any of it."

A vampire who remembered me. It was the stuff of nightmares.

But it eased the tightness in my throat all the same.

"Do you... have people who are missing you?" I asked.

He loosed a wry laugh. "Oh, I imagine there's a few."

Of course he did. He was strong, confident. Humorous at times, though I couldn't quite appreciate it. And attractive too, if I looked past those awful eyes and fangs—which around other vampires would probably be considered a good thing—with those broad shoulders and beautiful face. Who wouldn't want to know *his* name?

I envied a vampire. That was a new low. "I guess living so long, you have time to make a lot of friends."

At this, his laugh was more genuine. "A lot of enemies too. But in truth, my friends are few. When you live as long as I have… you have little patience for falsehoods, and the fickleness of friendship. Or at least the weak imitation most offer. But those that are true friends, whose bonds we've sealed in blood, I cherish them. I carry their names with me as they carry mine, even when we don't see each other for many years."

I shivered again. The sudden closeness from our conversation was unnerving. Worse was the fact I had the irrational urge to ask him more about his home. In some ways, it sounded similar to the way I'd grown up, before Greymere. Not that I'd had any *true* friends.

"We're nearly there." There was a reassuring note in his voice, one too gentle for my liking.

A moment later, an inn came into view as we crested a small hill. Smoke billowed from the chimney, just like Raphael had said. The windows were lit with an inviting yellow glow, promising warmth and shelter.

"You purchased disguise cards, correct?"

"I did."

He pulled Alphonse off to the side, sheltering us under the dense branches of a tree.

I brushed my fingers as dry as I could before pulling the deck from the holder I'd manufactured. Not as fancy as the usual leather ones, but since I hadn't had so much as a needle to shape it, it was acceptable. I flipped through and held out the disguise card to Raphael.

Better this than trying to enthrall anyone we came across. Less disconcerting too. The card would last for a week or so, unless dispelled by a witch. It wasn't very powerful magic, but all the card needed to do was change Raphael's eyes from the telltale red and darken his hair so it was no longer such a striking white.

Disguise cards were fairly popular in Eurobis. Mother had kept a thick deck made entirely of disguise cards. She, like most, used the magic for perfecting her face, removing blemishes, adjusting her lips to just the right amount of plumpness or thinness, depending on what was the current style.

Remember, my little princess. It doesn't matter what you are, only what others think *you are.*

Certain witches could see through disguises, and others could cast magic to dispel the enchantments, but out here it was unlikely we'd find anyone like that.

"You'll have to be the one to cast it, of course," he cajoled when I took too long, staring at the deck.

Right. Another reason to keep me around. Though voids had no magic of their own, they could unlock the magic stored in cards. Vampires, on the other hand, couldn't do even that. As if their very existences were incapable of channeling magic.

Greymere blocked all mystical abilities, which meant it had been ages since I'd felt the tingle of magic at my fingertips. I twisted in my seat and lifted the card between us.

There wasn't much to using the cards—all it took was a shred of will to power them up. The writing on the card faded into nothing, the enchanted paper turning white as magic bristled in the air between us. My heart filled at the sensation. I loved the electric sensation of casting magic. I hadn't felt it in ages, but it was as familiar as the last time I'd used it. It twisted around Raphael, who shut his eyes as the spell activated. His hair darkened from white all the way to a gleaming black. His eyes snapped open as the magic finally settled, the tingle on my arms fading away.

Blue eyes.

"I take it by your expression the card failed."

"No, it worked." But such a weak card... it should've gone for the easiest route, darkening his eyes a shade to a less suspicious brown, shifting the white of his hair to bright blond. Not... this. Maybe vampires made magic work differently. Another puzzle I wouldn't get to work out. "Let's go."

Raphael signaled Alphonse with a tap of his heels forward.

The inn had a friendly look about it, despite the rain. Any shelter would've looked marvelous in the downpour. The brick exterior was old but well maintained, a nice path leading to the front.

The entire space was charming. The scent of herbs and meat drifted in from the left, where there was a dining area similar to the tavern we'd been in earlier. To the right was a staircase, no doubt leading to the rooms upstairs.

But the biggest surprise was the boy who stood behind the desk. *Thomas*.

"Samantha! What a surprise."

Chapter 11

"Thomas," I exclaimed.

The boy from the card shop grinned, a dimple appearing on one side of his mouth. "Tom, remember?"

"How wonderful you two know each other's *names*," Raphael drawled.

I shifted on my feet, unsure why I felt so uncomfortable. Thomas's gaze drifted from me to the vampire who stood at my side, smile collapsing slightly. He didn't run away screaming; the disguise card worked fine. But he certainly wasn't relaxed as Raphael stared him down.

"This is, um, my brother Mark," I said quickly. "We got caught in the rain and were hoping we could spend the night here."

The dimple returned in force. "You're in the right place! The Royal Badger is always happy to give lovely, weary travelers a place to rest. Why don't I get you a hot meal first?"

"I'll go tend to Alphonse. Don't wait for me." Raphael disappeared back out into the rain, leaving me with Thomas, who relaxed immediately at his departure.

Thomas maneuvered out from the behind desk and gave me a wide grin. "Why don't I take your cloak so it can dry?" He looked from my face to lower, eyeing my soaked clothes.

That did sound nice. Until I glanced down and flushed, immediately crossing my arms over my cloak, pulling it tight. The water had truly soaked me; my blouse was transparent as it clung to me, leaving me utterly exposed save for my chest wrappings. "I'll just sit close to the fire."

Thomas at least had the manners to look ashamed of having been caught ogling. Part of me wanted to retreat immediately up to whatever room we could get and order supper there. But... well, I'd been on display, and he'd looked. That was just what boys did. Right? It didn't matter that I didn't like it. He hadn't actually harmed me in any way.

"I'll get you a dry blanket, of course, so you can wrap it around yourself."

"Oh. That'd be great."

He went to the back and came back with a bundle of fabric. I accepted with a twinge of guilt for my earlier thoughts about him, and shrugged off my cloak, facing away while I slipped the dry blanket over my shoulders. Thomas told someone to bring the cloak up to what would be our room and led me over to the dining hall. He sat us at the bar top. I didn't like having my back to the room, but I wasn't sure what to say. With Raphael, it was almost easier to push back. With Nelson and the guards of Greymere, I'd known my place not to say anything. But with a random boy... was it wrong to assert what I wanted? He'd think me paranoid, and I had no desire to draw attention.

Thomas was oblivious to my turmoil over our seats and instead cheerfully spoke. "You've gotta try Cook's lamb. It's the best thing ever."

Cook. Obviously, it wasn't the same cook as Greymere, but the moniker had me thinking of my time in Greymere. Of Cook serving out an unending sentence because no one cared enough to see justice done.

Despite the fact I was soaked and shivering, despite the fact I'd slept on the forest floor beside a vampire for several days, I wouldn't trade my current fate for my old one. No matter how terrible the cost had been.

He flagged down the server and ordered for us. Food appeared a moment later. Enticing spices wafted over from the two plates, making me acutely aware of my hunger.

"So, Sam, you didn't tell me you were headed this way."

"You didn't ask." I smiled, hoping it was at least half as simple and charming as his was.

The dimple showed his approval. "Fair enough. I guess I was too distracted. Where are you headed?"

"Apante."

"The City of Answers," he mused, using the more common nickname. "What answers are you looking for?"

Whatever the vampire wants. Of course I couldn't tell him that, so I made up a lie about seeking my fortune. He made a joke, and the conversation flowed easily while I devoured the lamb in front of me. Lamb had never been my favorite meat growing up, but gods, I'd once sworn when I got out of Greymere, I'd never be picky again. Food was for survival. I didn't need more than that.

Distantly, I wondered what was taking Raphael so long. Thomas was talkative, and he didn't notice as my mind wandered, and my responses stopped being full sentences and more a rotating sequence of nods and *mhmms*. A nice boy. That's what he was, through and through. Even as inexperienced as I was, I could tell he was flirting. A nice boy was flirting with me. It was like I was watching it happen to someone else. Someone who had another life, who hadn't seen the violence I had.

I tried to savor the attention, to put on the thought that I was in some way desirable. It fit like a pair of trousers fashioned from an old grain bag—too itchy, too close to the skin, too constricting.

I should have been charmed, but all I could think was I'd rather have eaten my meal in solitary silence.

"Let me get you something good for dessert." Thomas was up and around the counter, ducking into the kitchen before I could protest.

For a brief moment, my mind flickered to the pie from yesterday. To my stubborn refusal while Raphael sat there. Well, maybe today I *would* have the pie.

But Thomas returned with just a pair of goblets. He seemed to consider both glasses for a second before carefully setting one in front of me.

"It's a special dessert wine," he explained with a gleam in his eye. "On the house, of course."

I thanked him, though the truth was I didn't much care for wine. I'd had it only as a small child, sampling from my mother's cup. My impression from Nelson's drinking was not favorable. I took a single sip to be polite and then set it down.

Thomas cast me a crestfallen look. His handsome face was made mulish with the expression, which was just a bit too exaggerated to be charming. "You don't like it? It's a, uh, specialty of the town I grew up in."

The town, I recalled from his many tangents, was about a day's journey away. "I'm not much for wine."

"You'll like it," he insisted. "It's a bit of an acquired taste, but everyone likes it once they finish their first glass."

I squirmed, slightly uncomfortable with how pushy he was. It would be foolish to offend Thomas when he had been so kind. I just didn't really want to drink the wine.

VASILISA DRAKE

Wants are secondary to needs, I reminded myself. Being rude to a current host wasn't just rude, it was stupid. Drawing attention by being stubborn when we were already passing through late at night, when a vampire was in their midst, was foolish.

I lifted my drink back from the table and readied to take another sip.

The wine was snatched from my hands before it reached my lips.

I jerked back, straight into a hard—familiar—chest. Raphael had suddenly returned and now stood behind my seat. And he'd taken the dessert wine.

"My ward doesn't have the constitution for this drink."

I sputtered a protest, but the wine was already at Raphael's lips. Vampires don't drink. But Raphael took a sip all the same, watching Thomas over the rim of the glass. He grimaced.

"It's foul."

I wanted to bury my head in my hands at his rudeness, but it got worse. He dumped the wine behind the counter. I stared up at the vampire in horror. Although now he didn't look like the vampire I'd come to know. His dark hair gleamed in the low light, his blue eyes fixed on Thomas as he leaned over, a chilling smile on his face.

The tips of Thomas's ears flared bright red. Anger? Or embarrassment?

Either way, I was mortified. "*Mark*," I hissed.

"Apologies for the delay. Alphonse took some time to settle, but I'm here now and ready for a meal." His gaze was fixed squarely on Thomas, menace radiating off him.

"Of... of course," Thomas stammered. "I'll go and get that for you."

Raphael slid into the seat next to me. "Excellent. Then you can join me and Sam."

Sitting pressed between Thomas and Raphael sounded worse than anything Greymere had come up with. I stood, clutching the blanket around me as if to save me from the awkwardness. "Actually, I'm exhausted, *brother*. I'll just head up to rest."

Raphael nodded. Too easily. "Of course. Have a tray sent upstairs," he ordered Thomas, before turning to me. "Let's head to bed."

Chapter 12

The room was just large enough to fit a small table and chair, along with a freshly made bed. A bright fire roared in the corner, heating the space. The room was a palace compared to where I'd stayed at Greymere. The only issue with the space was that Raphael and I both were in it, alone.

"It'd be worth the gold for a second room," I groused. "You can always just enthrall someone into giving you more."

"How quickly you've changed your mind about my powers," Raphael mused.

I was willing to throw away a lot of morals if it meant not spending the night locked in the same four walls with a vampire. Yes, we'd slept near each other in the forest, by necessity. But spending the night in a tiny room with him?

"I'd rather spend the night with Alphonse."

Raphael snorted. "And I'm sure the stable boys who are sipping spirits in the empty stall would love your company. But that's not going to happen."

"Then you should be the one to leave. You're a creature of the night." I hated the way fear turned my voice petulant. I sounded like a whining child.

"I could go out and hunt for a more suitable dinner, if you prefer." He gestured to the tray that had been sent up shortly after. It was the worst looking goat leg I'd ever seen, courtesy of Thomas. Of course, Raphael had no intention of eating it. He'd planned to sit with us just to torture me, I was certain.

At my silence he arched a brow. "You're even considering it. You find sharing a bed with me so distasteful?"

There was another reason I didn't want to sleep in the bed, but I couldn't make myself voice it. Couldn't make myself admit how scared I felt.

"So be it."

I tensed, but Raphael simply moved to the window and unlocked it, letting an icy chill into the room. In a single leap, he jumped from the window.

I sped over to the open window to see for myself, but he'd disappeared into the night. I relatched the window. On the table by the spot where Raphael stood was a dry, folded tunic. I glanced towards the latched window once more before changing and adjusting the fireplace, setting my original clothing to dry. Then I stripped the bed of the largest blanket and pillow and slipped under the frame.

My sleep was fitful. Red eyes haunted it, twisting into blue ones. I woke just after dawn and crawled out from my hiding spot, mussing the bed so no one would know where I'd slept.

No sign of Raphael. I heated the food from last night over the low flames of the fire and ate it as breakfast before heading down. The inn was quiet. No sign of the staff, aside from an older woman who swept the main floor. I wandered outside, looking for the vampire. *Surely he wouldn't have taken off on his own.* The thought caused me more distress than I expected. I resolved to check the stables. To make sure he hadn't slipped away on our single horse.

Instead of Raphael, I found Thomas.

Kissing a girl.

I must've made a sound, because both broke apart. Her blouse was unlaced slightly, and she hastily tied it while giggling at Thomas. Vaguely, I recalled her from the night before. Now, she darted past me and out of the barn.

I avoided Thomas's eyes, moving over to Alphonse, who was still in his paddock. My chest unclenched at the sight of the horse. Why I was so shocked to see Thomas kissing another, I wasn't quite sure. Was it because he'd flirted with me in town and last night? Had I thought it meant more? Not really. I knew there couldn't be more. But I also only knew what "more" was in vague terms. There had been no affection in Greymere, no pretty words, no soft lips against my own. It was a world apart from how Tom lived.

I expected Thomas to disappear like the girl had, but instead he came closer, crowding me as I petted the horse.

"Err, good morning."

"Morning, Sam." He grinned at me, the dimple appearing the same as it had last night when he'd flirted with me.

The dimple annoyed me just a bit more than it had yesterday.

"Have you seen my brother?"

"Not a trace." His grin widened. "Good thing for us. You disappeared so fast, Sam. I was hoping we'd have a chance to get to know each other."

"I think you know enough women." My words came out pointy, like tiny, ineffective daggers.

"Aww, that's just Amy. She likes to tease me a little. It's nothing."

"I don't care," I said sincerely. "I just think it's a little strange to act the way you do when you're with her."

"Don't be jealous, Sam." He placed a hand on my shoulder, pushing me slightly so I had to look at him. I barely hid my flinch. "I'd much rather get to know you than talk to her."

"That wasn't talking." I tried to shrug his hand off, but it only drifted lower. I squirmed slightly.

"Thought I'd have the chance to get to know you better last night, but you disappeared on me," he chastised, ignoring my correction the same way he ignored the fact I definitely didn't want him touching me.

The accusation in his voice rankled, but he had a point. I *had* been rude. He'd fed me, given me a special dessert which I hadn't gotten to drink because of Raphael, and I'd left.

"We'll be leaving soon anyway, so it doesn't matter." And really, it didn't. I didn't like that Thomas was two-faced about women, but I didn't want him. "I'm just going to get Alphonse ready while I wait for him." Never mind the fact I didn't know how to set up a horse's tack. I just wanted the boy gone.

"Oh, he's probably going to be a while. I bet he went for his own roll in the hay, if you know what I mean. Gives us some time." He winked.

My stomach twisted. Could Thomas have been right? Without his red eyes, he certainly passed for gorgeous, and could've had his pick of women at any stray tavern he'd gone off to.

Then again, he'd probably just enthrall them and steal their blood rather than go for a "roll in the hay" as Thomas put it.

Or both.

Somehow both was worse.

"He'll be back soon," I said with false confidence.

"Then we should make the best of the time we have."

He leaned in. I leaned away. My back immediately landed against a wooden post, trapping me. I felt all at once too trapped, too claustrophobic, but the words to explain why Thomas should back away wouldn't find their way off my tongue.

His palms were on my hips, pinning me.

Trapped.

A flash of darkness and Raphael was there, powerful hands on either side of Thomas's head.

A twist. A *crack*! And Thomas fell to the floor.

His eyes looked up at me, unseeing, accusing.

Dead.

I raised my gaze to stare at Raphael in open-mouthed shock.

"How could you?" My words wobbled off my tongue.

His eyes may have been blue, but there was nothing human in them. "It's not all that hard, given my superior strength."

"He was just a boy!" I was close to screaming, but the words came out hollow.

"He was an irritating nuisance. He had no value."

"He was human."

"He was weak. I was strong. I wanted him dead, so he's dead. It's not complicated."

I looked from the corpse to Raphael. "You'd kill me that easily," I rasped. "Just another weak human."

"Ah, but right now, I have use of you."

"And if I cease to be useful?"

"Then you'd best take care not to," was his chilling response.

He pushed past me and readied Alphonse. When he led the horse from the paddock, I could only stare, my body numb.

"Listen to me, Samara. You can tell yourself I killed him because I'm an evil vampire. Or because I found his voice irritating and the wine he gave you smelled suspicious, or simply because I didn't care for the way he looked for any excuse to put his hands on you. It matters not. He's dead, and you still have to travel with me. As long as you're in my care, you're *mine*. No one else's."

My body was still numb as he pulled me atop the horse. I couldn't help but look back at Thomas's eyes. I wanted to reach for him, for what reason, I wasn't sure. But Raphael moved us away quickly.

We reached the City of Answers the next day.

Chapter 13

Apante was glorious.

Unlike Greymere, which was little more than... well, like its namesake, a gray block of stone, the former Witch Kingdom capital was filled with tall, colorful buildings. Multi-colored glass windows reflected rainbows onto the streets. Where the village had been overwhelming with a few scattered visitors, the City of Answers boasted hundreds of travelers that arrived every day.

Raphael and I blended in with the crowd. With the disguise magic in place and hood over his head, Raphael was able to move easily through the streets. Unnervingly so—if anything, he had more ease with the vendors than I did. He strolled up to a cart and returned with breakfast in the form of shaved meat, wrapped in a flat bread. The food of peasants—my mother would never have let me eat something so unrefined, especially with my hands.

It was delicious.

"You still haven't told me what you need me to ask," I reminded Raphael, glancing up at him between bites of food.

Alphonse was settled into a stable at the front of the city. The streets were too crowded for people to move easily through with a horse, so we walked side by side, just as we had in the forest.

"Patience, dove."

I huffed. We needed to request an audience with the Librarians. Then, I'd hold up my end of the bargain, and we'd go our separate ways.

I'd be alone. Again.

Trumpets sounded. The mass of people parted on cue, with Raphael and I getting swept to the side. With my short stature, it was hard to see past the crowds, but curiosity compelled me forward. A few moments later, I understood what the commotion was. Brilliant white horses marched forward, two by two, led by a large stallion that carried Prince Marcel the Bountiful.

Women cheered loudly at the sight of him, and then everyone turned frantic as he tossed handfuls of coins out to the crowds. A few coins turned into a hundred by the time they landed. Children dove between the adults, keen eyes working with tiny fingers to try to win against each other.

As he passed us, he tossed a handful right at us. Perhaps I should've reached—I was hardly any better off than the beggars on the street, only a few of Raphael's stolen coins lining my purse. Instead, all I could do was stare.

He had the same chestnut hair as all those years ago, his eyes kind and guileless. The people of Eurobis might fear their Storm-Blooded King, but they *loved* Marcel. His smile was broad, disguise magic perfecting his teeth that had been crooked as a child.

Twelve years was a long, long time. I hadn't felt the years stolen from me as acutely until the moment his gaze slid over our section.

There was no recognition when he turned away to throw more coins to the other side.

A relief, of course, that no one from the royal family recognized me, but not an unexpected one. I was a nobody. Besides, as a precaution, I'd used a card to disguise myself before we entered the city in case word had spread from Greymere. My hair was a color that seemed fashionable with the women of the day—lavender—my eyes an average blue. The remainder of the magic I used to twist my features just slightly, changing my nose and chin enough that Raphael had rolled his eyes at me.

"Is that the type of boy you like? Not a nice village one, but a royal one?"

Of course the vampire missed nothing. Still, I couldn't force myself to turn away until the accompanying entourage of carriages and horses totally blocked my view.

As long as he didn't guess the real reason I was staring at the prince, I was safe.

"You killed the nice village one, remember?"

Raphael grinned like he was proud of the murder, his smile flashing too-sharp canines that even magic couldn't fix. I looked away, disgusted.

With him, or with myself, I wasn't sure. I didn't forgive him for the murder, but I was able to make myself look past it with disturbing ease. Like with Nelson. Maybe Thomas wouldn't have killed me, but it felt like survival all the same. Raphael, for all his monstrous traits, had kept me safe and gotten me to the city.

"Come on." I shoved past our neighbors, turning from the crowd even while others remained to watch. "We won't get to any Librarians today. This must be his pilgrimage."

"His pilgrimage?" Raphael asked.

I snorted. Something I knew about Eurobis that the vampire didn't. The list shouldn't have been as short as it was, considering it was my kingdom. But that's what a long life got him, and a decade of servitude had gotten me.

"Not sure why I should tell you," I said, half-heartedly.

"You definitely shouldn't," Raphael agreed. "But perhaps I could answer a question for you in exchange for soothing my curiosity."

A BARGAIN SO BLOODY

We were past the crowds now. Somehow, even though I was the one who had pushed to leave, Raphael was once again leading. Like he couldn't help himself.

"Anything?" I asked, considering.

That was a powerful offer. Tempting.

"As long as telling you would not endanger my kingdom," he corrected.

"That's hardly fair, since you want to know state secrets."

Raphael rolled his disguised eyes at me. "I could simply enthrall another off the street to tell me."

"Then why don't you?" I countered.

"Perhaps because I want you to be the one to tell me. Though if you'd like to use that as your question, by all means."

Fine. He made a fair point, and I might as well get something from it. "The pilgrimage is a trip made after the royal heir turns eighteen. There's meant to be a specific prophecy for every ruler for the next thousand years. It's the only time the royal family is allowed to ask the Librarians for counsel. If they attempt at any other time, their requests are ignored, even though the Librarians will hear other requests." The ruling line didn't get to choose what question the Librarians answered, either.

"Because of what the royals did to seers."

"What the seers made them do," I corrected, just as I'd been taught.

It was said Apante had previously been the capital of Eurobis because that was where seers were strongest. But several hundred years ago, some king had decided to build up Ulryne as the new capital, right in the center of the continent—as far from the vampires as possible. Seers were immediately outlawed.

Raphael scoffed. "Just because some king felt threatened that someone knew more than he did."

"It's said to be a betrayal of the throne to have powers greater than that of the king." That's what we were taught. It was pedantic to argue with the vampire over the point. Even as a child, those two things had sounded similar to me, though my mother had insisted there was a difference.

All witches must pay a tithe to the king. Yet the seers give it only at their discretion. They may say no to the king, but yes to a peasant who asked. It was treasonous, she'd told me. She never said a single thing against the royal family—or at least, not against King Vaughn.

"And for that so-called betrayal, he ordered them all put to death." There was no mistaking the disgust in Raphael's voice, the curl in his lips. "But still they grasp on to slivers of that power."

It was hard to argue that point.

Before the seers had been killed, they had stored their magic in the Great Library. Even now, all these years later, their cards remained. The Librarians, though not seers themselves, guarded that knowledge, along with more traditional books, and dedicated themselves to understanding the world around us. Any witch or void could ask for their guidance—once. Because of the exile, even the king himself would be turned away if he asked for any more than what he'd been given during his pilgrimage.

Marcel was already eighteen.

It had felt like my life had frozen while I'd been in Greymere. That obviously wasn't the case.

"My turn." I could've asked him for vampire weaknesses or something useful, but one question had bothered me for days. "Why did you let yourself get captured?"

"Let?" Raphael drawled. "What makes you think I let myself get chained in copper and shoved into a dark prison?"

"Don't play dumb. You can enthrall humans, and I've seen you fight. Or rather, I've seen you kill. It's not even fair to call those *fights*."

Raphael was quiet for a long beat. I wondered if he'd go back on his word.

"You're observant, I'll give you that," he eventually said with something that bordered on respect in his tone.

"Well?" I prodded.

"I was looking for something. I was led to believe I'd find it near the witch prison. When I didn't find it, I decided to let some pompous guards think they'd found me, and enthralled them into imprisoning me rather than attempting to decapitate me."

"But why? What were you looking for?"

"I've answered your question. If you wanted more details, you should've been more specific."

I huffed a breath in frustration. He'd let them put him in copper shackles, turning him weak as a mortal while they whipped him for days? His thrall might have stopped the first set of guards from decapitating him, but a new set could have done so. I still wasn't convinced his thrall worked in Greymere—he'd have been defenseless. For a vampire who planned to live a "very long time," he'd risked coming to a bloody end in chains. What under the gods's sun could he have been looking for?

"Is this what your question to the Librarians is about?"

Raphael didn't answer. I hid my grin and took it as a yes.

I should've dropped it. Once I asked the question, my bargain was fulfilled, and we'd go our separate ways.

But the vampire was a puzzle. And I was terrible at resisting puzzles.

Chapter 14

The markets of Apante weren't as famous as the Great Library—they weren't called the Great Markets, after all—but they still far exceeded anything I'd ever seen. Colors exploded from every stall, vendors shouting bargains and enticements in a joyful cacophony. The noise hurt my ears, but there was so much life in it I forced myself forward. For years, the only yelling I'd heard had been from pain. Here, there was every other emotion on display—greed and pride, pleasure as customers inspected beautiful goods, good-natured bartering at every stall.

We had time to spare, since Prince Marcel would likely spend the day with the Librarians. Until he left tomorrow, we'd be unable to get an audience with them. We'd have to put in a request tomorrow, and if I was lucky, we'd be seen the same day.

One more day. Then we'd part ways.

There was a lovely deck holder that caught my eye. The case was surrounded in delicate beading, with bright blue and reds forming a pattern. It slotted along a belt that continued the same pattern, with sturdy leather that could fit all kinds of tinkering tools in addition to the deck. It would do a much better job holding the pile of cards than my makeshift pouch, that much was for certain.

Raphael, of course, caught me looking.

"Should I thrall him into giving it to you?" he offered, humor in his eyes.

I forced us to continue on. "It's pointless where I'm headed." For more than one reason.

"So you *have* decided to join the Monastery."

Was he joking? "I'm an exile," I hissed, keeping my voice so quiet only his vampire hearing would pick up on it. "It's not like I have any other option."

There were three main powers in the Witch Kingdom. The Crown, of course, set in Ulryne. The Great Library of Apante was another, because even outlawing seers didn't diminish their power. But the Monastery was different. Despite the name, it was really a network of churches that stretched throughout the kingdom. It claimed all of Eurobis as its seat of power, since the gods, too, claimed all of the continent.

The Monastery would take in anyone on the condition they forsook the use of magic—criminal, pauper, princess. All you had to do was devote yourself fully to the gods and forsake any use of magic. Converts put their faith solely in the gods, and, supposedly, were rewarded for it eternally. Since voids already lacked magic, they weren't giving up as much. But I'd also give up use of enchantments stored in cards.

"Surely you'll miss the magic."

I forced myself to still, hating how easily the vampire saw inside me. "Where I was before"—I avoided saying *Greymere* lest anyone accidentally eavesdropping pay closer attention—"I had no access to magic. This will hardly be a big adjustment."

Except I loved the sensation of using magic. I had loved it even in the years I'd been forced to go without. I reveled in feeling it around me as we walked through the markets. The electric spires dancing over my skin when I cast a card felt like armor. Giving up that protection, after everything...

Still, I'd be safe. The Monastery allowed criminals to join because it stripped you of your identity, including any past sins, when you joined. You gave up all markers of individuality. Not just magic, but ostentatious displays of wealth like the beaded toolbelt.

"There are other options," Raphael insisted.

I snorted and walked faster. Somehow, it was less fun to look at the wares available now that reality had sunk in. No matter what I did, I'd never own any of them. "What life could I have? I've missed my chance at any apprenticeship. And I'd be living a life looking over my shoulder, waiting for them to throw me in the dungeons. Or worse."

"You could continue with me. Come to my realm."

I actually managed to laugh at that. It had to be a joke. "A human? Find sanctuary in the Vampire Kingdom?"

"It's not so uncommon," he said mildly.

"Because *your kind* use us as chattel," I snapped. "Just a food source for any hungry vampire to drink from."

"You wouldn't be. If you came with me, I'd see to that."

"And what power do you have to promise that?" I demanded. Whoever Raphael was in the vampire world, he was expendable if he'd been sent into the heart of the Witch Kingdom alone. Especially given the way he'd risked his life on his quest. I forced myself to dismiss the offer before it took root in me, like a weed. I belonged among my own kind, at the Monastery.

Raphael didn't answer, didn't say a word arguing that I was wrong.

"It's for the best." I wasn't sure why it sounded like I was trying to convince him, when it was the obvious truth.

My gaze tipped to the Monastery of Apante. From the market, I could see the bright white tower. It stood out in stark relief from the other colorful buildings that adorned the city.

It was the only place in the kingdom where a void could hold even a small measure of power.

A BARGAIN SO BLOODY

Without power, you were nothing.

As predicted, Prince Marcel left the next morning. Raphael and I watched from the shade of the forest outside the city where we'd camped. Every inn seemed to be filled with visitors who had anticipated the prince's arrival and wanted to get a glimpse of him, and the last thing I wanted was to find the one single room available and share it with Raphael.

That morning, three dozen horses and three golden stagecoaches exited the city gates. Once the echoes of their footsteps faded, we returned to the city. I placed my request with the administrators of the Great Library and returned in the evening for my appointment.

The sun was setting by the time we returned. A line wrapped around the building, promising a long wait despite any appointment.

"Will you tell me your question now?" I asked as we trudged slowly along. Apparently, having an appointment was just the first step in seeing the Librarians. "Or do you plan to get through the wards and ask for yourself?"

The ancient wards that guarded the Great Library wouldn't be fooled by a little disguise magic. It would've been nice if the Librarians shared whatever ancient magic let them bespell the building to block vampires from entering with the rest of Eurobis. Perhaps the knowledge of how had been lost with the oracles.

Raphael sighed, as if having to rely on a human was such a heavy burden. Then he bent his towering frame down and whispered his question in my ear: "You're going to ask precisely how one can gain possession of the Black Grimoire as soon as reasonably possible."

His hot breath grazed the side of my face, and I blinked, barely able to process. I jerked back, desperate for some distance between us. "That's your question? What does it even mean? The Black Grimoire doesn't exist."

The Black Grimoire was nothing but a myth. It wasn't even a common myth, so I remembered nothing but the barest facts: the book existed and could only be used by a *special* kind of witch not seen in ages. That alone was enough to discount a tale—no witch had claim to an entire branch of magic. Grimoires, books of magic, did exist, and were often passed between bloodlines of powerful witches. Unlike cards, the magic in them couldn't be used by voids, and was more instructional than transactional.

What would possess a vampire to ask about a fairy tale?

"The phrasing is critical," Raphael said, ignoring my question. "If you don't ask for precise terms, they will respond with useless ambiguity. If you forget to give a time frame, the answer will be equally useless. Do you understand?"

"I'm not an idiot," I groused. I committed the nonsensical question to memory.

"I didn't say you were," he said smoothly, not moving out of my space in the slightest.

"But I want to know *why*." Why I was wasting my one allotted question on a myth.

But Raphael would say no more. He left my side once we moved a few more paces forward, no doubt lurking in the shadows, to avoid tripping any vampire sensors. It was half an hour more before I was finally to the front of the line. An extra five minutes, because the balding man in front of me wouldn't stop complaining. Apparently, he didn't appreciate the answer he'd gotten and was demanding another audience.

"Sir, you do not have an appointment." The hooded Librarian who stood at the entrance was half as tall and half as thin as the portly figure. Her voice was gentle, like a spring breeze. Her uniform was a bright sky blue, a thin chain of links clasping the shoulders together.

"I don't need one! I told you, girl, I was here the other day, and the Librarian was wrong."

"The Librarians are not wrong." A bold claim, but delivered without an ounce of ego. Like it was simply a fact—witches had magic, Eurobis had three moons, and the Librarians had all the answers.

Frustrated, the man made a critical mistake. Since arguing wasn't getting him what he wanted, he tried to force his way past. He threw a hand on the girl's shoulder and pushed. I braced for the Librarian to stumble back. She couldn't match his physical strength. Instead, it was the man who bounced back as if repelled by an invisible force field.

"Sylvester Norag, you are not welcome in the Great Library." Her voice thickened—no, that wasn't the right word. It was more like several voices spoke at once, some higher pitched, some lower. The hair on the back of my neck tingled.

She lifted an arm in front of her, a single card lifted between her fingers.

"You are not welcome anywhere in Eurobis."

Powerful magic flew from the card. A beam of light engulfed Sylvester, swallowing his body. I tucked my head into the crook of my elbow to block out the blinding glare.

When I looked up, there was no trace of the balding man. Only ashes remained, fading into the dirt of the floor.

I gaped.

"Next, please," the Librarian chirped.

CHAPTER 15

My eagerness to take the final steps towards the Great Library was greatly diminished by the thought that I, too, would be vaporized if they found out I was helping a vampire.

From the friendly face that peeked out behind the bright blue hood of the junior Librarian, despite all their knowledge, that particular secret was safe.

"Name?" she asked, with all the courtesy of a hostess at one of the tea shops.

"Samara." I didn't dare give a false name here.

"Samara..." She trailed off expectantly.

I swallowed, forcing my tongue to work. "Samara Koisemi." A name I hadn't claimed in many years.

VASILISA DRAKE

She nodded in acknowledgment, but didn't show any particular recognition while she canted her head as if listening for something. Though I couldn't hear anything, she nodded once more and extended an arm in invitation.

"Right this way, Samara Koisemi."

Entering the threshold of the Great Library was no less remarkable than entering another world. The smell of parchment hit me, unmistakable and enticing. Towers of bookshelves stretched higher than should've been possible given the height of the building. Books floated freely between shelves up high, zipping from one spot to another without so much as a rustle of the pages. In fact, the entire space was quiet.

My guide moved ahead. I hurried my steps so as not to lose her, but I couldn't stop my head from swiveling from side to side. She led me around the perimeter of the room—just as the stacks stretched high, a large staircase filled the center, allowing Librarians to move to lower levels. They wore varying shades of blue, from the same bright color of my guide to a dark navy.

"Do I ask you my question?" I whispered.

"No, Samara Koisemi." It unnerved me to hear my name over and over. It was the name of a criminal, and just the sound of it felt like an accusation. "I am only an apprentice, still learning the language of the Library. You will meet one of our journeymen."

She eventually led me to a table and sat me down. A male with a cloak two shades darker, with a slightly thicker chain holding the clasps together, sat across from me. The blue hood shrouded his face.

The journeyman.

He regarded me with only the mildest curiosity. Likely a baseline of interest the Librarians had for all things outside of books.

"What is your question?"

My question. I would only ever have one question, one chance to use the oracle magic stored in the Great Library, and not only was I giving it up for a vampire, but I was also giving it up for a myth.

No. I was giving it up for my *freedom*.

I repeated the exact words Raphael had breathed in my ear, making sure to let them out at a slow measured pace so I didn't mess up the order. The Library didn't allow for corrections if a tongue twisted over the wrong word. "In precise terms, how can one gain possession of the Black Grimoire, as soon as reasonably possible?"

The journeyman jolted back as if I'd used an electric card on him. His hood fell away, revealing an average face, lips gaping at me like a kraken out of water.

"That question," he breathed. "How do you know about that? *Why* would you ask that?"

I frowned at his strong reaction. I'd expected the journeyman to laugh at me. His reaction said there was more truth to the stories than I realized.

"Just curious," I hedged.

"Choose another question." He ground out the demand through clenched teeth.

I frowned. "I don't have another question. I want this one answered."

More accurately, I really didn't want to go back to Raphael without an answer.

"Something else," he hissed. "Ask us how to make your fortune. Ask us where to find the one you will wed. Or how to avoid your death."

I contemplated for a moment. If I asked him to tell me how to evade any potential threats and start a new life, the Librarians would eagerly give me an answer. Or I could ask if my mother's soul was at peace in the blessed fields or lost to the ninth hell as I feared.

I forced myself to look the journeyman directly in the eyes. I would use my question for Raphael's myth hunt. Though from the journeyman's reaction, it wasn't as much of a myth as I had been told growing up. "You agreed to my petition. I'm owed an answer to my question."

I hoped he wouldn't incinerate me on the spot, the way the apprentice had that unruly man at the door. But then, he'd tried to break the rules. He'd been greedy. I only wanted the answer they'd agreed to give me. "This is my only question."

The journeyman narrowed his eyes, grinding his teeth in frustration. But the magic of the Great Library won over, and his lips were forced open. He spoke with the same overlaying voices as I'd heard before, the hive mind magic of the Librarians channeling through him.

"Go north, to the marshes, to the abandoned temple of Anagenni. The Black Grimoire was entombed there seven hundred and seventy-seven years ago. It is locked away behind a statue of the patron goddess, guarded by traps even we do not know, so only the worthy may take possession of the book." The voice faded, and the journeyman glared at me. "You have your answer. Now begone."

I didn't need to be told twice. I scurried from the library with a nimbleness the most wily of rats would've envied. Still, I couldn't resist looking back at the library as I left. The books, the knowledge stored there, forever to be out of my reach because I'd given the vampire my question.

A question that left me with dozens of my own.

Anagenni. What was she the goddess of? Mother hadn't been especially pious, but in the Witch Kingdom, witches and voids alike used the pantheon like spices—a pinch of luck from Lixa, a prayer for health to Askli. Flourishes on the magic we used. It was common to see icons scattered throughout, but no one made formal temples to the gods these days. Why bother, when even voids had magic at their fingertips? Only the Monastery was different.

I darted through the exit, around the apprentice who had escorted me inside. A line still rounded the building. There would be no shortage of people with questions this night, nor any other.

VASILISA DRAKE

I scanned the darkness for Raphael, but neither red nor blue eyes peeked out in the dark.

That was fine. Uncertain how long the library would take, we'd arranged a meeting point for midnight.

But... I had thought perhaps he might be waiting for me.

Fool, I scolded myself.

Maybe that was why I took my time reaching the arranged spot, studying the city at night.

Witch lights lined the street, enchanted so the markets could stay open well past dark. Of course, the types of markets available at Apante changed with the setting of the sun. People looked to feed all manner of appetites at night, judging by the crooning calls coming from certain buildings. I couldn't help but look at one of the pleasure halls as I passed, wondering what it would be like to have that closeness with another. The stolen coins were heavy in my pocket, beckoning even though I'd never let myself give in. Not when I didn't have a way to get more coins.

A pair of oiled figures made eyes at me as I passed, one male, one female. Their bronzed bodies were displayed despite the slight chill of the night, golden fringed gossamer accenting their allure. Whatever they saw in me, they knew I was a target. It wasn't that either of their inviting smiles interested me in particular, but part of me wanted desperately to sate the curiosity that had built over the years. I'd gone from a girl to a woman in name only in Greymere. I was ignorant, but I *knew* I was ignorant, and that was worse.

A BARGAIN SO BLOODY

The lightness of my coin purse prevailed, and the two shifted their attention to more promising potential customers. I pressed on. I paused only once more, to listen to a street performer singing. She was dressed in gossamer silks, making eyes with every audience member even while her mind was clearly occupied with the music. Her voice dipped to low tones, cutting through the other noise in the city. When the song ended and she bowed, it was met with little applause.

I wished I could spare a coin to give her.

The old capital boasted another wonder beyond the Great Library—a beautiful garden, dedicated to an old, forgotten queen. Enormous amounts of magic must have gone into shaping it. The garden took up the entire eastern quarter of the Apante. The entrance was a brilliant marble gate that could only have been made from magic. The twin winged figures carved from the marble looked almost human, but it was the beautiful kind of human you'd die for. I passed through the gates, following the path. The space wasn't entirely deserted, but it was substantially emptier. The gentle wind rustling through the trees drowned out any quiet conversations. I wandered farther, taking in the space. Like the forests I'd slept in, but so much more deliberate. No two trees were alike, different variants that must have been magically spliced by a witch gifted in plant magic. Or more accurately, a team of them.

Even at night, several trees were blooming. The blossoms filled the air with a pleasing scent. Despite the size of the space, branches hung low, making the garden feel private. I was a woman alone at night in a relatively empty space, so I stayed on guard, but there was no sign of anyone else. I found a bench braced against a decorative boulder, carved to look like the three moons atop each other.

I was really alone, at last.

And then I wasn't.

There was no sound that gave him away, no movement in the shadows. But an awareness came into my periphery all the same.

"You remembered me, I see." I was surprised by the annoyance in my own voice. Since when had a vampire *not* being around been a problem?

Raphael sat down on the bench next to me, legs kicked out in front without a care. "I've been here the entire time."

"More likely you were off killing time in one of the pleasure halls."

I wasn't sure why I said it. Raphael was too focused on his mission, whatever it was, to give in to such base pleasures. I might believe vampires could feel desires like that, to a degree, but it was hard to imagine Raphael paying to sleep with a mortal. Even if his appearance rivaled any of the most successful courtesans, his voice a sweet caress that even now tempted me more than any of the others had—though he would likely kill me if I voiced the comparison.

A BARGAIN SO BLOODY

Maybe I said it because I'd thought if his mission was so important, he'd be there when I got out of the Great Library no matter what we'd said about waiting to meet here. That he'd be eager for me to return with his answer.

But he hadn't. I'd been alone.

"I believe that's what *you* were considering."

I flushed. So he was telling the truth about being there. And he was watching closely. *Why had he kept his distance? What would he have done if I did enter the pleasure halls?* "Hardly. It's senseless."

"It's pleasure."

"It's pointless." Survival was all that mattered. Curiosities and desires be damned.

"The point is enjoyment." There was that note again in his voice. As though he thought to say something more but held back.

In a bid to escape the conversation, I stood from the bench and began to meander along the path. Raphael was at my side in an instant, but at least he didn't argue the point further. It was one thing to wonder what a man's body would feel like. It was another to have Raphael know I had those musings.

"You saw the Librarians," he said, letting the subject drop.

"I did." I repeated the answer I'd gotten from the journeyman and watched the vampire's face for any sign of what the information meant, but his expression betrayed nothing beyond a patient tilt of his head. "He wasn't inclined to answer, but the magic bound him to. Why?"

"Because that's how the magic of the Great Library works. Once they agree to a request, they have no choice but to honor it."

I rolled my eyes. "I know *that*. Why did he want to fight against his sacred vows? What *is* the Black Grimoire?"

Our feet padded along the dirt path for several minutes. I was determined not to break the silence first.

Just when I thought he'd let us walk in silence until dawn, he drew a breath to answer. "The Black Grimoire contains magic of death and undeath. In the hands of the right witch, it's a dangerous weapon."

I frowned. No witch had magic that controlled death. Not that I'd ever heard of. "Why do you want it?"

That, he refused to answer. He continued on the path, regarding the trees with a thoughtful expression.

"So you'll go to the marshes, then?" I wasn't sure why I peppered him with so many questions. A sort of ache settled in my chest. I felt like a kid, desperately trying to get my mother's attention before she left for the latest ball while I stayed holed up in her rooms. She was going to leave, no matter what I did. But if she was looking at me, speaking to me, I could pretend there was no ball, and I wouldn't spend the night all alone.

"I will."

"Do you even know *how* to find the temple?"

"I'll manage."

"It said only the worthy could take it. Do you really think that's you?" A vampire, stealing a mythical witch's grimoire?

His lips curled up. "Worried for me, dove?"

More like I'm worried for myself. "Why do you call me that?" Of all the mysteries Raphael offered, this was one I'd ached to untangle. If I didn't ask now, I might never know.

"Because you remind me of a little bird, between the rapid flutter of your heart and clear desire to spread your wings."

I swallowed down any response to that. How could this monster see me so clearly? Was I transparent? Or did he truly... know me? Before long, our path led us back to the main gate. One of the twin angels faced inwards. It felt like it was looking right at me, accusing, demanding to know why I'd brought a vampire into their garden.

I was stuck wondering why I was reluctant to see him leave.

"This is it, then." I looked up at the three moons. "You'll have several hours of darkness to travel."

"I do." Raphael didn't follow my gaze to the moons. Instead, he kept looking at me. The blue began to fade from his eyes, the red returning as the disguise magic wore out. "You're certain you wish to go to the Monastery." His voice didn't raise at the end like a question, but it felt like one.

"It's the best place for me."

Raphael said nothing. I looked back and swallowed. Not from fear, though. Another emotion filled my chest. It was strange and terrible, but the vampire was the closest thing I'd had to a friend in the past decade.

Maybe longer.

"You'll let me go this time?" I joked.

He didn't return my smile. "If that is what you wish."

Why was it hard to make the words come out? "It is."

Raphael nodded once, his white hair sweeping forward as he dipped his chin. Then he turned without another glance and disappeared into the night.

Once more, I was alone.

Chapter 16

I SPENT A NIGHT on the streets. Or more accurately, on a roof.

Though Raphael had left me with a few coins, spending them on something as luxurious as a roof over my head seemed wasteful. The vampire had disappeared into the darkness, and I didn't want to walk out into the woods by myself.

I was no stranger to hidden sleeping spots. I woke early with the rising sun and readied to say something to the vampire.

But of course, I was alone once more.

How... familiar.

Not for much longer. I would break away from that loneliness. Joining the Monastery would change everything. If they could forgive killers and thieves, surely allying with a vampire—briefly—and some mild treason could be overlooked.

The gods were the big picture sort, right?

I should have headed directly to the white tower, but instead I found myself wandering through the city. I loathed the change that came over me. With the vampire nearby, I'd begun to walk the way my mother taught me—shoulders back, head high. *The same way Raphael walked*, I thought ruefully. After all, if anyone made a move for me, he'd deal with them viciously. More to the point, with him by my side, no one would make a move to begin with.

Without him, I returned to my old defenses. Head down, hood pulled up. My shoulders hunched as I wove between crowds, taking quick steps to avoid lingering long enough for someone to mark me as a target. Always move with a purpose, even if you have none. It was true everywhere from prisons to castles.

Magic hummed in the air. Would I miss it, in the Monastery? As a void, I had none. I shouldn't feel any kind of loss. By rights, magic didn't belong to me. But I wasn't sure I'd ever understand how the followers of the sect scorned something so lovely.

By midday, I'd ceased my wandering and headed to the building. The white tower was easy to find. The building was larger at the base before rising into an obelisk, perhaps a quarter the size of the Great Library.

I knocked. Once. Twice. Then, after a long moment, I lifted my hand for a third desperate time.

The door opened inward. A woman greeted me. She wore the simple white robes of all devotees, with clasps at the shoulders and a golden belt cinching the waist.

"Yes?" she said expectantly.

I swallowed. What do people say? Did they fall to their knees, begging to join? Did they have pretty euphemisms?

"I'd... I'd like to join the Monastery."

The smile that broke across her face was brighter than the noonday sun. "Then welcome, friend. Join us."

She moved so I could come inside, then offered to take my cloak. I was reluctant to part with it, but I wanted to make a good impression, so I let her.

"I'm Slyne, a devotee of Lixa."

I plastered a smile on my face that felt utterly unnatural. "I'm Samara."

The inside of the Monastery was as crowded as the Great Library, but instead of books, there were statues, formed in the likeness of every deity of the pantheon, of every size and shape hewn from gray marble lining the halls: Dolor, the thorned god of suffering, Isolde, the goddess of the night skies; and other gods I didn't even recognize. While the Monastery paid its respects to every deity, the average witch only learned a few key figures. The unseeing eyes of the statues seemed to follow us as we moved farther into the tower.

I think I preferred the books.

"You've come at a good time," Slyne tossed over her shoulder as we went up the stairs. "We're enjoying a lunch after morning worship."

"Is that okay?" I asked, nervous.

"Of course," Slyne assured me. "Void and witch alike, all are welcomed once they renounce any power beyond the gods." The words came out rehearsed. Somehow, it was more unnerving than the overlapping voices that spoke through the Librarian. At least then the magic was more obvious. Then again, even Slyne's words were backwards—hadn't I told Raphael haughtily that a witch's powers were *from* the gods?

Don't be so prejudiced, I chastised myself. Yes, most people looked down on the Monastery. I was letting my own biases twist me when I needed to focus on winning them over. After all, those same people would also look down on *me*. For escaping my sentence at Greymere, and worse, for making a deal with a vampire to do so.

But I couldn't regret either. Now that I had finally reached the Monastery.

Slyne came to a door several floors up and opened it, ushering me inside. The space was nothing like what I'd expected. It was... comfortable. People of all shapes and sizes lounged, spread between a few chaises, a long table that was piled with food, and even the floor, where they played with... cards. *Unenchanted* cards.

"Everyone, this is Samara. She's come to pledge herself to the gods."

A chorus of *Hello, Samara* came from the room before Slyne began a flurry of introductions I had no hope of following. A finger point, a face, a name, and a deity, thirty times over. I nodded and tried to adjust my smile so it felt a little less forced. My neck hurt from the stiffness of my shoulders, but I willed the tension away.

Slyne led me deeper into the room, a door shutting with a low *thud* as she sat next to me at the dining table. She wasted no time piling a plate high with food and placing it in front of me. I tried to remember the names of the others at the table, but I could do little more than answer their questions between small bites of the food. It was warm and filling, if plain. Not that I would ever complain about a meal that didn't poison me.

"So, what made you seek deliverance with the gods?" one of the younger girls asked from across the table. A devotee of Dolor, if I remembered right.

I swallowed down a bite of food, trying to remember what I'd come up with. A lie would eventually be discovered, but divulging the entire truth was too dangerous. "I was in a bad spot for a long time. I realized magic would never save me." After all, I was a void, and Greymere muted all magic. "The Monastery is known to be welcoming"—*desperate for recruits*—"so I thought I'd attempt to be worthy of their *deliverance*."

A round of head bobbing said my answer was acceptable. But the Dolor girl's lips curved in a patronizing smirk.

"Of course. Any magic that isn't gifted from the gods will only leave you worse off. Even if people are so corrupted they use it without a second thought."

Slyne shifted next to me. "Vora, you know each of us who comes has been touched by magic. What matters is renouncing it."

Still, Vora's reproach stirred enough pointed glances that I grew self-conscious. *What? Oh. My disguise magic.* My hair was still an unnatural lavender.

Shame stung my cheeks. The room felt hot, and I wanted to shrink in on the chair. I'd been so happy to finally be able to use magic, I'd forgotten to remove it. I was lucky Slyne hadn't turned me away on the spot.

I was amid a sea of plainness unseen in most of the continent. Browns, beiges, blonds. None of the bright colors so many indulged in. I willed the magic to fade, anxiously checking a lock of hair. Black once more.

"Your gods-given hair is lovely," Slyne said, warm as ever.

Vora's smile was victorious. "Not to worry. The gods will see you repent."

The others tittered at the comment.

"Of course. I'm eager to repent." I was eager to be *accepted*.

A BARGAIN SO BLOODY

"The gods take in all who repent," a boy to my left murmured.

After that, things were surprisingly comfortable. Hours passed. I said little, more comfortable listening and observing. Everything was far more normal than I'd expected. Okay, the fact there were statues on every flat surface was a little odd. Vora made a few more comments that might have been considered barbs at certain *godless heathens* in their company, but Slyne ignored them, and I followed suit. They joked. They smiled widely, even with mouthfuls of food. They were people. My own kind of people.

Not like that vampire.

Sure, I still felt like I was on the outside. But I wouldn't be greedy. I'd make them see my value. I'd devote myself to any god I was told, and they'd learn I could be counted on. I'd belong... eventually.

Over the course of the afternoon, I moved from the table to the floor, where a crowd had formed. A pile of cards—non-magical cards—was set between a group of acolytes. They traded the cards back and forth. Instead of magic-imbued symbols, they had different color dots on them, marking them with numbers and shapes. The cards were slammed down without care, then shuffled between food-flecked fingers.

My stomach twisted. I forced my expression to remain neutral.

"Want to play?" one of the girls offered.

I shook my head. "I'll watch for now. I'm still learning the rules." The cards were a mockery of the magic the Witch Kingdom held dear. *Does King Vaughn know?* Surely he wouldn't tolerate this. Even the servants in Greymere had never done anything so obscene.

She shrugged and returned her focus to the game. I rubbed a hand over my chest, to the spot where I'd hidden the enchanted cards I still carried. If they found me with them, they'd think it was just as blasphemous. I'd have to get rid of them—soon, once they accepted me. But no matter how logical, I couldn't make myself part with my only form of protection until I had a better one.

If a little disguise magic offended Vora, I didn't want to know what they'd think of the small deck I had. *I should have traded them before I came here.* My skin grew clammy at the thought, but I'd hidden things before. This would be fine.

I distracted myself, trying to puzzle out the rules of the different games they played while keeping an ear on the various conversations in the room. In a way, much of it was normal. Gossip, musings, egos competing immodestly. Me, listening, trying to make sense of a world where no one would tell me what rules I was at risk of breaking. Just like how I grew up.

Slyne took a spot by me on the floor sometime later. "The initiation will happen at dusk. Have you thought of who you'll devote yourself to?"

"I was considering the goddess Anagenni." The words popped from my mouth before I had a chance to consider what it meant to devote myself to a goddess I'd never heard of.

She frowned. "I don't know this goddess. What is she the goddess of?"

I was hoping Slyne would've known. Really, Slyne should have known—she'd obviously been in the Monastery for some time, by the way the others regarded her, including Vora. And the Monastery had statues to even the tiny god Thiox, who was the patron god of spoiled food.

"Oh, she's a goddess my mother was fond of," I lied. "How did you come to devote yourself to Lixa?"

Slyne allowed me to change the subject, and launched into a long story of how Lixa had guided her to the Monastery.

"I knew it was divine luck," she whispered conspiratorially. "I worried I'd be punished for such hubris, but when I met Devoin, I confided in him, and he agreed. He said I was meant to find the Monastery and shepherd others onto the true path."

"Devoin?" I asked.

"Devoin is this Monastery's head priest. Our leader," she clarified, the fondness in her voice obvious. "He should be here soon. He'll oversee your initiation."

Right. *That*. "The initiation... what's it like?" I hoped I sounded eager and curious, rather than worried.

She just gave me a cryptic smile. "Courage, Samara. The gods will make all things clear."

That was not reassuring.

The door creaked opened. A man walked in, older than the acolytes by some years. He was older, but far from feeble, a man in his prime or just starting to go past it. We weren't the only ones to turn. The entire room seemed magnetized as the man strode in. Slyne helped me to my feet and led me over by the crook of my arm.

"Devoin." Her voice took on a slightly different note, more girlish. "I'm pleased to say another has found their way towards the true path. May I present Samara, our next acolyte."

He looked only at Slyne, a broad grin tipping his lips. "You've done well."

She beamed.

He continued to smile as he turned his attention to me, but it didn't have the same warmth. "As for whether you've found your way... that's for the gods to determine."

Chapter 17

When I'd arrived, Slyne had led me up the tower. For the initiation, we ventured below ground. Devoin led the way, Slyne trailing right behind with my arm still locked in hers. A few others followed. The older members, I noted. Maybe only those who had a certain ranking could come to the Monastery?

Nerves frayed under my skin, but I forced myself to match Slyne's steps, breathing deeply through my nose.

I survived Greymere.

It'll just be some prayers. I'll repeat what they say, and it'll be fine.

And if it's not... I can handle it.

Whatever it cost, it'd be a small price for safety. For belonging.

The basement level was different from the rest of the spaces I'd seen. The stairs led to a wide, circular room. As with every other room, statues lined the space, but these were larger, at least eight feet tall, and carved from dark stone. They were carved with the same magical perfection as the ones at the front of the garden, but I forced myself to ignore it. Hanging braziers punctuated the space between the statues, casting the room in a low glow that reminded me of the dark halls I'd spent the past years in.

This was different. It was my choice to be here.

Devoin stood in the center. Slyne nudged me forward before taking a post in front of a statue, matching where the others scattered around.

"You've come to seek sanctuary in the temple of the gods, the true rulers of the realm. Do you wish for their deliverance?" Devoin intoned. His words were pious, but there was something in the tone that rankled. A coating of superiority that followed each one out, that said, *I have what you want.*

I forced myself to hold my head high. "I do."

He turned away and went to a pillar at the back while he continued to talk, his voice bouncing off the statues. "It is easy to make claims with words. You must prove your devotion. You have harmed yourself over and over with years of greedy magic use. Even now, I feel it clinging to you." The cards were hot against my skin. "It makes me wonder if you're beyond saving."

A hushed silence fell in the chamber. I glanced around, but none of the acolytes met my gaze. "I'll do it. Whatever it is, just give me a chance." *Just please, don't find the cards...*

"As I said, the gods do not trust the words of the corrupt. You must show them you are truly repentant. And as the priest of this city's Monastery, I will guide you to their forgiveness."

He turned back, the braziers casting him in a fearsome light.

"Kneel."

I dropped to my knees, the cold stone pressing against my shins. Devoin wasn't much taller than me, even at my short stature. Now, I had to crane my neck up to see him as he walked back to the center of the space.

"Do you admit only gods can save you?"

"Yes." The word flew from my mouth, as unabashed as my earlier begging.

Yes. Accept me. Let me belong.

The priest's face didn't change. "Beliefs are defined by actions, not words. You must make your body mirror the state of your soul. Only then will you understand the unbearable pain the gods are saving you from."

"Remove your shirt."

I hesitated.

"Do you want to be part of us or not?" Devoin demanded.

I have to do this. I reached for the hems of my new blouse. My flesh wasn't beautiful, but it wasn't shameful. The band of fabric still pressed my breasts together. Devoin's gaze pressed into me as I lifted my shirt. But no matter how careful I'd been, I couldn't stop the movement from dislodging one of the cards I'd pressed against my skin.

The tension in the room rose as all eyes fell to the enchanted card that fell to the ground.

This was it. They'd kick me out for sure now. I'd wasted my chance.

I hunched my shoulders, bracing for the yelling.

But Devoin's voice didn't change from that even, pious tone. "It seems you have extra sins to atone for. Now, impress the gods."

He held out his arm, right in front of my face. My stomach twisted in comprehension. With shaky fingers, I grasped the handle of the tool he'd retrieved from the other side of the room. Several knotted strands of rope dangled from the handle. From this close, I could smell the hint of copper that soaked the rope. How many times had it been used?

My arm felt impossibly heavy as I took it from his hand and lifted the handle above my head. Blindly, I let it fly. Even though I was braced, I gasped at the contact. It *hurt*.

"I said *impress* them."

A BARGAIN SO BLOODY

I lifted the scourge once more and hit myself as hard as I could. Pain exploded across my back, and I dropped the handle. My eyes watered, burning me.

"Again."

I picked it up and hit myself. I tried to avoid the same spot, but with all the tails, the whip seemed to hit every part of my back.

"Again."

My knuckles were white around the whip, but I obeyed. *You have to do this. You have to prove you're one of them*. This time, I didn't drop it.

"Again."

On it went. The pain stopped being so shocking, and instead grew consuming. I couldn't sink into it, not the way I could when Nelson would beat me. Because I had to participate. I had to hit myself as hard as possible, over and over, to earn Devoin's approval. If my blows grew weak, he simply said, "Do better." Those were the worst—the pain that was worthless. It earned me nothing.

But still, I hit myself. Because I would earn their approval. No one gave anything for free. At least here, the cost was clear. Hit after hit. My chest bent lower to the ground, the card directly on the floor between Devoin and me growing hazier with every blow.

"Again."

How many had it been? Ten strokes? Twenty? Sweat coated my palms and the rest of my body, making it hard to grasp the handle. Slyne met my gaze for the briefest moment when I looked up. I wasn't sure what I wanted to see there.

It was that same, warm, encouraging smile as when she'd led me in for lunch. The rest wore expressions mirroring the statues they stood in front of. The same people I'd laughed with, if briefly, only hours before.

"Again," Devoin said.

So again the ropes slammed into me. Was it even my own arm moving? It was hard to tell.

Then again.

And again.

I beat myself over and over at his command. I thought there was no end to the pain, until one split my skin wide open. I cried out at that, for the first time, the flail falling from my grasp as I bent over. Tears ran freely from my eyes. My brain tried to tell me to reach for the handle, to keep obeying. Instead, I crossed my hands over my chest, my forehead falling at Devoin's feet while my entire body shook.

"You have taken yourself as far as you could," Devoin said.

Was his voice gentle? Or was everything just distant? Hope bloomed in my chest. I'd done it. I'd maimed myself to his satisfaction. I'd endured and shown them I belonged—

"So I will take you the rest of the way and lead you to the gods' forgiveness."

I couldn't force my body up, but I twisted my head, finding his eyes.

They didn't seem benevolent or spiritual. Not even impassive.

They seemed... victorious.

I'd seen the same eyes on Nelson. Too many times.

How was this different from Greymere?

Devoin lifted the scourge in his hand. The swish of it whispering through the air lasted an hour. When it hit me, I screamed. It was a sound I'd never made before. A sound I hadn't known I could make.

Raphael didn't yell like this when they beat him.

Is this the same thing he went through? As a vampire, a mortal enemy of the witches? Was that the same as my fate?

"Stop!" I begged when he lifted it again. "Please. Mercy!"

"You must accept that pain is the will of the gods. As long as you fight it, you cannot be one of us," Nelson said.

No. Devoin?

He hit me again, harder. Blood splattered from the blow, landing in front of me. My mind seized on the drops. The red haze of memory grabbed me.

Blood and blood and blood. Flesh torn apart. The cries for mercy, cut off as her corpse was shredded—

More drops joined it.

The drops of red turned to a sea, blood flowing. There was screaming. My own? My memories? No—other.

VASILISA DRAKE

A thud. Another thud.

In my vision, Devoin collapsed.

His body—his head was gone, blood flowing from the neck.

I lifted my head.

Bodies.

Bodies everywhere. Bloody, brutal kills. As bloody as I remembered. Even as I looked, I didn't really *see*. My memories laid over the scene, a wave of déjà vu choking me.

But there was a difference. In the present, one figure still stood. Slashes of blood colored him red from his hair to his torso.

I should've tried to run. Should've been terrified of the monster.

One desperate arm untangled from my chest, reaching forward.

"You came..." Nothing more than a whisper of a question.

Any response was lost as my vision blurred and I collapsed.

Chapter 18

I WOKE, FIRST SLOWLY, then as awareness teased at my edges, I grabbed it and slammed my eyes open. Fear chased away any drowsiness. *Defenseless*. Where was I? I craned my neck up from where I lay prone. Above me was an angled wooden roof. Under me, something I hadn't slept on in ages—a bed.

I tried to prop myself up on my elbows, the blanket covering my back falling to reveal I was shirtless. My chest was wrapped in fresh bandages. My back ached like it had been ripped open.

Which it had been.

Memories crashed into me. My hand flew to my throat, then over the bandages as my movements grew more frantic. "My necklace." My voice was a raw rasp, but all I could do was push through the pain and twist to try to locate it. Was it lost forever?

No, no, no. Anything but *that*.

"On the table. Now, be still, lest you undo all my hard work."

My head jerked at the sound of a voice. Raphael stood in the entrance of the room, propped against the doorframe. He was back to white hair and red eyes, though something about him was different.

Exhausted. He looked exhausted. His hair was unkempt, eyes sunk farther in with dark rings around them. His shoulders were partially slumped, as though he'd been standing too long in that spot. Even after they'd spent days whipping him raw, he hadn't seemed this rough.

Something I now understood in a visceral way.

He lifted his chin to the other side of the bed. I twisted my neck, my head already spinning from the small amount of movement. Relief flooded my throat, letting me breathe again. The bedside table held a pathetically small stack of cards and the necklace I'd retrieved from Greymere and carried hidden on the journey.

I reached for the necklace, but the movement was too much. Raphael crossed the room and handed the chain to me. I snatched it once it was within reach, wrapping my fingers around the cool metal as I tried to make sense of my immediate situation. I didn't hear any noise aside from the crickets outside, so we were unlikely to be in an inn. A window was cracked open, letting the night breeze in.

"Your handiwork?" I croaked, pointing weakly at my wrappings.

The vampire grimaced. "You've been unconscious for three days. Your body's been fighting an infection, which the salve has mostly dealt with."

A fresh awareness of the bandages came over me. *Raphael* had dressed my wounds—multiple times, if he was putting salve on.

"Where are we?" I asked to distract myself from the thought. Since Raphael stood next to the bed, I had to crane my neck to face him.

"An abandoned house, about an hour's ride from the city."

"Was it abandoned when you got here?"

"Does it matter?" he growled. "Anyway, now that you're awake, we can be done with this."

I was going to ask what he meant, but I could only stare as he lifted his wrist to his mouth and bit down, scoring his wrist with a fang. He extended his arm in my direction, inches from my mouth.

Blood beaded on the skin, an invitation.

I tried to inch back, but it was hard with my back still wounded.

"Drink. It will heal you."

I shook my head, decisive and disgusted. "I'd rather die." Screw surviving. Not at that cost. I hadn't known there was a line for me before—team up with a vampire to escape my sentence? Fine. But become one of those abominations?

Raphael didn't *look* like an abomination, but I knew just how deadly he was. Even if it felt unfair to judge him for being deadly protecting *me*.

His gaze narrowed on me. "Do you know what others would do for this gift?" He actually sounded affronted.

"I don't care. Never, Raphael. *Never*."

He rolled his eyes. "You know drinking my blood won't turn you into a vampire, don't you? For that, I'd also need to drain your blood."

"It doesn't matter. I don't want any of *that* in me."

Frustration etched over his features. "Back to thinking of me as a monster, I see. Even though it was your fellow humans who beat you like an animal."

I flinched at his words. Shame filled me, twofold. For one, he was wrong. I wasn't a victim. I'd done it to myself. Or at least I had, until Devoin took over.

All because I wanted to prove I was worthy.

And again... I did consider him a monster. In the most literal sense: Vampires were animated after death and consumed the life-force of others with their teeth.

But I wasn't so naïve that I couldn't see there were monsters made in life too.

I forced my shoulders to relax, if only because squeezing them hurt. "I begin to wonder if there is anyone who isn't a monster." *Nelson. Devoin.* "I am... grateful for what you did. But this is my line. Please respect it."

I readied for him to argue that I was being stupid again. That he knew better, and I should stop being foolish. Though I couldn't fathom why he cared if I lived or died. I'd served my purpose.

He exhaled in resignation and slid into the chair by my bed. "Very well. If you insist. Though I'm going to need to change your bandages. You sweat through them before your fever broke."

He left and returned a moment later with a jar of salve. A single whiff told me it was higher quality than anything I'd ever touched at Greymere.

It would've been easiest if I rolled onto my stomach. Even propping myself up on the pillow hurt. But that felt too vulnerable, and I couldn't feel vulnerable now. Not around anyone. It was a massive effort to sit up enough for Raphael to slide behind me. Sweat covered my forehead by the time I managed, my breath coming in shallow pants.

Raphael simply waited. Then slid behind me on the bed and began to remove the bandages. I clutched the thin sheet for—modesty? Support?

The salve stung when he applied it, and a hiss escaped me. But despite that, his touch was... gentle.

The vampire, with the same hands that tore heads from shoulders, could be gentle. I hadn't known any kind of gentleness for so long that I found the sensation unnerving. Maybe because of the pain I was acutely aware of every point of contact, every whisper of his palm against my skin. Despite the pain, I wanted to lean into the touch.

Because I wanted any touch while in this shape? Or because I wanted his?

"What a reversal," Raphael mused.

Despite myself, my lips twitched. *Indeed*. Then it faded. "Yours was much worse than mine." The sight of his back flayed open would haunt me no matter how long I lived.

"It's hardly a competition," he retorted.

"You'd never have begged the way I did." I wasn't sure why the words came out. Wasn't sure why I could taste the bitterness in them.

His fingers stilled at my back. I twisted to look around and regretted it. His ruby eyes were *blazing*.

"Raphael?" I said quietly.

"You should *never* have had to beg." The words were as vicious as a slice from the scourge, but the anger in them wasn't directed at me. "They beat you like a blood-damned animal."

I turned away. Tears pricked my eyes. He was angry, on my behalf. Was I so pathetic that it was a comfort? But his pity was misplaced. "I did it to myself."

"You had no way of knowing what they would do to you."

I shook my head. "No. I mean I did it. Devoin—the priest. He told me I had to prove to the gods that... I don't know, that only they could save me? That I was unworthy?

I made it worse by sneaking the cards in. I should've sold them before going to the Monastery."

"He knew you were desperate, and he used that to degrade you. To punish you for needing help. Any excuse they gave you—as if the gods give a fuck how much you suffer in their names. As for the cards, of course you had the cards. Every fucking mortal who's not one of their cultists carries a deck. You had no knowledge of what to expect, that it would make it worse."

A tear threatened to escape as he spoke. I rubbed a palm across my eyes to stop it. "I still agreed."

"You told him to stop. And no one intervened."

I recalled the way I'd looked at Slyne, desperate. The way she'd looked back, confident that things were exactly as they should be. "He was their leader."

"And they're dead for following him blindly," Raphael replied.

They were. Bloody, bloody deaths. I'd seen him kill before. Nelson, the guards, Tom. But those had been quick, clean kills. What happened in the Monastery was a slaughter.

Would I be a traitor if I didn't mourn their deaths?

"Is that why you took us an hour from Apante?"

"I thought it wise for us to not be around in case questions were asked," Raphael agreed. "Not that anything they would do could truly threaten me, but in your condition..."

Weak.

"How did you hear me? I thought you were leaving for the marshes."

"I decided to remain in the city for a little longer. Vampire's prerogative." There was a casualness to the words that rang false to my ear, but I was too weary to interrogate it. Raphael closed the lid of the salve and began to wrap my back once more.

"Why?"

Why did you save me? Why bother? Why are you angry on my behalf? I'm a human. I mean nothing to you.

I don't mean anything to anyone. Not anymore.

"I suppose because I wanted to," he said with utter nonchalance, the bed shifting as he rose and walked to the door.

A whim. That's all my life was for him.

Any further questions were cut off as my stomach let out a loud groan. Raphael's head tilted at the sound. I flushed. Of course I was hungry. I'd slept for three days. Familiar pangs pierced me. How quickly I'd forgotten the sensation after traveling with the vampire for a time.

"I'll address that," he said, leaving the room before I could respond.

In the distance, I heard a series of clangs, curses, and eventually footsteps when he returned maybe half an hour later, carrying a plate.

A vampire is actually serving me a meal. Maybe I really was dead.

He placed the plate in front of me.

I looked at it.

Then I looked up at him, in horror.

"All that effort to save me and you're going to poison me?"

"Only cowards resort to poison," Raphael groused.

"Then what do you call this?"

The plate held a horrific mix of foods—berries, meats, beans, and at least two bones—bound together by something that might have started as eggs but was now closer to charcoal.

"I call it *food*. Now eat, Samara. Your body's healing relies on you using that mouth to masticate, not argue."

I gave the mound of "food" an experimental shove with a fork. "Don't vampires start out as humans, or is that just a myth?"

Raphael sank into the chair next to me. For the first time, his gaze seemed deliberately pointed away from me. His cheeks were just a touch brighter than I was accustomed to seeing on the pale vampire. "You go six hundred years without cooking and show me how good you are."

Six hundred years. But still... he'd done it. For me.

There was something nearly sweet about it.

Not sweet enough to counter the fumes rising from the plate, but sweet all the same.

"It's blood or eggs. Pick one," Raphael snapped, when I kept moving the food on the plate, trying to find some part that looked less noxious than another.

I picked the eggs.

Chapter 19

We spent several days in the house. Raphael certainly seemed annoyed at how slowly I was healing. No, annoyed wasn't the right word. It was too mild for the expression that passed over his eyes every time I strained my back in some overly ambitious movement.

Despite whatever he felt, he made no move to rush me—or to leave and set off on his own. He brought food to the cabin but, mercifully, made no additional meals once I could stand to move through the kitchen. In a sense, his cooking really was healing. It motivated me to get well enough to save me from any of his further attempts to cook "eggs."

The cabin was humble. The dust that covered the furniture alleviated my initial concerns that he'd murdered the previous occupant.

The days were slow, with nothing to do but sit around and heal. Raphael ushered me back to bed the moment I started breathing hard, informing me with no small amount of authority that "humans need extensive rest."

"How would you know?" I grumbled when he made that declaration once again.

Raphael arched a single white eyebrow in my direction. "I *was* a human once, you know."

Six hundred years ago. All vampires were turned humans. From a corrupt magic or what else, I couldn't say. Yet it was hard to picture Raphael that way. That he ever could have felt as I did now: feeble, weak.

The reply was an invitation.

Did I want to know more about him? I *shouldn't*.

But I did.

"What were you like, as a human?"

Raphael stretched out on the chair beside my bed. From this angle, I could see his profile. It was late at night, so the window in the room was drawn. The light of the moons shone through, casting shadows on the planes of his face.

"I'd like to say much the same. Being a vampire doesn't change one's fundamental nature. But I suppose the years have made me warier. More self-reliant. As a mortal, I was... optimistic."

He said *optimistic* the way I said *vampire* or *monster*. But as often as I called him a monster in my head, when the word passed my lips, all I could see were the human men who had delighted in my torment.

"Don't look so surprised. Times were different then. Kingdoms were younger, magic was wilder. All one had to do was look around and see a world of possibilities at their fingertips. I had a good life and knew little hardship. Dragons wove through the skies, and as a boy I dreamed I'd ride one. Instead, I wound up on a different path."

The path of a vampire. But before that... I tried to picture him, a small, ruddy-faced boy with bright blue eyes that dreamed of taming mythical beasts. Perhaps he was right that his nature hadn't changed—arrogant as hell.

"What made you choose to become a vampire?"

Something in his face shuddered, but he didn't end the conversation the way he usually did when that look appeared. "It wasn't exactly a choice. Or maybe it was, but it didn't feel like one at the time."

I frowned. "Do you regret it?"

He grinned, fangs glinting in the moonlight. "Trying to cast me in a role where I'm some poor misunderstood vampire that despises his nature? I'm stronger, faster, eternal. There's freedom in that—in having the strength and time to do anything you wish."

So what do *you want?* I bit back the question. It felt too personal.

Silence stretched. I knew it was my turn to share, but my throat was suddenly too dry to speak. Anxious, I fiddled with the chain around my neck. Raphael noted the movement and lifted his chin in its direction.

"What is that?"

I wrapped my palm around the pendant. The metal was cool against my too-warm skin. It felt odd to wear it instead of hiding it on my body, but there were only the two of us here, and Raphael wouldn't recognize it. "It was my father's. It's the only thing he ever gave me."

I certainly hadn't been given a shred of his magic.

"Is he alive?"

I hesitated. "Yes."

I didn't have more to give him than that, and mercifully, Raphael didn't press.

I dozed for a little after that, and when I woke, light trickled through the curtains. I ran my fingers over the necklace. The chain was tied together; it had broken at some point. I was lucky Raphael had thought to grab it at all. It was the one possession I had from either of my parents, from the life I had before I was sentenced to Greymere.

The pendant was an oval, overlarge in my tiny palm without being heavy. Four planes of brightly painted metal decorated the shape. The broken chain bothered me, but maybe I could fix it.

I eyed the cabin, considering. A space like this would need a lot of little repairs. Magic could be used for that kind of thing, but tracking down the right spell and trading for it each time would be annoying, so I wagered the previous owner would've kept manual tools. It took a few different guesses, but eventually I found an old toolkit. More than that, I found supplies that called to me: metal wiring, gloves, a magnifying piece, and more.

I grinned and took my haul back to the bedroom. As loath as I was to admit it, my back still ached when I walked despite the healing salve. I'd stopped Raphael from applying it after the first night I'd awoken, but my reach was limited, and the fever had lowered my strength further. I propped the pillow against the headboard and set to work repairing the chain. It was a delicate process since several links had been damaged. I could've shortened it and made my life easier, but I couldn't bear to throw away any of the pieces. Finally, when I finished with the necklace, I began to fiddle with the other pieces I'd found.

The day passed quickly with my tinkering. The only sign of time passing was the slight changing in the light of the room. Raphael slid into the room at one point, as he so often did, returning from wherever he went during the day. I debated stopping, his presence making me self-conscious. But I was bored, and my fingers were eager to have something to do.

Besides, I'd bathed around the damned vampire. This shouldn't leave me feeling any more exposed.

Raphael didn't say a word, except to briefly leave and return with some leftovers at one point. Only when dawn began to bleed through the window did I set my tools aside on the table behind my bed, a strange satisfaction in me.

It was possibly the first time I'd done something for myself, rather than just to survive since... I couldn't recall when.

The next night, when I awoke, my pile of supplies was significantly increased.

"Did you steal these?" I asked Raphael, my excitement turning what should've been an accusation into curiosity.

"Does it matter? I've done worse."

So I spent the next few days experimenting with the different supplies while Raphael watched me work. I made rat traps, like at the prison, except this time I had food to bait them with. They weren't strictly necessary, but there was a satisfaction in finally perfecting the design. Next, I worked the wire into lock picks I tested around the cabin. The copper cuffs, I modified on the rare occasion Raphael was out of the room, though he must've known I had them, but in my eagerness, I broke the locking mechanism. Sloppy.

I wasn't sure why he let me keep them, but they made me feel safer, even if they wouldn't be any good unless I could reform the metal into another shape. When I started on a new belt, he left his post at my bedside and returned a moment later with a small pouch.

"Here. I meant to give this to you earlier."

Curious, I opened the bag and gasped, stunned at what I was holding. It was the same belt I'd admired for a moment too long in the city market. Finely crafted, it would rival anything used at court. It was even more beautiful than I recalled, and up close, I could see just how carefully it had been stitched. Unconsciously, my fingers traced each row of beads as I lifted the belt to the light.

Suddenly self-conscious, I looked at Raphael. He had something resembling a smile on his lips, or at least a ghost of one. Like he was happy his gift pleased me. He'd seen me admiring it, and even knowing we'd part, he purchased it. Or thralled the human into giving it to him.

Why did he even bother?

All at once I felt awkward and unsure what to say. It was a strangely thoughtful gift—one that said he hadn't expected me to really join the Monastery.

It was the only gift I'd received since I was a child. Sufficient words spoiled on my tongue, and the most I managed was a mumbled thanks while clutching the belt tight between my fingers.

"I'm pleased you like it."

I nodded once more and returned to my projects. I had better luck understanding the mechanics of a lock than what would compel a vampire to give me a gift.

Over the next days, my back healed. After a few weeks, I could move without sharp pain. My energy returned.

But neither of us discussed what would happen after.

Instead, once I was feeling brave, I asked, "Who's Anagenni?"

We were sitting in the bedroom again. At first, Raphael had watched me in constant silence. I was the one who broke it, and now we spoke about different things while I worked. Well, Raphael did much of the talking, at my request. He told me of travels, of different parts of the kingdom even I hadn't heard of. He said nothing of the Vampire Kingdom, but sometimes he'd allude to things which would set my curiosity ablaze.

"Even the Monastery didn't know," I continued when he said nothing.

Raphael snorted. "I suppose those fanatics wouldn't. Anagenni is the goddess of death. The vampires revere her."

I balked. "Why would the Witch Kingdom have a temple to a vampire god?"

"I didn't say she's a vampire goddess. Just that we revere her while you all have shunned her for the past few centuries."

Ironic. The undying creatures worshiped death, while the mortals forsook her.

"Are you really going to go to her temple in the marshes? Whatever the Black Grimoire is, you're not a witch. It's useless to you."

"*We* are going to the marshes," he said, like it was a forgone conclusion.

I blinked at him. The past few days, we'd been in a domestic stasis, tinkering, talking. I hadn't considered... no, I hadn't let myself consider what would happen after.

VASILISA DRAKE

"You're healed enough now. We leave tomorrow."

Chapter 20

Raphael, for all his disappearances in our time at the cabin, hadn't bothered to steal another horse, which meant I was back to riding on Alphonse with him. He had, however, picked up a choice few cards, including one that enchanted the horse's legs to be able to handle the wet terrain.

Since he couldn't cast the cards himself, surely that meant he'd expected me to come with him. Imperious vampire.

But I went with him anyway. I couldn't stay in Apante after Raphael had just killed the highest-ranking members of the Apante Monastery, which was the only place that could shelter me. My next best hope was to follow him north, and once he accomplished his goal, convince him to deposit me in a village where I could build a life undetected. Eventually, the king's men would likely find me, and I'd need to run and find somewhere new or be caught, but I didn't have a better option yet.

He rode with uncharacteristic gentleness. Whether it was because of the marsh's terrain or that he had some lingering concern about my wellbeing... it was easier to believe the former.

We reached the temple a few days later. There was no mistaking the sight. Buried in the depths of the marshes was a temple perhaps half the size of the Monastery and a third as tall. It was made of shiny black stone that had withstood the elements. Even covered in years of vines and shrouded in mists, it radiated power. Something in me felt compelled to see the inside in a way I hadn't felt at the Great Library or the Monastery.

Another puzzle.

"You'll wait here," Raphael declared, dismounting from Alphonse with ease.

"I most certainly will not," I retorted. "And let an ogre have me for lunch?"

"You don't have enough meat to entice an ogre to expend the effort."

I looked around dramatically. "Ah, yes. Because ogres in the marshes have so many options, they're picky about which weak little humans they snack on."

"There'll be traps. It's too dangerous."

A BARGAIN SO BLOODY

I frowned. "You sound like you've been inside before."

A beat. "I have."

So it wasn't luck that led us so easily to the temple. Still, why? Were things so different hundreds of years ago that vampires ventured into the Witch Kingdom for temples?

Or was it from his life... before?

"Then you'll keep me safe," I countered. "You're the one who's constantly been saying I'm safer with you than without you."

Raphael hesitated. Indecision warred inside him—he obviously wasn't used to me challenging him on his plans. Especially not me asserting any kind of trust in him. But I did trust the vampire—to a point. And more than that, I wanted to go inside that temple, the way a child wants to run down a long, empty corridor.

And I really didn't want to find out which of us was right about ogre preferences.

I could see the moment I won him over. "Step where I step. And don't touch *anything*," he warned while helping me off the horse.

I rolled my eyes and followed him inside.

THE TEMPLE WAS DARK.

There was barely any other way to describe it. Despite the aged appearance, inside was all sleek black stone. Unnatural, glistening stone, all one piece rather than blocks, as though the temple had been carved from onyx.

Raphael moved cautiously inside, but with his vampire vision, the dark wasn't an issue. Me, I had to improvise. I'd snagged a branch from the marsh and concentrated, using one of the fire cards to light it. The magic had to work uphill to keep the waterlogged wood alight. The light was dim, barely enough for me to see the area directly in front of me. If Raphael stopped abruptly, I'd probably knock into him.

The air pricked against my skin. Gooseflesh pebbled on my arms as we moved past the entryway. The magic was thick in the air.

At the first fork, Raphael didn't hesitate to go left.

"How do you know your way around?" I asked, my words echoing off the walls.

He paused, briefly running his fingers against the wall. Could he feel the magic radiating off of the stone as I could? "All that matters is I do. Now, do *exactly* as I do."

He pressed a palm into the stone again, and to my shock, the wall rippled like it was made of water. On the floor, the stone lit up splashes of red and blue. He moved deftly over them. Each lit spot sparkled slightly when his foot bore down on it. He only touched the red ones.

I slid my hand against the wall, trying to find the exact spot he'd used. The stone was firm, but when I pressed, it rippled for me, just as it had for him.

But that wasn't all.

The tingling sensation of magic moved to a faster vibration, like I was shaking even as my body stood still. Like the ripples moved from the wall into me.

Like something was waking up.

"Little dove," Raphael hissed, snapping me from the sensation. "Stop dawdling."

"I'm not dawdling," I grumbled, matching my steps to the red spots. As my foot landed, sparks flew and then the area behind me darkened. The vibrations no longer filled my body. I turned back and lifted my torch to look, but the path behind us was back to normal. Since it reacted to me, it wasn't Raphael somehow using magic to navigate, but rather the temple's own magic.

He paused at the next intersection, as if considering.

To the left.

I wasn't sure where the thought came from, only that it was sudden, strange, and certain, but a second later, Raphael shifted and went down the path to our left.

A lucky guess. That was all.

The hall was identical to the one before, except there were three levers planted in the stone. Here, once again, Raphael seemingly knew just what to do. He pulled the first and third one.

Nothing happened, but he began to walk forward.

"What was the point of that?" I asked. I wanted to get a closer look at the lever system, to see how it worked, but he'd have a conniption.

"If I didn't do that, the floor would've swallowed us whole as we walked across," he said tersely.

"Really?" I frowned. I knew objects could be enchanted, but only temporarily. This place likely had been uninhabited for centuries, so how was this magic still working?

"This is the temple of a goddess. The same way the prison swallowed magic, her temple *breathes* it."

Greymere drove witches mad by blocking their abilities. How would a witch react to the opposite? They should surely be drawn to magic like this, yet the place was abandoned. The Monastery had taken over the place of most temples, utterly devoid of magic by comparison.

Raphael turned the next corner but didn't advance. He stopped so abruptly I nearly hit him. Confused, I peered past his arm, trying to see.

There was nothing.

More accurately, from the torchlight, there was nothing directly in front of the archway but a massive dark hole.

"What part of the wall do you have to press now?" I asked.

"None. This isn't a magical trap."

I frowned. "Then how do we get by?"

He pointed to the right, and I leaned forward to see what he was looking at. At the very edge, jutting from the wall, was a small lip, maybe three-quarters the length of my foot. It ran as far as I could see.

"We're not..."

"We are."

I swallowed. "What happens if we fall?"

"My suggestion is *don't*."

That didn't make me feel any better. "But if we do?"

"You get impaled on one of the spikes below."

Wonderful.

I could've insisted I stay here and wait for him to come back. Of course, if he took too long, the fire would go out and I'd have no way to find my way back. But there was something about the temple. Something that was drawing me deeper and deeper in.

He turned back to face me. "You can stay here," he said, reading my hesitation.

I shook my head. "I can manage."

"I'll hold the torch for you, then."

Before I could ask how, Raphael disappeared.

A breeze hit my face.

No, not a breeze. I stared at the spot where Raphael had been standing. In his place, at eye level with me, was a large bat.

He flapped towards my hands, an indication to give him the torch.

I was still staring at the creature in front of me.

"You can turn into a *bat*?"

He dove at my hands again, more impatient.

I'd never sleep well again. Not if vampires could turn into random animals.

Well... if I impaled myself on a spike in the pit, it wouldn't matter.

VASILISA DRAKE

I lifted the torch to him, uncertain if his small, clawed feet could grasp it, but they managed, digging so hard into the wood it dented. Apparently, vampire strength extended to other forms. He moved from the edge to the space over the chasm, lighting the ledge for me. I stepped onto the lip, pressing my weight towards the wall. My heart slammed against my ribs, but I mastered my breathing and slowly moved one foot forward, then the other. Bat-Raphael lit the way, a few paces ahead. I didn't dare look any farther. I didn't want to know how far I had to go. The stone was smooth, and the slick sweat of my palms meant I couldn't even fool myself into thinking I had any kind of grip.

When faced with a terrifying situation, the only thing to do was keep moving. So that was what I did, one slow foot drag at a time. It could've been an hour for all I knew. When I eased around another corner, I dared to let myself believe I might actually make it. I was close. So close. Raphael flew closer, the beating of his wings cooling the sweat beading on my neck. The torch seemed to be growing dimmer, but perhaps that was just my nerves. It lit the space immediately in front of me, so I stepped there, then again and again.

I'm going to make it.

Then the dim light sputtered out.

And I was in the dark.

Clinging to the wall.

Chapter 21

Panic seized me. Any chance of controlling my breathing died as I began to hyperventilate.

I'm going to die here.

I'd thought it would be worth it. That I needed to continue on this journey. Stupid. Survival above all else. Now I would die for my godsdamned curiosity.

"Samara. Slow your heart."

"Raphael?"

"I'm right here, just a few feet to to your left. You're nearly there."

"I-I can't," I stammered. It was hard to even speak between breaths.

"You can," he insisted. "Keep going."

Hesitantly, I slid my foot forward. Into the dark. But just like in the light, the path was smooth. I moved my other foot, and resumed inching.

"That's it." His voice was soothing, like the night sky. "Just a bit more."

I followed the sound of his voice, my galloping heart slowing to a canter.

"Good. Nearly there. Now just step forward and you'll make it."

Just another step. That was all I had to do. My foot slid off as the lip ended. I was there. I tried to hook my leg to catch the opening.

I lost my balance.

I was going to fall. The awareness hit me a second before I began to drop—an immediate, absolute certainty that I was done for. My hands slipped off as I fought to regain my balance, my foot trying to come back but missing, and I was falling, falling, falling—

Strong hands snatched me from the air itself. Raphael threw me back against his body, sending us both tumbling. I landed atop him. There was no light save the faint, unnatural glow of his red eyes.

In the dark, every other sense became more acute. This close, I inhaled his scent with my rapid breaths. Cedar, spice, and something more dangerous than the dark. My fingers gripped the fabric of his shirt, like he was the only thing stopping me from falling into the pit.

"Told you that you'd make it."

A BARGAIN SO BLOODY

I didn't have to see his mouth to know it was curved into a smile. Me, I couldn't smile right now. Not with my heart still slamming in my throat. I couldn't even force my fingers to unclench from where they were still fists in his shirt. My head told me I should be getting off him, that if I was close enough to feel the rise and fall of his chest beneath me, I was too, too close. But my legs were shaking too much for me to move.

"You caught me." Three words. The most I could manage in this position.

"I did," he agreed. Like it was nothing.

Like of course he had saved me from certain death, and how could I even doubt it?

How, indeed.

"As much as I enjoy having a woman on top of me, we should continue."

His teasing jolted me out of the remnants of panic that had caged me. My chest was flush against his, my legs sprawled over him. Even riding together on Alphonse didn't compare to this. I scrambled to stand, pressing my hands into his chest to leverage myself up, but in the dark I was moving blindly. His hands rose to my sides, steadying as he guided me up, and I told myself my heart was pounding only because I'd nearly fallen to my death, not because of his touch.

"The torch?" I asked.

Wood brushed my fingers as he offered me the discarded branch. It took a moment to figure out which card I needed, but eventually I managed to relight the flame. It was even smaller than before, as if the magic struggled to stir this deep in the temple. I stuck closer to Raphael as we ventured farther.

Even as the shock faded from the prior trap, I couldn't let go of one thing. "You can turn into a bat."

"Yes." *And your point is?* was the silent continuation.

I recalled the time we'd been in the inn, and he'd let himself out the window. I'd looked and seen no sign of the vampire. But I hadn't been looking for a bat.

"Why didn't you tell me?"

His steps slowed as we hit another trap. "I'll tell you my secrets as soon as you start volunteering your own."

Absently, my fingers threaded around the pendant on my neck. Fair enough.

But still... "Can all vampires do that?"

"No."

That was a small relief.

We continued along the winding path. We crossed a few more traps that Raphael navigated—sliding tiles, trick walls—but no more near-death experiences. At some point, we started going down, the ground beneath us sloped.

"We're here," Raphael announced.

Even if he hadn't said so, the change was obvious. The pitch black of the hallway changed as blue glyphs covered the walls. At first, they were sparse, thickening as we went deeper. The runes glowed, lighting the space enough that

I could finally see. Few knew Old Runyk of runes, but my mother had made me learn the basics at a young age. *Power*, one said. *Death*, said another. The rest, I couldn't decipher, but their magic charged the space. Even the air felt different, like it was charged on a stormy day and waiting for lightning to strike. The hallway was wide enough for us to walk side-by-side, so I could better see the path ahead. The runes seemed to call me forward, a siren song that was hard to resist.

I lifted a hand to them, wanting to trace the magical shape with my fingertips.

Raphael snatched my hand back. "Remember what I said—don't touch anything."

I drew my hand back from the wall, but Raphael didn't release his grip. He pulled me forward while I glanced wistfully at the wall.

Then I shook myself. What was I thinking? This temple was devoted to the goddess of death, and she seemed intent on killing trespassers. Why would I try to activate the magic guarding the heart of the temple? It was thoughtless, and I was never thoughtless. The magic seemed to cast a haze over my mind, and even the vague awareness of it wasn't enough to stop the desire.

The blue glow bounced off the black stone, brightening as the long hallway widened the farther we went. Conspicuously empty.

Until it wasn't.

It was really here.

Even with the Librarian's assurances, I hadn't really believed we'd find the Black Grimoire. It was a myth, lost to time. Yet there, at the end of the hallway, a book sat on a black stone lectern that seemed to be carved from the floor. Whatever magic was in the temple and the runes was magnified tenfold here, a magnetic pull tugging us closer.

Raphael's pace increased. His face reflected something nearing surprise—as if he, too, hadn't expected to find it here. In a matter of moments, we stood before the book, shoulder to shoulder.

The cover was ornate, inlaid with shining black stones that formed the shape of a skull, twin rubies in the eye sockets. The grimoire itself wasn't so large, but it practically pulsed with magic. Raphael lifted a hand toward it, then withdrew his fingers suddenly, as if burned. He let out a vulgar curse, something I'd never heard from him before.

"I can't touch it," he hissed. "It's enchanted so no vampire can."

I pulled my hand from his grip and flashed him a grin. "Good thing the *weak little human* is here, then."

Raphael glanced between the book and me. I forced my fingers to clench at my sides, when all they wanted to do was grab for it.

"Fine. But Samara—"

I was already reaching for the book. The second my fingers grazed the cover, its magic slammed into me. Touching the wall had been like something waking up inside me. Touching the book was like *I* was waking up after sleeping for years. Sensation overwhelmed me, blocking out the rest of my senses. There was no sound, no sight, only the book between my hands, beckoning me, as if to say, *At last, I am found*.

I need more. I had to get more of this, whatever it was. It was the same as being a void when you used enchanted cards for the first time, except a thousand times more potent. All the magic I could ever crave, all the *power*, and it lay just inside this book.

Unable to stop myself, I began to lift the cover.

Distantly, I heard a voice cry out, "Samara, no!" but it was too late.

Three things happened at once.

First, as I opened the book, the magic soured. What had been lively and joyful turned dark, as if it were disgusted with me.

Second, I was knocked to the ground, the book falling from my grip.

Third, Raphael cried out as a *whoosh* cut through the air. The book gone, I glanced up in time to see arrows spring from every side of the room. Right toward the spot I'd been standing. Raphael had shielded me and absorbed the blows.

Chapter 22

I pushed myself out from under Raphael.

His body was riddled with arrows. Blood coated the ground. So much blood. He lay face down in it.

No, no, no. Not again.

I lifted to my knees, checking him over. At least a dozen arrows covered his back.

I'd be dead if they'd have hit me.

Perhaps he'd done it because he was a vampire, invulnerable to simple arrows. He had accelerated healing. Surely, if I removed the arrows he'd be fine...

"Are you okay?" It was a stupid question, but I just wanted him to say *yes*. Yes, he was fine. Yes, he was an extremely powerful vampire, and what would fell a mortal was no match for him and his ego.

The only answer was a groan.

I swallowed. Even if he could heal, he wouldn't do it with the arrows inside him. I maneuvered around, taking care not to aggravate the wounds. Arrow wounds were tricky, because taking the head out ripped the flesh on the inside. There was a special way to get them out... *Think, Samara*. I'd seen it somewhere. A book, as a child? I'd need something that could hook around the point. I withdrew the contents of my skirt pockets, thanking the gods I hadn't left everything on Alphonse. In the days I'd spent tinkering, I'd made a few different objects. One had to work... *there*. What I'd intended to use to make a kit for picking locks. Now, I twisted the metal into a new shape, a long stem with a loop at the end, which I lined with the leather to hopefully protect his body from the worst of the arrows.

"This will hurt," I warned.

Raphael didn't answer, but his back tensed. I swallowed and set to work, snapping off part of the arrow shafts and working out the pieces. It was slow. If I rushed, I risked breaking off the tips inside his back. I didn't dare move him and jostle them further. Raphael grunted through his teeth as I worked, trying to hold steady for me. My fingers grew slick with his blood. I wiped them on my skirt, returning to the task. *Don't think about the blood. Just get them out*. For once, memories didn't take me. Only the pressing need to get the arrows out.

I stole glances at the ripped flesh, hoping it would miraculously knit together. When the last of the arrows were removed, I helped lift Raphael, moving us away from the center of the hall. I didn't want to risk the arrows coming for us again, but something told me as long as I didn't open the grimoire again, we'd be safe. The book was... aware. Of that, I was certain. If it didn't want a vampire to touch it, perhaps opening it had elevated its awareness to the point it detected a vampire—a threat—in the space.

But none of that mattered if Raphael died here.

There was an alcove a short distance past the lectern, with no glowing glyphs on the wall. He was heavy, so it was a struggle to move him that far. By his pained exhale, I wasn't doing a very good job. Still, with reserves of strength I didn't know I had, I managed to reach the alcove.

"Can I set you against the wall here without setting off another trap?" I asked quickly.

The slight dip of his head was either a nod or he was about to pass out. I propped him against the obsidian wall. The swirling storm in my chest refused to stop.

"You'll heal, right?"

"It's cursed copper." The words came out strained.

Panic swept through me. "But you're a vampire. You'll heal. Right?"

He strained to lift his head up, dull, hooded eyes looking back at me.

A BARGAIN SO BLOODY

"Not without blood."

I bit back a curse. He'd never make it out in this condition to feed. And I didn't stand a chance at going out to get him an animal. Even if I could navigate the traps on the way out, I doubted that would be enough. He'd once said animal blood was barely enough to survive on. To heal wounds of this magnitude, it wouldn't suffice.

No choice.

"Feed on me."

It was hard to tell which of us was more surprised by my words. His eyes widened, pain forgotten for the moment while he took me in. As for me, all I could see was that moment playing over and over in my mind, the impact of the floor as I was slammed to the ground while he shielded my body with his own.

"Before I change my mind," I said with impatience, trying to hide my urgency. Hadn't I sworn I'd die before I ever let a vampire drink my blood? Not after *that* night. But here I was, offering, instead of leaving him to die.

"You're sure?" he rasped.

"You're bleeding out. I'm pretty godsdamned sure!"

The promise of blood roused him from his stupor. Still, this weak, he could do little to move from where he was propped against the wall. I sank to my knees in front of him, kneeling between his legs. I steeled my core, readying for the pain that would come. I'd endured worse. And he'd saved me twice over. I owed him a debt.

VASILISA DRAKE

Was the debt really the only reason I didn't want Raphael to die? He bent his head, red eyes glowing in the dark. Lithe fingers brushed my hair away, tickling my shoulder blades.

His breath burned hot against my skin. I fought a shiver. *Fear? Worry for him?* His hands gripped my shoulder for stability. I was grateful for the brace, because if he didn't hold me in place I might bolt before allowing him to do this.

He lowered his mouth to my neck.

And I let the vampire bite me.

Chapter 23

A gasp flew from my mouth when his fangs pressed into my neck, twin points digging into my flesh.

I'd expected pain. I'd braced for it as stoically as I could manage. And maybe there was some, the slightest pinprick.

But it was erased as a tide of heat rose inside me at the contact.

His fingers clenched my arms tighter, as though to hold me in place, but I couldn't have moved away if I wanted to. My eyes shut as I gave in to the sensation. It was unlike anything I'd ever experienced before.

Bliss.

That was the only word for it. I arched in his grip, urging him to drink me deeper. My chest pressed against him, my nipples pebbling into stiff peaks. My body warmed throughout, my thighs squeezing together as desire pooled between my legs. The only thing I knew was pleasure, and I never wanted it to stop. *It feels so, so good*. I'd give him everything just to have more of this.

Raphael abruptly shoved me away, ripping his fangs from my neck.

I blinked, the daze receding.

He wiped his mouth with the back of his hand, pupils blown wide as they flicked between my neck and my expression. I slammed my own palm over the spot he'd bitten, but the wounds were already healing. Under my palm, my pulse raced. I tried and failed to tame my shallow breaths, leaning back on my heels as we stared at each other.

"Your taste... you're without parallel."

The words were a caress in the worst way because Raphael didn't even seem to realize he'd said them. His slight rasp raked over my body, which still throbbed with need. I'd never experienced any approximation for what he'd just stirred in me, and all at once I felt lost.

I let a vampire feed on me.

Horror. *I should be feeling horror*. But none came.

"So did it work?" I demanded, trying to stir the panic I'd felt just moments ago while he'd seemed on the brink of death. It was like I was drugged. The frantic energy I knew should be there was just out of reach, while it was all I could do not to ask him to bite me again.

Raphael rolled his neck.

"It did."

He rose to his feet and offered me a hand. I pushed myself up from the ground without taking it, trying to hide my sway. Of course, he noticed. To avoid meeting his gaze, I demanded he turn around, and I inspected his back.

Unmarred.

It was startling. I'd expected some healing, but this was... well, it was like magic. The skin appeared as though it had never been broken, had never taken a dozen copper arrows directly, even as his blood coated the floor.

We returned to the glowing hallway.

"Don't open the Black Grimoire, but pick it up," he ordered as the book we'd abandoned on the floor came into view.

"You sure it won't set off another trap?"

"You removed it from its resting place. The worst of the protective magic should be gone, and most of it will fade once we leave."

I lifted the grimoire into my arms, clutching it to my chest to avoid temptation. Its edges were stained with blood now.

"How do we get out?" There was no chance I could make it over that chasm again.

"That's the easy part."

VASILISA DRAKE

The easy part turned out to be a secret passage that Raphael activated with a few careful touches of the runes on the wall. It led us down a winding corridor, one without the perfect angles of the rest of the temple. My torch was dead; I had to clutch the tattered back of his shirt to avoid stumbling. I fought the inane urge to spread my fingers over the freshly mended skin, as if I could convince myself the arrows had never been there.

That the bite had never happened.

That I'd never offered to let a vampire feed on me.

We hit what seemed to be a dead end just a few minutes later, but with a couple more touches, the barrier disappeared. Moonlight splintered past Raphael. I'd been about to ask why we didn't just enter through whatever passage when I tilted my head and realized exactly where the opening led.

Into nothing.

More accurately, we were at least twenty feet in the air. Before I could ask Raphael just how we were supposed to get down, he jumped.

I shrieked and clapped a hand over my mouth, edging tentatively closer so I could peer out.

And there was Raphael. Not splattered against the ground, but standing tall, waving to me while the silver light of the moons danced through his hair and bounced off his skin.

"Jump down," he called.

I shook my head, trembling slightly while I gripped the book for stability. Its gentle thrum of magic did little to steady me. *Blame it on the blood loss*. "I can't! I'll break my neck."

"I'll catch you," he assured me. "Trust me."

Trust a vampire to save my life.

A third time.

I jumped.

Air whooshed past me, blowing my hair away. I tucked my legs in and shut my eyes, bracing for death or at least several broken bones.

Contact.

But not with the ground. Strong, steady arms held me, one under my knees, the other supporting my back. I slowly unclenched my face, forcing my eyelids to open.

Raphael grinned down at me. "Told you."

I blew out a breath, trying to calm my racing heart as I tried to process the fact we'd not only survived this crazy adventure, but we also had the lost Black Grimoire with us.

Raphael made no move to drop me as he surveyed our surroundings. I found myself relaxing in his arms, breathing in his cedar scent like I could wrap it around me and hold it close. The rise and fall of his chest was gentle, even if no heart beat inside it.

No heartbeat. Because he's a vampire. *Who you let drink your blood.*

"Put me down," I demanded.

Raphael gently lowered me to the ground, and I turned away from him. Alphonse, to my immense relief, had not been eaten by an ogre in our absence. I slid the Black Grimoire into Alphonse's saddlebag. It took my hands an extra moment to release the book, but I let it go with a caress against the edges. Maybe because I'd nearly died half a dozen times getting it.

Raphael didn't miss the movement. "Do you know Old Runyk?"

He must have seen me reading the walls in the temple. Though it begged the question: How did Raphael know it? "A little. I studied as a child, but it's been many years since I've come across it. Do you?"

"Only enough to recognize it." Raphael considered me, clearly weighing something more. "Do you think you could learn to read the grimoire?"

I scoffed by reflex, then looked back at the book. Could I? I hadn't studied anything academic in ages. "It would be useless without a witch who can use the grimoire."

Raphael nodded, reluctantly, letting the subject drop. Neither of us moved onto Alphonse.

Now what?

I'd gone with Raphael on this little retrieval quest—not realizing exactly how perilous the abandoned temple would be—because he'd taken care of me while I healed,

A BARGAIN SO BLOODY

and I was out of options. The Monastery would never take me back, and no matter how I wanted to survive, there was no way I could put myself through that again.

But without Raphael around... at best, I could hope to reach some farm out on the edges of the kingdom that could use a pair of hands only used to rat catching. Would I be safe there? They might not look for me specifically, but every once in a while, they tracked criminals via magical means. They would find me. Without the Monastery to stand in their way, I'd eventually be found and executed. I had no money, no skills, no refuge.

"What is it?" Raphael asked.

I have nowhere to go. "I'm... not sure what my next steps are." For years, I'd worked towards my goal of starting a new life at the Monastery. Now I was lost. Each step seemed to edge me closer and closer to the precipice of a cliff. I fingered the flap of the saddlebag, even now wanting to soothe myself by holding the grimoire.

"There's more to Eurobis than the Witch Kingdom," Raphael said, voice soft.

I glanced at him, then realized: "You mean the lands beyond the Vampire Kingdom?"

Raphael's expression said that wasn't quite what he meant, but now that the idea hit me, new air filled my lungs. I'd never considered moving beyond the Witch Kingdom, because the vampires had us locked in. There was no way out except through their domain, and no one would choose that.

But I had a vampire. "Could you get me safe passage through the Vampire Kingdom and out to the west?" No soldier in the king's army would ever be able to hunt me down there.

"I... could." Raphael seemed to hesitate, unlike his usual, assured speech.

I was too relieved to care. I drew myself up onto the horse and tried not to tense when Raphael sat behind me once more, his hand coming across my middle to hold me steady as we began to move.

"You're uneasy," he said. "Why?"

Was my body so obvious? "I'm fine."

He snorted and stalled Alphonse. "That's a lie."

I was uneasy because the vampire was holding me again, and unlike before, I couldn't ask him to just let me down. Nor did his steadying touch feel like it had when we'd first been forced to ride together, like something I had to endure for survival.

It felt like something I might want.

The way he'd looked at me after feeding...

"Won't you have trouble being this close to my neck?" I blurted.

"I'll restrain myself," he replied.

That didn't make me feel better.

"Relax, Samara. I won't bite you again."

Finally, the tension in my shoulders eased. There was quiet determination in his words, and I found myself trusting them. At least, until he added—

"Not without permission, anyway."

He clicked his heels, and Alphonse began to move again before I could finish stammering my vows that that would never, ever, ever happen again. Even as his reassurance made me recall exactly how my body had heated when he'd bitten me, the pleasure his fangs had wrought that had me imagining a repeat.

Never.

Raphael's assurances weren't exactly convincing. I managed to keep quiet until we hit the edge of the marshes, when I finally dared ask: "Now what?"

"Now," Raphael said, "you come home to Damerel with me."

To the Vampire Kingdom.

Chapter 24

Snowfall stalled our trip.

We completed two days's journey before the snow began. This late in spring? A bad omen. A sign something was amiss.

Like a human willingly going to the Vampire Kingdom.

Temporarily, at least. Raphael insisted it would be safe to rest there for at least a few days. I wasn't fond of the plan by any means, but I needed supplies. I'd used almost all the cards available and had only a few coins left. Going to the Vampire Kingdom was terrifying, but the promise of a new life where no one knew me—or wanted me dead—was enticing enough to make me look past it. And while I had reservations about being in the home of other vampires, a part of me trusted Raphael would be true to his word and keep me safe.

With the Black Grimoire in our possession—and no more disguise cards—Raphael refused to consider going near any human settlement. Which presented a problem, since unlike the vampire, I was decidedly *not* impervious to the cold. I'd used the enchanted warmth card on my cloak days before, when the cold had first settled around us, but its magic was waning. Fortunately, one of the cards I'd traded for in the first village had been a shelter card.

Unfortunately, the "shelter" that sprang from the enchantment wasn't the inn-sized tent promised in the picture. It was a tent, with a ceiling maybe two feet tall, twice as wide, and four times as long. A threadbare folded blanket appeared at its center.

It was a glorified sleeping bag.

"That d-dealer ripped me off," I groused between chattering teeth. "We'll ha-have to find an inn. Or at least a h-house." It was so cold my fingers were turning an even starker white. I didn't care who Raphael had to thrall to get us somewhere warm.

"This will be fine," Raphael said. "The storm doesn't seem too bad. It should break overnight."

I hated that I recognized by the tone of his voice there'd be no arguing. Unwilling to stay out in the cold a minute longer, I slid into the tent. It was hardly better than being outside, except there was no snow in the tent.

VASILISA DRAKE

I'd used up all the fire cards in the temple and didn't stand a chance of making a flame without magic. I curled up, pressing my body as close together as possible. Whatever could be said about Greymere, it had never been cold like this. In fact, growing up as I had, I'd never known cold like this at all. Any chill that permeated the great halls was quickly chased off with a heating spell. I clutched the tattered blanket closer. It was a poor substitute for real warmth.

The cold made it hard to think or feel. I had to resign myself to the fact it would be a long night. But I'd survive it. Probably. I shut my eyes and prepared to rest.

Then the entrance of the tent jostled.

My eyes flew open as Raphael moved through the small entrance.

"What are you d-doing?"

"You'll hardly avoid freezing to death with this tent alone."

I blinked at him, and in the time it took my ice-addled brain to process, he had slid beside me in the minuscule tent. His arm pinned me down, his body curved around my back. The thin blanket of my cloak was the only barrier between us.

"I'll b-be okay," I protested, even as I felt some of the chill ease. Vampires didn't produce quite as much body heat as a normal human, or so I suspected. It had been so long since I'd pressed myself against another human, I struggled to recall.

"Humans. So delicate."

I wasn't sure if he meant the fact I was weak to the cold or that I was objecting to huddling for warmth with a vampire. I made a sound with the back of my throat and squeezed my eyes shut, trying to fall asleep.

It was not forthcoming. Even with Raphael and the tent, I couldn't stop shivering.

"You're still too cold."

"I'm f-fine."

He snorted. "I've worked too hard to keep you alive to let some snow destroy you, dove."

He reached for the blankets, and I yelped a protest. But my half-frozen fingers clutching the blanket were no match for Raphael, who with a deftness that shouldn't have been possible, maneuvered himself under the thin fabric.

The barrier was gone.

"This is inap-p-propriate," I chattered. It was an utterly inane protest, but it was the only thing my iced-over brain could think of to try to articulate that *this should not be happening*.

"You freed a vampire from the most secure prison in the Witch Kingdom and stole a sacred grimoire from a goddess's temple, and now you expect me to believe you're worried about propriety?"

"Yes." It was petulant. It was my only defense against the foreign sensations curling around my center. I'd never had this awareness before, not the way I'd felt since when

VASILISA DRAKE

Raphael fed on me in the temple. It was like my eyes had opened to an entire world, and I was desperate to keep my eyes shut because it was a vampire opening my eyes to that world.

The past few days's ride had been agony. While I'd once reveled in the admission Raphael made about our riding impacting him, now that I understood it intimately, there was no revelry, only shame.

"Too bad, Samara. We both know you're a survivor first. And that's all this is—survival." His words were soft steel, each one a counter to the arguments in my head.

The trouble was, it didn't feel like survival. Survival was unpleasant and brutal. It was catching rats and having my scraps of food spat in. It was making myself small and staying unnoticed. It was serving a sentence for a crime I didn't commit. It was taking blows to prove I was worthy of the gods's grace.

Whatever survival was, it wasn't the warm embrace of a male and bone-deep awareness that, against all odds, I was safe. Because no matter what predator lurked in the woods, there was none worse than the one in bed with me. And this one was devoted to keeping me safe—for now, anyway.

Every spot Raphael touched me felt like a brand, his skin scalding me. He was so godsdamned *large*. The tent wasn't big to begin with, but with him inside, there seemed to be no space that wasn't part of him. His arm was heavy across my stomach. He didn't deliberately press against me, but it was only natural our legs brushed, the backs of my thighs pressed against the tree trunks he called legs. Hard, firm muscle. A protective barrier from the chill. The spice of his scent filled the air, and it immediately brought me back to the temple. To the way he'd been so close against me when he'd bit my neck. I tried to despise the memory, but my body remembered a very different story. Even in the cold, heat rose between my legs that had me squeezing my thighs and willing my thoughts to change, burying my nose in the blankets to stifle the scent. But magic-produced blankets had no smell of their own.

When Raphael sighed in exasperation, his breath tickled the back of my neck. Right over the spot he'd bitten.

"Whatever you're thinking, I suggest you stop and just sleep."

My eyes flew open.

How did he know?

"I'm not thinking anything," I hissed, noting my teeth no longer chattered.

I felt, more than heard, the rumble of his chuckle. "Now, we both know you're not capable of having less than ten thoughts in a second, Samara."

"Well, I'm not having any right now."

"I can scent the truth." His whispered words sent a shiver down my spine—and not from the cold.

"You... you can smell when someone is telling the truth?"

He chuckled, a low, strained sound. "I can scent the evidence from you that your thoughts are a bit, let's say, amorous."

I flushed, my cheeks suddenly warm against the frigid air. "There's nothing to scent." *Dear gods, please let there be nothing to scent.* I squeezed my thighs, trying to will my desire away. In doing so, I accidentally brushed closer to Raphael, something moving against my back.

My cheeks weren't just warm. They were blazing.

"If it makes you feel better, you're not the only one affected." There was that low, strained chuckle again.

"There's nothing to scent, I told you. Your nose must be defective."

"There's not a part of me that's defective, I assure you. Though I do love how easily you lie," he mused. "Not a talent I ever acquired."

"You've probably never had to." I wasn't sure why I said it. The cold, the exhaustion, the proximity where I wasn't meeting his gaze. Or just because I didn't want to discuss my *other* thoughts any further.

"There've been times I wanted to," Raphael admitted. "But vampires aren't capable of telling untruths."

I shifted slightly at his answer and immediately regretted it. Because it was obvious, I wasn't the only one having *thoughts* in the tent.

"You expect me to believe vampires are always honest?" I countered, trying to move the conversation past any chance to mention we both knew I'd just felt his erection press into me.

"Not hardly. We merely cannot tell untruths, and that's not the same thing. In the vampire courts, twisting words is a great game, though I can't say it's one I care for."

Not unlike the courts of King Vaughn, then. My mother had been a master at the game—until she'd lost grievously.

"But you lie when you thrall people. You tell them they see things that aren't there."

"That's different. It's less a lie and more of a command on the mind."

Some good that was, then. Instead of trying to poke holes in the logic of vampire magic, I asked, "What's Damerel like?"

"Damerel sits inside the Western Vampire Kingdom. It's—"

"Wait." Another jerk before I could stop myself, and a loosening of breath from Raphael I wanted to drink in even though I made myself ignore it and the accompanying pulse at my back. "What do you mean *Western* Vampire Kingdom?"

"There are three realms ruled by vampires," Raphael explained. He didn't seem surprised I wasn't aware of this. "The North, the West, and the South. The West, seated at Damerel, is the strongest. The South is the most populous and richest. The North is... I suppose *unusual* is the most succinct way to describe it."

I didn't want succinct, but I forced myself to process what he'd said. Multiple Vampire Kingdoms. I'd never considered it.

"Damerel," he continued, "is inside a mountain. Its walls are carved from the mountain stone itself, allowing people to shelter themselves from the sun. It could be considered a palace from that view, but it's the size of a city, with three layers. The base is the common folk, then the merchants and commerce levels, and then the seat of the Crown, where the aristocrats and king live."

We'd be going to the base of a mountain. I tried to imagine it but came up empty; all I could picture was Greymere. It was hard to read Raphael's tone. He described the mountain-city in neutral terms. There wasn't any longing in his voice, nor any contempt.

"Is it home?"

There was a long pause. So long I wondered if perhaps the vampire had gone to sleep. But then—

"I confess to you, I think I've forgotten the meaning of the word."

Perhaps the vampire and I were more alike than I'd realized.

PART II

Chapter 25

The Western Vampire Kingdom looked no different from the Witch Kingdom. We reached it in another day, though I didn't realize it was so close until the terrain turned from grass to rock as we approached the mountain range.

I'd expected grand, dark spires, a sprawling palace like in the Witch Kingdom capital, vampires patrolling the grounds, with pointed fangs and questions for intruders. At least some other foreboding signs that we had reached what I'd been raised to believe was the seat of evil in Eurobis.

A BARGAIN SO BLOODY

The entrance to Damerel was little more than a cave. Raphael tied Alphonse to a tree at the base of the mountain.

"We can't leave him," I protested. Not just because it was foolish to leave a perfectly good horse behind. I'd grown attached to the horse on our journey, and I'd need him when I departed in a few days.

"I'll send someone to collect him," Raphael assured me with confidence that would've convinced me he was lying if not for the fact he'd just told me vampires couldn't lie. For the first time, I considered perhaps Raphael wasn't some common vampire, but perhaps one of the aristocrats he'd mentioned.

Then again, he'd been captured and sent to Greymere. No one had come for him, nor had he reached out to anyone who might be looking for him. I dismissed the thought. He must have meant a friend. Though it was harder to imagine him having friends than him being an aristocrat.

Before we entered, I cast the anti-thrall card I'd bargained for weeks ago. Raphael rolled his eyes.

"You won't need that," he said with a scoff.

"You can't be too careful." Just because *his* weak thrall didn't work on me didn't mean I wouldn't be in danger from others. I needed every protection possible, even if I would be gone in a few days.

He seemed to debate a retort but thought better of it. Given all his reassurances I'd be safe here for a few days, I'd almost expected more of a protest.

I clutched the modified copper cuffs in my skirt as we moved in, taking mental inventory of the precious few cards I had in my deck. There weren't many, and hardly any would be useful against a vampire. I had the cursed copper shackles, but given they were broken, and vampires were both faster and stronger, they were as good as shiny paperweights. *Defenseless.* I loathed the feeling. I swallowed down my worries as the darkness engulfed us.

The stone became smoother the deeper we went. I wasn't sure if I should expect the oppressive uniform stone of Greymere or the mystical marks from the Temple of Anagenni, but what I found was neither.

In what felt like a few short steps, the cave walls turned into elegant, plastered designs. Raphael moved with purpose, and I hurried after him. In the span of no more than an hour, we were in halls that rivaled those in Ulryne. No—though my memories were fogged by time, they were quite possibly even finer. Rich reds and purples, ornamented with gold designs.

For a moment, I could almost imagine the place was familiar.

Until we reached the first vampire.

Somehow, I'd gotten used to the sight of red eyes on Raphael's face. I'd let him place his fangs on me. Touched him and let him touch me. Felt his unbeating heart at my back as we rode for hundreds of miles.

But if I'd thought that acceptance would carry over to any other vampire, it was quickly erased.

In a few frantic heartbeats, several things happened at once.

The vampire, dressed like a nobleman, bowed at the hips towards us—towards Raphael. His crimson gaze slid to me, and all at once I was back *there*, covered in blood, blood, blood. I pawed at my pocket for the copper cuffs, trying to change my helpless nature. I only succeeded in scratching myself on a rough edge.

The distant awareness of pain was nothing compared to how my body reacted as the stranger's nostrils flared at the scent of my blood. He moved fast, imperceptibly fast to my human eyes, as he surged towards me.

I screamed.

And then the vampire was flying across the hallway. The perfectly ornamented red-and-purple walls caved in as the vampire collided.

Raphael lunged after the vampire, baring his teeth like a wild animal. He lifted the vampire with a single hand.

"Mine," he snarled.

Chapter 26

Raphael released the vampire, letting his body crumple to the ground. The vampire was still alive. He'd attack Raphael. Gods, Raphael could get hurt. I was rooted in my spot, unable to slow my heart enough to think past the roaring in my head that bleated *Danger, danger, danger!*

But the vampire didn't rise to attack Raphael. He prostrated himself, bracing his hands on the ground with his bowed head.

"You raised those hands at her," Raphael snarled. His voice... I'd heard it like that only in the echoes of my nightmares of the Monastery initiation. "You reached for what was mine with those hands."

"My king! I apologize. I did not realize she was yours. The scent of her blood overtook me. I forgot myself."

My king, the vampire had called him.

I trembled at the word. *King*.

Enemy.

"See that you never do so again." Raphael's voice was colder than I'd ever heard it. "And let this serve as a reminder."

He gripped the vampire's wrists from the floor, and in one sickening movement Raphael ripped the vampire's hands off.

The vampire howled. Raphael flung the dismembered hands down the hall, a trail of red, red, red blood spraying over the walls.

"Should you or anyone else lay a hand on what's mine, let your lives be forfeit. You live only as a warning to them."

The vampire on the floor babbled his agreement, but Raphael was already facing me once more. I tore my gaze from the sobbing vampire to face him. His gaze was still icy, utterly opposite to how he'd been the night before. He grabbed my wounded wrist and lifted it high. I stared up in confusion, then gasped as he lifted my palm to his lips and gave it a lick.

But he wasn't looking at me. Around us, a crowd had gathered. He removed his mouth, but held my arm high, as though I were some trophy.

King.

"This woman is mine. No one is to touch her." He addressed them easily, like it was his birthright. "To do so is to forfeit your right to a quick and easy death."

No. It couldn't be. The way he'd been beaten, captured... there was no way I'd been traveling for weeks with the king of vampires. My mind scrambled for any other explanation, grasping at vapors.

But the crowd all dipped to a knee in deference.

When they rose, all I could see was the sea of red. We were surrounded on both sides, hungry eyes looking at me, bright, wanting. *Oh gods.* My heart was a frantic drum beating in alarm faster and faster. The sharp inhale of my breaths turned into me choking. I couldn't get the air out fast enough before I sucked more in. My gaze swung wildly from eyes to eyes to eyes. I tried to shut mine, but they were still there, a vision of red, red, red all around me.

My knees buckled. Someone grabbed my arms before I fell. Raphael. Concern was etched on that now familiar face.

But all I saw were the red eyes.

The blood.

I fainted.

When I came to, all the vampires were gone.

All except Raphael. He stood across the room, arms folded. He'd changed, bathed. His white hair was slicked back, his face freshly shaven. He'd traded the stolen cloak and tunic for clothing befitting of royalty.

The room matched his station. It was a sprawling space, with a hearth on the far side where a small fire blazed, and two distinct seating areas: one in front, and one by me. I was lying on a low couch made of purple velvet. My fingers traced the texture, trying to ground myself in the surroundings.

"Tell me it's a misunderstanding," I croaked.

Raphael said nothing.

The fog cleared and an incessant need pressed against my chest. "Tell me."

Raphael shook his head. "I cannot."

"The vampire... he called you his king."

"He did," Raphael agreed. "Because I'm the Vampire King of the West."

Gods, I'd been such a fool. His strength, his *arrogance*. I'd spent enough time with royalty. I should've recognized it. Yet Raphael was also worlds apart from the king I'd known. He hadn't ordered me about. He'd treated me, at times, like a partner. If not an equal, then a close enough approximation.

I swallowed down the thought, the events that had transpired between Greymere and Damerel bouncing around my throbbing head. "You *licked* me."

Raphael's posture was stiff. "My apologies. I pride myself on keeping my word, and while I did in letter, I did not in spirit. I needed to seal the wound, and I wanted to show them."

"Show them what? That I'm *yours*?"

Mine, he'd called me. I hadn't belonged to anyone in so, so long. Even though it was for show, I'd come closer to belonging in that instance than I had in the past decade.

"Vampires respect claims like that. Your blood... certain blood is more attractive to vampires. You should take care not to bleed, but by daybreak, all will know what I've said and heed my words."

I shuddered and forced myself up onto my elbows. "Why is my blood so enticing? Is there a way I could change it?" I anxiously ran my fingers over the edge of the settee.

"You can't change what you are," he said softly. "You don't need to."

"I'm *human*, Raphael. I'm going to bleed. I'll be dead in a minute if one of them attacks." *Them*. Not *you*. Somehow Raphael was different from other vampires to my mind. Or maybe that was how I'd reconciled it. "You said I'd be safe here. I was a fool to believe you."

It was less a rebuke of him and more one of me. How had I been so desperate that I'd trust a vampire—the vampire king, no less—to protect me? "I need to leave. Now."

Had I really thought I could be safer here than with my own kind? Even for a few days?

"You are safe here," Raphael insisted. With vampire speed, he moved from his perch across the room to my side. He dropped to his knees, sinking to meet me at eye level. "Anyone who makes you feel any other way dies. I vow this, Samara. The only reason Lucas's head is on his shoulders is because I want him to spread the message."

It was impossible to hold his gaze at this distance. Half-lying down in an unfamiliar room, I felt vulnerable.

No, I felt vulnerable because when he said words like that, I wanted to believe him.

"You don't need to send a message. I'm not staying."

"You need rest," he countered. "Supplies. A few days of real food, not whatever small mammal I drain for you. Sturdy clothing. Maps. Remember your plan?"

Valid points. But that didn't change the fact he was the king of vampires. "What I need is the truth. You lied to me," I accused.

Raphael arched a brow. "How, dove? I cannot tell untruths."

"You deceived me, then," I corrected. "I never would have let you out of that cell if I'd known you were their godsdamned king."

Raphael's voice dropped low. "You would have done anything to leave that prison, and we both know it."

I looked away, not able to meet the truth in his eyes. "Just show me how to get out of this place. If it'll take too long to get maps, I can go without, or I'll just hide out in the

Witch Kingdom." Anxiety caged my heart and constricted it into shallow, shallow beats that left me dizzy.

"Nothing has changed, Samara. You would be found and executed for escaping your sentence."

There was sense in Raphael's words, but I couldn't get the sight of all those vampires out of my mind. I'd thought one was terrifying. Dozens—hundreds—maybe thousands. Just the thought made it hard to breathe again. "Your vampires won't just tolerate a human walking around."

Raphael snorted, dismissing the argument. "They'll tolerate anything I tell them to or suffer the consequences of their treason. Besides, you are hardly the only mortal here."

Yes, me and the other humans they kept for food. It was well known the vampires stole humans from the bordering towns to keep themselves fed. And that was to make me feel better? "I'd rather take my chances against the king's witches."

"You can't go back there," he said with infuriating patience.

I frowned. "Am I to be your captive, then? Not allowed to leave?"

Did I imagine his hesitation? "You would die, Samara. I gave my word I would protect you—that means not letting you go off to your death."

I looked away, scanning the room. "Then I'll stay here. Give me whatever supplies the *vampire king* is willing to part with in exchange for helping you retrieve the grimoire, and I'll be on my way." At the thought of the grimoire, my fingers twitched. "Where is the grimoire anyway?"

His head cocked at the sudden question. "Safe." Raphael regarded me for a moment. No doubt he saw I was unsatisfied by the answer. Taking pity on me, he moved and pointed to a table his body had blocked across the room.

Something in me unclenched, just slightly, when I laid eyes on it.

"There's another option," Raphael said slowly, like he didn't want to startle me.

My shoulders tensed. "What?"

"Before I tell you, I want you to answer a question for me. Do you trust me to keep you safe?"

The word *no* was on the tip of my tongue before I even considered the question. Safe wasn't a word that had applied to me in a long, long time. But as Raphael stared at me, red eyes warm and utterly still while he waited for my answer, it wasn't so easy to spit the word out.

"I don't know if I believe there's such a thing as safety," I admitted.

To my surprise, he didn't tell me I was wrong. "That's a fair answer, so let me change the question. Do you think anyone will do a better job keeping you safe than I would?"

"No," I conceded.

Raphael nodded. "That's right. As long as you're here with me, dove, you're mine. And I protect what's mine, dove. Ruthlessly."

Ruthlessly. With dismembered hands and decapitated bodies. The thought should be chilling, especially given my aversion to violence. But... violence done to protect me felt altogether different than violence done against me. *Hypocrite*.

"Then let me place another card in your hand. Instead of scurrying off in a few days, you could stay longer and do one more task for me."

I should say he was insane. Say there was no possible reason I'd stay. "What task?"

Raphael flashed a grin, just for a moment. "You could translate the grimoire for me."

I blinked. Of all the things I'd expected... my gaze immediately landed on the enchanted book once more. I wanted to know its secrets, even if they were useless to a void like me.

"I told you I barely remember Old Runyk." I'd had a knack for languages as a girl, something my mother had hoped would impress my father, but most of what I'd learned was forgotten.

"I have a library that would be at your disposal. I'm confident with enough time, you could decipher the text."

"Why would I do that?" I demanded. What use did a vampire have for a witch-less grimoire?

"Because, if you do that, I'll pay you five hundred gold pieces. Enough to not just start a new life as a beggar in the west, but to live like a queen."

The offer was tantalizing. *Too good to be true.* "If you have hundreds of gold pieces lying around, you should give them to me anyway for getting you the grimoire. If not for me, you wouldn't have been able to take it from the temple," I reminded him.

"If you wanted payment for helping me retrieve the grimoire, you should have negotiated before," he countered, with a smirk that made me want to hit him. "This is my offer. Five hundred gold pieces for the translation. While you work on it, you'll live here, under my protection."

But I'd still be working on his behalf. This was witch magic. It didn't belong in a Vampire Kingdom. I didn't belong here. "It's treason."

Raphael made a valiant effort to resist rolling his eyes. "Breaking me out of prison wasn't?"

I flinched. "That was survival."

"Then survive here, Samara," he urged. "Thrive here. You've never had a chance to know yourself—I'll give you that, and more."

My heart slowed, the panic somehow easing, impossibly. For twelve years, my only thought had been how to survive the trials of each day. The only part of me I recognized now was the rat who would gnaw off a limb to survive. *Could I betray my kingdom for the chance to find out I was something more?*

"One thousand gold pieces," I countered.

"A queenly sum indeed," Raphael said, without so much as balking at the number. "It's a bargain, then."

I swallowed. For the second time, I'd made a deal with the vampire.

"Now, there's someone I'd like you to meet."

Chapter 27

If I'd hoped Raphael might give me a few days in private to acclimate to the subterranean kingdom, I was to be sorely disappointed. Once I could stand, he ordered me up and off the settee. We were in a sitting room that was as large as twenty cells in Greymere put together, and an explosion of color. A velvet green couch, a rich scarlet bedspread, chairs covered in navy fabric. Like Greymere, there was a distinct lack of windows. Before forcing me to face the kingdom once more, however, Raphael led me to a bathing chamber. The room was a marvel of quartz and marble, a large tub at the center filled with steaming water.

I glanced at Raphael.

He left the room, latching the door shut behind him.

Any hesitation was overwhelmingly defeated by the prospect of bathing in warm water. I stripped my dirty traveling clothes as carefully as I could while speeding towards the tub. The heat of the bath engulfed me, and I began scrubbing my body as best I could.

Then my eyes landed on a shelf across from the tub.

At least fifty crystal bottles were nestled closely together. Curious, I got out of the tub, already missing the warm water. Once I removed the stopper from one, I inhaled deeply.

Bergamot.

Rich citrus with a hint of tartness I could *feel* on my tongue. My heart nearly stopped. It was utterly decadent, and I was hungry for more. I wafted it over, taking the deepest inhale I had in ages. It was the complete opposite of everything I'd been surrounded by for so long.

Sense abandoned me. I snatched half a dozen bottles of perfumed bathing oils and poured them one by one into the tub, watching the water go from light blue to navy to violet. Different notes rubbed against my senses, each of them exotic and luxurious, each of them a world apart from vampires and darkness and blood. Part of me longed to dive under the water and drink them until I drowned a happy, aromatic death. I savored the cacophony of perfumes and soaked myself, wishing I could stay forever.

Sense eventually won out, and when my skin wrinkled to the point I looked like a proper crone, I forced myself to rise from the tub. Water slid away, steam wrapping around me as I found a fluffy white towel on the rack to dry myself with. My dirty clothes lay in a pile on the floor, utterly unappealing compared to the luxury of the towel.

A neatly folded assortment of fabric I hadn't noticed before, however, sat on a shelf beyond the tub. A cinched tunic and trousers, like those for riding.

I finished drying and wrung my hair with my hands. My fingers tried and failed to comb my black hair into a semblance of order. The tunic slipped over my shoulders easily, a loose style that didn't require much cinching. I tied the embroidered belt with my deck over it and sourced my remaining defenses from my pockets. The trousers didn't offer a spot for the cuffs. I considered switching back, but the clothes were in tatters. I hesitated and reburied the broken shackles, resolving to figure it out later. There was a large mirror covering one wall, and I wiped my fingers against the steamed-over glass to take a look.

My skin was pink from the heat of the bath. My hair had a shine to it from the water and the oils. The clothes didn't quite fit, the neck a bit too wide for my narrow shoulders, the trousers requiring me to pull the ties tight, but I looked more normal than I had in ages.

A knock sounded on the door. *Raphael*. I swallowed. I couldn't hide here forever.

I opened the door.

Raphael had his mouth open, as if he'd been about to say something, but as the steam flew out around me, his mouth shut, and he wrinkled his nose.

Given that even to my own nose I had a cloying amount of scents strewn on me, it was probably painful for a vampire to be near me. Well, good.

"You were always complaining I smelled," I reminded him.

"Now you don't smell like yourself at all," he said with what bordered on a petulant sigh.

Wasn't that the entire point? Guilt pricked at me all the same. I supposed I should feel bad about wasting all the perfume. Yes, it had been nice to imagine a life where I was surrounded by decadence, but that's not what I was meant for. I was a mortal driven to seek refuge in the Vampire Kingdom. I didn't deserve nice things like this.

"I'll be more mindful," I murmured, resolving to not take such things again. I looked at the floor. Fancy bath oils weren't for girls like me, anyway.

"If you like it, use it all," he replied in an instant. "Just perhaps... not all at once."

I lifted my gaze and gave Raphael a tentative smile. He nodded, approving of something he saw in me.

"What now?" I asked.

"Now we let Amalthea find us."

Amalthea.

A BARGAIN SO BLOODY

I repeated the lyrical name in my mind as we walked through the hallways. *Amalthea*. It was an elegant name. A lady's name. The name of Raphael's lady? Before, it would never have occurred to me that vampires could take lovers. Now, I was consumed by the thought of Raphael belonging to another.

The thought had never crossed my mind.

My gut twisted.

"Something wrong?" Raphael asked as I fell behind a step.

I hurried to catch up. Awful clenching in my stomach aside, I didn't dare fall away from the protection of the vampire king.

"No, no. I was just thinking perhaps I could, um, *not* go to meet this vampire Amalthea."

Raphael chuckled. "Amalthea's not a vampire."

I stumbled.

"She's not?"

"Damerel is home to more than just vampires. If it wasn't, we would starve."

That was true, but it didn't make me feel better. Obviously there were humans the vampires fed on, but just by the way Raphael spoke of her, I knew there was more to this Amalthea. "So she's a void, like me?"

"Amalthea is a witch."

A witch? In the Vampire Kingdom? All I could do was blink in surprise as Raphael threw open a massive wooden door. Gone were the carpeted palace halls, replaced by packed dirt. The cavern was large and mostly empty, with a weapons rack at either end of the space, and a few benches. In the center was a woman. Nobility of some kind, judging by her posture and finery.

"Amalthea," Raphael said in greeting.

"Raphael," she replied, without any of the deference that should have come from speaking to a king. "You know, just because I knew you'd be here didn't mean I knew when. I've been waiting for half a day. And it's so dusty here. You might have arranged a luncheon for this introduction."

Raphael shrugged. "Then you should have found us at luncheon."

The witch blew out an exasperated breath. "You know that's not how it works. I saw us *here*."

I at once understood why Amalthea, a witch, was in the Vampire Kingdom.

Amalthea wasn't just a witch.

She was an oracle.

Chapter 28

"Then you know what we're about to do, and you still came dressed like this?" Raphael sounded exasperated.

That in itself was about as shocking as being in the presence of an oracle. Raphael was never anything as mundane as *exasperated*.

"I accounted for that. I weighed my desire to do your bidding exactly with my desire to make an impression, and the latter won."

Amalthea was a voluptuous woman, elegantly dressed in large swaths of flowing fabric. Unlike my practical wool, hers were layers and layers of gauze, intricately embroidered in varying patterns. Her hair was silver, with shocks of white and blue lowlights that matched her gray eyes. Or gray eye, rather. A decorated glass orb sat in the left socket, moving with the right one as she appraised me in turn. Her face was made of circles, with round lips, full cheeks, and puffy eyes, which gave her a youthful appearance. Her skin had the warm tones under it that the vampires lacked.

Yet she was as unnatural as the vampires. A witch who could see in the future.

Raphael had brought up the Witch Kingdom's treatment of seers at Apante. Was she the reason?

"So you believe you can undermine my plans."

I would have quaked if Raphael had spoken that way to me, with icy accusation. Amalthea gave the vampire king a dismissive wave. "Relax, Your Majesty. I thought of that."

On unspoken cue, the doors behind us opened once more. My spine stiffened at once. If Amalthea was the consummate witch, the male who stepped in was utterly vampiric. His skin was the color of the running moon, his hair a shade lighter and slicked back before tying off at the nape. He wore a uniform of some kind, black with a purple emblem on the shoulder. While Amalthea was close to my height, this vampire was nearly as tall as Raphael, and more muscular.

He bowed to Raphael immediately.

"My king, I understand you have need of me."

"Iademos," Raphael acknowledged. "I'm afraid once again our witch has decided she knew better and brought you here. I didn't yet want vampires around—" He cut off with a glance at me and turned to Amalthea. "It's unwise to go against my wishes, Oracle."

Though he faced Amalthea, I didn't take my eyes off the vampire in the room. My fingers shook slightly, longing for the comfort of the copper cuffs I'd left in the bathing suite. The vampire spared me the barest glance before focusing on Amalthea, annoyance obvious on his features. But restrained annoyance, like when a friend has played a joke, rather than vampire annoyance where they contemplate tearing you limb from limb.

I tried to steady my heart and failed.

"Even when you are wrong? Surely our king hasn't changed that much on this journey." The witch's voice was lilting, like she was singing instead of insulting her king. "She will be living among vampires. She cannot be cloistered away. You trust Demos above all others, so who better than your right hand to join us? He's much better with a blade than I am, in any case."

"Fine," Raphael bit off. "I leave her in both of your care." An ominous current ran between the words.

Iademos nodded gravely. Though I wasn't facing Amalthea, I suspected her response was less deferential.

"You're leaving?" I didn't mean for my words to come out as a whisper. Panic spidered over my skin, constricting my chest. *He was leaving me with another vampire?*

Raphael faced me. "I have matters to attend to. Despite her many faults, Amalthea is correct. I trust Iademos above any other in this mountain, or all of Eurobis. I planned to hold off the introduction, but since Amalthea has deemed herself an incompetent teacher"—an indignant huff from the seer—"they will both be with you when I am not." He reached into the folds of his cloak and pulled out a short scabbard. "Learn this weapon. You will *not* need it here, but it will give you comfort to have and know how to use it, given your future plans."

My plans to leave, once I finished translating. I took the blade and pulled it from its oiled sheath, testing the weight in my hand. It wasn't gold, but the color was similar. Bronze? Raphael nodded once with satisfaction and left without further word.

I swallowed.

What now?

Amalthea approached me without any of the hesitation that constantly rattled inside me.

"In His Majesty's hurry to play nursemaid, he forgot all his manners." She ignored a pointed cough from Iademos. "My name is Amalthea, court seer to the Vampire Kingdom of the West and resident know-it-all. Or if not all, at least the interesting parts. That disapproving fanged menace is Iademos, right hand to the Vampire King of the West and general of Damerel's army."

She looked at me expectantly. *Right. This is the part where I introduce myself.* "I'm Samara. No fancy titles, I'm afraid. Just a stray Raphael picked up."

Amalthea laughed, and Iademos's lip curled into something that might have been a repressed smile.

"Oh, you're much more than that. You're the first human Raphael's ever claimed as his Chosen."

I blinked. "What?"

Iademos cleared his throat. "What Amalthea means is you're our king's guest. That in itself grants you status."

"Like his right hand and an illegal witch as babysitters?"

"*Illegal witch*?" Amalthea repeated, tone thunderous.

I looked down, embarrassed. That was the term I'd always heard used to refer to seers, and it had slipped out before I'd thought through the implications.

"There's no such thing as illegal magic, any more than there are illegal clouds. Magic chooses its form, and we obey. Only a fool attempts to restrict the existence of kinds of magic. There will always be a reckoning for such hubris." The words were almost a growl by the time Amalthea finished speaking.

"I'm sorry," I said quickly. "I didn't mean—that was rude of me."

Amalthea's expression softened at once, the thunderstorm gone as quickly as it had come. "I'll bear no grudge, Samara. I've had worse said about me and done to me." She lifted a hand to her face, where her glass eye looked back at me. "You'd be wise to remember what I've said."

I nodded. "Can I ask how you came to be here?"

"Of course. And because I like you, I'll even answer. Here, come and sit."

"The king told us—rather told you—to train her," Iademos chastised.

Amalthea waved him away. Where the vampire guard frightened me and was clearly not one to be trifled with, Amalthea treated him like an annoying sibling. "Learning about her new home is important training for Samara. There'll be plenty enough time for you to show off all your little drills later. Not that there's much to say—stick them with the sharp end. Nothing to it."

Iademos ground his jaw. I kept my eyes on him even as Amalthea dragged me over to a bench.

"Won't you get us refreshments?" she asked saccharinely.

"That's not my—fine." He huffed and left the room.

Amalthea flashed me a victorious smile.

"Is it wise to needle him like that?" I asked, unable to help myself.

"Oh, Demos likes it. He has the rest of the castle too well-trained. A person can only take so much bowing and scraping before they want to fling themselves off a cliff. I keep him sane."

I had the distinct impression Amalthea was doing her best to drive the guard insane. Still, I was glad to have a reprieve. Even if Raphael trusted him, it was impossible to relax around a vampire. An oracle was difficult enough.

"Where were we? Ah yes, how I came to be here. It was a combination of factors. My parents were voids, and my powers were late to manifest. By the time it became obvious I was an oracle, they couldn't bear to see me killed. For a time, they tried to hide me from the village, but a young witch has to practice their powers. One little gaffe on my part and the village was demanding my head. They fled with me in the middle of the night, and after a time we made it here. Or nearly, I should say. My mother didn't survive the journey, and my father died soon after."

"A vampire killed him?" Sympathy twisted in my stomach.

She shook her head. "No. His heart simply stopped one day soon after we arrived. In any case, that's my tale."

"Are there many witches who come to the vampire lands?"

"Not many. More voids, looking to be turned." At my horrified look, she grinned. "Immortality and supernatural strength are a seductive combination. Mortals serve in the kingdom, and if their service is exceptional, they can earn the king's blessing to turn."

I swallowed. "Is that why you serve Raphael? Because you want to be a vampire?"

"No. I've seen enough of my fate to not want more," she said, a touch quiet. "I serve Raphael because he's a decisive, fair king. Besides, it's forbidden to turn a witch. Immortality, supernatural strength, *and* magic? Even the gods would condemn that."

I didn't presume to know what the gods would and wouldn't condemn, especially if Amalthea was implying vampires weren't condemned by the gods.

Heresy.

"So you're telling me humans just... come to live and work in the Vampire Kingdom?" My tone was heavy with skepticism. "The vampires just let them do their jobs instead of feeding off them? Next you'll tell me you have orcs over for tea every week."

"Only once a month," Amalthea replied immediately.

I laughed before I could help myself.

"See? There you are. I knew there was a girl with a sense of humor under that skittish exterior."

"Skittish?" I snorted. "What human wouldn't be terrified when surrounded by vampires?"

Amalthea gestured at me, gossamer fabric flaring. "A human *under the protection of their king*. Vampires revere hierarchy, and King Raphael sits squarely at the top. You're his. No one would dare try to steal from the king," she explained. "Besides, the vampires don't feed indiscriminately outside of designated times. You of all humans have nothing to worry about."

Despite her assurances, I remembered the time a vampire had bitten me. The vampire king. The way I—no, my body—reacted.

"You expect me to believe they can control themselves? They're little more than animals." I forced contempt I didn't feel into my words, chasing away the memories of the bite.

Amalthea frowned. "Is that really what you think?"

No. Not about Raphael. But I could still see it—the blood, the throat ripped open. *Blood and blood and—*

Amalthea pressed my hands into hers. "Gracious, stop shaking. He'll lambaste me for distressing you."

I shook the memories off as well as her hands. "I'm not going to run off and tattle to Raphael." The thought was preposterous.

Amalthea took a long drag of her tea, her smallest finger extended as she dipped the cup back. "It'll hardly matter, dear. He'll know. He drank your blood, after all."

CHAPTER 29

I gaped at Amalthea. *"What?"*

"What have you done now, Thea?"

I flinched at the sudden sound of Iademos's voice. He'd returned carrying a tray of tea and biscuits, and I hadn't heard so much as the packed dirt crunch under his boots.

He set the tray between us and leaned against the wall. There was enough space to sit, but I was thankful. He could clearly sense how uncomfortable I was and was giving me some distance.

But my discomfort was overwhelmed by the sheer number of questions threatening to bubble over.

"What do you mean? He can feel what I feel because he drank my blood?"

"Well, yes," Amalthea said.

"Thea, it's not for us to tell her this."

"It's my blood, so I certainly think I'm entitled to know what it means," I snapped.

She looked between me and Iademos. "You have a point. It's simple, when King Raphael drinks someone's blood, a link is formed. He'll be able to sense your emotions for the rest of your life."

"Is that how it works for all vampires?" Gods, the taking of blood was an invasion, but this was beyond any horror I'd imagine.

"No, not at all. Very few vampires have that ability. I understand it's rather overwhelming, given how much vampires drink. He's not taken from the source in over a hundred years." She paused, gauging the effect of her words on me. "And those he'd taken in the past out of necessity, he killed shortly after so he wouldn't be bothered."

My skin turned to ice.

"Biscuit?" she offered.

I took the biscuit. Then I ate three more after the first made me acutely aware of how hungry I was. "If Raphael is going to kill me because of my pesky emotions, I might as well die with a full stomach." Crumbs sputtered at the corner of my mouth around the words, any semblance of manners forgotten.

Amalthea's eyes flew wide. "Oh, no. I'm sure he wouldn't."

I wasn't. Right now, he needed me to translate the grimoire, or so he claimed. But a few months or years from now? When he was sick of being bombarded with my fear and stress and all those pesky mortal emotions?

But I'd ask Raphael directly about it later. There had to be a way to sever the link... besides the obvious. Him not mentioning it had to be deliberate though. If it was easy to sever whatever bond had formed, he'd have done so by now. Right?

"Now, where were we?" Amalthea said, obviously eager to change the subject.

"Before mentioning Raphael's killed every human whose blood he drank, you were telling me the vampires and humans coexist peacefully."

The witch winced. "I'm not saying there's never any... friction. But generally, yes, it's peaceful. The vampires here aren't starving by any means, so there's little danger from them. Feeding tends to occur only from donors."

I frowned. "Donors?"

"Humans who offer up their blood to vampires," she clarified.

I jerked back. "Why would anyone do such a thing?"

"For gold, mainly," Amalthea explained. "There are many jobs open to humans here, but since blood donating is one thing vampires can't do, it's a lucrative avenue. From my understanding, it can be pleasurable work."

The memory of Raphael's fangs buried in my neck and the sensations it brought burned through me once more. I drained my teacup to the dregs, desperate for anything else to focus on.

"Ready to train, then?" she asked as I set the cup back down on the platter.

I stood. "Please."

But Amalthea didn't stand with me. Instead, Iademos pushed off the wall.

I hadn't forgotten the vampire was there, not quite, but I'd managed to relax temporarily. Now, I squared my shoulders and unsheathed the dagger. I doubted I'd be able to even scratch the vampire with it if I tried. Gods, I hated being weak.

Raphael trusts him. I tried to repeat the words enough to calm myself, but I had no doubt the vampire heard every quickening beat.

"You won't be using that today," the vampire said. At my confused look, he explained, "For one, you're liable to cut yourself with it without training."

"And for another?" I asked.

"It's a cursed copper alloy, which means in the extremely unlikely event you struck me with it, it would... prick. Use this instead." He walked to the rack of weapons and tossed me a short wooden blade. I scrambled—and failed—to catch it.

"We have our work cut out for us," Iademos said dryly.

I glared.

He grinned. "That's better. Can't fight off enemies if your tail is tucked betwixt your legs."

I didn't believe it was possible for me to tolerate a vampire besides Raphael, but Iademos almost made me question that belief. He was relaxed, and careful to give me space. He wasn't treating me like I was prey or overly delicate.

He took a practice dagger for himself and flipped it in his hands, waiting for me to settle my grip on the training stick he'd thrown my way.

"A dagger's not a great weapon if you're in a head-on confrontation. It doesn't have the reach of a sword, but it also doesn't require the muscles or years of training." That explained why Raphael had picked it for me. From the looks of the larger practice swords, I'd struggle to lift one, let alone defend myself with it. "What's good is that you can use it to maneuver when your opponent is close and surprise them. With your size and sex, you'll be underestimated in just about any fight—which is *the male's fault*," he emphasized after Amalthea made an annoyed sound, "not yours."

I wasn't offended by blunt lessons. I'd learned at a young age just how much of a liability being a girl could be, and I'd learned since then that I would use any tool available to me to survive.

"We'll make sure to use it to your advantage," he continued. "Now, I'm going to show you the basics."

So the general did. From a distance. He demonstrated and ran me through several drills. He always stayed within my line of sight, avoiding sudden movements. I was grateful for that, even if I likely would have benefited from more corrections.

The hours passed. A thin sheen of sweat coated my forehead, my body exhausted from the repetitive movements, but I was determined to practice without complaint. I'd spent a lifetime wishing for protection in different forms—in magic, in my mother, in the Monastery—and I was tired of it. For the past weeks, I'd relied on a vampire to keep me safe. And Raphael had, but Raphael wouldn't always be there, and more than that, I didn't *want* to need his protection. In a few weeks or months, however long it took to translate the grimoire, I'd be setting off into an unknown territory. I needed to stop looking outwardly and start building my own defenses. So even though my shoulder was on fire, my wrist aching from the abrupt use, I continued.

It was Amalthea who finally said it was enough.

"I can keep going," I said quickly. "I don't have anything else to do."

Iademos shook his head. "As much as I hate to say it, Thea is right. Overdo it and you won't be able to move your arms tomorrow."

I was unprepared for the disappointment that pierced me. Even though they had a point, it felt like a failure.

"Each day, Amalthea or I will work with you on building strength. A dagger may not require the strength of a broadsword, but you still need some muscle to pierce the skin." He ran his gaze up and down, but there was nothing to it beyond a blunt appraisal.

"We'll have you ready to carve the hearts of vampires out in no time," Amalthea assured me, the bloodthirsty promise leaving her lips with a smile. "But you and I have another trial ahead of us."

I put the practice dagger back on the stand. "We do?"

"We do," she confirmed. "We have a ball to get ready for."

CHAPTER 30

Iademos took his leave while Amalthea stood and dusted off her immaculate skirts.

"What ball?" *Vampires have balls?*

She read my expression with ease. "Courts always have balls, do they not? Our king has been gone for weeks with no word. It's only right to have one to commemorate his return."

"But... I don't need to go to that." I didn't need to be around vampires any more than absolutely necessary. A ball was not, by any measure, necessary.

"Raphael claimed you. It's only right you make an appearance. Besides, people are curious about you."

Just what I needed: vampires interested in me.

"And you must be curious about them as well."

"I'm really not," I insisted. I knew everything I needed to: They were dangerous predators, and voids like me were their ideal prey. As for the ball itself, well, I'd never been to one, though I'd watched from the corner of the room as my mother prepared to attend, layering disguise magic on top until her appearance transformed, making her unrecognizable—and in the eyes of a child, just a little scary.

My heart ached, in that fleeting moment, to be a child again and watching her. When the scariest thing was seeing her lips turn from pink to purple, her lashes long enough to graze her magically sharpened cheekbones when she batted her eyes.

She shrugged. "Well, too bad. You're going."

"Why?" I demanded, collecting my dagger from the bench.

"Because *I'm* not missing the ball, and Raphael left you in my care. Do you really want to sit by yourself in a room with a chair barricading the door shut because you're terrified to be alone in the Vampire Kingdom?"

I glared. That was exactly what I intended, even if I'd come to see just how outmatched I was against vampire strength. "That's a low blow."

"Low blows work," Amalthea countered. "Now, we've barely enough time to get ready, so let's go."

"How long?" I asked, alarmed.

"Less than three hours."

A BARGAIN SO BLOODY

Amalthea navigated the twisting hallways of Damerel with ease. I froze at the first pair of vampires we crossed paths with, but the witch just tugged on my arm to keep me moving while the vampires bowed their heads in respect—at *us*. Humans.

"Here we are."

I didn't recognize the hall where Amalthea's rooms were, but that didn't say much. Despite the fact we were under a mountain, the hallways were every bit the labyrinth as the castle in Ulryne.

"These are your chambers?"

"They are," she replied, tossing the doors wide.

To say Amalthea's room was chaotic was to greatly understate the level of disarray. Dresses hung off every elevated surface, from the changing screen to the wingback chairs by the fire to the low table in the middle of the room. The floor was a viper's nest of shoes of every description, from practical, fur-lined boots I'd have killed to have in the prison to heels that rivaled the dagger I was anxiously clutching. That was not to say Amalthea used her room as one big closet. It was also part library, with books scattered throughout, left open to specific pages, and garden, with the remaining floor space eaten up by luscious purple and blue flowers that matched her hair.

"Don't mind the mess," she chirped, taking a big step over a particularly dangerous mountain of flats.

I thought of my mother's immaculate chambers, which never had so much as a stocking out to be gawked at. "No problem."

She pointed off to the side. "There's a bathing room over there. You can wash up and then we'll have some fun. Here, take this. It's clean."

She picked a ball of fabric from her dresser, and I unfurled it. A satin robe. Despite the wrinkled state, it actually seemed to have been laundered.

"Thanks."

I ducked into the bathroom and stifled a laugh when I saw the shelving. It seemed I wasn't the only one with a penchant for perfumes. Amalthea had dozens of half-empty bottles, some stacked on top of each other to fit. This time, I abstained, washing my body quickly before returning to Amalthea.

"Now, let's see what we've got. Sit," she instructed.

In my time freshening up, she'd unearthed both a stool and vanity that I hadn't noticed. Obediently, I sat. Iademos may have been the general, but Amalthea certainly liked to give orders.

"I just love your hair," she mused, running her fingers through it. "I'm going to have fun with you, Sam."

She grinned at me in the mirror, gray eye brimming with mischief. Everything she did was with complete ease. Like having me in her room getting ready for a ball was no big deal. Was this what it was like to have friends? Despite the bizarre circumstances, I was touched. My eyes burned.

"What's this? None of this," she said quickly. She brushed away the tears that threatened to form.

"It's just... you're so *nice* to me." She'd been ordered to babysit, but Amalthea had immediately embraced me, teasing, joking, teaching.

She shrugged. "I know we're going to be friends."

"Act like this and it's a self-fulfilling prophecy," I joked.

"Aren't all prophecies?" she replied glibly. "But even if we weren't, it's in my best interest to be on your good side. I'm rather invested in surviving."

I frowned. "I don't see how I could make a difference in anyone's survival."

The witch lifted a brush from the vanity and began to run it through my hair. "Maybe not today," she half-agreed, seeming far too focused on my hair as she answered. Taming the wild strands of my hair was no simple task. My hair was naturally straight, but nights spent sleeping on the forest floor without so much as a comb meant I'd made do with my fingers and little else.

A thought occurred to me. "When you say you know... you mean you got a feeling, or you saw with your magic?"

She divided my hair into sections, not answering immediately for the first time since I'd met her. Had I committed some social blunder by asking? Some witches were intensely personal about their magic—my mother made it a rule to never ask for details, though in private she seemed to know everything. The last thing I wanted to do was offend one of the only non-vampires in the castle.

"It's a sense, mostly," she said at last. "Sometimes my power is clear. For example, I knew Raphael would be in the training room. Swear the male doesn't believe in giving word because he wants to make sure my magic 'stays sharp' or some nonsense," she grumbled. "I get visions of the future. An image, a scene. But I have no way of knowing when."

I watched her in the mirror, steadfast in her work on my hair. When I tried to grab another brush to help her, she swatted my hands away. "When I was a child, I wanted a little sister to dress like a doll. It seems my fantasies are at last to be fulfilled."

"I suppose Iademos isn't willing to let you oil his hair?"

Amalthea barked a laugh so abruptly that she yanked on my hair. "You really do have a humor about you when you're coaxed from your shell. That's good. Raphael could use some laughter."

"You... you speak of him very casually." I called him Raphael because that was all I'd known him as—the captured vampire I'd partnered with to escape Greymere. But here, he was a king.

She lifted her shoulders as if it was utterly inconsequential. "He is who he is, no matter what he's called. In court, of course, I show proper decorum. But as his adviser, it does no good to be falling over myself constantly and making sure I'm addressing him correctly and not cutting him off and curtsying for exactly fifteen seconds when he enters a room."

"You're his adviser," I repeated.

"If a king's council's duty is to warn him of future dangers, there could be none better than a witch who can see the future."

That made sense. If anything, it was a wonder the witch king hadn't repaired relationships with the oracles to use their magic to his own benefit.

The thought felt like a betrayal, so instead I focused more on analyzing what I'd seen of Raphael and Amalthea. It was obvious they were familiar with each other. Was there something more there? I'd assumed vampires nurtured the same disdain for witches that witches held for them, but perhaps that loathing went only one way.

Perhaps Amalthea and Raphael truly were close.

The thought made my stomach sour, and not just because it was antithetical to what I'd been taught as a child.

"There." She poured some oil from a bottle into her palms and ran her fingers through my freshly brushed hair. "Lovely. Now we can start on your face."

She reached around me and pulled open a drawer. Dozens of tiny containers and brushes filled the area, clattering as they rolled around. She selected one of the rolling bottles with practiced precision and uncorked it so I could look inside.

"Disguise cards are hard to come by, so I get by with colored powders. Turn," she instructed.

I spun on the seat. Two things became obvious very quickly: Amalthea had been completely serious about wanting a doll to dress up, and despite her ability to see the future, she was utterly indecisive. She pulled a powder up, compared the coloring with my own, and then switched to another. The process repeated several times until she settled on her selections. With my eyes closed, all my attention was drawn to the feather-light sensation as she brushed over my forehead, my cheeks, my neck. My eyelids got an obscene amount of attention. The brush was almost ticklish, and when my face quirked on reflex, Amalthea quickly ordered me to "not interrupt her work."

At last, the witch was satisfied with her efforts. She turned me back to the mirror. I'd expected to be painted like an autumn tree. Instead, I found I still looked like myself. My lips were lined and slightly darker, my eyes more attention-grabbing, but since I was among the few in Damerel who didn't have red eyes, it hardly mattered.

She turned her arsenal on herself, plucking fresh brushes and covering her face in quick strokes. In what seemed to be a matter of seconds, she had given herself light blue eyeshadow and a matching navy lip.

"If you can do it that fast, why did it take so long for me?"

She grinned. "Because I was having fun."

It seemed indulgent, but it was hard to judge when Amalthea seemed so giddy. Despite the hardship she'd seen in her life, Amalthea had a certain gaiety that seemed utterly natural. Her smiles were quick, and complemented by crinkled eyes. In contrast, each time I returned her smile I felt like a fraud.

"Let me slip something on for the evening and then we'll sort out your gown. You're going to be spectacular, Sam."

She ducked from the mirror and began searching the floor. Heaps of fabric were lifted and quickly discarded until she was three-quarters across the room and appeared satisfied at last. She disappeared behind the silk screen, her previous dress falling over the screen to the ground in a pile.

Since the use of the screen was no doubt for my benefit, the state of the room made more sense. When she reemerged, everything above her clavicle was bare. Her dress began above her breasts, and midnight blue fabric pooled down, cinched only at the waist. Like all her clothes, it was ornately embroidered with long billowing sleeves that ran from mid-shoulder down below her hands.

"How did you decide?" I asked, curious. Well, curious and desperate to delay our attendance at the ball.

"It's been at least a season since I was seen in this gown," she explained. "The exposed neck is the fashion of the court among the powerful and the flirtatious. It can be an invitation for a bite. Or it can be a declaration that no one would be able to take from you and challenging any to try. The color is simply because I look wonderful in this shade of blue."

I swallowed, unable to focus on the blue while her neck and shoulders were exposed. "How do you know which is which?"

"Attitude," she chirped. She strode over to me as if the floor wasn't littered by uneven mountains of clothes. "Now, our proportions are too different for me to lend you anything. First thing tomorrow, I'll ensure a fresh wardrobe is started for you. But tonight, it's a special enough occasion we can use this."

Another flourish and Amalthea revealed her stack of cards from another drawer. It was easily a hundred cards thick, exponentially larger than my own paltry deck. She thumbed through them haphazardly. "No, no... where is it... no... ah! Here we are." She slid the deck back into its hiding place and lifted a card triumphantly between her fingers.

My brows drew together. "You can't be serious."

It was a creation card. Creation magic was extremely rare and coveted, because unlike most temporary enchantments, that which it created was permanent. At its purest, the power enabled the caster to create whatever was in their mind. Like all cards, they came in different strengths and assortments. Prince Marcel the Bountiful had a kind of creation magic. It only allowed him to multiply that which he already had, but even that was considered an incredible feat. Reading the symbols on this card, this card was limited, but even still, it was outrageous to propose using it for something as mundane as a dress.

I pulled back, trying to reason with Amalthea. "It's too much. Better for me to skip or wear what I am now if I really must attend."

"It's imperative you send the right message. Wearing some ill-fitted castoff or thrown-together day dress—sorry—is decidedly *not* the right message."

"Amalthea, families would work for years to afford a card half that powerful."

"You know, you can call me Thea," she replied as if that was the only part she heard.

"Thea," I echoed, trying out the nickname. "Be sensible. This extravagance is beyond anything a void should dream of, let alone do."

She cocked a hip out, the dark fabric swaying with the movement. "You're the king's Chosen. The only thing you need to dream of is your dress. Or, if you prefer, I can conjure it for you."

The gleam in her eyes said she liked that idea more by the second. I yanked the card from her fingers, which she let go easily with a triumphant grin.

"Only because I'm afraid of what you'd put me in," I grumbled.

She huffed. "I have excellent taste, I'll have you know."

I left my position in front of the mirror and carefully pulled my current dress off, casting a mournful look at the comfortable fabric. I'd never used a creation card before, never even held one, but magic was always intuitive. I shut my eyes and tried to think of what I would wear. I didn't have a clue what the fashions were these days, let alone the vampire styles beyond what little Amalthea had told me. I pushed a general idea to the card, hoping like with disguise magic it would fill in the blanks. *I am not one of them.* The magic traced over my body, wrapping around me. *I am not prey.* Fabric appeared with a sparkle of light, unformed yet as the magic read my intentions.

I don't want them to touch me.

When the dress finally materialized, I stepped out for Thea to see.

She blinked at me, for the first time slightly off-kilter.

"Well, that's definitely sending a message." She recovered and drew closer, offering me a hand. "I'd daresay you're as ready as you'll ever be. Won't Raphael be surprised to see you!"

Chapter 31

It took nearly half an hour to navigate the winding maze of the mountain castle's halls, to say nothing of the added complication of the shoes Amalthea had lent me. After years going barefoot and wishing for proper footwear, I found myself wishing I could kick the pointy-heeled torture devices off. The thick calluses of my feet weren't made for such fine things. I tried to map the castle in my mind as Amalthea led me, arm linked with mine. The halls were almost entirely empty, and as we approached the ballroom, I realized why.

When Amalthea declared we had three hours to get ready, she clearly had no intention for us to arrive on time.

"It sounds like the ball started hours ago," I whispered to her.

She gave me an amused look, gray eye twinkling with mirth. "But of course. You couldn't be seen arriving first, after all. That dress deserves an audience."

I wasn't so sure.

The dress was exactly what I'd wanted, but I never would have been able to picture it. Now that the magic had taken the essence of my thoughts and made it physical, I was unsure if it had been such a wise idea to let those feelings guide the creation magic.

The skirts flowed around me, the bodice and sleeves heavy. I'd seen myself in the mirror before leaving.

If Raphael hates it, perhaps I'll get to leave the ball immediately.

A servant opened the door, and with no further instruction, the herald announced our arrival. "Presenting the seer of the court and adviser to King Raphael, Lady Amalthea, and King Raphael's claimed human, Lady Samara!"

A hush fell over the space. Or perhaps there was no silence, but rather no noise that could surmount the roaring in my ears as hundreds of pairs of eyes stared up at me.

Prey. To them, I was prey.

My vision swam, bouncing from group to group, a sea of white hair, pale skin, and red eyes surrounding me.

Then my gaze landed on one particular figure.

Raphael.

A BARGAIN SO BLOODY

At once, he became all I could see. He was dressed in more finery than I'd ever seen. Like Amalthea, his neck was exposed—and there was no doubt in my mind this was not an invitation, but a threat. The fashion was unlike anything I'd ever seen in the Witch Kingdom. He was dressed entirely in black, with rich silk stretching from his shoulders down to billowing cuff sleeves. The garment was inlaid with rubies that glinted under the chandelier's light, a large one pinning a matching cape to his back. A fearsome crown sat atop his head. Severe silver spikes went unadorned, marking him as a king who needed no such finery.

He looked more like himself than I'd ever seen him, yet at the same time he was unrecognizable from the vampire I'd slept next to in the woods.

When I first saw him, I thought he looked shocked to see me. All traces of surprise were gone now, and instead the slightest glint of satisfaction shone on his face, from the light of his eyes to the slight upturn of his lips.

He strode to the base of the stairs, expectant.

"Oh good, I was worried he might be angry I brought you," Amalthea whispered.

Her words gave me enough of a jolt to ground me back in the moment. Yes, I was in a ballroom with vampires, but damn me to the eighth hell, I was already in a castle surrounded by them. I'd known what I was walking into, even if the sight was discomfiting. We began to descend the stairs.

My gaze remained trained on Raphael.

When we reached him, he turned his attention to Amalthea.

"You and I will speak later." The barest threat underlaid the words, but it was enough that Amalthea quickly excused herself as she was "utterly parched."

He extended a hand to me, and I grabbed it like a lifeline.

"I wasn't expecting you," he said so quietly I had to strain to hear.

"I gathered as much. I can go," I said quickly, but Raphael shook his head before I finished.

"No. Better that they see you for what you are."

"A weak human?" My skepticism was plain.

"Untouchable." He cocked his head slightly to the side. "This is quite the dress. It suits you."

I was instantly flustered. Who was this Raphael? He was direct and ferocious, as he'd ever been. There was a silkiness to his words—that, and the way he was dressed not as a disheveled ex-prisoner but as royalty—that made me feel strange.

My dress was utterly opposite to vampire fashion. I'd begged the creation card for one thing: *I don't want vampires to touch me.*

The magic translated that into a dress that was closer to armor than the flowing form Amalthea wore. A metal collar covered my neck, winding down into chains that held up the bodice, which was made of metal sheets that molded to my form. The sleeves and skirt were still feminine, covering my body in a way that let me move freely. The entire piece was copper of varying shades. It wouldn't actually hurt vampires—creation magic couldn't create enchanted items—but just as Amalthea had wanted, it sent a message.

I'm not one of you.

To complete the look, I'd added the cursed copper shackles as cuffs. They were useless as weapons, but they worked just fine as a warning.

"Dance with me," Raphael said.

I blinked up at him. "Why?"

He grinned. "If you're in my arms, I can keep an eye on you, since it seems Amalthea can't be trusted to not give into her whims." He made some gestures, and music billowed over the chatter. I hadn't been able to hear it properly, but now that I could, it was all I could do to not sway my body with the sounds.

Waves of notes surrounded me, and I was greedy for them. It had been so long, so damnably long. My chest tightened as the music crescendo swelled, climbing, climbing, and then crashing over me. When the song ended and another began, my throat was dry.

Raphael cocked his head, studying me like I was something all too interesting. *Could he feel what the music meant to me?*

"Talk to me, Samara."

How to explain what it was to go years and years with nothing but screams and insults to break up hours of bleak silence? That having my senses filled with something so beautiful, so lovely, and alive, made my knees want to buckle?

"Perhaps we will dance later," he murmured, guiding me away from the dance floor.

I struggled to focus on his words when all I wanted was to find the source of the music and sit at the feet of whoever made it. "I... I like music."

The three words were hard to get out. Music was mine. It was private, secret. Making myself give that up to a male who should have been my mortal enemy felt wrong.

And yet some part of me wanted him to know me.

"Do you play?" he asked, oblivious to my internal struggle.

I pursed my lips. "No. My mother said it wasn't proper for someone of my status. She was convinced I was to be a lady, who had others playing music on command."

Raphael didn't say anything to that, and with the silence, I found myself wanting to give voice to a memory. "When she was away, I'd try to make my own instruments. The closest I came was a flute made from a carrot. Of course, there was no quiet way to play my carrot-flute, so I was quickly discovered."

"And then?" Raphael said as I trailed off. We were being watched from behind cups and tilted heads. Raphael didn't pay an iota of attention to the onlookers as we moved around the room. His attention was entirely on me.

"She had it tossed in the evening stew."

Raphael drew up short. "That was cruel."

I shrugged, the chains over my shoulders making a soft sound. "It wasn't meant to be. She did it for my own good."

Raphael didn't reply to that, but I sensed he had more to say. We'd nearly reached the refreshment table when a male vampire approached.

"Greetings, Your Majesty," the noble said. His elevated status was obvious from the finely made clothing and comfort with which he moved through the room.

"Lazarus," Raphael acknowledged.

"It's wonderful to see you back at Damerel," Lazarus crooned. "And you've taken a human."

I didn't want to meet any vampires, but as with all predators, any display of weakness would just arouse those deadly instincts. When the vampire looked at me, I didn't shrink away. Instead, I straightened my spine, resisting the urge to fiddle with my cursed copper cuffs as I fixed my feet under the dress into the same formation Iademos had drilled into me earlier that day.

Raphael inclined his head. Obviously, his taciturn habits were part of his nature, not personal as I'd once assumed.

"We're all so *curious* about her," Lazarus continued, paying no mind to Raphael's lack of response. "And everything that transpired while you were gone. Was your quest successful? Are we once more *safe* from the abomination?" The noble managed to drip his honeyed words in the barest hint of contempt.

Raphael smiled, but all I saw were fangs I was glad not to have pointed at me. "All is as I wish it to be."

Lazarus was quick to make his excuses while I tried to puzzle out his words. Raphael had been on a quest to get the Black Grimoire. He'd been waylaid and mistakenly gone to Greymere instead of the marshes. But what abomination? The Grimoire? It was an odd term, and Raphael hadn't attempted to burn it or anything.

Perhaps the true reason for Raphael's time away wasn't widespread. But that still begged the question: What did they all think Raphael meant to do in the Witch Kingdom?

We continued, landing at the refreshments table. Several vampires eyed their king but thought better of approaching. The long table at the edge of the room was piled high with glasses, a pyramid of champagne flutes on one side of an ice sculpture that wasn't fine enough to be magic made. The other side held a matching tower of chalices filled with deep red liquid. My stomach revolted at the sight.

Raphael extended a glass of golden champagne to me. "Here."

I shook my head.

"You're not thirsty?"

"I don't imbibe." I'd never really had the chance. Any spirits that made their way to Greymere were quickly hoarded by Nelson and distributed among his favored few.

The behavior that followed did more to frighten me than inspire envy. Those were nights to hide in the farthest, coldest corners of the prison. Losing my senses in the midst of all these vampires from the same drink? That was what my nightmares were made of.

"Water, then." He gave some small signal and a servant—human—approached. He instructed him to bring fresh spring water and dismissed him with a turned shoulder.

The sight rankled. "Are all humans in your kingdom servants?"

Raphael arched a brow at me. "Anyone who tried to treat Amalthea as a servant would find themselves laughed out of castle and country."

"All *voids*, then?"

"We all serve something higher, do we not?" he drawled. "But no. Otherwise this table would be covered in blood mead."

The table was divided between both drinks. Yet there were no humans in attendance among the nobility. There were hundreds in attendance, but Amalthea was alone in her not-pure-white hair.

"Look closer," Raphael said in my ear.

I stiffened as the heat of his breath caressed me, the tingle curling down the back of my neck. I hadn't realized we were so close. But I obeyed, examining those nearest to us more carefully. A pair of women chattering behind feathered fans, hiding their necks. A trio of men, gathered around a high-top table, one gesturing wildly as he recounted some story. I cocked my head, trying to make sense of what I saw. All had cropped white hair of slightly varying lengths, and each had red eyes... but my attention snagged on the one on the right. His eyes seemed just a shade less vibrant. His skin didn't have the same blue tint as the others had. And perhaps most telling, he was older. Maybe sixty, sixty-five, if I were to lay a bet.

There was only one explanation.

"No," I breathed.

"Oh, yes."

By the sixth hell. Bad enough they wanted to be vampires, but they even aped their appearance. Amalthea had said disguise cards were difficult to come by, so they must have spent a magical fortune in a Vampire Kingdom to match their appearances.

"All the time?"

"Mostly for special occasions, council meetings, and so on. Perhaps ten or twenty percent at most among the gentry are human. The nobles are a mix of long-standing houses and appointed posts. Obviously, humans can only rise in position from the latter, and when your competition has an endless amount of time to reach a post, you're at a disadvantage. Make no mistake, the humans you find among them are some of the craftiest creatures in this room."

"And so they want to fit in, for the vampires to forget they're not like them?"

"As if the chasm between immortal and mortal is so easily crossed," Raphael said with the barest snort. "The endless drum of their beating hearts and labored breaths will always give them away."

I swallowed and put a half step of distance between us. He was right. Vampires were a world apart.

A servant returned with a crystal glass of icy water on a tray, a boon in the heat of the crowd. It wasn't the same servant, but he looked familiar. Not from Damerel, though. I hadn't learned any faces here. I tried to place him while he extended a tray towards me.

"For you, Lady Samara," he said with a respectful half bow. His gaze was on the floor.

For a moment I just stared. Was my mind playing tricks on me? The face I imagined I hadn't seen for many years, and only in shadows.

Raphael took the glass and handed it to me when I made no move to take it.

"Thank you," I said, as the human servant retreated. *A mistake. You mistook that other servant for another.* I ignored Raphael's curious look and tried to return to the subject. "Amalthea doesn't bother. Trying to look more like a vampire, I mean."

"The fates themselves could not convince Amalthea to do anything she didn't want to."

"I've known her only a short time, and I find that to be a fair assessment," I agreed.

We spoke a little more but were eventually interrupted. More sycophants, much like Lazarus. Honeyed words, talks of politics and policies mixed in with cloying praise for Raphael: his sense of justice, his dedication to the kingdom, his wit, his majestic presence. Some might bear a grain of truth, but I suspected the same words would have been applied to a lobotomized rooster if it wore the crown. Some things didn't change.

I occupied my mind by studying the celebrants of the room, both those who approached and anyone else in my line of sight. With each one, I made it a game to figure out if they were vampire or human. Most were vampires, as Raphael said. As I practiced, I got better at picking out the humans from the bunch. The clothing was the same style… but seldom quite as grand. The difference between a civil servant and a titled inheritor. They lacked the utter stillness the vampires were capable of, the grace that came when you moved with no excessive flourishes. There were differences in the red eyes, but while the vampires seemed to nearly glow as they sipped the blood mead, the humans were always lackluster.

Disdain swept through me. How quickly they begged to be rid of their humanity. Not just that, their individuality. I loathed the part of me that understood. Was it so different from the court of the Witch King, where courtiers constantly competed to dress in the latest fashion, or raced to tell the king the latest gossip? Was I any better, even if I was only here temporarily?

Many had chosen this. They had given up the second-class life of a mortal without magic in an enchanted kingdom to try to rise another way. I wanted to believe that made me different. But my choices had led me here too. If it was a matter of survival, would I disguise myself as a vampire? I couldn't deny it. I'd let one feed on me, claim me.

I would *never* let one turn me. That difference would have to be enough.

A nasally voice caught my attention.

"And will she be joining us for the Tri-Lunar Eclipse Ceremony?" a female noble asked. Vampire. Definitely vampire. Her hair was up, her bodice cut low. She angled her neck as if beckoning. If ever there was someone inviting a bite, it was this female. *Did vampires even bite other vampires?* What was the point?

"Perhaps," Raphael said noncommittally.

They must mean me. I edged closer to Raphael. I didn't feel particularly threatened, but I didn't care for the hungry look in her eyes. Though it wasn't quite directed at me.

"Oh, it'll be so exciting," her companion added, punctuating her words with a demure flap of her fan. Her neck was covered in a high lace collar. "It'll be my first one."

"You *never* forget your first," the first vampire said with a wink. "Mine was just barely three hundred years ago, and I've been waiting for the next one since."

What exactly *was* the Tri-Lunar Eclipse Ceremony?

VASILISA DRAKE

The conversation dripped in cultural innuendos I lacked context for. The focus drifted back to politics, and eventually, the two females were replaced by others, all attempting to curry favor with the returned king. There was no more time for Raphael and me to talk, and I found I missed the comfort that small talk had offered.

At least, I could have used the distraction. Without it, my mind kept returning to the human servant from before, unable to relax.

Chapter 32

Someone jiggled the doorknob of my room the next morning. *Intruder.* My body stiffened at the thought. *Someone is trying to get in.*

"Samara?"

Thea. It was only Amalthea. I slid the Black Grimoire off my lap and shut the heavy tome, trailing my fingers over it.

"Coming!" I called through the heavy wooden door. I untucked the chair from the handle and slid away the desk I'd set to reinforce it. Finally, I twisted the key and unlocked the door.

Amalthea cast a curious glance at the pile of furniture as she stepped inside. "Redecorating?" she asked lightly.

I tried to smile. She didn't give me reassurances I wouldn't believe, and I was thankful.

"I didn't mean to barge in on you, but I was wondering if you wanted to have breakfast with me before training."

"That would be nice." I meant to sound warm and sincere, mirroring the witch's tone, but instead I sounded stupefied. I'd slept fitfully after the ball and finally gave up on sleep sometime in the early hours. It hadn't occurred to me anyone would offer to have breakfast with me. "I got distracted trying to read that." I pointed to the grimoire.

Amalthea's gaze followed my gesture. Her eyebrows shot up. "You're reading *that* book?"

"Trying," I grumbled. The truth was, I barely remembered the shape of the common runes in Old Runyk, let alone the meaning. They were similar to the common tongue, but the sounds assigned to half the letters were different, the diphthongs a mess, and I struggled to so much as write my name in it let alone understand a magical book. "Raphael mentioned there's a library that might help?"

"Raphael. Raphael wanted you to translate *that* book?" It was the second time she'd said that as if she meant to put several expletives after it. "By the sixth hell, where did you even find that thing?"

I frowned at her. "The marshes. Given that it's what he went all the way to the Witch Kingdom to seek out, it only makes sense we brought it back. The whole reason I'm here is because he offered me a thousand gold pieces

A BARGAIN SO BLOODY

to translate it." A task I wasn't sure I was up to, based on my limited success this morning.

But I wanted to succeed. Was determined to.

Amalthea shifted on her feet like she didn't even want to be in the same room as the grimoire. She didn't immediately correct me or agree with me, which meant one thing: She was keeping something from me and weighing how much to share. A cutting reminder that even though she had been all smiles while we dressed the night before, we weren't confidants.

"Amalthea, what were you and everyone expecting Raphael to do while he went to the Witch Kingdom?" I waited a beat, and when she stayed silent, I pressed on: "Raphael said he was looking for something and wound up in Greymere, and I assumed it was due to bad information. But you're a seer—if he has you guiding him to the grimoire, he shouldn't be at risk of that. And last night, a noble mentioned something about an 'abomination.'" I let the words hang. I could believe Lazarus didn't know the truth, but Raphael had said himself he trusted Amalthea. Besides, wouldn't he have at least consulted his court seer before setting off?

Still, Amalthea said nothing. She simply stood there, arms crossed protectively over her abdomen, not meeting my gaze.

My throat stiffened, all at once swollen by hurt and frustration.

"I think I'll take breakfast alone." I turned back to the settee.

Thea grabbed my wrist. "Wait."

I turned back, and she pulled me across the room to sit by the fire. Her gaze flickered back between the grimoire and me. "You're correct about several things. Raphael did go to Greymere based on the information I gave him, but it wasn't about the Black Grimoire. I can't even find that book with my sight. It's cloaked in too many centuries of magic for a single seer to find. Frankly, I'm confused as to what he even wants with it—vampires and witches alike are loath to be around it. It gives me the creeps just being in the room. If anyone knew Raphael had it in his possession, that he'd actually sought it out, there would be questions."

Questions from whom? "But that doesn't tell me what you sent him looking for."

"Right. There's a creature that appears every few hundred years. Mortal enemy to the vampires. Raphael isn't just king because he's strong—he's king because when this creature appears, he hunts it down and guarantees the safety of all Vampire Kingdoms."

A creature that vampires were scared of... either I should be scared of it too, or I should hope Raphael was unsuccessful in finding it. But it was clear from Thea's tone she believed in whatever mission Raphael had been on.

"Sam, the truth is, I'm at a loss about what to think now that the book is in Damerel, and Raphael isn't answering any of my questions either." She heaved a sigh. "Now, can we please get breakfast? We can go to the library after and get all the dusty old tomes you like—but don't tell them what you're working on."

I stood reluctantly, looking back at the grimoire which still beckoned from the opposite end of the room.

"Sam, I promise no one wants to be near that book."

"Alright," I agreed.

But I turned back and tucked the grimoire between the couch pillows all the same, hiding it from view when I really wished I could have taken it with me.

"What is your business?"

An ancient-looking vampire peered down from an elevated countertop. His skin sagged slightly, his red eyes rimmed with bloodshot whites. Unlike everyone else who looked at Amalthea with a healthy dose of respect, the librarian's brusque tone said he was irritated with both of us. To the right of his podium was an iron gate. Amalthea had explained on the way over that the librarian answered to no one but the king, so entry was at the librarian's discretion. And that it was best not to tell him what we were looking for. Even if he didn't know about the grimoire, no vampire wanted anything to do with sharing hard-won witch knowledge.

"I'm showing the king's Chosen all of the kingdom's wonders," Amalthea said, unperturbed by the librarian's tone.

His face didn't so much as twitch in acknowledgment.

"If you please." Her imperious tone made it clear that it was not a request.

The vampire still didn't say a word in recognition, but he pulled a lever, and the ceiling-high iron gate swung open.

"Do vampires age?" I murmured as quietly as I could when we passed.

Amalthea shot me a stunned look, but it was the vampire librarian who answered. "I was old when I turned, girl. Now, the years pass like seconds."

In short, he'd looked that way when he'd turned, which was also a long time ago. I tried to fight off the flush at my rudeness. "I suppose I know so little about vampires. Are there books for me to learn more about them?"

An ancient, bushy white brow rose as the librarian slowly extended his arm towards the open door. The answer was obvious.

"We'll find you some," Amalthea assured me, tugging me the rest of the way inside.

Amalthea led me on a quick tour of the library, which mainly meant gesturing broadly at several thousand books at a time. The library was utterly non-magical but no less wondrous than the one in Apante. Shelves were carved into the stone, towering to dangerous heights. "Histories here, novels over there, plays because those are different, skilled workbooks are in this section, religious studies on the gods basically take up this entire wall..."

"Where *would* books on vampires be?" I hadn't lied—I did want to find some books about how vampires worked. Specifically, I wanted to know how to break the bond between Raphael and me.

"That's a bit broad."

"Their powers, then." *And how to counteract them.*

Amalthea considered me and then eyed the rest of the library. "I know just the book. I'll bring it to you tomorrow. In the meantime, let's find what you need to translate that cursed thing." She was careful not to mention exactly what I was translating. Not when a vampire could overhear.

Unlike the bustle of the Great Library, the library of Damerel was silent. Our footsteps were swallowed by plush carpet as we moved forward. Amalthea navigated the space with ease.

"I don't suppose you've seen the books I need?" I asked hopefully.

She cast me a rueful smile. "Not quite. But I spent enough time here when I arrived at Damerel that I learned a lot."

She eventually located the stack of books she wanted. They were buried in the farthest corner of the library, dust covering the tops. I frowned. These books would have been prized in the king's library, but here, they seemed to be kept almost reluctantly. Why were they so disdained?

Simply because they were witch books or specifically about Old Runyk? Thea offered me a piddling selection of books, and I picked the four that were the most promising. Nothing as simple as a dictionary, unfortunately, but the four were enough to leave me better equipped to translate the grimoire.

We split the books into two piles between us.

"I don't understand why everyone is so scared of that book," I said softly as we headed towards the entrance.

She cocked her head at me. "You know how grimoires work, right?"

As much as any void could. "They're like cookbooks. Witches record spells that work in them."

"Not quite. That is true, but witches also imbue magic in them. Unlike enchanted cards, however, only witches with the corresponding skill set can use them. And in most cases, the magic doesn't fade. Grimoires are guarded jealously in families and often fought over as an inheritance." She paused at a shelf and grabbed two more books, putting them on top of our piles. "I'd always heard they can take on a life of their own, with enough time. Not sentient, exactly, but something like it. They don't like witches outside their bloodline touching them."

I frowned. "But there's no witch who has control over death magic."

Thea said nothing while I continued to ponder what she'd said about grimoires. Even if there were such a witch, this grimoire had been left in a tomb for who knows how long. The Black Grimoire must have been different, which was why it had become part of witch folklore.

Another puzzle piece fitting into a picture I couldn't quite see.

We reached the entryway. Amalthea attempted to stride through, leaving me speeding along behind her, but the librarian wasn't fooled by the books she had placed atop our piles.

"Halt," the librarian hissed. "She can't look at those books."

Amalthea arched a brow at the librarian. "Your king says she can do exactly that."

"She certainly can't take them," he continued, indignant.

The tone made me want to cower and apologize. Amalthea felt nothing of the sort.

"I suggest you try telling King Raphael that. Maybe he'll realize it's time for a new librarian," she said breezily, hooking my arm and pulling me away while the ancient vampire sputtered.

We disappeared down the hall before any further complaints could be made. Once we turned a corner, I shared a glance with Amalthea.

On silent cue, we both burst out laughing.

"By the eighth hell, you have no fear," I said between giggles. The way she'd stared the vampire down and invoked Raphael's name. Given she hadn't even known about the grimoire until two hours ago, there was no chance Raphael had said any such thing.

She pressed her fingertips to her lips, trying to regain control. "Of him? No. Of Demos when we show up late? Maybe."

Chapter 33

As the days passed, a routine emerged. Amalthea met me at my rooms each morning and we ate a light breakfast before joining Demos for training. I still struggled to relax around the vampire, but he proved himself a patient teacher—if somewhat exacting. But then, that's what I wanted. There was no point in practicing to be sloppy. Even if I didn't know how to use it yet, I carried the dagger everywhere with me on the jeweled belt Raphael had gifted me.

After practice, we would eat again, with Raphael occasionally joining us, and then I'd retreat to my rooms to work on my two projects: translating the grimoire and learning everything I could about vampires. Mercifully, I was spared any more balls.

The grimoire was addictive. Just touching it gave me the same rush as using enchanted cards. If Amalthea was to be believed about certain grimoires having an awareness, no doubt this one did. Even Raphael didn't care to be around it, but me, I loved it. For a void like me who adored magic since I'd never have any of my own, being around the enchanted tome was energizing. I was still in the first few pages, able to grasp only the barest framework. So far, I'd learned the owner of the book was devoted to Anagenni. Not a surprise. The rough translation for a devotee was *necromancer*, which used the same suffix as other witchkind used in Old Runyk. Their origin, their purpose, that I still hadn't made sense of. Every word translated was hard-won—and some I couldn't get—but I enjoyed the task.

My other task was more daunting. Amalthea gave me two books: one on vampire powers and the other on vampire society. At first, just holding the first book Amalthea had given me made my hands shake so badly I could scarcely open it. Raphael had actually come to check on me with some vague pretext—he hadn't acknowledged the fact he'd felt my panic through whatever mental link was between us.

All the more reason I had to study the vampires. My mother had instilled in me that knowledge was a kind of power no one could take from you. She had meant knowledge of other courtiers and their political machinations. I had favored book learning even as a child. Though I'd never wanted to interact with vampires, if this was my life, staying ignorant was more likely to shorten it than anything else.

The book on vampire powers was more a running list of the varied abilities vampires had. It seemed there were as many vampire abilities as witches' magics: turning into a bat, flight, invisibility, telepathy. But despite the wide range, few vampires actually had any powers, which was some small relief. The mental link between a vampire and those they bit was also rare. The book mentioned it was possible to learn to block it, but offered no details, to my frustration.

The other book on vampire society was slightly more reassuring. Vampires were terrifying, and nothing would change my mind. But they weren't the mindless beasts I'd thought. I'd seen the truth of that while I'd traveled with Raphael, and training with Demos proved he wasn't a complete exception. Raphael had mentioned he had advisers, and the kingdom was filled with civil servants, but it went beyond that. The entirety of vampire society was strictly hierarchical, with every individual neatly slotting into their respective place. Vampires revered strength—the strongest led, the rest obeyed. They were also extremely territorial. From what I read, vampires respected each other's claims. If they didn't, they were quickly excised from society or killed.

VASILISA DRAKE

Between what I'd read and my training, I slowly became more confident. Despite the gentle cajoling from Amalthea and Demos, I didn't *want* to be scared all the time. So I pushed myself. I made the walk to Amalthea's some mornings for breakfast, instead of the other way around. I let Demos put his hands on my arms to correct my form. I didn't make eye contact with vampires in the halls or attempt to get to know them, but I tried to force myself not to sprint if I was caught in the halls when one came by. Even when the halls were empty, I felt like there were eyes on me, watching, waiting, but I fought the urge to hunch my shoulders and cower.

A life of fear was not a life. Raphael never sprinted away from enemies—and, well, Raphael likely knew he would always win the fight. But I was under his protection while I worked for him, and everything I learned told me that should keep me safe for now. I tried to trust in that.

That was why, a couple weeks later, when I finished training for the day, I didn't go straight back to my rooms.

A sound caught my attention going down the hall. Not noise but... as I went farther down the winding hall, the sound grew louder and clearer. Music notes. Memories of the night at the ball, of my first time hearing music in years, made my chest tighten. And here it was again—a different tune, but no less beguiling. Eventually, I wound up in a small alcove above a small theater. I could peer down and see the form of the musician. The world disappeared around me as I listened. My heart pounded in time with the rhythm of the music. The tune was a lively, jovial thing. And while joy was a long-forgotten emotion to someone as wretched as me, the music made the emotion echo in my chest. I wrapped my palm around the wrought-iron railing, the metal digging into my palm as I remained transfixed. When one song ended, another began. Hours must have passed, but they felt like the barest seconds.

When the final notes faded, I went back to my room in a daze.

Music.

Glorious music, unlike anything I'd heard in ages. The music in the ball had shocked me, but the memory had been layered with anxiety around the vampires. But there on the balcony, it had just been me and the sounds, wrapping through my blood and making it hum.

And then the next day, I returned.

A different performer was present, this one playing a large wooden instrument with strings as tall as me. Once again, all my senses shut off one by one until all I focused on was the music, entirely different, mournful and grand.

Each day I went back, drawn like a moth to a pyromancer's flame. When it became obvious I was losing too many hours, I packed my research materials with me, hastily scribbling the passage I was working on in the grimoire with my translation aids. I hid myself in the alcove and relished in the depth of music. No screams, no curses, no vile threats. No miserable silence that haunted you, worse than any of the other sounds, making you realize just how alone you were. The music was a comfort I desperately needed. And so I went back, each day, listening, working, lowering my guard as I let the notes wash over me.

Until that proved to be a mistake.

"So this is what became of you."

I jolted. Between the passage I was working on and the day's musician—a pianist who played songs like rolling waves—I had entirely forgotten my surroundings. Towering over me was the servant I'd seen weeks ago at the ball, the one I'd recognized and convinced myself I'd been mistaken when I didn't see him again. His appearance was nothing remarkable: brown eyes, brown hair, a nose that was neither too long nor too short, a stature that was slightly smaller than usual for a man but still larger than me. He was in his early fifties, maybe, but with the long life of witches, he was in his prime.

In the moment at the ball, it had been so easy to convince myself it wasn't him. Just a brief moment with a common-looking man. His appearance was as I remembered, but his demeanor was entirely different.

Now, the aura around the spymaster was as I remembered, like oil seeped from the air he breathed, dark and destroying.

I stood immediately, my hand clumsily reaching for the bronze dagger in the sheath at my side.

The servant arched a brow. "Now, none of that. You'll only hurt yourself, Samara. I simply came to say hello."

"I don't believe you."

The servant spread his arms wide. "Now, Samara. I'm simply happy to see you doing well."

I wished I was more confident in my training. Wished I was like Raphael who could kill without remorse. "Because trusting the king's spymaster is in my best interest, Titus?"

"At least I haven't abandoned my country," Titus drawled.

"My country abandoned me first," I hissed. My knuckles strained around my dagger. The exact opposite to the light, secure grip Demos had tried to train me on.

Titus *tsked*. "Now, now. A little time in Greymere for a void is nothing. It's not like you're a witch."

Greymere was hell. But there was no point in arguing the matter. He was simply goading me. "I just want a fresh start, Titus."

"A fresh start. For you, of all people?" He took a step forward, but I had no room to go back. "I simply find it interesting that their demon king has taken an interest in you. I wonder if he'd be as charitable if he knew who you really were?"

My grip loosened, and he seized the opportunity to snatch my dagger. It fit easily in his hand, and he twirled his hand up to point the blade at me.

I swallowed, and satisfaction rolled over the spymaster's lips at the sight.

"I'm not a threat to you," I said softly.

"On that, I agree perfectly." He was too close. His scent of bitter almonds made me breathe through my mouth. "You're an opportunity."

"An opportunity?" I bit my tongue on the echo.

His grin was serpentine. Patient, but all too satisfied he'd piqued my interest. "You're the king's Chosen, girl. You could do the Crown a great service in your role."

I wanted to ask what he meant, but this time I kept silent. Titus sighed, as if annoyed I wasn't playing the proper role in this conversation.

"You could help me deal a blow to their kingdom. One they wouldn't recover from."

Now I couldn't hold back my cursed curiosity. "What do you intend?"

But as I'd known, spies delighted in withholding information, not sharing it. "Leave those details to me. But if you did agree, I could return you to the safety of the Witch Kingdom. Not your home, certainly, but I could put you in a village somewhere and ensure no one ever sought you there. Doesn't that sound lovely?"

I could go back. No. I shook off the thought, not taking my eyes off Titus for a moment. I couldn't betray Raphael.

Yes, I believed the vampires were evil, but... maybe they weren't as evil as I always thought. And I certainly didn't trust Titus. "I just want to be left alone."

"Left alone? Or left as the vampire king's pet?" he asked snidely.

I glared but said nothing.

"What a spoiled pet, I suppose. The vampires are so nice to you. Not like the bad ones you knew before... I bet you've convinced yourself they're *different*."

His patronizing tone made the hair on my neck bristle.

"You should learn more about your new owners, Samara Koisemi. See more of the mountain. Learn what lies in the rot of their kingdom. And when you can no longer lie to yourself, and remember your true allegiances, I'll be back." He tossed the dagger at my feet. "I'm a wonderful ally, girl. But remember: The king's shadowed hand is a terrible enemy to have. Something your mother should have known."

Titus fingered a card at his side and disappeared. Music washed over me, making me acutely aware that it had been absent in the past minutes of our conversation. Had he slowed time, or simply put us in a bubble with some magic?

My mind was divided in two. One part wanted to puzzle through the logistics of what had just happened. How was he here? What was his endgame? Would he follow through on his threats? Should I be helping him?

The other part was screaming, screaming, screaming.

Raphael appeared before me, and I stared through him. He scanned the surroundings, looking for some invisible threat, nostrils flaring. Did he scent Titus's bitter almond scent, or was the spymaster more careful than that?

The part of my brain that wasn't screaming, screaming, screaming noted his appearance: the crown on his head that was absent when he joined Amalthea and I for a meal; his clothing elegant, though his clothes were askance, as if he'd run here abruptly.

His chest didn't heave, not like mine, but his eyes were a bit wild.

When no threat materialized, he reined it in. In any other moment, it would have been fascinating to watch. The way his posture changed, his movements slowed, non-threatening as he approached me. Nothing more concerning than the straightening of his cuffs as he asked, "Is everything alright?"

His voice, low but strong, cut through the panicked haze in my head. Against my will, I swayed slightly.

He crossed the five paces between us immediately and braced my upper arms between his hands.

"Samara."

His hold was steadying. My skin felt clammy all around, my back suddenly aching like I'd spent three days on my feet. I forced my shoulders down as I steadied while he supported me.

A BARGAIN SO BLOODY

"How'd you get here so quickly?" I asked, still stunned. One moment, Titus had been confronting me. Now, Raphael was in front of me, and I was prepared.

"I sensed something was wrong. Not physically," he clarified.

Right. The bond.

"Now tell me what aggrieves you." *So I can destroy it.* The words went unspoken, but the offer felt as blatant as if he'd said them.

King Stormblood's spymaster is in your midst and wants me to help him plot against you.

The words caught in my throat. It invited questions—how did I know the spymaster? How did he know me? I didn't dare answer either. Why hadn't I mentioned suspecting seeing him at the ball? Raphael might decide I was in league with Titus before I could defend myself.

I was useful to Raphael, and maybe, just maybe, he harbored some affection for me. *The vampire king's pet*, Titus had called me. But the creature who had slaughtered dozens on our travel would kill any threat to his kingdom.

I couldn't tell him.

However much I wanted to trust him and his friends, survival came first. And Titus had reminded me just how precarious that was.

"The... it was the music."

Raphael cocked his head at me, his grip loosening just slightly. "The music."

I swallowed, trying to scrounge up something convincing. Could he sense that I was lying, or just the anxiety and fear twisting through me? "I haven't heard this style of music before. It's intense. Loud." Loud noises were hard; sometimes they reminded me of the screams in Greymere. There was more than one instrument playing. One hit the keys with such intensity the walls nearly shook, the other was a mournful string tone that stirred something I wasn't sure what to do with.

The best lies were rooted in the truth.

"I'll remove the musicians at once," he said.

I winced at the thought I'd ruined what was likely a prestigious post from talented musicians. "It's not bad," I clarified. "But what I like about music is it awakens something in me. Sometimes it's so light and peaceful its foreign after everything. And sometimes it's like holding up a mirror that shows my worst memories."

Raphael studied my face for another beat. I forced myself to hold his gaze, to not dart my eyes to the corner like I ached to do.

Then he lowered to his knees in front of me. I tried to jolt back, but he caught my fingers in his hand before I moved far.

He lifted a blade between us—my cursed bronze blade. It had been between my feet where Titus had thrown it. Where it made no sense of being if I was simply listening to music like I'd claimed.

But Raphael didn't call me on the obvious lie. "You dropped this," was all he said.

Blisters were already forming on his palm as he wrapped my fingers around it, pressing my palm into a firm grip.

I clenched the blade like a lifeline.

"Thank you," I murmured. "For coming."

Raphael slowly let go, his burned fingers trailing over the back of my hand before dropping to his side.

"Of course."

Chapter 34

I hadn't seen Titus again in the past two weeks, but he'd done his job and ruined any semblance of peace I'd found. His words got under my skin—not just the threat, but the insinuation there was more to learn about the kingdom. In the hours before daybreak, sleep constantly evaded me while guilt twisted in my gut. It was a betrayal not to tell Raphael that King Stormblood's spymaster was lurking in their midst, but I had no way to explain myself without casting suspicions on how I knew him. Even if I managed a convincing lie, when confronted, Titus would tell them everything.

Hopefully, if Titus was going to do something, Amalthea would see it, and I wouldn't have to intervene. That was the point of having an oracle, right?

That morning, as I lay in the nest I'd made under the bed, the guilt was especially terrible. My stomach seemed unable to unclench. I tried to sit up and everything seemed to shift. I slumped against my pillow, pulling my legs closer against me. Something felt really wrong.

I lifted the blanket.

Blood.

Between my thighs.

I'm going to be sick.

Bang! Bang! Bang!

"Samara? Open the door."

Raphael. "One minute!" I called. I forced myself to ignore the pain and slid out from under the bed, grabbing my pillow and blanket. Why it was critical to not let Raphael know I was sleeping under the bed while I wanted to curl into a ball and hold my stomach could only be attributed to whatever fragment of pride I still had. My entire center of gravity seemed to shift as I stood, my feet wobbling as I started towards the barricaded door.

"I'm coming in," he declared.

"Wait—"

But the locked door was already swinging open, the furniture I'd lodged against it splintering as he pushed his way inside.

Of course. Why had I deluded myself into thinking some measly wooden furniture would protect me from vampire strength? I felt like heaving. Raphael stood in the doorway, impeccably dressed, while I stood from halfway across the room with my loose bedclothes hanging off me.

He inhaled sharply through his nose. "Oh."

And then he was gone, the door shut behind him.

I crumpled to the floor, bile in my throat, my stomach still miserably cramping. My thoughts were fuzzy, like I was high in the air without the ability to draw a deep breath. Instinct took over, and I rushed to the toilet. I sank to my knees on the cool stone and heaved, expelling everything inside me. Footsteps sounded beside me, and I tried to lift my head to react, but all at once there were fingers on my back, through my hair.

"It's okay," Raphael said. "You're okay."

"I'm bleeding," I hissed. My lower area ached like a cramp rather than a cut.

He pulled my hair away, one hand on the small of my back as I clutched the sides of the basin. "I know. I've sent for a healer—a human one. She'll be here soon. I can get Amalthea as well, if you'd find comfort in her presence."

Finally, I lifted my head, but it was impossible to fully meet Raphael's eyes. "Maybe later."

It was mortifying enough to be like this around Raphael. I debated sending him away, but that was the last thing I wanted, and I didn't have enough pride to push

A BARGAIN SO BLOODY

him away. He stayed at my side for several long moments until I felt certain I wouldn't vomit again.

"There's a change of clothes on the stool." He gestured to the side of the room. "I'll be right outside. Unless you want me to stay?"

I shook my head. Raphael left the room, and I took a few moments to note the blood seemed to have stopped. Was it from training too hard? I'd never experienced anything like this before. The cramps had eased slightly, but I wanted to get back under the bed as soon as possible. Maybe I could rest a little more before training. Just the thought of running through drills with Iademos made me want to vomit again.

I briefly washed my pelvis and thighs, then put on the loose dress he'd left me. When I opened the door, there were two figures. Raphael was joined by a woman with graying dark hair and an apron that had a dozen pockets so overflowing I wondered how it stayed up. A thin sheen of sweat dotted her brow as she shifted on her feet, the scent of herbs wafting over me as she neared.

"Hello, dear. My name is Charlotte. Raphael says you had need of a healer?" She gestured to the bed for me to sit. I went to the settee instead, but Raphael beat me there and dragged the massive piece of furniture away from the wall and over to the fireplace with startling ease. I'd have marveled more if my abdomen wasn't begging for me to sit down.

Once I settled on the plush cushion with Charlotte in front of me, Raphael was at my back. Just as well. I didn't need to look at him while the healer examined me.

"I'm bleeding. But I wasn't cut." Confusion shaded my voice. In all my time at Greymere, nothing like that had happened, and I'd endured far worse than the past weeks of training.

"How old are you, dear?"

"Twenty years." At least, I didn't think my birthday had passed yet. *Why did it matter?*

"And how are you feeling?" she asked.

It was so strange to have someone ask that. I didn't want to appear weak. "I'm bleeding," I repeated. "But I'm doing alright." *Kind of.*

"The truth, dove," Raphael interrupted.

I winced.

"I need to know how you're doing to best help you, dear," Charlotte assured me. "Do you know what your monthly cycle is?"

The words stirred some memories of my mother talking with her lady's maids, but nothing specific. I shook my head.

Charlotte explained in short, factual sentences what a monthly cycle was, and the fact it apparently happened every month or so to mortals from a young age.

I wanted to vomit all over again. "Every month? But this has never happened to me before."

She pursed her lips as she studied me. "It's... unusual, to say the least, for one of your age to have not yet had a cycle."

"She didn't have it because she was malnourished for the entirety of her adolescence," Raphael interrupted. "I'd wager this is the first time in her life she's properly eaten."

"It's best if the patient answers, Your Majesty." It wasn't quite a rebuke, but something like it. Charlotte focused her attention solely on me.

"I... it wasn't possible to eat much these past years." Another cramp seized my stomach. Raphael's hand was immediately on my shoulder, gently pressing, distracting me from the pain.

"So how are you feeling now?" she asked again.

"Terrible, to be honest. My stomach hurts like someone is twisting a knife in it, my head feels like it's going to float away, my back is sore, and I think I'd vomit again except there's nothing left in my stomach."

Charlotte just nodded along. "It's to be expected, I'm afraid. I can mix you a drink to help abate the symptoms, but the body needs what it needs. I take it you don't know much about handling your cycle?"

I shook my head once more. The healer launched into extensive details on symptomatology, expectations, and hygiene. By the time she finished, I was almost grateful to Greymere for keeping me so starved it had never happened before. Almost.

VASILISA DRAKE

The healer mixed up a brew before going, and under her—and Raphael's—watchful gaze I drained every foul-tasting drop. I'd certainly had worse. Foul-tasting medicine was a novelty, though. When sick as a child, a witch trained in healing magic would tend to me. There was, of course, no such thing in Greymere, but there was no medicine either. The bitter drink felt like a kind of penance, as though because I suffered through the foul taste I would deserve the healing it offered.

The healer departed with promises to check on me tomorrow. Or any time I needed, or wanted to be checked-on—"Even in the middle of the day," she added, when Raphael didn't look pleased with her answer.

"You should go to bed," he said once the door shut.

I was exhausted, but there was no way I could sleep right now. Certainly no way I'd crawl under the bedframe with Raphael here. "Can you send for Amalthea?"

"If you wish. But both the healer and I advise you to rest."

"Amalthea's presence will help me rest."

Raphael chortled. "The last thing Amalthea brings to any room is tranquility." But he heeded my wishes all the same. He stepped out, summoning a messenger to fetch Amalthea, and stayed, lingering in the doorjamb until the seer arrived.

A BARGAIN SO BLOODY

Amalthea arrived with a basket of gifts. She dismissed Raphael with a wave of her hand and strode into the room, dress billowing around her.

"I have just the thing," she declared.

"The healer already gave me a brew."

She waved my words away the same way she'd shooed Raphael from the room. "Bah. This is better than anything a healer could give you. Here." She lifted a smaller box from the basket she'd set on the ground between us.

I took the box, curious, and lifted the lid. Rows of small brown desserts, decorated with different colored sugar, lined the bottom.

"It's chocolate. Trust me," she encouraged. Not knowing what those words meant for someone like me.

But... I did. At least in this. I took one and nibbled on an edge. An explosion of flavor coated my mouth, bitter yet enticing. I took another bite while Amalthea reached over and plopped one whole in her mouth.

I continued on the chocolates. I didn't exactly like the taste, but I couldn't stop eating them. My fingers were quickly painted brown. Amalthea managed to avoid making such a mess, despite eating at least as many. When the box was finally empty, I turned it over in my hands, antsy. The pile of splintered furniture, my onetime source of protection, taunted me. The hinges were askew, and from experience, I knew a lock brutishly opened like that would need delicate repair.

I hated to ask favors, but I'd never sleep another night like this. "Thea, do you think it would be possible to get someone to fix the door today?"

Amalthea pursed her lips and twisted her neck to see the destruction from Raphael's entry. "I guess Raphael was... motivated. If he felt your pain through the bond, I doubt anything would have stopped him."

The bond again. "So can it be fixed?"

"Of course, Sam. But you should know, even without a door, everyone would respect your space. You're the king's Chosen."

Not everyone. Not Titus. I tried not to let my skepticism show, but must have failed miserably, because Thea quickly added, "Let me see to that right now, actually."

She got up, and I examined the rest of the contents of the basket. Under the box was a book, a stone, and a bell. I lifted the bell in my hand, the gold metal glinting against the firelight. A summoning bell.

"That's tied to me," Amalthea explained, returning a moment later. "More suitable than having Raphael sending servants to fetch me."

Summoning bells were tied to an individual and called them over a short distance. My mother had given one away once, in affection, and told me to think long and hard before doing so. Beyond that, I'd only ever seen them tied to servants before.

But Amalthea wasn't my servant. Maybe she really was my friend.

"And what are these for?"

"That," she said, pointing at the stone, "goes into the fire. It's not enchanted, but that kind of rock stores heat very well. You take it out a bit before you intend to sleep, and it warms the bed. Before I started taking the tea, it was my best friend during my cycle. The book is to entertain you when you're bored."

The stone I appreciated. The book... "I have enough entertainment for me with the grimoire."

Amalthea grimaced. "That's hardly fun. This will help pass the time."

I was about to protest I had no such need for entertainment, not when there was work to be done, when her words made me remember what I was supposed to be doing right now. "Gods, Amalthea. I need to get to the training room! Demos will—"

"*Demos* will understand," she interrupted. "He's a hardass, but he's not a complete barbarian, Sam. We can resume in a few days when the worst has passed."

"That's not necessary," I protested. "I'm not grievously ill. I'm confident others have fought in worse."

Amalthea lifted the stone from the basket and placed it at the edge of the fireplace. "Maybe so, but that doesn't mean you have to. You're training in self-defense, Sam, not going to war. Just because theoretical 'others' had it worse doesn't mean you shouldn't take care of yourself."

I wanted to explain that was exactly what it meant, but I lacked the words that wouldn't sound petulant. Amalthea, rightfully used to winning every argument, settled back in her chair with another book. I didn't take the grimoire out, but I didn't pick up the novel either, instead choosing to study the book on vampire powers. Maybe it wasn't the worst thing that the mental link had brought Raphael to me, but the intimacy bothered me. Hours passed. The door got fixed—by a vampire—and when he left, Amalthea helped barricade the door once more for me.

At some point, I drifted off to sleep. More accurately, I succumbed to the exhaustion like my body begged me to. When I awoke, it was a fight to lift my eyelids. The room was dark, save the dwindling orange embers from the fireplace. The book I'd been working through was splayed open on my chest. I cracked my neck, trying to orient myself to my setting.

And realized I wasn't alone.

"You always do this," I groused.

"Do what?" the Vampire King of the West asked.

"Watch me sleep."

I didn't have to see him to know he was smirking. "Someone needs to keep an eye on you."

But why is it you? "Where's Amalthea?"

"I sent her back to her rooms to rest. If it helps, she had to be persuaded." Raphael tossed another log on the fire, jostling the others around until the fire grew brighter.

A BARGAIN SO BLOODY

Then he pulled the heating stone Amalthea had placed inside with his bare hand and tucked it into the bed. I wondered if it would still be warm if I pulled it under the bedframe, where I actually slept. He lit the other lights in the room, allowing my human eyes to adjust.

My attention landed not on him—or the barricade that had been carefully reconstructed with more order than Amalthea had been capable of—but on a silver rolling cart piled high past the entryway.

"Raphael," I said slowly, "what is that?"

"Oh, that." He shrugged. "Amalthea mentioned you might like them and find the taste soothing."

That was a pile of chocolate balls piled at least as tall as a child, ornately arranged as if fit for display in the great hall. It probably weighed more than me.

Raphael said the last words I expected to hear from a king. "Let me serve you."

I didn't have the heart to admit I'd already eaten half my weight in chocolate, so I dutifully put one of the truffles in my mouth. In fact, I was developing quite a taste for the sweet. "I take it by the fact I can eat it, you didn't cook it yourself."

Raphael grinned, settling onto the sofa next to me, his legs kicked out and ankles crossed while he tucked his hands behind his head. "Here, I have servants for those needs."

I plopped another one in, savoring the taste. These were more decadent than the box Amalthea had given me, with a little fruit paste inside. Raphael watched me swallow, his gaze pinned to my face. My body warmed at his watchful gaze, and I cast about for something to say. "Maybe I should call Amalthea back to share."

Raphael seemed to note the tiny golden bell on the end table for the first time. He frowned. "She *gave* you a summoning bell? By blood, she must like you. She refused to have one made for me."

"Something tells me the chocolate might go a long way with her. Or shoes, from what I've seen." A strange cramp wove through my stomach at the idea of Raphael gifting her shoes or desserts, but I didn't want to cause discord between the two.

He snorted. "I pay her enough she can buy all the chocolate and dresses she likes. She simply prefers you. Can't say I blame her."

We sat like that for several moments. It wasn't entirely uncomfortable. Raphael and I had walked and rode for hours at a time without a word passing between us. But then, it had been about survival. I'd thought him a monster, but at least I stood a chance with him as my monster. Now, however, as the fire warmed my toes, and I sat curled up in the corner of the settee with him at the other end, the vampire sprawled without a care, it was obvious: this was something more than survival. After a time, the fire lowered again, and Raphael put another log on it.

"You've been reading, I see," he said, breaking the silence.

Right. I was still holding the book on vampire powers against my chest. I lifted my head to study his face. Was he annoyed I wasn't working on the translation he'd offered me a thousand gold pieces for? "I've been working on the grimoire," I promised. "It's slow, but I'm making progress." I probably should have given him a status update sooner, but he hadn't asked, and I hadn't translated anything meaningful enough to warrant a report.

"I'm more intrigued by your current reading material."

Panic flared inside me. Would he think I was spying on them? Trying to use my position to gain knowledge about vampires? The encounter with Titus had left me paranoid.

"It's a simple question, dove. Relax."

I swallowed. Fine. He wanted to know why I was reading about vampire powers. "So you really can sense what I'm feeling?"

"You wear your fears on your face, you know."

That wasn't a denial. It had taken me weeks to work up the courage; I wasn't letting him slip away with sly words so easily. "Is it true?"

A beat. Then—"Yes."

I chewed at my cheek, waiting for more of a response. He didn't elaborate.

"Amalthea told me," I prodded.

He tilted his head back and sighed. "Amalthea has a big mouth. Is she also the source of your reading material?"

I nodded, but I wouldn't let him change the subject. "So you form a mental link with everyone you bite?"

"Theoretically."

"Don't make me guess, Raphael," I said. "What does that mean?"

"It means I don't make a habit of biting living sources. Or if they start out alive when I'm drinking, I drain them so my own thoughts aren't muddied with others."

Gods. Just when I'd fooled myself into thinking he wasn't monstrous.

"Again, Samara, relax. I have no intention of killing you because of the bond. The others... it's irritating having your mind crowded by others. It's a power that's driven lesser vampires to madness."

"You shouldn't have had anything to drink from me if it was such a burden," I hissed. My anger was borne of fear. Raphael might not be lying right now, but he could change his mind.

He arched a single white brow at me. "You'll recall I didn't have much of a choice."

"So you wouldn't drink from me again, given the chance?"

"It hardly matters, dove. Once is all it takes to forge the link."

That wasn't an answer. Which with Raphael, was an answer. Yes, he'd drink from me if there was an invitation. I wasn't sure how to feel about that. Disgusted? That's what my brain said my reaction should be. But talking of the bite made me recall exactly how it had felt, something I'd worked hard to forget. If I asked him to bite me, would he?

Ask him? I was losing my mind. I didn't know how much he could tell from the mental link, but by the curious stare he was giving me, it was far too much.

"How can we break the bond?" I asked. "I haven't come across any answers in this." *Yet.*

He skimmed the title once more and then—*did he just roll his eyes*? "You won't find such an answer in that book. The bond is permanent."

Great. "And what if my emotions annoy you?" *Will you kill me then?*

Raphael appeared unconcerned with the possibility. "You don't need to worry over such a thing."

"What if there was a way to block you from my feelings?" I pressed. "This book mentions mental shielding, but it offers no details."

"There's no need," he insisted.

Because if I ever bothered him, he *would* kill me. Just like how he'd killed Thomas. Because he wanted to. "Do you know how to do it?"

He gave a beleaguered sigh. "I've just told you there's no need. Why do you belabor the point, dove?"

Because I know by the way you're avoiding the question, it means yes, you do. "If you can truly feel my emotions, then you must know I'm worried you're going to change your mind about being shackled to my human grievances for the rest of my natural life."

"I can feel you, Samara." He turned fully to me now, his gaze pinning me. "I feel it all, but as I told you, your emotions are blatant when I'm near you. You're worried, yes, and curious about this puzzle. I feel it in my chest the same way I can hear your own heart racing now, the way you swallow to clear your throat to levy another argument."

My heart was racing. Part of it was the worry that Raphael would kill me to end the bond, but that was distant to the pounding in my chest I felt as he looked at me. We were scant inches apart now. His shirt was slightly unbuttoned, his neck exposed in vampire fashion. His arm was braced along the back of the couch, fingers close enough to graze my shoulders by accident when he twitched. Not that I'd noticed the vampire twitching before. I was more aware of each brush of those fingers than any lingering cramps.

I leaned away, looked away. Forced myself to believe that my heart was racing only out of self-preservation, because this was feeling more like self-destruction.

"Train me. Or at least tell me how, and I can practice on my own."

He looked at me, examining not just my face but my whole person. As if weighing something.

Then, simply: "No."

Chapter 35

"Better," Demos said. "Again."

I nodded and lunged for the training dummy again. It had been three weeks since I'd had my cycle. I'd reluctantly rested, as instructed, and the moment Charlotte cleared me to resume exercise I'd thrown myself into it with renewed vigor. I was determined to train my body, especially since Raphael categorically refused to work with me on the mental training.

It's a safety precaution, he'd said. *It's better for me to know if you're in pain or afraid.*

I didn't agree. It was better for my fears to be my own, not exposed to a vampire who might tire of them at any moment. Which was why when I stabbed the training dummy for the twentieth time that morning, I was picturing a certain vampire king.

"Sam, you keep that up and the poor thing won't be able to have any training-bag-children," Amalthea called from the sidelines after I landed a rather low blow.

I took that as praise and readied for another swipe. I was so, so tired of being weak. I was getting stronger, physically at least. Amalthea had gifted me new training leathers just last week, after my body no longer fit comfortably into the old ones. My ribs were covered in a layer of fat and muscle, my fists no longer shaking as the punches lacked any weight. But even as I viciously attacked the training dummy, I knew the anger that fueled me was simply a cover for fear. An inanimate opponent was one thing. A bigger, stronger opponent was another.

The shame of how easily Titus had disarmed me lingered.

I hadn't gone back to the alcove to listen to the music since. Each day, on the way back from training, I wandered near, wishing I was braver. Wrapping myself in the music made me feel so alive, so free. But now when I thought of being there, all I could picture was Titus and his threats. I studied in my room, my dagger never more than an arm's distance away.

"Let's take a break," Iademos announced.

"I can keep going."

I wanted to keep going. Wanted to stop being so godsdamned weak.

"You say that every day," he chided. It was true. "Your body needs rest as much as it needs exercise."

Fine. I returned my training dagger to the rack, and we joined Amalthea for lunch. Today, it was a tray of sandwiches filled with things like cured meat, scrambled kobold eggs, vegetables, and a succulent spread. Demos, of course, didn't partake. More pity him.

While we ate, Amalthea regaled us both with the latest court gossip. Unlike the solitary life I'd carved for myself, Amalthea spent her evenings around various members of vampire society, attending dinners, soirées, and, last night, gambling parties.

"I can't believe they let you play," Demos grumbled.

"Are you suggesting I cheat?" Amalthea retorted primly.

"That's exactly what I'm suggesting," he replied.

She slammed her plate down in indignation. "I'll have you know, even if I didn't cheat, I would win."

"So... you do cheat?" I asked.

She shifted her ireful gaze towards me. "Not you too."

"That's not a denial," Demos pointed out.

"Is it cheating when they listen to my heartbeat to try to figure out if I'm nervous? Or stay utterly still when a mortal would at least fidget? Of course not. So using my gifts isn't cheating."

Demos rolled his eyes. "Who did you fleece this time?"

"Lazarus. He had it coming."

Lazarus. I remembered the name. The vampire from the ball, the one who mentioned the abomination. Thinking of the ball made me think of Titus, and thinking of Titus made me remember his taunt—that I didn't know enough about the Vampire Kingdom. That I let them treat me like a pet, never to be taken out. Goading words, but there was a grain of truth. I'd barely seen a fraction of the castle—what did I really know about Damerel? What did I *want* to know?

I wasn't going to be here for long. I was getting close to finishing the first part of the grimoire.

And yet I could still hear Titus's voice: *You should learn more about your new owners, Samara Koisemi. See more of the mountain.*

"I... I'd like to see more of the city," I said, interrupting the current bickering between Demos and Amalthea.

Both turned to me, and I shrank, my shoulders curling in on reflex.

"What changed?" Amalthea asked. "You've declined every other invitation I'd given you."

That was true. Because Amalthea's invitations involved spending an evening in fine dresses that didn't quite fit around vampire nobles, and I'd prefer an evening solving the mysteries of the Black Grimoire any day over that. "I didn't say I wanted to talk to anyone. Just... see what it's like."

And just like that, Amalthea was won over. "You couldn't have a better tour guide. Let's get out of here."

Demos grabbed the witch's wrist as she sprang up. Unlike me, she didn't stiffen at the contact, just glared back.

"Not so fast. Do you really think Raphael wants her wandering around? She's the king's Chosen."

"She's the king's Chosen, so if she wants to parade naked down Main Street, she damn well can," Amalthea retorted. "You've been tutoring her for weeks. Do you have so little faith in your skills to think even if she was attacked, *even if* we weren't glued to her side, she couldn't fend off an attacker?"

She was quickly regretting her request. "Guys—"

"Fine," Demos snapped, looking at me. "You can go. If you beat Amalthea in a sparring match. Thea, no going easy on Sam."

"Fine. Sam, let's do this." She jerked out of his grip and marched over to the weapons rack and plucked up a random short sword.

"I said no going easy. Take the staff."

Amalthea's sound of exasperation carried as she dropped the training sword and picked up a wooden staff. I hadn't fought against one of those yet. She turned back, and for the first time I realized she was in a loose blouse and trousers instead of her usual ornately embroidered dresses. Fashionable for training clothes, but still... different. Had she known this was coming? I didn't have time to process the implication, because Amalthea had grabbed my usual practice weapon and tossed it to me.

Actually, it wasn't going to me, but was aimed squarely at Demos's head. He snatched it from the air with vampire reflexes and extended it to me, hilt first.

"Oops. Guess my aim is a little off."

"Enough playing," Demos groused.

Her staff was a little taller than she was, her feet already in a fighting stance while she maneuvered the stave in quick circles. I stood reluctantly, no longer so confident in the skills I'd learned. Drills were one thing, but I hadn't attempted any kind of sparring yet. "Demos, I don't think I can win."

"You may not," he agreed.

Well, wasn't that comforting?

"But if you already have doubts, you've lost before you've begun," he continued. "Amalthea is good with a staff, but she's rusty. She rarely practices, because with her foresight, she rightfully reasons she can avoid almost any deadly confrontation. But that will give you an edge. You're smaller, faster. A staff gives her reach, so you'll have to get in close. Just remember, the dagger isn't your only weapon. Even if she does win, it'll be good practice."

He gave me a quick pat on the shoulder and shoved me forward. I stumbled, trying to find my balance. It was the first time he'd touched me outside of the slight corrections of my form.

"Ready?" she asked.

No. "Yes."

"First to a killing blow wins. Begin," Demos said.

Amalthea lunged for me. I barely managed to clumsily shift out of the way in time to right myself as her staff jabbed at me again. Amalthea might cheat at cards, but it became immediately apparent she wasn't about to go easy on me. She was relentless, and all I could do was move back, trying to avoid getting knocked out by her staff.

"Fight back," she said as she thrust in my direction.

I kept dancing around, looking for an opening. This wasn't a simple puzzle where I had as much time as I needed for a solution—I had to try to think, fast, while Amalthea advanced.

I wouldn't win. Not while I kept retreating.

The next time her staff came down, I lifted my wooden practice sword. The weapons collided, but I managed to shove her stave up.

"Good," Demos called.

Good. Or very bad. Because Amalthea redoubled her efforts, her staff moving quickly. I managed to block several blows, getting close enough her staff couldn't build the momentum it was meant to. But I wasn't perfect. Her wooden pole knocked into my forearms once when I misjudged the angle, and pain reverberated up to my shoulder.

Feel it later. Fight now.

Vicious instinct drove me, unlike any that had awakened in me before. Sweat dripped down my neck, my chest pounding against the tight fighting leathers. Amalthea was also growing tired, her round face covered in a thin sheen. Had her movements slowed? She'd been chasing me for as long as I'd been running.

A heavy blow to my leg alerted me to the fact that, no, Amalthea was not utterly exhausted.

Shit. I lifted my dagger again, but it wasn't made to fight against a staff. I went back on the defensive, dodging blocks, jumping backwards while I tried to formulate a plan. Amalthea followed me, as expected, but her blows fell into a pattern. Head, chest, leg, chest, head, chest, leg. She'd switch sides or angles, but as her body tired, so did her mind.

Now. When the next chest blow came, I was ready. Instead of dodging, I deflected. Not fighting her staff but shifting it enough to make her need to adjust her balance. Surprise at the broken pattern made her stumble to regain balance, just barely. I swung my right leg out, sweeping under her left.

She fell. I dropped my dagger and grabbed the staff, my hands opposite hers, and shoved back until she was pinned under me. I pressed down against her clavicle.

Hard.

Harder.

"Yield," Amalthea sputtered. "I yield."

I blinked. Sparring. *We're just sparring.* I scrambled off Amalthea, offering her an arm to stand. She took it and grinned at me, her eye twinkling with pride. "Well played, Sam."

"For someone blessed with foresight, you should've seen that move coming," Demos said, coming over to us. "Maybe we should have Sam give you lessons."

"Just for that, first round at Tilda's is on you," she groused. "If you're satisfied, then, I'm going to scrub this dirt off. We'll go out this evening."

True to her word, Amalthea disappeared off to her rooms to wash the dirt of the training floor off her back. Demos stayed with me for a little after to walk me through some of my mistakes.

"You did well, all considered," he said as he finished.

I swallowed. I'd barely won against a human. If a vampire came at me, I'd be dead. I said as much.

"Sam, no one is going to attack you," he assured me. "I know the Witch Kingdom has prejudices about vampires, but we're rational creatures. A bit emotional, a touch capricious, and yes, we drink blood. But beyond that, have any of us behaved in a way that truly frightened you?"

Yes. Years ago. But I didn't want to answer that. "If you think I'm safe walking around Damerel, then why make me spar with Amalthea?"

He grinned, the first real boyish look I'd ever seen on the vampire general. "Because it's time someone other than me knocked that witch on her ass."

Considering she was getting her way, I wasn't entirely sure that's what had happened, but I nodded along anyway.

If that was what worked for the two of them, so be it.

Damned if it made any sense to me.

Wherever Tilda's was, we weren't going there first. Amalthea pulled me, arm in arm, while Demos trailed behind us glaring at passersby. The mountain had three levels, which Raphael had explained. The top part, the castle, was actually home to very few members of vampire society. The second was where almost all commerce took place. Vampire nobility also lived in the center ring of the second level. The third and final level housed the commoners, mainly vampires since most humans worked in noble houses. By most, Amalthea estimated, that was around ninety-five percent of the population.

"How do vampires even have nobility?" I asked. "If vampires can't procreate, can't create a bloodline, you can't inherit titles."

Amalthea shook her head. "They do have bloodlines. Vampires are tied together through their lineage. If a noble wants to add someone to their house, they petition Raphael to turn the human and take them in. Not all vampires belong to a noble house, but there are also clans among the commoners, distant relatives without power."

What a strange system. "So that's how they get around not having children," I murmured.

Amalthea didn't say anything to that, which was odd, because she hadn't stopped talking since she appeared at my door this afternoon with an ornate change of clothes, and shoes that pinched my feet enough that I suspected all was not strictly forgiven from the sparring ring.

"What aren't you telling me? I thought vampires are infertile."

"It's true, vampires can't conceive naturally," Demos said, joining the conversation. "But the desire for children is strong enough some have taken to a… workaround. If a child is turned, they'll grow normally until reaching maturity. They live in a half-state, taking both food and blood as sustenance. They bear the weaknesses of both vampires and humans, so they tend to be guarded jealously by their parents."

"Their vampire parents," I clarified. "They're turning babies?"

Horror roiled inside me.

"No one would turn an infant," Amalthea assured me. "But that's more due to the fact it's forbidden to turn a witch, and they must wait long enough to be certain they're a void."

By seven, then. Most witch children showed signs of their powers by their fourth birthday, but some took longer, needing a trigger to reveal their powers. Seven was considered the cutoff, when even the most hopeful parents resigned themselves to their child's fate as an unremarkable void. Ironic—a vampire would rejoice to have a void, while a mortal parent would mourn.

My seventh birthday hadn't been a happy one.

"You'll find it's not so different from any other city," Amalthea continued, chasing away the uneasy subject with an airy wave of her hand. "This is Dressmaker's Way, my favorite street to peruse."

The road was lined with dozens of shops matching the namesake, glass windows displaying styles I'd seen Amalthea wearing weeks ago. Although we were inside the mountain, it was surprisingly bright. Demos had explained the city had devised a system of sustainable torchlight that allowed streetlights encased in glass to line the roads. Inside them, oil was replenished from a central source. Part of me wanted to ask to see that mechanism, or at least look at one up close, but I was too embarrassed to ask for such an inconvenience. There was an ingenuity to many parts of the city. When you didn't have magic, you had to be clever in other ways.

The dresses, made without so much as an enchanted bobbin, must take ages. The one to my left had an ornate bird perched on the shoulder and sleeve, tail feathers winding down around the hips.

"You could try it on," Amalthea said. "Or perhaps have something custom made. They'd certainly welcome you as a walk-in."

Likely because Amalthea struck me as a frequent and generous patron of the shops.

"Spare me," Demos grumbled, walking past us. Amalthea kicked out her leg, trying to catch the general unaware, but he didn't trip or so much as stumble. "I doubt this is what Samara wanted to see."

"What *do* you want to see?" Amalthea asked.

Want wasn't the right word. "The humans. The ones you said donate their blood."

The thought turned my stomach, but I wanted to believe it wasn't as bad as I imagined. That Titus was wrong. That I could see with my own eyes what went on and disprove what I'd feared all my life.

My two companions exchanged a look. I could read the stiff expression on Iademos's face. It said: *Absolutely not*. Amalthea, who normally would've been contrary, for once seemed aligned.

"I deserve to see how the other voids are treated," I pressed. I deserved to see the role everyone thought I fulfilled for Raphael.

"It's not that we aren't willing to take you," Amalthea gentled, "but it's obvious you're particularly, let's say, sensitive to these things. Even the thought of blood drinking turns your pale skin ghost-white. Damerel has many wonderful things to offer. Let's show you those for now."

Demos nodded in agreement, and we set off to continue the tour of the commerce section.

But I didn't agree.

CHAPTER 36

TILDA'S WAS A BOISTEROUS tavern located in the narrow wedge at the side of the mountain.

Amalthea and Demos were greeted warmly, by name, when we arrived. The serving girl, a vampire with her hair tied back into two parts, gave me a curious look. In fact, the entire bar was filled with vampires. There were two levels: the main floor, and a second that ringed around the top. No one had to tell me it was a popular location. I hadn't been this surrounded since the ball, maybe not even then. My heart pounded, breaths growing shallow. Amalthea held my hand, giving a reassuring pulse as she maneuvered us inside.

"You wanted to see the kingdom? This is *the* place to be."

A band played on the raised platform across from the bar top. A trio of players, two vampires, one human, took up the stage. One had a small fiddle, the other an instrument unlike any I'd ever seen, with billowing folds going in and out and white keys on the side. The human moved around the stage, crooning.

Demos secured us a table right by the stage that was surprisingly vacant, then left to get us the round of drinks Amalthea reminded him he owed us. I sat with my back to the wall, trying to focus on the music instead of my increasing nerves.

Amalthea gave me a concerned look. Guilt pricked at me. I was the one who had insisted on going out. It wasn't fair for me to ruin the fun for others, but being surrounded by vampires—increasingly inebriated vampires—wasn't something I could just put out of my mind.

"The Vampire Kingdom is rather musical," I said over the din.

"It is?" she said, leaning in.

I gestured to the stage. "I mean, everywhere you go there's someone playing. Each day, a new performer takes the stage in the castle." Not that I'd let myself enjoy it these past few weeks.

"Oh." A strange look came into her eyes. "That's a new development. Raphael's become quite the patron of the arts as of late."

I frowned. She'd laced meaning into the last of her words, but I couldn't guess what she was referring to. "Why is that?"

She tilted her head towards me. "Perhaps because you mentioned you liked it at the ball. That was when he sent a missive inviting musicians from all over to perform."

For me? Was Amalthea right, and Raphael had sourced dozens of musicians just for me to listen to, because I'd confided in him my love of music? But he'd made no mention. Hadn't asked me if I'd noticed.

Though with the blood bond, he must have sensed it—how my mind struggled to accept the joy I felt when I listened to a violinist dip their bow or a guitarist twist their fingers over the strings.

Something warm and light swirled in my stomach, much like when a song resonated in a way that set it apart from others.

I didn't have the time to reply before Demos returned, setting two glasses of wine on the table between us while he kept a mug of something more to his taste in his left hand.

"Where's my ale?" she groused.

"I thought you'd like something more refined," he said innocently.

"I'll show you refined." She lifted her hand and made a vulgar gesture that had me recoiling. But she lifted the glass anyway and took a long drag.

I didn't drink from mine. The two fell into an easy banter and didn't take offense at my silence. My attention roamed from their latest argument to the music, and over to our surroundings. I hadn't spent much time in mortal bars, naturally. But aside from the fact there was no real food served, and everyone had the same white hair, it wasn't altogether so different from what I imagined. Packs of men came in, slapping each other on the back as they eyed groups of women. One table held a competitive game of dice, judging from the crowd built around it that seemed to cheer and bemoan the rolls with equal enthusiasm. Unlike the castle, where nearly all the servants were human, here the vampires worked as well. One serving girl polished glasses while chatting, her posture easy as a young-looking vampire leaned against the door.

And then he walked in.

Raphael wasn't wearing the regalia I'd become accustomed to seeing him in within the castle walls, but there was no mistaking him as anything but an extremely powerful predator. He strolled into Tilda's without an ounce of hesitation. The room didn't come to a halt, not exactly, but it did quiet, the closest to him bowing as he walked past them.

Right over to us.

"You found us quickly," Amalthea grumbled, finishing off her first glass of wine.

Raphael slid into the seat next to me, his body sprawling. His arm came around the back of my chair, not quite touching me, but close enough if I leaned back it would be. "Demos sent word before you left."

The witch's expression would have turned a lesser vampire to ash. Her sweet face looked so fearsome I couldn't help but giggle.

"Enjoying yourself?" he asked softly, while Amalthea and Demos got into another argument over nothing.

Because of the bond, I was sure he could feel the maelstrom of emotions swirling inside me. But something in me had relaxed, just slightly, the moment he'd walked in. As if instinctively, I accepted I was completely safe. "Yes."

Suddenly, a cry went up in the room. "A round of drinks on the house, to honor King Raphael keeping the kingdom safe from the scourge yet again!"

The scourge. I twisted away from Raphael to study the speaker. The bartender, a stout woman with large biceps, hefted four mugs in each hand, liquid sloshing inside them. A cheer went up and the free alcohol was quickly distributed. Around us, mugs clinked together. A serving girl brought our table a fresh round, including two towering mugs of non-blood ale for Amalthea and me.

"Water," he told the serving girl, who nodded with vampiric speed.

Demos regaled Raphael with the story of how we'd wound up here, and the look Raphael gave me when he heard how I swept Amalthea's leg... some long-forgotten embers of pride glowed in my chest. Before long, it was the general and witch volleying back and forth while Raphael and I listened. The waitress brought back a glass of icy water for me, and I took a large gulp, relishing the cool liquid. The bar wasn't uncomfortably stuffy, but I'd grown much warmer since Raphael had filled the seat next to me.

"I have a question for you," Raphael said, while the two were immersed in a debate over some recent political debacle.

"A question for a question."

"Deal. Why do you not partake in drink?"

The untouched ale and wine were still in front of me. I ran my fingers over the rim of one, trying to gather my thoughts. "Shipments would come to Greymere each month. When they included liquors, fights would break out over them. Nelson—the one who found us when we escaped—he was nasty. Cruel. Petty. Since he was also in charge, he always got at least one bottle. He'd drink the whole thing down. It was understandable. No one wanted to be in Greymere, exactly, but not all the servants were sentenced like I was. Sometimes it was a good way to dispose of an unwanted noble son, like in Nelson's case." He'd been arrogant. Thought himself better than the rest of us and never let us forget it. "He'd drink a whole bottle in a night, and it would change him. Instead of being so ornery and nasty, he was... *nice*." I dripped the syllable in every ounce of derision I could. I remembered the first time I'd been around, as a child. I'd learned to hide better when he got like that. "I associate it with him. That drunken, out-of-control bumbling. I never want to be *anything* like him."

Raphael was silent for a moment. I kept my gaze trained on the glass in front of me, not meeting his gaze.

"You could *never* be anything like him."

"You didn't know him," I countered.

"I know his type. And all the liquor in the world couldn't malform you like that." A pause. "I'm not saying you have to drink. But if you wanted to indulge, I would watch over you."

I twisted my lips. "It doesn't exactly seem pleasant."

Raphael shrugged. "At its most extreme, it's not. But many enjoy it in moderation. Even if you wind up knowing you don't like it, it's a shame to let one bastard—who was a bastard sober, from the sound of it—take away part of life."

That was Raphael, always able to cut to the heart of the matter so quickly. Was I being unfair to myself by refusing to submit to any pleasure out of fear? I wrapped my fingers around the stem of the glass, tipping it towards me. The pale-yellow liquid caught the lights of the tavern, a vaguely citric smell wafting over.

Finally, I looked at the vampire king. "You'll watch over me if I drink?"

"I'll always watch over you."

I took a sip.

The world didn't end. My mouth tingled slightly at the sensation, adjusting. "I don't feel any different."

"A child wouldn't even feel that little," he teased.

So I took another sip. More confident this time. Then a third as I realized I did like the taste. I didn't rush to drain the glass, but soon enough it was finished. I joined in to break up the latest fight between Amalthea and Demos—apparently, the two even had opposite opinions on appropriate bathing temperatures.

"Does it matter as long as you can take a bath?" I interjected. "I went twelve years without being able to."

"You certainly smelled like it," Raphael added, nostrils flaring in memory.

"Just as well, so you wouldn't want to bite me. Vampires are *so* sensitive."

Demos snorted. "I'm not the one who called bathing in anything less than scalding water 'unspeakably cruel.'"

"I'm simply saying, if you have the option of a better experience, there's no reason to deny yourself," Amalthea countered, then focused on me. "You never talk about your life before. How you wound up where you did."

There was an implicit question there that left my three companions looking at me expectantly. Normally, I avoided any mention of how Raphael had found me—or the time before. I assumed Raphael had given them some description, but since I hadn't told him much either... "I was sentenced when I was eight."

"Sentenced... to prison?"

I shook my head. There was a distinction—proper prisoners got to sit around, at least. Got regular meals. "To serve the prison. Greymere drives witches mad, so only voids can work there, but a life cut off from magic is inconvenient even for voids. Most serve short terms. It's a miserable, filthy place." Maybe the drink was affecting me. Or perhaps I just wanted to be able to tell someone. "I was sentenced to serve fifteen years, and then I could be released. Or so I thought. The night Raphael and I escaped, I found out that was a lie. They had no intention of letting me go."

"But you were a child." Amalthea's voice was soft with horror. "What could possibly have been so terrible you were sent there?"

I took another pull of ale, savoring the burn down my throat. With every sip, it was easier to understand why others liked it. "Such is the king's justice."

"Not all kings," Raphael growled.

I hadn't looked at him while speaking. His expression was fierce, nearly terrifying. But I knew, in my bones, it wasn't directed at me but at the injustices I'd faced. There was a comfort in that, in someone being angry at the old wounds I'd thought long since scarred over.

The night continued. I spoke no more of my past, but Demos and Raphael took turns telling stories from theirs. The two had known each other for over half a millennium,

A BARGAIN SO BLOODY

which left plenty of fodder for entertaining tales. I listened and drank more, eager to chase away the memories that had stirred. The wine made it easy.

"I think you had a bit much," Raphael said as I stumbled out the door ahead of him, catching myself on the wooden frame.

"I fuh—" *Hiccup*. "Feel great."

And then I nearly landed face-first onto the stone walkway. Powerful arms scooped me up, and before I knew it, I was pressed against Raphael's chest, one arm cradling my back, the other under my legs. I nestled into his hold, liking the way his scent wrapped around me. There was a low rumble in his chest, and something like, "Go on ahead without us."

Amalthea's and Demos's voices were distant as they bid us goodbye. I twisted to look over at them and then back at Raphael. He was wearing an expression that was utterly foreign to me, so soft and concerned. His white brows furrowed as he looked down at me, the red eyes I'd once found terrifying were warm with affection. Gods, that wine was good. He had the slightest stubble covering the sharp planes of his face. I lifted a palm to his cheek, marveling at the prickly sensation. He halted while I ran my fingers over his skin. Vampire stillness. I liked that I was getting to touch him. I'd tried to stop noticing how beautiful he was—first, because he was a vampire. Then, because of everything else. But now, those parts of my brain were as quiet as the empty streets.

"I forget human tolerance is vastly lower than a vampire's," he said, the low tone of his voice washing over me.

I curled in closer, dropping my hand to his neck. "Drank less than Thea."

The rumble of his chest was soothing. "Sometimes I wonder if Thea might be part fish."

My brain was too slow to understand what he was saying exactly, but it was with that same dry humor I'd come to recognize so I laughed all the same. And then suddenly I was all too tired and too comfortable to stay awake. I dozed for what could have been hours or minutes, waking up only as we reached my (recently replaced) door. The little rest I'd had left me wide awake and even more aware of the male who carried me.

"You smell so nice," I murmured, savoring the closeness. It felt so right. "I wish I could taste you."

His fingers tensed around my legs. "And here I so often think that about you."

"You did," I remind him. "You said I was perfect."

"This is true."

Which part—that you said it, or that it's true? "I shouldn't have let you."

"Because of the bond?"

I giggled. "No. Because of how it felt."

It was a predator whose eyes pinned me in place, but for once I wasn't scared. "And how was that, Samara?"

"Alive. Connected." I shivered at the memory. "I thought it would be painful. Thought I'd die before I let

A BARGAIN SO BLOODY

a vampire bite me. But sometimes, when I lay in bed, I wonder if I'd die if I don't get bitten again. If that's the only way to feel so gloriously alive. My body ached in ways I'd never known possible, my skin felt tight. For the first time, I felt like I understood what it was to be a woman. I wanted you, Raphael. More than anything. I'd have given you anything."

Raphael set me on the bed, gently, and took several steps back. "The bite sometimes makes humans... *react*, Samara. That's all."

I shook my head. "I'd never felt anything like that before."

"Surely you've felt *something* like that. From a kiss, a caress."

I laughed, a bit loud in the quiet of the room. "Raphael, when would I have ever kissed *anyone*? Do you think Nelson was the kind to whisper sweet nothings? That any in Greymere were?"

There was nothing human about the growl that left his mouth. He prowled closer. "Did they ever hurt you, Samara? Mark my words, I'll go back and slaughter them all if you say so."

"Not like that. Nelson was the worst, but even he never..." I trailed off, not wanting to let him haunt my evening any more. I'd never been assaulted, but it hadn't been chivalry that kept me safe. "In all ways, I'm ignorant, Raphael." I paused. "Ignorant... but curious."

Feeling braver than I ever had before, I reached my hand out again, crossing the space between us. I ran the back of my hand down his chest. Beneath the fabric, I felt his muscles. Solid. Strong. Would his bare flesh feel the same? Raphael caught my wrist, pinning it against him.

"You can feel my emotions right now, can't you?" I asked.

His face was strained. "I think you should sleep, Samara. You're going to be exhausted tomorrow."

"Then you can," I said, ignoring his statement. "If you couldn't, you'd deny it. If you can feel it, you know," I said with relief. "I don't need to tell you." I didn't need to admit how desperately I wanted Raphael in that moment. How I'd looked at him over and over, wanting, not even letting myself accept how badly I did.

Now here he was, tantalizingly close. The top of his shirt was unbuttoned, showing an expanse of hard muscle. I tilted my head back at Raphael, who stood right in front of the bed.

The desire brewing inside me was as heady a mixture as the ale. "Won't you give this to me?"

A low sound shuddered through him. "No, dove. Not like this."

He stepped back and I stood, stumbling into him. He caught me quickly, arms wrapped around me, steadying. I clung to the lapels of his shirt. "Don't you want me?" I whimpered. Was I so undesirable, that even tossing myself at this male, he was repulsed?

"Samara..." His thumb stroked the side of my face. "If you tell me you want something with a clear head, anything in my power, it's yours. But not tonight. Not when you would wake up hating me more than you already do." He gently guided me back to the bed. My body protested, but I lacked the words to tell him he was wrong. Maybe because I knew he wasn't. I wouldn't find this courage again. It wasn't even real courage, just borrowed from the intoxicating mix of attention and alcohol. A mix that let me look past the fact the one man I'd ever wondered about like this was the king of vampires. That let me ignore the fact I'd be leaving.

Suddenly, I was annoyed at Raphael. It was bad enough I'd trusted him to drink and now made a fool of myself. But what was my reward for being foolish? Shame, and a heated body that didn't understand the denial.

"Sleep, little dove. Or you'll regret it all in the morning."

I harrumphed, crossing my arms over my chest. Then I rolled farther and farther until I reached the edge. Then I grabbed my pillow and rolled off the bed entirely.

"Samara," Raphael said.

"I'm not sleeping up there," I said petulantly.

Raphael leaned over the bed, looking down at me. The sight made me giggle. "Because I'm here?" he asked.

"No."

Even drunk, I expected mockery. What kind of person couldn't sleep in a bed? "I can't sleep in this bed."

He frowned. "I'll get you another mattress."

I shook my head. "I can't sleep in *any* bed."

"You slept in one at the cabin," he pointed out.

True. It had been another world. With my back wrecked, there'd been no other option. And the cabin was different enough that it hadn't stirred memories with the same viciousness. But here, the halls, the finery... despite being a world apart, it was all too similar. "I was lying in bed when they came. That night." The night they'd come for Mother. Raphael's body went still in my periphery, but I was lost to the memory.

"Traitors," the guards had snarled when they barged through the chamber doors. The same guards I'd known all my life, who had smiled when I passed by. "Ungrateful whore."

"I did try," I added quickly, the words stumbling over each other as they left my mouth. "But I couldn't sleep. Even in Greymere, I was in the habit of hiding myself somewhere different each night. I can't sleep if I feel exposed." In a bed, waiting for anyone to come in and grab me. Tears pricked my eyes, hating my weakness. Obviously, Raphael had known I was weak compared to him, but he had no idea just how pathetic I was. And here I was, telling him.

I braced for the revulsion, the derision.

He lifted up, disappearing from view. Leaving? No. Another pillow dropped to the floor, and he pushed it under the bed.

"Then we won't sleep on the bed," he announced.

"W-we?" I stammered.

He dropped down, sliding under the bed. The bed was elevated, enough that I could comfortably slip under each night and be hidden by the long, draping bedspread. Raphael, in contrast, filled the space. "Of course. I said I would watch over you, Samara. What would keep you safer than sleeping at my side?"

It was an overreach of logic, the kind of declaration that only made sense because Raphael said it with such arrogance, and the glasses of wine and ale had a way of muddling my mind.

And because I wanted it to be true.

Chapter 37

I WAS WARMER THAN usual. Eyes squeezed shut, I relished in it. Even though I took a blanket under the bed with me, it was still a bit cold and hard to rest, and I was eager to get out from under the bed each morning. But today, the warmth made it just a bit more comfortable, and I curled deeper under the blanket even as awareness tingled at the edges of my mind. There was the slightest thrumming behind my forehead I wanted to chase away with more sleep.

Except I wasn't curling into the blanket.

The pulsing pain in my head was the least of the unpleasantness as my eyes snapped open, and I realized I wasn't alone.

I was with Raphael.

Under my bed, rubbing my backside into him for comfort.

After making an advance on him last night.

And being summarily rebuffed.

Fire gods, if there's any mercy, just turn me to ash now.

"I'd say good morning, but you know I don't lie," Raphael said, quiet laughter accenting the words.

I tried to reply, but all that came out was a groan. I tugged the pillow over my head.

"I feel like something an ogre threw up," I whimpered. Why in the skies did people drink if in addition to making fools of themselves, they had to remember it and feel physical pain at the reminder?

"That's to be expected when you try to keep up with Amalthea your first night out."

"I'm never drinking again," I vowed. Nothing good came of it.

"At least you tried and found out for yourself, rather than letting fear stop you."

Right. I got to try drinking. But not the other things I'd attempted. No doubt he felt my shame this morning, beneath the general malaise. At least he was kind enough to pretend otherwise.

Still, Raphael was right. In some small way, I'd conquered my fears. And I'd only done it because I'd known he was there, watching over me.

"Thank you." My reply was quiet, not just because the pillow muffled me. "And... thank you for staying." Even if part of me wished he was gone and spared me the indignity of waking up remembering exactly how I'd propositioned the vampire king while waking up next to him.

"Of course, Samara."

The only thing worse than getting up and facing the day would be lingering in bed, the humiliation of last night hanging over me. I got out from under the bed, pulling the blanket and pillow and fixing them askew on the bed so it would look like I'd been in it. After all these weeks, it was a rote habit.

"Why do you do that?" Raphael asked.

I rolled my eyes, then regretted it when it made my head throb. "So they won't know." Because it was one thing to be so afraid I slept under a bed and another to advertise it to a castle full of predators, including the maids who entered my room each day to make the bed. Shame swirled in my gut over what I'd confessed last night to Raphael. What kind of weak-willed child couldn't even sleep in a bed?

It was harder to confess without the alcohol lubricating my words.

Maybe that's why people drink. Despite the shame and the headache, it let them be honest.

I fled to the bathroom. The water was tepid and did little to ease the soreness that permeated my entire body. Amalthea was right, hot water really was superior. Not that this would be a day to taunt Demos. My feet wobbled when I got out and dressed. I pulled my hair back into a thick plait. It had turned wild from the night, and I didn't have the energy to try to tame the knots. And because every time I pulled at the tangles, my headache compounded.

Hoping Raphael had finally left, I exited the washroom.

And there he was, appearing utterly relaxed as he sat on the settee. His legs were crossed as he spread out on the plush velvet, completely at home. Then again, the entire castle was his home. I was just staying here, for now. He thumbed through my notes.

"If you're feeling even a fraction of what I am, you should tell me how to block the bond." I was grateful his vampire hearing meant I didn't have to speak too loudly, because even my own voice was painful.

"I have just the antidote, but you won't accept it." He lifted his wrist towards me. Right. Vampire blood. "I sent for Charlotte, and she offered that instead." He pointed to a glass of putrid-looking liquid freshly set next to the bed.

My chest fluttered at the thoughtfulness of the gesture, even as when I lifted it to my lips, I had to fight to swallow it without spewing the liquid back in the cup. While I drank as quickly as my stomach would allow, Raphael leafed through my notes. I kept them tucked away, but not completely hidden.

"I've been making progress," I assured him. The reminder of my purpose here compelled me to justify my progress. "It's slow, but it will go faster once I get more familiar with the language."

Raphael made a sound of acknowledgment, setting the papers aside. He seemed strangely disinterested in what I had to say. But wasn't the whole point of me being here translating the book? I hid my frown. The puzzle pieces weren't fitting together. Raphael wouldn't have gone through all that trouble for something that was unimportant, surely. Last night, I'd trusted Raphael more than I had anyone in a very long time. And yet... things weren't adding up. Something was being kept from me, I was certain.

"You're right," he said, interrupting my ruminations.

"Huh?"

"I will teach you how to block the bond. Meet me in my rooms at midnight tomorrow."

Raphael swept out of the room, and I stared at his back for a long moment. Then my gaze swept to the clock on the mantel and realized I was tremendously late for practice.

I hurried down the halls, which were filled with servants, vampire and human alike. On reflex, I scanned for Titus, but just as with prior weeks, the spymaster was nowhere to be seen. I couldn't fight the feeling I was being watched, but maybe that had more to do with the fact the vampire king was seen leaving my bedroom. I had no doubts vampires were as relentless gossips as humans. My mother would've been aghast. Moreso if she knew I'd offered myself to the male last night—and had been rebuffed. Her imaginary rebuke faded as I rushed as much as possible without resorting to sprinting.

When I opened the room to the training arena, Amalthea and Demos were already there. More than that, they were sparring. Unlike the practice sticks Demos and I used, they had real weapons, and they were fast. Demos wasn't using his vampire speed, but he was still winning.

I watched for a moment. Amalthea often wore a serene, teasing expression, her round face cherubic. But in the heat of battle, she was fierce. I'd not noticed when we'd sparred, too focused on dodging her stave.

Now, she wore fighting leathers and a leaf-shaped blade about the length of her arm. Demos wore his standard black. His blade was similarly dark. Odd. It didn't reflect light, as if it was painted. I'd never seen him with a weapon drawn. In fact, in many ways, despite knowing his status, I'd come to conceptualize him as a teacher, a friend.

Iademos was a warrior. A vampire warrior.

And then he won. The tip of his blade was at her throat, a hairsbreadth from cutting her. Amalthea dropped her arm in submission, but her expression was annoyed. They didn't seem aware I was here.

"You're slow today," he said. "This sloppiness could get you killed."

She moved the blade away with the back of her forearm. "We don't all metabolize alcohol so quickly."

"Amalthea, you're being pathetic."

Anger rolled in my belly, sudden and riotous. "Don't say that to her," I snapped.

Both heads turned to me in sync, eyes wide. I stepped into the training arena, my hands curling into fists. The sight of the vampire with his blade at my friend's throat, browbeating her... Something foreign and monstrous in me roared.

"Apologize to her," I snarled.

"Amalthea, I apologize," Demos said immediately, not looking away from me.

Some of the anger inside me uncoiled, appeased.

Amalthea looked between us. "Sam, it's okay. Really. You know how Demos is. And I give as good as I get." She elbowed the vampire, but he was still looking at me.

I flushed. All at once, it was obvious I'd overreacted. "I'm sorry. I... I don't feel right." I tried to catalog my feelings and figure out where I'd gone wrong. Was it the fact Titus had reminded me how weak I was? The memories from last night? Or had something in me always been fragile, at the brink of breaking?

The uncertainty made my breaths come shallow.

Amalthea came over and ran her hand lightly over my arm. "It's okay, Sam. No apology needed. Demos and I can get a little caustic, but we can try to tone it down."

I shook my head. "No, no. Something came over me, but I'm fine now." It was only a half-lie. The sudden black rage had passed, but I felt miles from *fine*. "You're in training leathers," I remarked, desperate to change the subject.

"Amalthea lost a bet last night, so she's agreed to train with you," Demos explained.

I wanted to ask the subject of the bet, but I still felt weird for snapping at Demos so I just accepted it with a nod. Demos began to walk us through a new series of drills with real blades, and I welcomed the distraction. It was nice to train with someone else, especially since Amalthea, even hungover, had better form than me. Demos worked with me like nothing had happened, the whole incident forgotten.

But it wasn't. Something had changed in the way he watched me.

I wasn't sure I liked it.

When I got back to my room, something was… off. It took me a moment to pinpoint what had changed: my bed. The spread was the same, the four post pillars identical, but the slightest wood frame peeked out from under the draped blanket. A note was on my bedside table.

VASILISA DRAKE

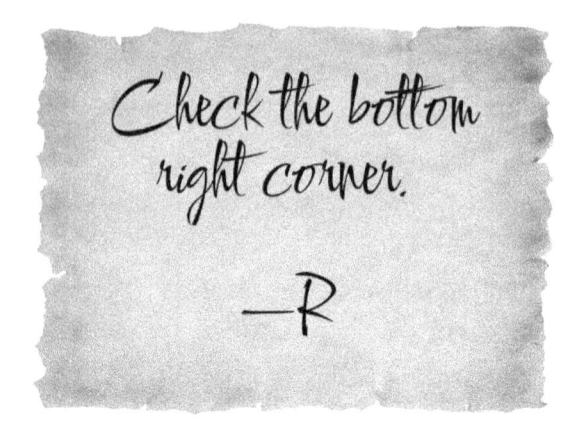

> *Check the bottom right corner.*
>
> *—R*

I did as instructed. Before, my bed had been elevated on four posts. Now, under the mattress, the wooden frame extended all the way to the ground. On the far right side, opposite the entryway, there was a small locking mechanism. I admired the elegance of it. The way it was set up, I wouldn't have noticed it if Raphael hadn't pointed it out. When I maneuvered the siding, the wooden panel dropped away, surprisingly lightweight.

That was the least of the marvels the bed now contained. Inside were two pillows and a properly fitted blanket. I pressed my palm into the blanket. More than that, Raphael had something done so the carpet under the bed was even softer. Inside was a small clock. I frowned, peering farther in.

Although the wood appeared solid from the outside, light was able to get through. I eased my body under. More than that, the carved base was strategically cut so I could see if anyone came into the room. Before, I'd kept the covers from the main bed pulled so I wouldn't be seen if anyone came in, but like this I wouldn't need to, and instead could feel secure that I wasn't blind to anybody coming.

The bed compartment was a stunning feat of engineering. How was it possible it had all been done in a day?

A second note fell from one of the pillows.

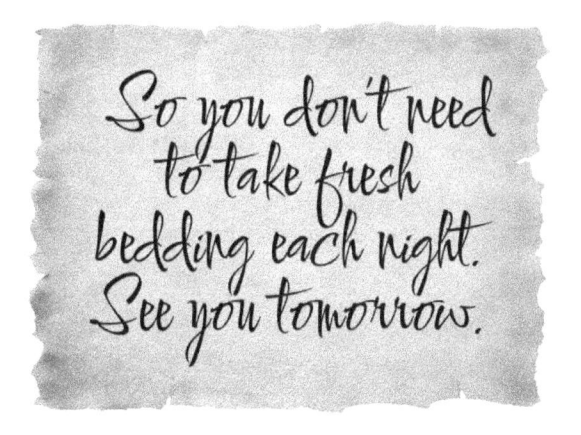

> So you don't need to take fresh bedding each night. See you tomorrow.

There was no possibility Raphael missed my wave of gratitude through our mental link. And though I liked my privacy... maybe that wasn't the worst thing.

Chapter 38

I knocked on the door of Raphael's chambers, then tapped my foot impatiently when I didn't hear a response.

I'd never been to his chambers before; Raphael had never actually told me where his private quarters were. When I'd ask Amalthea, she'd burst out laughing.

"Surely you're joking."

Do I seem like I'm trying to surprise Raphael in bed? I wanted to retort. But just the thought made me flush. Besides, he'd rejected me. He didn't want me. All the wine in the world wouldn't convince me that was a good idea. *"It's where he said to meet him."*

"But... don't you know where his rooms are?"

A BARGAIN SO BLOODY

I shook my head. Wandering into the vampire king's chambers wasn't on my limited list of activities I was comfortable doing. *"Why would I?"*

I knocked again. When there was no answer, I cast a glance about the hallway. It was the time we'd agreed to meet.

I threw the door to his chambers open.

And blinked at the scene before me. Demos was in the room, dressed in his uniform, his arms crossed as he stood in front of Raphael, who was turned a quarter away from me.

Raphael was naked.

Well, he had a towel around his hips. His hair was damp, the water dripping from the white tips over his jawline. His chest was on full display and bore no sign of the whips at Greymere. His skin was unbroken, stretching over hard muscle. He was perched on the edge of a massive desk, his hands gripping into the wood, flexing the muscles of his arms.

My skin grew hot and tight when I realized I was interrupting. Gods, and I thought him and Amalthea...

"I'll come back another time," I squeaked.

Demos didn't look at me as he said, "We can continue this conversation another time."

"No. The matter is closed." Raphael's voice brooked no room for argument.

I was missing context, but clearly I was interrupting Vampire Kingdom business, not some rendezvous. I was curious, because of course I was, but I chased the emotion away. *Their politics don't concern you.*

"You can't just ignore this," Demos said through clenched teeth.

"I'm not," Raphael snapped. His gaze flashed towards me, then back at Demos as the blade of his tone dulled just a fraction. "What I'm doing is refusing to discuss it at this time and ordering you not to investigate further."

Demos turned away from his king, not waiting for a proper dismissal, and brushed past me. His expression was cold and unfriendly, unlike the neutral expression I knew from our daily practice. He had too much restraint to slam the door given he was however-many hundreds of years old instead of a toddler, but the solid *thud* it shut with was enough for me to register how he felt about Raphael's response to whatever argument.

"Good evening to you," he drawled.

"Don't 'good evening' me," I blubbered. "You're indecent!"

He arched a brow at me, making no move to cover himself. "I'm not the one who barged in."

"You told me to meet you in your chambers at this time," I reminded him. "*And* I knocked."

Raphael shrugged, unrepentant. His bare shoulders *really* shouldn't look that good doing something as mundane as shrugging, but I watched every flex of his muscles against my will. "Demos caught me while I was bathing. No sense of timing with that one." He gave a *what-can-you-do* sigh that was distinctly un-kingly as he brushed his wet hair back with one hand.

"You have preternatural speed. You could dress in seconds." I hoped the annoyance in my tone would disguise the fact I was having a very hard time not looking at Raphael like this.

"What can I say? I like to take my time." But he did push off the desk and cross the room, grabbing some dark clothing and disappearing into another room. He did not, however, shut the door.

I worked very hard not to think about Raphael dressing in the next room, and studied his chambers. They were similar to my own: a sitting room and office, with a grand desk that would have been more impressive if it wasn't covered in mountains of parchment. The door where he'd disappeared was likely the washroom, and another shut door that was certainly his sleeping quarters. The decorations were different from my own, darker colors, less ornamentation but still luxurious.

Raphael reappeared, mercifully clothed. Kind of. His hair was still wet, skewed in a half-dozen directions like he'd shook it in a towel. His clothing was simply a pair of woven charcoal-gray slacks and a deep mauve silk shirt that was only partly buttoned. Different from his usual black. I studied him for a heartbeat too long before he cleared his throat.

Oh. Right. I was annoyed at him. It took a second to recall the emotions that had me pounding on the door, but once I did, I was seething all over.

"You put me next door to you?" I demanded.

"Finished looking and straight to business," he said mildly.

I ignored the remark. "How did I not know you were stationed across the hall?"

"Perhaps you simply aren't overly observant," he offered.

I didn't exactly patrol the hallways, but that wasn't enough to convince me. If I didn't know, it was because he didn't *want* me to know. All these weeks, and I hadn't seen him enter or leave once. The bastard had offered to *walk me to my rooms* on more than one occasion.

"Why am I sleeping across from you, Raphael? You know what people are going to think," I hissed.

Raphael drew closer from across the room, until he was right in front of me. There was something lethal about him in this state, half-dressed, hair still wet. And yet his red eyes were utterly focused on me. "What are they going to think, dove?"

Was he going to make me spell it out? "That I—that you—we—*ergh*!" I was too flustered to get the words out. Kings used the chambers near them for favored mistresses. It would seem like I was placed near him to meet his *physical* needs.

By the smirk that threatened the left corner of his lips, he knew exactly what I was referring to. He just enjoyed torturing me.

"You know exactly what they're going to think," I groused.

Raphael cocked a brow. "I'm not in the habit of letting gossip dictate my actions. Besides, do you really care what a bunch of vampires think of your sexual proclivities?"

Sexual proclivities. If a pit straight to the second hell could open in the floor then and there, I'd prostrate myself in thanks to the god of circles himself.

"You could have put me near Amalthea," I sputtered.

"You're safest near *me*." He took a step closer. "You're my Chosen, Samara. Or at least you are in their eyes, because that's what keeps you safe in my kingdom."

My understanding of being one of his Chosen only meant, for vampire society, I was off limits for anyone but Raphael to drink from. If that was true, there was no reason for me to have chambers across from him.

Not unless there was more to the title than that.

My cheeks heated. At once, the image of Raphael's undressed body arose, coupled with the thought of what others in the kingdom thought we'd be doing with such proximity.

And he'd let them think that!

"You're frustrated," Raphael remarked.

I tried to bite down on the emotion, but it was a lot easier to contort your face than your emotions. "This is why I need you to help me block the link."

"As I've told you, you wear every emotion on your face. Anyone who knows you could figure that out."

Anyone who knows me. For a long time, there'd been no one like that. Now, it seemed, I had a vampire who could read me as easily as a book. I couldn't be sure how I felt about that, mainly because I disliked it less than I was supposed to.

Raphael moved back behind his desk, putting some distance between us. "Join me."

I followed him and sank into one of the plush leather seats on the other side of the table. I gestured to the stacks of letters and missives. "Don't you have others who could take care of this for you?"

Raphael gave the piles a rueful smile. "Most of it, I delegate. But some things still require me to handle personally—though in six hundred years I've never developed an affinity for paperwork."

I could make out the familiar scrawl of the common tongue. Having gone a decade without reading or writing, my grasp was tenuous, but returning more each day as I studied Old Runyk and read the books Amalthea gave me. Or at least, the ones worthy of time.

"How much do you know about mental magic?" Raphael asked.

"I'm a void, so I'd say hardly anything."

Raphael steepled his fingers on the wood. "It's like this: With most magic, there's a physical manifestation that witches focus on. With mental magic, telepaths, truth-seekers, and similar, you instead have to focus on quieting your mind and seeing the magic there."

"But I'm not a witch," I reminded him.

"You'll be able to do this," he said with conviction. "It simply takes practice. The principle is the same as with other mental magic. Imagine in your mind a barrier around your thoughts. As though they're foiled in cursed copper, repelling me. Take one emotion and concentrate on stirring it, then hiding it from me."

It was impossible to concentrate while Raphael looked at me so I shut my eyes. I recalled the frustration from earlier and imagined winding it into a tight ball and covering it in glinting plates of copper. I drew a deep breath, trying to solidify the mental wall. It felt a bit silly, but I wanted my privacy, so I used all my concentration to try to follow Raphael's instructions.

"Frustration. You're trying too hard," he remarked.

"Isn't the entire point to practice?"

"Not if you want me to be blocked from your emotions throughout the day. Like this, you can try to hide specific feelings, but you're bound to slip. Try again."

I blew out a breath, focusing. This time, I picked something else—the shame that lingered over how I'd snapped at Demos. This time, instead of bundling it tight and trying to press it together, I let myself feel it but imagined a blanket of copper over it.

"Better," Raphael remarked. "I can feel it, but only if I try to dig into your mind."

Better. So we tried again. And again. It was difficult to practice something when you're supposed to make it effortless, and I had no way to know if it was working unless Raphael told me. Still, with every one-word-approval, I grew more confident that I could do this.

Time flew by. Surely Raphael had better things to do, but he didn't rush me, practicing until finally I slumped in the chair, a throbbing headache brewing between my brows.

I gave him a tired grin. "Now you won't have to deal with all my nuisance emotions."

Raphael didn't return it. "I've never minded, Samara. Not once."

When he said things like that, it got hard to look at him again. He got up and moved to a decanter across the room, pouring bright red liquid into a crystal glass. It wasn't the same dark shade the blood mead I'd seen other vampires drink. His throat bobbed as he swallowed.

A morbid question hit me. "Is it... good like that? Just at room temperature."

He set the glass down and arched a brow at me. "I'm surprised you're asking that."

I was too. A while ago, such a question would have been inconceivable. Just the thought of a vampire drinking blood was enough to make panic seize me. But with Raphael... there was something I wanted to trust. And I was curious. So I pulled a page from his book and waited in silence until he answered.

"It's not, which is why most vampires exclusively take a source directly. This is little better than animal blood for me."

I frowned. "What if you heated it over a fire?"

Raphael barked a laugh, as if I'd made a joke. I'd been completely serious. "That would hardly make it better. There's more to blood-taking than the temperature of it. I'm afraid if I elaborated, you'd run screaming from my room."

I snorted. "Yes, run all the way across the hall to my room next door."

"See if this is more to your taste." He reached around and picked up a covered tray I'd failed to notice. The polished silver gleamed in the torchlight. I moved away from the piles of important papers and took a seat on the couch, behind a low table. Raphael set the tray in front of me and lifted the lid.

A single pie occupied the tray, still fresh from the oven.

"You keep pie in your room?"

"Only when I know you'll be here." Raphael didn't look at me as he said it, and it was good, because there was nothing I could do to hide the blush that coated my cheeks or cover the little thrill that went through me.

"Thank you," I murmured, lifting the fork from the tray to break the crust. It was utterly decadent, fresh-baked and sugar-filled. The tartness on my tongue was vivid, and I swallowed with pleasure. There was little ladylike in how I ate—not that Raphael complained. I devoured the pie and set the tray down, a satisfied hand on my bulging stomach.

"Training is hungry work," Raphael remarked with a hint of amusement.

"I feel rather like a dog that's been given a treat for performing a clever trick." Not undeserved, given the rigorous mental training he'd just put me through. Still, the image made me think of Titus's comments about me being a spoiled pet. I fought to keep that out of my emotions and off my face.

"You *are* rather clever," Raphael teased.

Titus's *spoiled pet* taunt came to mind, but I kicked it away. I hadn't seen him in weeks. Perhaps he'd departed from Damerel, whatever plan foiled.

We sat for a while, an easy silence between us. The castle could be utterly silent at times, given the quiet way vampires moved and noise insulation. In my rooms, sometimes it was too quiet. Sitting next to Raphael, it was comfortable.

"What changed your mind?" I eventually asked. "When I asked you weeks ago to train me, you refused. You said it would hinder your ability to keep me safe. So what changed?"

"Everything I said is still true. I do think you're safer if I can sense your emotions. That way I'd know if you felt you were in danger." Raphael leaned forward, resting his elbows on his knees as he looked ahead. "But... you wanted me to. It's hypocritical to tell you you're safe in my kingdom and yet curtail your wishes as if that wasn't true. Perhaps there is another part of me that was selfish. That looked for an excuse to hold on to the blood bond. But my desires should not win out over your own, not when I've promised you sanctuary, and that includes sanctuary from the king's whims. So, if you want something, and it's in my power to give it, I will give it."

I tried to make sense of what he'd just said. I swallowed.

"You really are doing it just to respect my wishes?" My wishes had never mattered to anyone before. Never been taken into consideration. Never had any power.

"Of course."

Of course. Like it made sense.

"Samara, if you tell me you want something, I will do what I can to please you. Why do you struggle to believe that?"

My stomach twisted. "I was raised to believe that the surest way to be denied something was to let another know you wanted it." An instrument. A hug. A family.

"That's a sad way to live." He didn't coat the words in a saccharine way another might have.

"It was a safe way." I took another bite of the pie, the granules of sugar melting on my tongue. *Delicious*. "Why was Demos upset earlier?"

My bid to change the subject wasn't subtle, nor appreciated by the pained expression on Raphael's face.

"He had... concerns." Raphael said the last word slowly, like he was trying very hard to make something complicated fit in a tidy little box.

I told myself I was disappointed in the vague answer only because I was curious, not because I was upset Raphael didn't confide in me. It didn't affect me; I'd be gone soon anyway.

"Ask me something else," he said, a peace offering.

"Tell me something," I countered. "Something... something someone wouldn't guess about you."

He grinned. "I find I'm curious to know what you would guess about me, but I'll play." A pause, and his expression grew a shade more serious. "I never wanted to be king."

"No?" I asked, surprised. I remembered how staunchly he'd told me he was glad he'd been turned into a vampire. I'd assumed Raphael wanted power. I would never want to turn, but the desire for strength? Recognition? That could be as seductive as safety.

He shook his head, leaning back on the couch. "In many ways, it feels like a choice forced upon me."

I shifted slightly so I was facing him more, tucking my feet under my legs. "How did you become king?" Could vampires inherit? They couldn't have children... organically. My stomach twisted at the thought of Raphael being one of those babes turned.

Raphael arched a brow. "The same way anyone gets anything in a world of monsters. By force. It was the only option that let me have what I wanted. But I own all my actions—every single bloody one."

I considered that. I'd felt trapped at Greymere, with only one path way forward. But I'd done something bloody in my own right to escape.

"I was the strongest, and I was the most ruthless," Raphael continued. "The years when I came to power... I didn't waste time on politicking. There are those who excel at it, and they have a place. But me? It was a brutal, brutal thing."

"What do you excel at, then?" My voice was soft.

He held my gaze. "Truthfully? Surviving. At any cost."

He was a survivor. Like me. It was hard to imagine us having anything in common, but when he said those words, I heard the savage truth. I recognized it like I recognized my fingertips.

We were closer now. In that moment, I didn't want to survive—I just *wanted*. My heart fluttered, the mental shields I'd worked on only half in place. There was no way Raphael missed that, and yet he was still so close.

But I'm leaving.

And I wouldn't survive Raphael.

"Will you tell me what it's like beyond Damerel?" I whispered.

If Raphael was surprised by my sudden conversation change, he didn't betray it. He pulled away and returned moments later with a giant scroll. He pulled the low table closer to the couch and laid the map open for us.

I blinked. I hadn't actually seen a map since childhood, and even that had only been due to the tutors my mother had insisted on.

The map itself was a work of art, but my eyes skipped over the ornamentation and tried to refit this map into my worldview. I didn't remember Eurobis being so large. I planted my finger on a mountain range in the middle. "Is this really Damerel?" The letters were curved in an ornate script. No map from the Witch Kingdom would have named the vampire capital.

He bent closer, shoulder to shoulder with me, even though he could see just fine with his vampire vision.

"Though I rule the so-called Vampire Kingdom of the West, we're more of a barrier between the two halves of the continent."

"So what's over there?" I moved my hand to the middle-left of the map.

"Other magical creatures capable of reasoning inhabit the rest of the continent. You'll find kobolds and ogres, but there are other beings of power who have claimed territory." Raphael moved his fingers to the back of my hand. I jolted at the contact but let him adjust my fingers to the north corner. "The shape-changers live here." He moved my hand down to a peninsula so narrow it could have been an island. "The Winged Ones are here. There are more magical mortals, like your witches, only they don't use magic in the same ways." He withdrew his fingers and gestured to the rest of the map. "The fae have several strongholds, constantly changing alliances. You would encounter them..." He trailed off uncharacteristically.

I'd encounter them when I left. "Do you think I could manage there? I'm just a void."

"I think you could *thrive*," he rasped. "It's not the Witch Kingdom, where you have magic or you're mud. There are many ways to live there."

I pursed my lips. I hadn't ever thought of it as unfair. It was just how things were. Besides, witches shared their magic with the rest of us through cards. That we paid for.

I turned away from the thought. "Have you spent much time in the rest of Eurobis?" He certainly knew about it.

"I cannot. The southern and northern kingdoms have closer ties. We trade through them, most often."

Trade. The Witch Kingdom was locked between those kingdoms; we had no one to trade with. Sometimes it disconcerted me how much more to the world there was now that I was ostensibly in the world of monsters.

And soon I'd get to see an entire new realm.

By myself.

"Would you... visit me, once I'm settled?" The thought, silly as it was, slipped through before I could catch it on my tongue. The late hour made it too easy to say these ridiculous things.

He drew closer, his cedar scent licking at my senses, our knees touching. "Samara, there is nowhere in this world I would not go if you wished me to."

He couldn't lie. I stilled, my body frozen while my heart raced faster and faster.

"Too much truth?" His tone was teasing, yet his eyes were still serious.

Yes. It wouldn't be a simple thing, wanting Raphael like this. It would destroy me. There was no denying it. Not after this night.

But it would turn me into what they thought, another human for the king to use. I had to translate the book and leave—

"Samara?"

I shook my head. "I can't do this."

He didn't play coy and ask what I meant. "I'll always respect your wishes."

The sentence held a hundred possibilities I was saying *no* to.

The man who called himself king of monsters would always respect my wishes.

"I have to go," I murmured, untucking my legs and pulling away. To avoid leaving on a bleak note, I summoned vexation I no longer felt and arched a brow at the vampire king. "I'm sure I'll be able to find my way back to my rooms from here."

Chapter 39

One of my books was missing. I frowned. I had been rotating through the books since the librarian apparently made a stink about them being gone for too long, but the one missing wasn't just any book, but the one I'd tucked my notes inside of. Had I returned the wrong book by mistake?

Amalthea was called away on court business. Normally, she accompanied me when I refreshed my stock of books. I debated waiting for her, but I was so close to getting this latest passage fully translated.

It had been coming more quickly, even though I was splitting my time between practicing my mental shields with Raphael, physical training with Demos, and translating. Progress had been the slowest on sparring, but Raphael appeared almost frustrated by how quickly I'd developed my mental shields.

Translating... I was close. There were a few gaps I could infer, but there was one term in the opening I couldn't grasp. Though I could translate other pages, the opening pages of a grimoire served as critical context for the mythical tome. I'd seen something similar to at least one of the mysterious glyphs in the missing book, I was certain.

This is the book of the necromancer. The witch who alone serves Anagenni, they who _____. Through the goddess's will, the necromancer has dominion over bone and blood, ____ and ____. The _____ bow to the necromancer.

I made a quick calculation and decided my desire to finish my work outweighed how uncomfortable the librarian made me.

The librarian was surprisingly absent from his post. I took that as a good omen and went inside, scurrying around the stacks of books to find the now familiar corner that held the Old Runyk books.

Where is it? I scanned the spines, but the book I was looking for wasn't there. I squatted low and pulled out each book one by one. Maybe it hadn't been reshelved? That would mean I'd have to ask the librarian, and just the thought sent a shiver down my spine. Maybe it had fallen behind a piece of furniture in my room.

"Looking for this?" an old, cracked voice said.

I jerked upright and turned.

The librarian stood just a few feet away. His appearance was every bit as ghastly as I remembered, skin as thin of the frailest parchment bound in the texts he guarded. But that wasn't what I focused on.

The missing book was in his hand.

"Oh, um, yes," I squeaked. "I didn't mean to return it. I wasn't done with the book."

"Of course," he said congenially.

He made no move to give me the book, so I was forced to walk to him and take it. I opened the front and frowned.

"Or were you looking for these?"

He held a few sheets of parchment aloft, covered in my drafted translations. Relief went through me at the realization I wouldn't need to start all over again.

"Yes, thank you." I held out my hand, but the librarian kept the papers lifted.

I looked up at him in confusion.

"Did you think," the librarian said mildly, "that I would not figure out what you were doing?"

I took a small step backwards. "I'm working on a project for the king."

The librarian barked a laugh, the sound like a crack of thunder. "Did you think I wouldn't know who you really serve? That I wouldn't recognize you for what you really are? As if the king would ever ask for this. When he learns what I've done, he'll reward me."

What he's done?

His voice turned into that hypnotic lull of a thrall. "Now stay still so I can kill you."

I barely had time to process the threat before the librarian lunged at me. It was nothing like the lunges Amalthea made when we sparred, or when Demos modeled his movements. This was a vampire's lunge, fast, deadly, and unstoppable.

The librarian grabbed my shoulders in his hands, nails digging in.

"Let go!" I cried.

Startled, his grip halted for a second. I had only the moment to reach into my deck and pull the one card I still had. Half a thought pulled the magic from the enchantment.

Bzzz!

A cloud of insects manifested between us, diving for the vampire.

The sound that came from the vampire was nothing human. He roared as the swarm of wasps attacked. His limbs swung wildly, attempting to swat them away.

They'd buy me scant seconds. They blocked his vision, but there was no chance I could run and escape in time.

There was only one move open to me.

I pulled the dagger from my belt, the bronze blade surprisingly light. The wasps continued to sting the vampire, but he was once more moving towards me.

I lunged.

And planted the blade squarely in his chest.

The ancient vampire crumpled to the ground.

His face turned from pale to the color of ash. His skin began to crumble, turning to dust and falling in until there was nothing left but bones and the clothes he'd worn. The wasps disappeared with the spell. My dagger clattered to the ground, no longer embedded in the flesh.

So this was how a vampire died.

A strange calm had come over me. I stood transfixed, watching as centuries of undeath faded into nothing.

I had done that.

Without thought, I smiled.

WHAT TRANSPIRED AFTER WAS a blur. Amalthea found me there, drawn by a vision.

"Samara! What happened?"

The story stumbled out of me, and she pulled me into her arms. I didn't manage to lift my arms, and her brows knitted together in concern. "We need to tell Raphael."

"Can you?" I asked. "I just want to go back to my room and work on the translation." I was so, so close to deciphering the last words of the critical first page.

Amalthea looked at me like I had lost it. "Sam, you shouldn't be alone right now. This... this would be a lot for anyone, but especially..."

Especially someone as fragile as me. She didn't say it, but I knew what she meant. Yet at the moment, I didn't feel fragile.

I didn't feel anything.

"Let's go to my rooms, and I'll tell Raphael to meet us there," she suggested.

Suddenly tired, I did as she bid. Raphael came immediately once she sent word, furious.

"How did this happen?" he snarled.

"Raphael," Amalthea said, her tone reproachful.

She had cleared one chair from the mountain of dresses it was buried under and given me a cup of tea.

I stared at Raphael. His eyes were wild.

He was dressed in court fashion, like he'd just run out of a meeting to get here.

"I felt nothing in the bond." His anger was on a tenuous leash.

I slumped in the chair. "Then it seems all my training has paid off. You were just wrong about me being safe here."

Raphael jerked back like I'd slapped him. I regretted the words, but they were true, weren't they?

"What happened?" he demanded.

It was Thea who answered, repeating everything I'd told her. Only when I had told her, I'd omitted the questions.

"Why did translating the grimoire make him want to kill me?" I asked.

Did you think I wouldn't know who you really serve? That I wouldn't recognize you for what you really are? The question... in the panic... I hadn't known what he meant. It made no sense given the context.

The two exchanged a look. Pieces fit in.

"He thought I serve the creature Raphael was sent to hunt, didn't he?" I pressed. *The necromancer*.

"He must have thought you served Anagenni," he explained with reluctance.

I frowned. "You said the vampires worship Anagenni."

"Vampires do revere Anagenni," Amalthea explained. "But it's not precisely true to say she is a beloved goddess. They fear her."

"But why?" Why wouldn't the undead love the goddess of death? What did they have to fear? Raphael clearly knew her well enough, but the librarian had rejected the idea his king would have anything to do with her grimoire.

Raphael came closer. "Don't think on this anymore, Samara. Vampires... they can go mad with age, making it impossible to puzzle out their motives."

My head slumped between my palms. "So I should just live in fear of the next vampire who goes crazy and attacks me?" Gods, what a hopeless thing.

"You're not going to live in fear." Raphael pulled my hands away, making me look up at him. "You're brave, Samara. You saved yourself. If any good can come of this, let it be that. You're not the same girl you were."

I gave a small snort and looked away. "I was terrified. I got lucky." Lucky I'd had the wasp card, lucky I'd yelled loud enough to startle the vampire, lucky I'd drawn the dagger in time and that it had landed true. "I'm not like you."

"*Of course* you were afraid. Samara, there's no bravery without fear. No courage is born untested. But you triumphed over a deadly, powerful foe. Not a fearful dove—but apparently a little viper," he said with what I might have dared consider admiration. "Take pride in that."

Brave. Courageous. Could those words really apply to me? Reconciling Raphael's view of my actions with my own was difficult. I studied the flames, thinking of how I'd felt when the vampire had turned to dust. For the first time, I'd felt like I was in control.

"You won, Samara. And if need be, you will again. Trust in that."

Chapter 40

I didn't waste time after the attack returning to translating. I'd worked slowly for two reasons—one, it had taken a while to get used to reading at all again, let alone in Old Runyk; the skills had atrophied. And two, which was shameful to admit, I'd lulled myself into a belief that I could take my time. A thousand gold pieces was worth working slowly for, and I had Amalthea for tea, and Demos for training, and Raphael... Raphael for everything else.

Finally, I'd finished the first passage in its entirety. I'd worked late nights... and early mornings. But the retrieved book let me piece together the word I couldn't get.

It wasn't a word that was common in Old Runyk. "Those who are without death," or simplified, "the undead." *Vampires*.

The implication was... terrifying. I'd asked Demos to forgo training so I could deliver the translation to Raphael. With this done, I could continue to work on the rest of the book... or let Raphael destroy it.

Demos didn't heckle me for skipping training like he would Amalthea. He'd been a bit off since the night I'd caught him in Raphael's chambers. Sometimes I caught him watching me. Not clinically studying my form, not like a vampire who was hungry. Just... watching. For what?

I considered us friendly, but not close enough to ask why he seemed to think I was due to sprout a second head.

"You've been doing well with your training," he offered while we walked down the halls. Guards stationed periodically nodded to both of us, after straightening their posture when their boss came into view.

"Really?" I chirped. The praise surprised me.

"I don't give empty compliments, and I can't lie," he said dryly.

I grinned. "Right." Praise from the king's general was high praise indeed.

"You came to us nearly emaciated and barely able to hold a stance, now you've managed to take down a vampire," he continued. "Remind me how that went down, again?"

I shivered at the memory, tucking my hands under my arms protectively. For some reason, I wished I had the grimoire with me, but there was no way I was taking it in front of other vampires after everything.

"It was fast. Honestly, most of it was instinct, the training paying off." The memory of the ancient librarian lunging for me played in my mind. "He said some weird stuff, taunted me. Then he charged. I was able to cast the wasp card, and I used the blade like you taught me. He was dust before my mind really caught up."

"Battles do tend to go fast," Demos acknowledged. "They can feel prolonged in the moment, especially for vampires who move at faster speeds, but in reality, even among mortals they rarely go more than five minutes." A pause. "It's surprising he didn't use his thrall on you."

Right. The terrifying power that let vampires compel mortals. *Why hadn't the librarian done so?* I had focused on translating the book as fast as I could and avoided thinking about that battle. Or... was it possible he had? He'd told me to stay still or something, but I'd thought it was some patronizing language since he was so confident he could kill me.

"Maybe he wanted to play with his prey, and underestimated me?"

Raphael had told me his thrall didn't work on me before. I'd thought that was just *him*, some quirk.

With the way Demos was probing, I decided not to volunteer that.

"Perhaps." He looked like he wanted to say something more, then shook his head. "In any case, you should be proud. When you leave the kingdom, you'll be a fearsome foe in your own right."

When you leave. "You sound like you're almost looking forward to it," I teased, ignoring the pang in my chest. I *wanted* to leave. I was working tirelessly to, and with this, I might be able to. So why didn't the thought fill me with joy?

"Or at least, you must be looking forward to having your afternoons back," I continued.

That broke through the ice around the general. He rolled his eyes. "At least Amalthea's been preoccupied with you. Once you leave, she'll be back to meddling with everything."

I hid a grin. Maybe Demos was wishing he could keep Amalthea training too. He was much harsher with her than me, but the oracle gave as good as she got—on the days she showed up. She mostly kept to their bargain, but as she reminded us both, she did have important work to do.

The hallways grew more crowded, the carpeting more ornate, as we neared the throne room. We passed a few offices, with those Raphael had mentioned he delegated work to, concentrating on different tasks. Some were vampires, but a few were humans in those ghastly vampire disguises.

Still not used to that.

"Just be warned, the king's been in a bit of a mood," Demos said.

I frowned. "Why?"

He looked at me like not only had I sprouted that second head, but it was a very stupid head. "The librarian attack."

"Oh. Right." Of course Raphael would be stressed—someone who had held an important post had gone insane. No doubt he was worried others might follow.

Demos led me through a side door rather than the main entrance, and explained we'd wait for court to adjourn, at which point I could talk to him. I had dressed in proper clothes rather than the training leathers Amalthea had fitted me with. The dress was vivid blue and slightly low-necked, as was appropriate for my "station" as Raphael's Chosen, and as ornate as I could manage for something I could put on myself.

I was woefully underdressed compared to most of the court.

We were a little to the left and in front of Raphael, standing back. He didn't look at us when we entered, so I took a second to study him. He sat on an elevated dais upon a high-backed throne made of solid silver. His crown was a matching metal, with rubies dotting the edge, his hair tamed back by the crown. His fingers were steepled on the arm. The only sign of boredom was his fourth finger tapping to a staccato. His posture was rigid, his expression not interested, but not insultingly bored. Dispassionate, perhaps.

The room held at least ten rows of long seats, mostly filled with nobles dressed in finery.

Two were standing towards the front of the room, petitioners seeking some resolution. Across from Demos and me were three vampires seated behind a slightly elevated bench: two vampires, and a human to the side. Their clothes weren't as ornate as the petitioners, but rather uniforms. I quickly surmised these were something akin to a jury that heard petitions. The first few petitions were surprisingly mundane. When matters escalated up for Raphael to deal with, he was collected, he let both parties speak. His rulings seemed generally fair, but of course, no one dared argue with their king.

I thought about how he'd confided he'd never wanted the crown, yet he was involved as a ruler. Though the first I'd seen had been wealthy nobles, as time went on I realized there were others who also sought resolutions. The process wasn't riveting, exactly, but it was a fascinating look at the kingdom. It had due process, a far-cry from the chaotic frenzy I'd always feared. Yes, some vampires were crazy—hence the recent attack on my life—but the kingdom had another side to it. I wasn't so blind I couldn't acknowledge that.

A human came forward. Unlike the others who roamed the halls, this one didn't disguise his species. He had hair the color of wet dirt, with silver flecks speckled throughout that complemented the sagging lines around his eyes and jowls. A pair of spectacles balanced on the bridge of his

A BARGAIN SO BLOODY

nose, so short and narrow I wondered how he didn't go cross-eyed. A vampiress who looked years younger, but could have easily been centuries older, stood at his side as if presenting him.

The court secretary cleared his throat. "Janessa of the Ash-Sworn clan petitions King Raphael to allow her to turn Crowley Adinamos to one of the night people, and live as a member of her clan."

The night people. A vampire?

Demos tensed besides me, but I stared at Raphael. He extended a hand, waving them to continue. He hadn't directly responded to the other petitions, as they'd been to the court, but this power must exclusively reside with him.

"Tell us your service, Mister Adinamos."

Crowley cast a nervous glance back, then shuffled a few steps forward, wringing his hands.

"Your Highness," he stammered.

Your Majesty, I silently corrected.

"I've served the Ash-Sworn clan faithfully for more than thirty years. I've submitted papers outlining my contributions." He gestured to the secretary, who lifted a thick stack of parchment.

"I'll hear it from your mortal tongue," Raphael said without humor.

"O-of course." The stammering returned. "I didn't mean to imply—that is—I've worked hard, King Raphael. I've worked tirelessly as one of their actuaries for decades. There are books filled in the accounting I've done. My eyes have paid the price." He raised a hand to the spectacles on his face. "And my service is without barriers. I've given blood, when requested—as is my privilege!" he quickly clarified. "I have lived a life without magic, after you... err... graciously accepted me in your kingdom. That is of course its own reward. But my most ardent dream is to prove myself worthy of eternal service."

My stomach cramped. Demos quietly offered to escort me outside, but I waved him off. I wanted to see this. Needed to.

A human choosing to give up their humanity.

Crowley dithered through a few other accomplishments, pressing his glasses back now and again with his third finger. It was a ploy, perhaps, showing himself with mortal hair that was white only from age, mortal eyes strained from labor. A price he'd paid in hopes Raphael would wipe the slate clean and gift him immortality.

"And then"—Crowley's voice lifted in triumph—"the reason for my petition came. A fortnight ago, a young vampire was injured, not even ten. He had fallen into a ravine. His legs were broken, and he had no chance of climbing out. I aided him, provided him with blood, and returned him to his parents. I can think of no higher service I could offer than to remain in the kingdom's service forever."

At last, the man stopped speaking. There was utter silence in the room, as if everyone held a collective breath while awaiting Raphael's decision. Of course, most of the courtroom didn't need to breathe. Still, the silence was so bad I could imagine myself hearing Crowley's heartbeat, twin to my own racing one—with excitement, while mine ached with dread.

"I have considered your petition." Raphael spoke in that slow, unhurried tone I'd first heard from him, like unending night. "You make some valid arguments for why you deserve to be one of the blood. Your actions with the son are telling of your character. In fact, I believe though you demurred, the young vampire was none other than the heir to the clan you serve."

Did I imagine Crowley taking a half step backwards?

"You have my blessing." Raphael nodded to Janessa. "Turn him. Now."

Janessa looked surprised, as did everyone else in the room. Not blatantly whispering, but there were telling shifts of eyes, adjusted stances. Something was off.

"Didn't they want this?" I asked Demos under my breath.

"The turning is normally done in private," he explained. "But I'm sure Raphael has his reasons."

Lady Janessa stepped over to Crowley, taking center stage with him. They were on display. "Here, Your Majesty?" she murmured.

He gave a casual flick of his fingers, not deigning to repeat himself. He was still the picture of casual grace, but something in his eyes was cold.

VASILISA DRAKE

Once Janessa leaned over, I could look nowhere else. Bile coated the back of my throat, and I wondered if I'd made a grave mistake in not taking Demos up on his offer to stand outside.

But I stayed.

I had to see.

The vampiress brushed the human's hair away and bit into his soft, sagging skin. His lips parted, but he made no move to get away. I could imagine exactly why—and why this would be done in private.

He fell to the floor, and she went with him, kneeling as he lay in her lap.

She didn't let go with her fangs. He grew paler and paler, his skin almost the white of the vampire by the time she withdrew her lips.

With a nail, she clawed her own wrist open and drenched his parted lips in her blood. His chest was no longer rising and falling.

The air in the room was suddenly too thick, pressing in on all sides, but I couldn't look away.

She killed him. And now she was to resurrect him.

"Just one small matter," Raphael said.

All eyes swung to the king.

"Your Majesty?" she said, meekly. Perhaps turning was exhausting for the vampire?

"The boy Crowley saved—your nephew, as I recall. How did Crowley find him?"

She blinked. "I... that is a better question for Crowley, Your Majesty. Once he has turned, I've every hope he will be able to answer your queries to satisfaction."

"Naturally," Raphael replied easily. "Then perhaps this one will be more suited to your domain. How did your nephew get injured in the first place?"

Janessa looked pale, even paler than usual for a vampire. Blood was smeared over her lips, which were parted as she stared up from the floor at Raphael on the high throne. "It is not unusual for young vampires to overestimate—"

"Do *not* attempt to deceive me!" Raphael roared.

I flinched.

The entire room flinched.

"You stupid, stupid child," Raphael snarled. "You think you can manipulate your king into gifting your toy immortality?"

"Your Majesty, I only—"

"Silence!" Raphael snarled. "I'll tell you what you did. You convinced your nephew to leave his bed, then led him down to the ravine. You hurled him over the side. And while he cried, bones broken into splinters, betrayed by someone blood-bound to protect him, you extorted him. You told him if he vowed not to say a word of your sins, he could have some of that pathetic worm's blood. And why? Because you wanted your lover to be turned, and you'd both grown tired of waiting. You wanted to be absolutely sure I'd be so moved by his noble gesture, I would permit it." He leaned forward, his fingers curled over the arms of his throne. "Go on. Tell me I'm wrong."

The vampiress opened and closed her lips, but no sound passed. She couldn't lie.

"Of course," Raphael continued, "it turns out you're as conniving as you are stupid. You made him vow not to tell anyone, but once the fingers in his hands healed, he was able to write his responses."

The entire court was silent. I fought the urge to vomit. I'd thought there was nothing worse than giving up mortality to become a vampire—but Crowley had abandoned his humanity long before if he thought this was in any world justifiable.

Raphael had clearly known about this. Why go through this charade?

"Punishment should suit the misdeed. I've allowed you to turn him, to give him the eternal life he hungered for." A pause. "Snap his neck. Now."

"Mercy, Your Majesty!" She fell to her hands, pleading. "Punish me instead."

"Oh, I am." Raphael rose from his throne, taking one slow step down the dais at a time. "You will live." He took another step. "Knowing you took his years of service, and his reward is death from his own sire." Another step. "And you will live the rest of your life in exile." Another step. "You betrayed your own clan when you harmed your nephew. No vampire will let you take refuge with them now."

He stood in front of Janessa, who was crying on her hands and knees. I felt no pity at the sight, only hatred.

Raphael was doing something beyond cruel.

The newly made vampire would die.

This one would suffer.

Monsters.

"Break his neck now," he ordered. "You won't like it if I'm the one who takes my time, savoring his death."

Tears streamed down her face as she lifted Crowley's body. He was unconscious, but his lids flickered. Was he aware in this state?

Snap!

Janessa wailed.

The hatred that had fogged over me cleared with the sound of her screams. Suddenly, I didn't feel any more righteous anger.

I just felt sick.

"Get out." Raphael's voice was low and deadly, then he lifted his chin to address the room. "Everyone, out." He nudged the corpse, which was already decomposing to sand, with his foot. "And someone take this trash with them."

I vomited.

VASILISA DRAKE

Demos forced me out of the room with the rest of them and led me to a back chamber. I didn't want to see Raphael in this state, but since I'd made a point of going, there was no way I could just leave now.

The room was directly behind the throne room, an office of some kind. Raphael walked in a moment after us. He looked wearier than I'd seen him, but he straightened when he saw me notice.

"I'm sorry you had to see that." A brusque apology.

"Why?" The word made the bitter film of my sick coat my mouth once more. The taste seemed to coat my entire body.

He frowned. "I couldn't allow that to go unpunished. Not when they tried to manipulate their king, and certainly not when the cost of that was abuse of a youngling."

I shook my head, my arms crossed tight over my abdomen. The entire room stood between us. "That's not what I mean. I don't... I don't even disagree, really. If what you say is true, then death is certainly deserved. But why give them hope? Why make her be the one to do it? Why draw it out into a spectacle?" My voice rose as I spoke until I was near shouting.

"Because *this* is what they understand." Raphael didn't shout back, but his voice boomed through the room. "*This* is what vampires learn from. This is what stops them from doing worse. I stop them, little viper. You might not like what that looks like, but it must be done."

A BARGAIN SO BLOODY

"This may seem brutal, but it's not unusual for our culture," Demos added. "We're a bloody, brutal people. There's no use pretending otherwise."

I swallowed down another argument.

They were violent. Not just violent, but cruel, sadistic. Only controlled by someone stronger, crueler, as Raphael had shown.

"What did you come for?" Raphael asked. Then he turned to Demos. "*Why* did you bring her?"

Demos shrugged. Unlike me, to him, the execution was just another day. "She said it was important. For that translation she's doing."

The grimoire. The passage I'd finish translating.

This is the book of the necromancer. The witch who alone serves Anagenni, they who control all who have perished. Through the goddess's will, the necromancer has dominion over bone and blood, soul and spirit. The undead bow to the necromancer. One witch is gifted to the world every two hundred years with Anagenni's blessing. They alone can right the balance.

The undead bow to the necromancer.

Vampires. The necromancer, if they were real, could control vampires. The one creature that might be able to control them, and the grimoire was the key to their power.

Raphael had to suspect. But if I confirmed it, he might destroy the book.

"I..." I thought as fast as I could—the one strength I had over vampires was I could lie. I needed one Demos wouldn't call me on. I couldn't deny I'd come about the translation. "I decided to work from the back since I was having trouble at the front, and I found a spell I thought might be interesting." The best lies were rooted in truth. When struggling with the first passage, I *had* worked on a few of the spells. "It called for some ingredients, and I thought if we collected them, Amalthea could try to use it. Maybe the magical trace would help her find whoever it belongs to."

It wouldn't work, of course. The grimoire wasn't a simple cookbook anyone could take a page from.

Raphael gave me a long look, as if trying to understand why I'd propose such a stupid idea.

A drop of sweat slid from the back of my neck down my spine.

"Amalthea can't use the grimoire, unfortunately," Raphael said.

Demos sighed. "I could have guessed as much. You should have told me that was your important news. I'd have saved you this headache, and you could have trained."

I resisted the urge to wipe the perspiration from my brow. "My apologies. I'll keep at it."

But I wasn't sorry I missed training.

I wasn't sorry I'd seen this.

Chapter 41

I HAD AVOIDED THE alcove ever since Titus found me there. I missed the music, but a naïve part of me hoped that if I simply didn't encounter the spymaster again, he'd ignore me. He'd rightfully pointed out that if I told Raphael or anybody who he was, that would open more questions about how I knew, and those weren't questions I could afford to answer.

And now that I'd decided not to tell Raphael about the grimoire passage I'd translated, I was keeping even more secrets.

So, yes, I was naïve to think Titus would simply leave me be. And perhaps a little bit stupid.

Amalthea had offered—more like insisted—we go out to the second level and visit some of her favorite shops. She had offered to meet me at my rooms, but I offered to meet her closer to the tunnel that led to the lower level so she wouldn't need to trek all the way from court to my chambers.

"Waiting for someone?"

I swung around, expecting to see Titus. Instead, the only thing I saw was an empty hallway.

"You're a hard woman to get to these days, Samara Koisemi."

Titus's voice came from my left this time. Still, nothing. Disguise magic, then. The most potent disguise magic would allow the caster to become entirely invisible. As the king's spymaster, Titus would have access to all the best cards.

Titus was a witch. Likely a powerful one—nobody lesser could have risen to power in the Storm-blooded King's court. But what kind of magic he had, I couldn't be sure. Likely not disguise magic, since otherwise he would have used it more liberally. Not knowing a witch's magic was dangerous, especially when that witch was threatening you.

"Amalthea will be here any minute," I said. "You should go. I have nothing to say to you, except I'm not a threat to your mission." Whatever it was.

"Oh, Samara. And here I thought you'd be interested in hearing the king's offer to pardon you."

I was unable to stop myself from flinching at his words. "What?"

"Oh, did that get your attention?" Titus said coyly. "Home, Samara. Pardoned, with enough money to start your own household in Ulryne. You could go *home*."

He was suddenly very, very close. I couldn't see him, but I could smell his breath. I wrinkled my nose.

"Why would the king do that?" He'd been the one who sentenced me as a child.

"Yes, what could make up for treason on two counts? What service could you give the Crown that would let His Majesty overlook the fact you helped a vampire break out of Greymere?"

I could give Titus the Black Grimoire. I'd have to escape after, but giving Titus that tool could be enough to earn a pardon.

It would be a betrayal, however. And as much as Titus might technically serve the Crown, I didn't trust him. Not with that.

The pardon though? There was a very strong possibility it was a real offer. A tempting one.

"Righting that wrong would be a start," Titus finally said when it became clear I wouldn't answer. "Destroying the scourge of our kingdom. You'd be hailed as a *hero*, Koisemi. Your family name would be known for centuries for your bravery. You wouldn't just be pardoned, you'd be *welcomed* in court."

I wavered. For the briefest second, I considered what it would mean to be allowed to return home. Not surrounded by dangerous creatures who could kill me in a heartbeat. Ones who would maim children to get what they wanted. Instead, I could be among my own kind, living out of exile. Not a shameful life, but one I could live proudly in court, like my mother had always wanted

It cost me something to give that up and say, "I'm not interested. I've made a new life here." I had no intention of telling Titus my true plans were to go west of the kingdom.

"Look how keen you are to defend that life, even when it could be what kills you," Titus purred.

My spine stiffened. "Are you threatening me?"

"Me?" The spymaster made a sound of indignation. "How quick you are to forget that any of them would kill you in a heartbeat. Isn't that what nearly happened in the library just a few weeks ago?"

How did he know? Then again, he was a spy for a reason.

"The vampire was crazy." That's what Raphael had said—sometimes the old ones went insane.

"Do you really believe that?" Titus's laugh was cruel. "Or is that what you want to believe, because otherwise you betrayed your country for no reason? You're kept as a pet, a blood bag for their bastard king. You love being kept on a leash in a dark room."

Vampires couldn't lie. If Raphael said it, it must be true. Yet had he said the librarian had gone crazy? Or just that it happened sometimes? I tried to recall the exact wording.

"Open your eyes to the world you're living in, not the one you'd like to believe you are," Titus said. He was in front of me now. "I'll ask your answer again in one week, Samara. Even if you're as stupid as you appear, I expect your response may change."

I wish I could say Titus's offer hadn't haunted my visit with Amalthea, but it had. At my request, she'd shown me more of Damerel. But both she and Demos had refused to show me the parts I was most desperate to see: the blood donors.

Maybe desperate wasn't the right word. I didn't want to be reminded of the act. The memory of how it had felt with Raphael hadn't faded—his fangs buried in my neck, sensation ricocheting through my body. The shame of it, of being used to sustain another creature, the shame of how I would have let him take every last drop.

But I had to know. The three of them might have become my friends, but they were keeping some things secret. Titus's comments still lingered in my mind, seeds of doubt he'd masterfully planted. What if I really had blinded myself, let myself believe everything could be okay when I was sheltered from the truth?

That was why I doubled back after parting ways with Amalthea.

VASILISA DRAKE

Vampires and witches hadn't become mortal enemies simply because they were two tame, well-mannered species with slightly differing needs. They had warred over the years because vampires saw themselves at the top of the food chain and had taken and taken. Centuries ago, a great battle had broken out, and the Witch Kingdom emerged, having driven the vampires out of society. There had been a cost. We were surrounded on all sides, and lost access to the rest of the continent, as well as the ability to trade overseas. But it was for the best. That way, we were safe.

So, no, regardless of how much I'd come to trust Raphael, I couldn't believe voids had really given up everything and happily let vampires feed on them as needed.

Being in the second level felt different without the security of an escort. I pulled my cloak low over my head and clutched the bronze dagger in my hand.

I'd killed a vampire with that dagger. Gods, it was terrifying to be out alone, but I had to do this. I tried to remember what Raphael had said. No bravery without fear.

Well, I was afraid. But I had to know the truth, and that mattered more.

I knew exactly where to go: the district Amalthea was always careful to avoid. As I understood it, there had to be several different places for vampires to go drink, but much like restaurants cropped up in clusters in cities, so too did the vampire equivalent.

My stomach turned at the comparison, but I kept moving. The rule was the same in all cities—move with purpose, move fast.

Damerel held thousands of denizens, and the streets were moderately crowded at any time. I walked quickly, my heels digging into the dirt as I navigated the city.

An old wooden sign swung down from outside a building. Signs like that were used throughout witch cities—a dress from a seamstress, a necklace for a jeweler, a bed for an inn. This sign with a red droplet painted on it, there was no such sign in the Witch Kingdom. But I understood the meaning implicitly.

It was late, even for vampires. A pair of male vampires walked towards the building, arms braced around each other's shoulders.

"By blood, I'm starving," one said loudly to the other.

I flinched at the bold exclamation, praying the shadows held me tightly.

"Me too. I hope Sue's available tonight," the other replied.

The first vampire chuckled, craggy laugh carrying over to where I stood at the edge of an alleyway. "Sue's always available for you."

The two went in.

I didn't have a plan. I wanted to talk to some of the humans who worked there and find out what the truth was. See if they were really okay.

The building didn't have any windows, otherwise, I would have looked in them to get a sense of what I was walking into.

There was no choice. After a few more minutes of deliberation, I went inside.

The inside of the blood den was nothing I'd been prepared for. The building was grand, with columns at the entrance. Several vampires lingered around. A host stood at the front but paid me little mind. With my raven-black hair, I was obviously human, and therefore not a customer. I walked back. The entryway turned into a long hall with dozens of branching rooms. Women and men were posted at most, bodies curved invitingly against the doorway.

More than just their necks were exposed. Breasts were bare at minimum. I tried not to stare lest I get caught, but my cheeks were hot at the sight. Until I passed an occupied room, the velvet curtain not fully loose. The man sprawled out was entirely bare, appendages I'd only been vaguely aware of on display, and a vampire sat between his thighs... biting. I walked faster, my blood cold. I rounded a corner and pulled the curtain back slightly on a room to the left. No one was posted at the edge of it, but no sounds came from inside.

A girl was splayed backwards onto a low mattress.

Oh gods. I rushed over. She was my age, maybe a bit older, with beautiful, delicate features. Two punctures in her neck still dripped blood.

A BARGAIN SO BLOODY

I pressed my hand to her nose. Her breaths came faintly. I swallowed. She was alive.

Her eyes slowly opened, and she didn't seem at all startled I was leaning over her.

"Hey," I said urgently. "Wake up. Are you okay?"

"Back for more?" she purred.

I blinked at her. "I'm not a vampire."

She stared up at me and yawned. "Oh. Right. I don't know you. Who are you?"

"I'm Sam," I said quickly, trying to examine her body for wounds. And to my growing horror, I found them. There were bite marks all over, not just on her neck. "Are you okay?"

She didn't look it. Her skin was pale, her forehead glossy with dried sweat. "I feel great." She stretched her arms. "Reki just took a lot. He likes it rough, but he pays well."

My stomach twisted. "And you're okay with that?"

"Of course." She sighed into the mattress. "Nothing hurts when they bite."

I wanted to vomit. Her words were slow and slurred. Her eyes fluttered shut. I leaned over, trying to get a better look at her.

"Hey, who are you?"

I turned. An older woman stormed into the room. "You're not one of my courtesans."

"Does it matter?" I hissed. "She needs help!"

Concern crossed the woman's features. She pushed me aside and pressed her fingers to the base of the girl's throat.

The concern evaporated as she turned on me. "My girl is fine. Now, who are you? One of Marta's girls, trying to poach my best?"

If this was her best being "fine," I had serious concerns about the entirety of her operation. "I'm not with Marta. I came to check on how the girls are treated. I... work for King Raphael."

She arched a disbelieving brow at me, probably because I didn't sound like I believed the fumbled lie myself. "You're telling me the king ordered you to come here and check on how I run my business?"

Not exactly. In for a copper, in for a gold piece. Raphael never would have tolerated his orders being questioned though. He could say it was just because he was strong, but even when he was flayed open, bound by copper, he'd never lost the arrogance that kept his spine straight and his gaze level. I drew my shoulders back and stood eye-to-eye with the matron. If he could do it, I could at least pretend to have a fraction of his courage. "Are things so different here that you think the vampire king tolerates disobedience?" I forced my words to come out slowly, the way he so often did, and a zip of satisfaction went through me as the matron took a half step back.

"Of course not." Her tone had turned from accusatory to simply brusque. "I simply didn't realize who you were since you didn't identify yourself or come directly to me and instead slipped into one of our service rooms."

A BARGAIN SO BLOODY

I arched a brow at her, letting her bluster. "I'll be sure to let the king know you think his practices could be improved."

The matron paled. "No need for that. Why don't you join me in my office and tell me how I can be of service to the Crown?"

I allowed her to lead me deeper into the blood den. Unlike most of the rooms which only had a curtain, the matron's office was concealed by a heavy wooden door. She pushed it open and gestured to the two seats in front of her desk. I didn't want to sit with my back to the door. It would look strange to stand askance with the exit in sight, so I plopped down onto the very edge of the chair while the woman settled into a large plush chair that nearly drowned her. In the candlelight of the other room, I'd mistaken her hair for red, but now I saw it was more of a nutty brown. Her face was polished with the same cosmetics Amalthea used, but it was in heavy layers, the colors crumbling a bit at the edges of her lips and cheekbones. Unlike the minimal gossamer the workers wore, her chest was covered with a voluminous top that buttoned up as far as her chin and cinched at the wrists.

"I suppose I haven't introduced myself. I'm Latia, matron and owner of this blood den for more than thirty years. How may I be of service to the Crown?"

It would have been polite to introduce myself, but I couldn't even bring myself to give a fake name. "Describe your"—*disgusting, foul, exploitative*—"business for me."

Latia's puckered lips twitched downward at the simplicity of my question, but apparently my lie about being here on Raphael's orders held enough weight to stop her from voicing any more objections. "It's rather simple. Every human in Damerel is expected to contribute, and the most valuable asset any human has over vampires is fresh, warm blood. I recruit the girls—and men, of course—in order to provide a carefully cultivated selection that appeals to the higher echelons of vampire society. I've worked tirelessly to establish our humble little den. The vampire nobility know they can come to us for vibrant, well-nourished sustenance, and in return I make sure the compensation keeps all my people taken care of."

"So the vampires pay you and then you pass the coin on the workers?" I confirmed.

Latia shrugged. "Within reason. There are expenses to the upkeep of this establishment, their appearance, and so on. It's easier if I manage the money and they manage the clients, you see."

Latia's "within reason" and mine likely differed. Given the blissed-out state of the workers, though, they might not protest as much. "So all the vampires do is bite? No... touching?"

"Not hardly." She beamed. "Some dens keep the two services apart, but we want to keep our customers sated. *Those* needs often go together. Not always, of course, but there's something so wonderfully pleasant about the two combined, or so I'm told. I work hard to ensure our workers are appealing on all fronts."

Bile rose in my stomach. "And they're okay with that? The humans?"

A careless shrug. "One bite and no one is saying no. As I said, they're compensated."

I could believe that. Just the memory of Raphael's bite could turn my breathing shallow. But that had been different. Everything about Latia made my skin crawl. Perhaps even more so than the vampires. They were awful, yes, but they had to drink blood to survive. Latia had taken that hunger and turned it into a profit. I'd judged the humans for being fed on, but was she any better, facilitating deals while carefully covering her body, setting herself apart?

She continued: "Our vampire clientele only bite *with* permission *where* permitted. Each donor sets their own boundaries, within reason. The vampires are very careful. Nothing for the king to worry about, I assure you.

"How many humans do this work for you?" I asked.

"I cannot say arithmetic is my specialty." Latia furrowed her brow. "I have roughly fifty voids in employ, but as I said, we're rather exclusive. There are easily another forty dens, not counting private services, of course."

Too many. My stomach twisted. "And how many die every year from greedy vampires taking too much?"

Latia stiffened in her chair. "Any unexpected deaths are strictly dealt with."

"They are?"

She nodded. "Of course. The vampire is immediately banned from the premises, and any unpaid earnings go to the family. I pride myself on taking close care of my staff."

So one den closed the door, but thirty-nine were still open. Anger coursed through me. At Latia, at the hypothetical vampires, at Raphael for letting this happen. I got up from the seat with a sudden urge for a scalding bath. "I'll see myself out."

I didn't want to spend another second in that woman's company, or in that godscursed building. But before I could go, I needed to check on the girl I'd seen. Latia obviously didn't give a damn, but my conscience wouldn't let me go until I saw she was alright, no matter how badly my self-preserving side screeched at me to leave. I doubled back the way we came, trying to unwind the path we'd taken. Years surrounded by identical walls at Greymere had honed my sense of direction. I brushed the cloth screen aside, peering into the room. All the rooms looked the same, but I was pretty sure this one was correct.

"Hello?" I called from the edge of the room.

No answer. The bed was rumpled like I remembered. It was impossible to tell from the doorframe if anyone was in the bed. I went inside and crossed the room to the bed. What I'd thought was possibly the girl had been a pillow covered in discarded blankets. Relief. I should have felt relief. If she was gone, it meant she was well enough to stand, or someone had taken her. She wasn't lying dead as I'd feared.

Just get out, Samara. That self-preserving voice grew louder and louder. *Protect yourself*.

I'd done my best. I'd learned about the blood dens, and I reviled them. As unsavory as it was, I'd be naïve to consider anything a revelation. If I hadn't been so focused on learning about the grimoire and being scared of my own shadow, I'd have realized this without Titus rubbing my nose in it. My gaze snagged on layers of dried blood on the fitted sheets, dark splotches of red and brown underneath. I tugged the coverlet over and turned towards the door.

And there, blocking the doorway, was a vampire with hungry eyes and pointed fangs.

"Well, don't you smell delicious?"

Chapter 42

"I'm the king's Chosen," I blurted. It was the first thing that came to mind.

"Oh, is that the fantasy you offer?" The vampire stepped closer. He wasn't as big as Raphael or Demos, but he towered over me. My legs began to shake.

"No, I'm the king's," I repeated. On reflex, I took a step back and knocked into the bed.

"Then call me the king." His words came out a bit slow, his footfall at an awkward angle that lacked the usual vampire grace. He reminded me more of Nelson than Raphael. "Pretty thing. Haven't seen you at Latia's before."

"I'm telling you, don't come near me." My voice was growing louder, more desperate. The curtain no doubt muffled some sound, and the den was far from quiet, but why wasn't someone coming?

"Blood love the gimmicks she comes up with," the vampire swore appreciatively and continued his stumble-stroll towards me.

No. *I'm not defenseless.* Anger coursed through me. I had beaten the vampire in the library—narrowly. This one was at least partly incapacitated. I drew my dagger underneath the cover of my cloak and drew my feet apart into the fighting stance Demos had taught me. This vampire didn't yet realize—didn't believe—I was a threat.

You'll be underestimated in just about any fight. We'll make sure to use it to your advantage, Demos had told me on that first day.

Once I attacked him, he'd realize I wasn't some meek little donor. Which meant I only had one shot.

He was just two feet away when I closed the gap, thrusting the dagger as far as I could into his chest. Delight lit his features for a flicker of a second, thinking I was embracing him, but at the last fraction of a second he twisted, realizing what I was doing. Rage burned in those red eyes.

"You bitch!" he roared.

I had missed.

I was dead.

But as quickly as the realization came, the sight in front of me transformed.

The vampire was pushed aside and rammed into the wall on my left. Towering over him was Raphael, teeth bared.

"She. Wasn't. Lying," he snarled.

And then with a twist of his other hand, the vampire's head popped off the body and rolled across the floor.

Disgust and anger warred inside me. The vampire's blood spilled out, but only a second later the body decomposed into dust.

My chest heaved from the violent mix of emotions.

And while I composed myself, Raphael watched me.

"What are you doing here?" I hissed. "You... you just killed him." I wasn't shedding a tear for the vampire, but the sheer violence of Raphael's movements, decisive and powerful, made my puny stabbing look like child's play.

Before, he'd ordered the snap of a neck to make a point.

Now, he'd ripped this vampire's head off in fury.

"I will kill anyone who lays a hand on you." His words weren't composed the way they usually were, not the smooth silk of night sky but a thunderous storm cloud. "Now tell me what you're doing here."

The anger from before swelled up, but now, instead of being divided between Latia and the other blood dens and all vampires, it was concentrated solely on their king. "I said I wanted to see a blood den. You all refused."

Raphael prowled closer, but I didn't back away. "And this is the one you picked?"

I scoffed. "What, should I have found a less exploitative one?"

Raphael looked slightly affronted. "Exploitative? The humans are paid for their service. They're here willingly. You may not like their choices, but it doesn't make them wrong."

I couldn't even look at Raphael. "Of course they're willing. After the first bite, who would say no to a second?" Wasn't that what Latia had said? I crossed to the other side of the room, away from Raphael and the bloodied bed and the pile of ash-filled clothing.

But Raphael was at my heels.

"You did." His voice had eased some.

It was on the tip of my tongue to admit I had dreamed of that bite over and over, had imagined asking him to take from me again. Only sheer stubbornness had stopped me from making the request. But that confession would cost me. Giving in to my attraction to Raphael would ruin me. Letting him bite me? It would shred my very soul.

I made certain those emotions were tucked behind my mental barriers and said nothing, eyes weaving over the peeling wallpaper.

"What would you have us do instead?" Now he was at my back. His shadow met mine on the wall. "Vampires need blood, much the same as you need air or water."

"Why not just take from animals? You did fine when we traveled living like that."

Okay, perhaps not quite *fine* from what he had said. But surely that was better. Every vampire had started as a human. Didn't they see the betrayal in that?

Or were they all humans like Crowley had been, monsters who felt entitled to harm anyone necessary for their own gain?

"Why should we?" Raphael retorted. "There's an order to things."

"And that order will always have the weak at the bottom, and the strong taking what they wish from the top," I snapped, turning around abruptly.

I regretted it. Raphael was even closer than I'd realized. I had to stare up at him.

"I repeat, they are not *taken*. Every human here is in my kingdom willingly, giving their blood willingly. It could be much worse."

But it could be better. "And would they do this if they had a better option?"

"Did you serve in Greymere because it was your choice, Samara? Did they pay you a wage?"

I jerked back.

"*That* was slavery. *This* is a choice. There's a difference."

It was hardly a choice anyone in their right mind would make. The bites were addictive. Of course they stayed and let Latia offer their veins for any vampire with coin. "I never asked my question the other night. You owe me one, Raphael, so tell me truthfully: Do you really think this system is fair? Do you think it's safe? For all the words about choice, I told that vampire no and he was still going to feed on me. If he killed me, what then? Is it fair that at most he'd just be banned from this den and free to go to any other?"

Raphael was still, yet I swore I could feel the riot of emotions in him. "What he attempted... it will be dealt with."

"Dealt with?" I flung an arm in the direction of the wall. What had been fear when the vampire stalked towards me was crystallizing now as anger. "*Raphael, he's already dead*. And he's only dead because someone bigger and stronger than him stopped him. Because you took pity on me."

"Is that what you think?" He cocked his head. "That I pity you?"

I gave that the derisive snort it deserved. "You expect me to believe that's not what this is? At every turn, I'm weak, and you're strong. I'm there serving Nelson for years, and one day in, you kill him. I give myself to the Monastery, willing to debase myself for protection, and you kill them all too. Fifth hell, even now I freeze at the sight of blood. I let you feed me, clothe me, like a useless infant. I have no magic, just the barest grasp on a language of a book you don't even seem to care about. If it's not pity..." I trailed off. *Then what?* I wanted to scream.

"It is *not* pity." Raphael took a step forward, and now I inched back, pressed into the wall. "You don't see the events as I do. Twice, now, you've defended yourself from bigger, stronger foes. You work tirelessly to prove yourself. You claim you freeze, but I've seen you: when needed, you act. Your mind is always working, solving puzzles at a speed even I marvel at. In the temple, you removed a dozen arrows from my back when I was drenched in blood, so no, you do not 'freeze.' Surely food and clothing are the least I owe you for my life. I do not contend you were not afraid, Samara. But you do not let fear stop you."

He drew closer. I was caged between him and the wall. My heart thundered in my chest, but it wasn't fear now. Even the anger was distant. The panes of his face were in stark relief, eyes vivid and beguiling. The white strands of his hair fell toward me as he bent his head to look down.

"I do not pity you," Raphael repeated. "Little viper, I find you irresistible."

I scoffed. "That's madness."

"Because you make me mad," he growled. His words were like lightning in my veins, electrifying, terrifying. His hand came to my cheek, brushing my hair aside. All my thoughts halted. Moments ago, I'd feared death. Now, I wasn't sure what to expect. For Raphael to take me back to the castle, or to chastise me for being careless.

What I didn't expect was for him to kiss me.

He grabbed my cheeks and captured my lips. I stiffened in surprise, unsure and unsteady. I'd never kissed anyone. But Raphael was patient, coaxing. Desire stirred deep inside me, a wick catching fire with every brush of his tongue. He guided me, and my blood warmed, desperation lighting in my veins. His taste was potent and all at once it was everything to me. There was no room where a vampire had been killed, no enemy kingdoms, no spymaster dogging at my heels.

There was only me, Raphael, and this burning tension that had ignited.

Want him. It didn't matter I only had half a clue what I was doing. He drew me deeper into the kiss, his other hand coming around my side and pressing me against him. He tasted like darkness and temptation. I lifted my hands to his head, pulling him closer. He groaned against my lips at the movement, and I arched at the sound. More. I wanted more of that. My tongue curled in his mouth, a bold exploration.

Then it found the point of his fang. Copper colored the kiss at once.

I jerked back.

Blood.

Raphael didn't press me into another kiss, but he didn't move back. His red eyes were lit ruby red, the glow of a vampire who just had blood. Gods damn it. The taste remained in my own mouth. A strange tingle coated my lips, as if I could feel his absence.

Raphael kissed me.

I wanted him to do it again. Before common sense chased away the blissful feeling that had started in my body, before I remembered that the perfect, handsome face before me was normally topped by a crown.

He went still. Waiting. Assessing.

If I reached for him, he'd let me kiss him. Despite all my inexperience, I knew that with every fiber of my being.

"Raphael, you promised me one more answered question. Do you believe this system is fair, with the blood dens and the humans?" *The strong ruling the weak?*

I wished I could have been surprised when he finally gave his answer.

"Yes."

There was no more kissing after that.

And as Raphael escorted me back to my chambers—across from his own—I came to another conclusion.

It wouldn't be enough to translate the grimoire.

I would need to steal it.

The necromancer that Raphael had failed to locate—I'd find them. I'd give them the book.

I'd give the monsters something to fear.

Chapter 43

I HAD LIVED IN rags for the better part of my life at this point. Rags were bordering on an overstatement, actually, since even the most worn material was quickly commandeered by those bigger and stronger. There had been nights I'd wished more strongly for fresh, soft, dresses than I had food.

And I would happily have agreed to never wear anything but those rags again if it meant I didn't have to endure one more minute of this dress fitting. Between Amalthea's exacting sense of aesthetics and standing half-naked while two vampires worked to mold the tarps to me, tension had every muscle in my body on the brink of cramping.

"No, that's not quite right," Amalthea murmured to the seamstress for what must have been the tenth time since we'd arrived.

The seamstress obliged and moved the bodice a sliver higher.

It was three days after I'd first come here with Amalthea. Three days since I'd been cornered by Titus. Three days since I'd kissed Raphael in the blood den. Now, I was standing on a raised platform like a mannequin. Amalthea went back and forth over hemlines and skirt designs and sleeve shapes and everything else I'd never wanted to know about with the vampiress shop owner and head seamstress, Bertha. At my feet, another vampire was pinning the skirt in place.

I'd soaked the fabric of my back with how much I was sweating, but I endured it. Apparently there were no human dressmakers to help. *Thea is here*. I repeated those three words over and over again like a spell. *Thea is here, Thea is here*. She wouldn't let anything happen. And maybe I wanted to prove Titus wrong. To prove *myself* wrong.

When Amalthea had proposed dress shopping... it wasn't that I wanted for clothing by any stretch, but I hadn't wanted to disappoint her. Friendship was a foreign thing for me. The closest I'd come was a relationship with my half-brother, but that had been secret.

"Maybe a jot lower," Amalthea mused, and once again the shift was adjusted. "Sam, what do you think?"

I thought I'd rather skip whatever event this dress was intended for, but that would hurt Thea's feelings. Instead I said, "I'll defer to you." Because I couldn't tell the difference between this position and any of the past dozen.

The witch nodded.

A sharp pain hit my calf. "Ouch!"

"Oh, my lady, I'm... sorry..." The seamstress pinning my legs trailed off, seeming transfixed. She'd accidentally stuck me with a pin.

She was still, in the way only vampires could be, staring at the spot of blood that had spilled onto the fabric.

I was frozen like a rabbit that had realized it was all too close to a hungry kobold.

"Be more careful," Amalthea snapped. Her tone was harsher than I'd ever heard, but already the tingle of magic lit around me, the slight pain disappearing. In her hand was a now-blank card that must have contained the healing magic. She'd activated it almost immediately.

"Oh, my lady, I am so, so sorry," the vampire at my knees stammered. "It was an accident, I swear. Please don't tell the king!"

Bertha pushed the girl away. "My sincere apologies, Lady Samara. I assure you, I do not tolerate this sloppiness in my shop. I'll see that the girl is dealt with."

I stiffened at the tone in the seamstress's voice. "What do you mean by that?"

"A proper beating, I assure you. Something that will make an impression no matter the immortal healing. And of course, I'll pull out her fangs."

I stared at Bertha and her certainty faded a fraction. "I can pull the fangs out again if that's not to your satisfaction. Or would you like to administer a beating of your own as well?"

For a moment, I was so angry I was struck still. Always with this brutal, barbaric form of justice. When the shop owner parted her lips again to add whatever else to the girl's unending list of punishment, I found my voice.

"You won't be doing any of that."

The girl cringed.

"Of course, Lady Samara, I didn't mean to imply I would take away this privilege from King Raphael. If he prefers to take his justice personally, I would never dream of interfering."

Whatever the girl thought Raphael would do, it had her shaking. After what I'd seen in his court, I understood why. I'd never seen a vampire so afraid, not even Janessa when Raphael had ordered her lover's death. I thought of them as fearsome, near all-powerful creatures.

But looking at her peering up at me with beseeching eyes, lip quivering, all I could think was that I had no doubt looked the same way at Nelson more times than I cared to remember.

"To be clear," I said slowly, "in your view, justice for mistakenly pricking my skin with one of the several hundred pins currently wrapped around me warrants beating and mutilation." Before I could be misinterpreted again, I added, "Or worse. To you, that's fairness?"

Bertha clearly had no safe way to answer. She thought I wanted retribution, so she'd piled on as many horrors as she could manage. Telling me she wouldn't do anything went against all she knew.

"Of course, I am responsible for my staff." Her voice was considerably quieter now. "I will also submit myself to the will of the king. Even if he wishes to flay me—"

I winced because my back still bore the scars of those memories.

I cut her off: "None of that is going to happen. It was an accident. What's your name?" I asked the girl.

"J-Josephine," she whispered.

I nodded. "Josephine apologized. Amalthea healed me. That's all there is to it. There will be no beating, no defanging, no firing, no flaying. Is that understood?" I wasn't sure where this imperious tone had come from. Gods knew I'd never spoken for myself that way, but seeing Josephine... I straightened my spine as I stared at the shopkeeper.

"Of course," the shopkeeper said with considerably less enthusiasm than what she'd used to describe the punishment.

I'd have been more skeptical, but vampires couldn't lie.

"What are you all ogling at?" Amalthea snapped. I turned and saw every vampire was staring at me with that same stillness, the scent of my blood drawing their attention. I hadn't noticed, being so focused on the girl. "It's as though you ladies have never smelled blood before. Go to a blood den and stop acting like fools."

The onlookers collectively turned away at Amalthea's command.

I wanted to go home, but I had a point to prove. "Josephine, would you mind finishing pinning the hemline?"

Josephine's head bobbed up and down with vampiric speed. "At once, my lady!"

As much as I wanted to leave, I wouldn't let the shop owner blame Josephine for us leaving sooner than planned. I cast Amalthea a look to try to gauge what she thought of how I'd handled it, if I'd overstepped, but I couldn't read the expression on her face.

"It will be magnificent," the shopkeeper assured me when the draping was finished. I dipped my head in acknowledgment and finally stepped off the platform. Despite my brave front, I hadn't wanted vampire fingers on my skin any longer. I went behind the curtain and pulled on my dress from before. When I returned, a trio of vampire nobles tittered on the edges, eyeing me.

I looked from them to Amalthea, who heaved a beleaguered sigh before slightly turning her body towards them while still maintaining eye contact with me. "Ladies, surely you have better things to do than blatantly gossip all day."

"Perhaps we only wanted to get a glimpse at the fashion the king's Chosen has selected," one vampiress retorted.

"Perhaps," Amalthea echoed.

Perhaps was an easy enough way around their inability to lie.

"I'm sure it's nothing more interesting than any other ballgown," I said, coming to Amalthea's side. It was a little dismissive of Bertha, but I wasn't exactly feeling charitable.

"Is that not the gown she will wear for the Tri-Lunar Eclipse?" the same vampire said. She responded to Thea, not me, however.

The term… I'd heard it before. At the first ball. The vampire that had clung a little too closely to Raphael had mentioned the same event. Amalthea cut the conversation off by hooking my arm with hers and leading us from the shop. Once we had gone half a block, I finally asked her for details.

"Why is everyone so focused on me attending the Tri-Lunar Eclipse?"

Thea wove us expertly through the crowded streets. It was the middle of the night, which was effectively midday for vampires. "*Who* is everyone? Those ninnies?"

Okay, everyone was an exaggeration. But I spoke to hardly any vampires, and twice now it had come up. "Them, others," I said vaguely. "It seems important."

"It is," Thea admitted slowly, still shepherding me along. "It's a rare event. Eclipses hold particular significance in vampire culture, and the tri-lunar one is rare enough it's seen as quite the event. There's a whole assortment of customs, speeches given, and so on. Honestly, I think the vampires just want something to make a fuss about given their overly long lives."

It sounded like any other ball. But there was something a little *too* casual about her explanation. "That doesn't explain why they're so focused on me specifically," I pressed.

Thea didn't seem to want to answer based on the long pause before she spoke again. "As I said, there are customs. And one of them revolves around the king drinking from his Chosen. There's a whole lot to do with the symbol of power, prosperity, and on and on."

I stopped in the middle of the street, feet suddenly rooted in the spot. Thea halted abruptly with me since we still had our arms linked. "Raphael intends to drink from me? At this ceremony?"

"It *is* the custom," Amalthea said, voice carefully neutral. "Besides, being bitten isn't unpleasant, is it?"

I flushed. Worse than that, it was the opposite. "Raphael never said anything about this when he decided to claim me as his Chosen." He'd told me he wouldn't drink from me. But now he'd put me in a position where he had to. "If those are the terms, he should just *un*claim me."

Amalthea rolled her eye. "Samara, I promise you wouldn't find that status preferable in the slightest."

I frowned. "Why not? You aren't his Chosen or anything and no one bites you."

The oracle barked a laugh and tried to tug me forward. "Oh, there are a couple reasons for that, but that's a conversation for another time. Suffice it to say, you will remain Raphael's Chosen. He's not wrong that it's the best way to keep you safe. There's little to be done to sway the king from any course of action that he believes is done for your protection."

"I don't want him to drink from me. I won't let him."

"You will."

I flinched at the certainty in her tone. "I won't."

Amalthea faced me, but her gaze went foggy as if she wasn't really aware of her surroundings. "Samara, I see his fangs at your bare throat in the gown that was pinned today. The sky is lit above from starlight where you've bent your neck for him. He will take from you." She blinked and gave me an apologetic smile. "I don't like to do that, but sometimes there's comfort in knowing what's coming to pass."

I swallowed, my throat tight. So I was to accept it was a forgone conclusion?

"What about another donor? Couldn't he take from them?" I was desperate.

She shook her head and gave me a final, insistent pull. I no longer had the energy to force us to stay. "I told you what I saw, and I'm never wrong. That's one reason my kind is so hated."

"I don't hate you," I said quickly. The opposite. Thea hadn't just looked after my safety, but she'd worked hard to be my friend even though I was only here temporarily.

Even though I was going to betray all of them when I took the grimoire to the necromancer.

Thea gave me a sad smile, her remaining eye softening with sympathy. "If he took from another, it would be a grave insult, hurt your standing here permanently—Raphael doesn't drink from living donors anyway, so it's you or no one."

Was it really such a forgone conclusion? Raphael hadn't said a word. Did he expect to break his vows so easily?

"If I wasn't here, then he would have to drink from another," I protested.

"Sam." I hadn't heard Amalthea's voice so soft. "Raphael does not tolerate the bonds he forms with those he drinks from. The only time he drinks from a human is at the eclipse."

"So he can just not bond with them like in the past," I insisted.

She shook her head. "No, Sam. If he drinks another human, he makes sure there's no bond. He drains them completely."

The implication of her words hit me like a blow. Part of me wanted to lower my mental shields and push my displeasure towards him. Instead, I turned it inward, walking with Amalthea without really being there. Maybe Titus was right. I'd lived my entire life knowing vampires couldn't be trusted. Any so-called status I had here hinged on letting Raphael do anything he wanted to me, apparently.

I didn't belong here.

"He didn't tell me any of this." It hurt, like a twisted knife.

Amalthea increased our pace. "Perhaps he would have if you were not avoiding him." There was the barest note of something in her voice. Censure?

"I'm not avoiding him," I lied, even as I admitted to myself she might have had a point. Ever since he found me in the donor den that night, I'd taken care to avoid encountering Raphael. I took meals in my room, and insisted on having Amalthea walk me back to my rooms.

My cheeks heated at the memory of the night, part blush and part fury. I refused to meet the sidelong glance she cast my way. I wasn't fooling either of us, but unless her oracle vision had shown her what happened between the vampire king and me, I wasn't saying a word.

Amalthea seemed inclined to say more, but something caught her attention. She startled and tried to usher me down an alleyway.

"This is a better path," she said urgently.

I frowned. "But we're nearly back—"

My words broke off as I saw what Amalthea had tried to spare me. A small cluster of Damerel's denizens lingered around a corner, a few pinching noses. Two legs were splayed out on the ground, visible.

VASILISA DRAKE

I was already moving, Amalthea's urging to not look barely registered as I walked closer.

There, on the sidewalk, half in an alley, half out, was the mangled body of a girl. Her throat had been torn wide open, her head barely hanging on by the slightest tendon. Her entire front was painted red with blood, the scraps of fabric that had once been a sheer dress ripped to shreds.

I'd seen this girl. The one who'd been weak in bed at the donor den.

She was dead. A vampire had done this.

I'd seen this before.

Blood and blood and blood. A woman's flesh, torn apart. An arm flung to one edge of the arena, the arterial blood cascading through the air. The cries for mercy cut off as her corpse is shredded by the vampire's ruthless fangs. He's not biting her, he's mauling her. The once fine brocade of her gown is soaked through. When he drains her neck, he moves to other arteries, trying to pull more from her body. He rips apart her limbs like he's trying to crack open her body for any spare drop of blood. When he's done, my world has ended. There is no more of the woman who birthed me, who raised me. Just pieces of skin scattered in all corners of the arena. The others are cheering. All I can do is stare.

I keep staring. The two scenes overlapped in my mind. *She's dead because of me*. The accusation echoed through me. I wasn't even sure which woman I mean. Both? If I had told Raphael what I had seen more precisely, would he have been able to make sure she was safe?

A BARGAIN SO BLOODY

Or was this every human's fate at the hands of vampires?
Dead. Not just dead, but destroyed. Devoured.
For what? For some animal's snack?
Her sightless eyes met mine, accusing.
I have to get the necromancer the grimoire.

Chapter 44

"You're avoiding me."

I shrieked and nearly dropped my towel. When I'd entered the bathing chamber, my room had been empty. Now, Raphael was lounging on my bed, his hands tucked behind his head, flexing his biceps in the confines of his white shirt. His ankles were crossed, boots resting on the coverlet in a way that would have earned me an ear-ringing lecture from my mother.

In contrast, I was naked, save for the towel clutched perilously in one hand.

"Expecting privacy in my own room hardly counts as avoiding you," I snapped.

A BARGAIN SO BLOODY

Anger was good. Anger that let me cover the flush I felt encroaching on every inch of my body as Raphael arched a single eyebrow at me. The anger wasn't about Raphael in the room—it was about the mutilated corpse I'd seen yesterday. But having him here in my space made it impossible to wall away those emotions, so I chose to focus on the immediate ones that made my blood roar, not the memory.

Part of me wondered, *Did he like what he saw?* Now that I'd put on some fat and muscle, turning into a woman more substantial than the skin-and-bones waif he'd met in Greymere...

I tightened my mental shields and kicked the thought aside. That was the trouble with kissing vampire kings who looked like Raphael. You started to wonder if your body was pleasing rather than when you'd outlive your usefulness and would be abandoned once more.

"You walked in on me wearing a towel," he replied when he'd completed his appraisal. "I'd argue returning the favor should be expected."

Unfortunately, he finished his a second before I finished mine, and the curve of his lips let me know he was aware I'd been looking too.

I skirted the room to get to the changing screen, where my dress was perched.

"I'd rather you leave now."

"Eventually," he repeated.

No one made the vampire king do a single thing he didn't want to.

I blew out a breath of frustration. Either I grabbed my dress and marched across the room *again* to change in the bathing room with my tail between my legs, or I got out of my now-soaked towel and dressed in the same room as Raphael.

Even he can't see through solid objects, I chided myself. Still, it felt utterly intimate to be changing clothes with Raphael in the room. I threw the dress on and walked out from the screen so I could cross my arms over my chest and tell Raphael what I thought of him camping on my bed.

For a long moment, neither of us spoke.

"Amalthea mentioned you saw something unpleasant yesterday."

My fingers pressed harder into the flesh of my upper arms. The girl, massacred by a careless vampire. I didn't even know her name. Her killer probably didn't either. The scene where we'd found her body replayed over and over in my mind, but it was like I was a distant viewer. I saw it in my waking hours, and during what little sleep I'd had last night, I replayed a scenario where I'd done something different in the den and saved her.

I failed in each one.

"I didn't feel it, you know," Raphael continued. "I would have come if I'd felt it, but there wasn't even a ripple. It's impressive your shield didn't slip even when dealing with such a shock. You've been a quick study in learning to secure your emotions."

He called it impressive, yet neither of us was impressed. For me, it made sense. I'd spent my entire life suppressing my feelings in front of others, and in turn, to myself. And I'd had extra motivation to block out Raphael. Now that I planned to take the grimoire once I finished using his resources to translate it, it was all the more important I hid my true feelings. As exposed as I'd felt with only my towel for modesty, I felt completely exposed at the thought of Raphael feeling my emotions.

"And that's what bothers you. The fact you couldn't feel my emotions. Not that an innocent girl was mutilated by one of your citizens."

Raphael made no denial. "These things happen. *You* are my priority, not some random human who signed up as a donor."

Because in whatever moral compass he followed, the humans didn't matter. I did. Knowing whether I was upset was of paramount importance. But the fact I was upset one of my kind was killed by one of his meant nothing.

Titus was right.

"Fine," I snarled, my fingers curling into fists. "You want to know my emotions? Here."

They unfurled inside me. I hadn't simply locked them away from Raphael, but myself. Now, I let it all pour out of me. The anger. The disgust. The hatred for the one who had maimed that girl was overwhelming. I despised them all for being complicit. The ones who walked by. The ones who would let whatever vampire feed again. The ones who stole children, the ones who hurled them into ravines for their own gain. The hatred I'd known since childhood, the memories that had tormented me for years—I unleashed them too. Raphael recoiled, just slightly, as each one slammed into him.

The fear I felt walking around the halls of Damerel.

The helplessness when I saw her body.

The unending hatred for vampires.

And then, when they'd all landed true, I shoved my mental walls high, reeling back my errant emotions until they were tucked away in a tidy corner, the same place I put all the inconvenient feelings that got between me and survival.

Raphael looked to the other edge of the room, his gaze distant.

"Well?" I demanded, dissatisfied by the way he just sat there. "Did that please you? Did that voyeuristic look at my inner feelings satisfy your curiosity?"

Raphael didn't turn to look at me. Instead, with that terrifying, preternatural speed, he simply moved from the bed to the space in front of me in the time it took me to blink.

"I want you to be safe," he hissed. "I don't crave your fear out of some perverse desire to make sure you realize exactly how breakable you are, but to be there at your side so no one elsc does so."

I flinched. *Breakable*. Vampires couldn't lie. That's how he saw me.

Most days it was how I saw myself. Weak, breakable, pathetic. It made me scared. Made me cower around those stronger to appease them. Yet somehow, though I was no stronger than any other void, when Raphael said it, I didn't feel like I was confronted with a truth. I felt like I was presented with an injustice, and it made me furious.

"Don't think I've forgotten how you slipped out without an escort." His hands were around my biceps, not squeezing, but pressing in enough that I felt caged in. "Do you realize," he said with deadly calm, "how easily that could have been you? When you decided to sneak out into the dark corners of my city, did you not stop and realize just how monumentally *stupid* that was?"

Stupid. Breakable. So much for strong and clever. "Am I safe or am I not?" I retorted. "You tell me no one will touch me. You make these promises that you yourself don't seem to believe. They mean nothing."

His red eyes seared me. "Is that what you think?"

No. Yes. I don't know! I wanted to scream. "How simple the dividing line for you—if a human is worthy of your attention, then all should perish for looking at them. Yet if they live in your kingdom, with you as their ruler, trust you to care for them, they're fools in your eyes. Veins to be tapped for your real citizens to feast on."

Raphael scoffed. "Do you think your old king is any better?"

"I daresay he couldn't be worse. You take what you want, Raphael. You and all the vampires. I understand the hierarchy you've set. I'm to be paraded around as your personal meal next week. Amalthea told me—something you didn't bother to do."

"Amalthea said *what*?" Raphael growled.

"The Tri-Lunar Eclipse. She'd seen you at my neck, despite all your promises to never drink from me again." Raphael's lips parted as if to protest, but I continued on before he could interject. "Wasn't this your plan all along?"

"It was *not*," Raphael growled. "I had another plan."

"Oh?" I nearly snarled the word. "And was this plan to drink from another human and kill them?"

Raphael flinched as if I'd struck him.

But he didn't deny it.

I shook my head in disbelief. "You were going to kill someone. And you probably weren't even going to tell me. I'm upset because a human girl was killed, and you were *about to do the same thing*. So fine, Raphael. Drink from me. Claim my lifeblood if that's what will save some unlucky human's life, but know you're no different than any of the other monsters. The only difference is that you treat me a little better, and the others see me as your pet, so that when they kill a human in their bloodlust, it's one you don't have use for." I broke out of his grip with a tug of my shoulders. "Now, leave so I can get back to being *useful*, Your Majesty."

Raphael remained rooted in his spot. "Do you not see that you're different?"

As if this conversation hadn't proved he saw me as he did every other worthless mortal, except that I was *his*. "I'm useful, as we agreed." I gave the Black Grimoire a pointed look. "So I'd best get back to work."

Still, Raphael remained. "Have you had success in your translations?" His voice was soft, coaxing.

I didn't want small talk, but the quickest way to get rid of him was to pretend everything was fine. "It's slow. Slower than I expected, so I have nothing to show for it. I should get back to it," I repeated.

Raphael made no move to leave. He wasn't oblivious. He simply didn't care.

"By the fifth hell, Raphael, I want to be alone!" Apparently, I wasn't so good at pretending.

Finally, Raphael moved. We crossed in opposite directions, me moving to the couch where the grimoire was and him towards the door. When he reached the doorframe, he paused.

"I mean it," I said quietly from across the room. The urge to yell had passed in those few steps and now I could scarcely whisper. But no doubt he would hear every word. "I'll go with you to the ball. Just leave me be until then."

Raphael left.

I watched the door for several minutes, as if expecting him to come back.

To apologize? To say he'd find the vampire who murdered the donor and see justice done? To say he'd been wrong about the humans? About me? To say I didn't need to go to the ball?

I didn't know what I wanted from Raphael. Worse, I seemed to want *everything*, and everything was a delusion.

When I, at last, was confident he wasn't coming back, I opened the grimoire. I'd been lying to Raphael for weeks now. Since I'd translated the opening line and realized it was the key to undoing the vampires, I'd thought of little else. Some parts were hard to interpret—winding prose, detailed origins of the goddess Anagenni, the meaning of death and all other kinds of philosophical dribble that didn't mean anything concrete.

I slipped out the sheet where I'd translated the first true passage and traced my fingers over the dried ink on the parchment. I'd nearly memorized the words.

The undead bow to the necromancer. One witch is gifted to the world every two hundred years with Anagenni's blessing. They alone can right the balance.

At first, I'd concluded Raphael must not realize what he had in his possession if he was letting me translate it. In the days since, I'd dismissed the thought. This was why Raphael hunted them. Because vampires weren't stronger than all witches after all. That was why he'd taken the grimoire, so even if this necromancer rose to power they'd be weak. The book likely gave some hint of who it was or some secrets to their magic the vampires could use against them.

Somewhere out there was a witch who would be able to take on the vampires. To stop them from killing humans as they so pleased.

Once I finished, I planned to help them with the translated grimoire. But the truth was, I had no idea where to look. And every day wasted in searching would cost more lives.

I needed to do something more immediate to make the vampires realize they weren't so untouchable.

That us weak, breakable mortals could fight back instead of being fodder.

Hours later, when the castle was quiet, I slipped out of my room once more.

That was why I slid a small parchment with one word scribbled on it behind the false rock Titus had shown me.

Yes

Chapter 45

"You're going to die when you see the dress," Amalthea declared as she burst through the door the moment I opened it.

An eruption of red engulfed the space between us. I blinked at the color. It was startlingly bright, with layers and layers of skirts in a vibrant red hue.

The exact shade of freshly spilled blood.

Gods, I don't want to do this.

But time had run out. Tonight was the ceremony.

"They finished not a moment too soon," Amalthea continued, strolling into my room. "We've only hours before the eclipse." She was comfortable in my space, which made sense since I'd spent most of the past week holed up in my room. I went to training every morning, as instructed, using the practice to exhaust my body and escape the memories. I napped right after, the only decent sleep I got. Sometimes I hoped the music might help chase them away, but I didn't want to spend any time lingering in the halls before retreating to the safety of my room. Then Amalthea would knock on my door with supper and join me, carefully avoiding the topic she most wanted to discuss: my fight with Raphael. Any time she brought it up, I ended the conversation, so she learned to dance around it while filling the otherwise oppressive silence with lighthearted court gossip. This week, the focus had all been on the eclipse.

Which was tonight.

I swallowed. The last thing I'd said to Raphael was that I would go with him, but I hadn't heard a word since. A part of me still hoped he wouldn't take me up on it, would show me it wasn't as inevitable as Amalthea insisted. But her presence said otherwise.

"Let's get this over with." I hoped my vague disinterest would cover the fact the thought of the evening's ball made me increasingly nervous.

Amalthea gave me a look I couldn't quite decipher and gestured over to the vanity. I scratched my palms, anxious.

Could she see what was coming?

I hadn't heard back from Titus, but when I caved and checked yesterday, the note was gone. I'd thought he would make a move immediately, but I was waiting in suspense.

And in the interim, I was going to play the role of Raphael's Chosen in the bloodiest way possible.

Around Amalthea's side was a satchel of cosmetics. She spilled the contents over the counter, turning each bottle over, looking at me, and then discarding or setting aside the acceptable options until she had picked out a suitable selection for this occasion.

Normally I enjoyed talking with Amalthea, and she was eager to oblige, but both of us were fairly quiet. She murmured directions to me—close my eyes, open them, part my lips, shut them, tilt left, tilt right. Under her direction, my face transformed from plain to striking, with bright red sparkles around my eyelids, and sharp crimson on my lips. She artfully arranged my hair into a swept-up design, pinned in place with a silver ruby clip and ornamented with other jewels. To complete the ensemble, she clipped long, pinching earrings to my lobes.

"Now your dress," she instructed, pushing me to the bathroom to change. Too tired to argue, I slipped behind closed doors, shucked off my day-wear, and pulled the dress on. Amalthea entered the room and laced the gown, looking at me in the mirror.

This is what the king's Chosen would wear.

I hardly recognized myself. From my crown to my feet, I was bathed in red. My skin was pink, my face painted. It was as though I appraised a stranger—*beautiful*, I thought at once. A prize for a vampire.

I wanted to light the dress on fire.

Instead, I thanked Amalthea for everything, for arranging my makeup, for fixing my hair, for seeing the dress through. I thanked her even as I wanted to ask her why this was happening. To ask if her oracle powers could let her look to my past and find where it had all gone so wrong.

"You could come to my room while I finish getting ready," she offered as she gathered the cosmetics and went to the door.

I stood, awkward in my own space. "No thanks. I think I could use a little quiet before the commotion this evening."

"It's a celebration, not a commotion," she corrected, though I hardly saw the difference. She pressed her back against the door, giving me an understanding smile. "But I thought you'd say that. Raphael will be by in an hour—I'll see you at the ball. Save me a dance."

And then she was gone, the door clicking shut behind her as the lock fell into place.

I exhaled, the corset of the dress suddenly too restrictive for me to inhale properly.

"Women," said a contemptuous voice behind me.

I bit back a scream at the sound. *How?*

"Titus."

Invisible spiders crawled down my spine. It was unnerving to realize someone invisible lurked around you, and a thousand times worse to realize he had been in my bedroom. Amalthea hadn't had the door open long when she left, which meant he either slipped in at just the right moment... or he'd been here the entire time.

"My, and don't you sound pleased to see me, Samara." His voice had moved—not closer, but now at my other side. I forced myself not to flinch, to not give him the satisfaction. "Disappointed your little dress-up adventure was cut short?"

"What do you want?" I demanded.

The king's spy was in no hurry to answer my questions. "I despise that woman, you know. An abomination. You'd think the worst thing in the world would be being born useless without magic like the voids, but those heretics are worse. And here she is, proving we were right to hunt them down. Betraying her own kind, and for what? To spend hours preening in front of the mirror? Vapid, useless thing. A waste of magic."

I stiffened at his derogatory tone. I might be working with Titus now, but that didn't mean I no longer loathed him. "What is your counterproposal?" I cast my arms up theatrically, but really, I was trying to create space around myself so I could maneuver to the bed. The one blessing of this dress was the volume of the skirt gave me at least a little distance from the spy. "She'd be killed in the Witch Kingdom. Who could blame her for surviving?" There was also the fact Amalthea was the furthest thing from vapid I'd ever encountered—and the Witch Kingdom had its share of vapid courtiers. Thea spent hours each day in meetings, when she wasn't with me. She sat on a number of councils and advised Raphael. Additionally, she was acutely aware of the going-ons at every level of court, not just in aristocratic circles. Maids confided in her, dressmakers gossiped with her. Overbearing? At times. But vapid? *Never*.

"Then she should have died with dignity before she could shame our entire species," Titus snapped.

It was the first time his calm veneer had slipped.

Did I score a point? Or did I just make this situation more dangerous for myself?

"You're so quick to defend her, Samara. It makes me wonder about that little note you wrote me."

I swallowed, the sensation sharp and ugly. That was why he was here, after all. Of course he hadn't given me a warning. He enjoyed my fear far too much.

Not for the first time since I'd left the note, a wave of doubt hit me. But it was too late to go back on the plan. If I confessed that for months I'd not only known the Storm-blooded King's spymaster was in the kingdom but that I'd plotted against Raphael with him?

No matter what his affection, I'd be dead.

And when the memory of that girl came again, the doubt disappeared, replaced by that same, relentless anger that had been growing.

"She dressed you like his little meal." His voice was closer now. I could smell the sweet almonds on his breath.

"No different than putting a shiny red apple in a roast's mouth."

The slightest graze of the gossamer that wrapped my arms. I jerked my hand back.

"What do you want?" I demanded once more. "You may be invisible, but Raphael will be here soon, and he'll hear you. Not being able to see you won't stop him from following the sound of your heartbeat and ripping your head from your shoulders."

A pause.

Gods, I wish he would leave. I was beside my bed now, my hand aching to reach for the dagger under the pillow.

Titus had risked a lot to enter my rooms, with all the guards posted in the halls. He wasn't invincible, no matter how he acted. He wouldn't have come just to lecture me.

"Are you committed to this cause or not?"

I hesitated. I'd seen the cruelty of vampires firsthand, at every turn in my life. Raphael had condoned their actions.

I owed him nothing.

But still, I hesitated.

A folded piece of parchment fluttered to the floor in front of me, the royal seal stamped on it. I picked it up and opened it. The sprawling script, the golden ink. Exactly as I'd seen it in childhood.

"A pardon, Samara. All your sins forgiven."

A royal pardon. I could go home.

Wherever that is, part of me chastised.

But that louder part of me craved this. To finally be absolved of guilt and welcomed into the land of humans once more. Once I helped Titus, I would flee with the book and scour the Witch Kingdom without the threat of imprisonment.

The parchment disappeared again as Titus snatched it back. In its place, he set another item.

A card.

Not just any card. The purple edges said this was made by a toximancer, a witch specialized in poisons.

"What am I to do with this?" I made no move to pick it up.

Titus let out an aggrieved sigh, as though he could hardly believe he was still talking to me. "And here your one redeeming feature is you were thought to be clever. It's a poison card."

Obviously. "And what do you expect me to do? Use it on Raphael?"

"In a manner of speaking. Such a card would never work on a vampire. Their bodies are too strong. But if he were to ingest it directly, even the demon king himself couldn't withstand the toxins."

When he drinks from me.

This was why Titus had seen such an opportunity in me being the king's Chosen. With me, Raphael was vulnerable in a way he was with no other.

He hasn't drunk from the source in hundreds of years, Thea had said.

Yet he was to drink from me, just as Thea had seen. He was always meant to. If he was going to take my blood, as so many vampires took from humans in his kingdoms, he deserved this reckoning. Or was I always meant to betray him? Was that why she had seen it? My stomach churned, and I desperately wished for five minutes to think this through. Titus gave me no quarter.

"Besides. Just think what would happen if their kind knew who you really were. They'd hardly be so quick to welcome you, don't you agree?"

My stomach rolled again. I snatched up the poison card. Such a light thing, between my fingers. Barely the width of my palm. Yet the magic in it was deadly. The symbols on it left no doubt of that.

"What happens after?" I said quietly. "If I help carry out this plan, how will I escape?"

"I'll help you, of course," he said soothingly. No doubt that syrup of his voice was meant to make me look past the fact I didn't trust the spymaster one iota.

No, once I did this, I'd need to find my own way out. I glanced at the grimoire's hiding spot. I'd need to take that with me. Returning to my rooms would be a foolish move, but there was no other choice. I didn't trust Titus with it. If the necromancer really could stand against the vampires, they'd need all the help they could get.

"Tick-tock, Samara."

I activated the card.

Chapter 46

Raphael arrived at my door a scant hour later, and when I opened it, I thought I might cease breathing altogether.

He wore a black silk tunic draped over his shoulders in a wide vee, a stark contrast to his alabaster skin. Red jewels ornamented his skin—his fingers, his shoulders, his chest.

The same, glowing red of his eyes.

The same red as my dress.

An iron crown settled on his brow, menacing spikes that reminded me of vampire fangs. Its fierce, unyielding shape served as a contrast to the luxurious tailoring that engulfed him.

He was otherworldly.

And yet, my dress made me the perfect extension of his outfit.

"Samara. You look..." He trailed off.

I had never known Raphael to be at a loss for words. But there he was, staring at me like he'd never seen me before.

"I'm ready," I said, covering the fact his appearance had rendered me similarly speechless.

"Are you?" Raphael asked.

It was a good thing I was a human and could lie. I nodded.

Raphael extended an arm, and I just stared at it. I'd never actually hooked arms with a suitor. Not that Raphael was anything of the sort to me, not that he *could* ever be... but just that crook of an elbow made me ache for the life I could have had.

A life I could still have. With the pardon.

"I don't believe this tradition is any different in the Witch Kingdom," he prompted with dry humor.

Despite everything, I wanted to smile at the jest.

I slipped my arm around his and that was all it took. Raphael strode down the hallway, keeping to a pace I could manage in heels. No doubt he heard every fluttering beat of my heart as we grew closer to the ballroom. I hoped he continued to think it was simple nerves, not a warning bell of my betrayal.

Act normal, I willed myself. *Just go along with everything and let him bite you when the time is right.*

A BARGAIN SO BLOODY

We didn't go the way I expected. The hallway wrapped around and around as we rose to the very top of Damerel.

The ballroom was different than the one from the welcome ball. There was no staircase to descend from, only two massive twin doors, ornately carved from stone that were thrust open at our arrival, an abrupt trumpet cutting through the din that emanated from the room.

"His Majesty, King Raphael, First of His Name, Chosen of Anagenni, Ruler of the Vampire Kingdom of the West, and Lady Samara, the king's Chosen, have arrived!"

All eyes were on us at once, then quickly cast down as everyone bowed low.

For Raphael, of course.

He stepped forward, as was his right, and I followed along, helpless.

The room itself rose to a peak at the top. A grand chandelier, the size of my bed, hung from a massive chain, with crystals and candles that filled the space with light. It was a feat of engineering it held up. Parts of the mountain were cut away to reveal the outside world. A glimpse at the three red eclipses.

If I'd thought the last ball had prepared me for a crowd, I was sorely mistaken. The ballroom was larger than the other one, but it was even more filled with vampires and humans alike. There were many, many humans. Not just the ones who disguised themselves wistfully as vampires.

No, when I looked at them... I saw myself.

It took everything in me not to pull from Raphael's grip and run. "It seems I've complied with the dress code."

I ran a sweaty palm over the red full silk of my skirt. The humans were easy to identify—each of us wore red. Sleeveless dresses, vests with no undershirts. Pulse points exposed nearly everywhere. The fashion was ornate on humans and vampires alike, with the others cloaked in darker shades of gray and black.

Many wore black, but only Raphael was fully cloaked in the color—save the red jewels embroidered into his tunic.

"It is... symbolic," Raphael said carefully. His voice was quiet, but in a room full of vampire hearing, I doubted there was such thing as a private conversation.

Symbolic of the blood they would spill? My *poisoned* blood.

On some silent signal, the bows came to an end. Everyone watched us.

Oh gods, now? "Is this the part where you drink from me?" *Why had I refused to let Thea tell me any more of what was expected?*

Raphael adjusted and moved so he was directly in front of me without relinquishing our interlinked arms. His large frame blocked my view from the others.

"Now is the part where we dance."

He didn't break eye contact while he gestured to the band, and a fresh song started. I could hardly hear the first notes over the invisible cotton that clogged my ears.

He bent towards me, his breath caressing the shell of my ear. "They'll stop staring once we start dancing."

"I don't know the steps," I hissed under my breath.

This close, I could nearly feel the rumble of his low laughter. "Just move. I'll do the rest."

So I moved, needing no further convincing if it meant three hundred pairs of eyes would go elsewhere in the room. I swayed slightly, imitating what I recalled from the dances I'd observed in another life. It was more swaying and shuffling than anything as elegant as a waltz, but Raphael was true to his word. His hand slid into mine, lifting our palms while his other hand dipped lower, burning into my side while mine naturally moved to his bicep. I looked around as the others began to dance, and tried to mimic the movements to better fit the style of the Vampire Kingdom.

"You're thinking too hard," he mused.

"I'm trying to not step on your feet." The quip was out before I realized the irony. I was concerned about stepping on his feet... as if I didn't plan far greater harm.

I faltered in my shuffle-dance, but Raphael rescued me.

"Don't worry about them, little viper. They don't matter." The chandelier light caught the brutal iron of his crown as he moved easily in his improvised steps. "Only this matters. What you feel in this moment, what you're doing."

I tried to let them fade to the background, but my thoughts were now caught in another swirl. That was why Raphael resorted to another tactic—distracting me.

"Tell me your opinion of the music."

Now that we had settled into a rhythm, I let the notes entrance me. I'd spotted the small orchestra on the edge of the room when we'd arrived. The acoustics of the ballroom were excellent, the volume not distracting, but loud enough to drown out the worst of my thoughts. Dozens of instruments came together in a harmony that thrummed over my skin and made me want to move, even if my steps were still uncertain.

"They're skilled," I conceded.

"But do you like them?" he pressed.

On this, there was no need to lie. "I do." If I could have done nothing but sit in the empty ballroom with the music playing for eternity, I might have been content.

They didn't have music like this in the Witch Kingdom.

Once more, I pushed the thoughts of my old home away. *Keep acting natural.*

"Are there always so many for an event like this?" I lifted my chin in the direction of the small orchestra. It was disproportionate for the event, surely.

Raphael's lip quirked. "No."

"Then why?"

"For you. I brought them here for you." He spun me, and I managed to keep my balance while I twirled across the floor before winding up back in his arms, secured once more. "I wanted to show you another side of this kingdom."

"Another side?" I shut my eyes, trying to figure out what he meant. "Raphael, tell me, why are all the humans in red?"

The symbolism was obvious, but I wanted to hear it.

Wanted to make him paint the divide between us clearly.

"I told you it was symbolic."

Surely he didn't think I'd give in to such obvious evasion. "Symbolic of *what*?" I pressed.

He didn't need to breathe, but he sighed anyway. "The blood the humans offer, and the darkness that triumphs over them. While three red moons hang full, ripe, in the sky, while the dark sky surrounds them."

There were no pleasantries I could use to cover that truth. That would always be the chasm between us. The vampires were powerful, eternal. Humans nothing but fodder.

The song ended and another started. We kept moving, now in sync, even as I made the steps up.

"I do not wish to deceive you, little viper. My world is a brutal one. But I want to share it with you, nonetheless."

The name reminded me of the venom currently running through my veins. I hid my reaction and looked away.

"What if I don't want to be part of this world?" *What if this world is wrong?*

"Everywhere has its ugliness. Some places just cloak it better." The knot on his throat bobbed. "If you cannot find solace in my kingdom, then I will find you somewhere else, with all the gold you can carry. Yet I hope you would choose to stay at my side."

"But... I was only meant to stay a few days. Then to translate the grimoire." I forced myself not to give anything away when I mentioned the tome I'd already made progress translating.

"I only wish for your happiness." His eyes held me, making it impossible to look anywhere else.

Happy. Like it was so simple. "Why?"

The vampire king was quiet for a moment. Then—"I suppose a part of it is because you've known so little of it."

I couldn't look at him anymore, so I cast my gaze around the room. What was a normal amount of happiness for someone to have? How did you measure it? Had I had a happy childhood before Greymere? It had been better, surely, but happiness had been a superfluous pursuit in my mother's mind.

Happiness can be found at the bottom of a choice bottle, she'd once told me. *You're meant for more, my little princess.*

I wasn't happy. Maybe in fleeting moments here—but I was trading all those small moments for something more.

A purpose.

"And your life?" I challenged. "Is it happy?"

The silence that followed was a damning admission for a vampire who couldn't lie.

A BARGAIN SO BLOODY

We rotated around the room, my dress grazing the floor. The music swelled and fell as the dance ended. An invisible clock counted down the ceremony. Once we stopped moving, it hit me at once, the air suddenly impossibly thick.

"I need a moment." I broke away from Raphael, uncertain of my destination. I pushed through a throng of onlookers, keeping my eyes down as I tried to find any exit. The grand entrance was on the opposite side of the room but—*there*, an opening.

I stepped out onto the balcony. The opening led directly to a balcony carved from the stone. It was empty. I went farther, for a moment, stunned by where I was.

The night sent clear, cool air into my lungs. This was the first time I'd been outside in *months*. I inhaled deeply, savoring it. If things went wrong, it could be the last time I was outside.

The view was glorious. I moved to the stone wall that provided a barrier from tumbling down, careful not to lean over. Several peaks were in view, close in height, just far enough away that if I closed one eye and reached, I might think I'd be able to touch their spires. Snow sprinkled their tops, but with the heat from the crowd still warming me, I didn't mind the chill. Even if I'd been shivering, I'd have endured it just to have a few moments to gather my thoughts.

But I was not alone for long.

"You don't have to stand that far away," I murmured.

Demos stepped forward from the doorway. I'd said I needed a moment, and Raphael had given it to me. He had not, however, left me without guard. The king's general wore all black, as all the vampires did, but it was ornamented. The uniform of a soldier rather than formal clothing.

"I'm surprised you're not with Thea." It was nonsensical, but it happened to be the first thing that came to mind. I was worried if I was left in silence with my thoughts the deception would be plain on my face.

He stood six feet to my side, looking out over the cliffs. "Why would I be with her?"

Because you're always looking at her. "You're friends, are you not?"

"I'm to guard *you*." His tone was controlled.

"I'm sure no vampire would dare touch the king's Chosen at the Tri-Lunar Eclipse." I kept my tone dry, but my heart pounded, daring him to contradict me.

"There are other threats," Demos said.

A shiver went down my spine, not just from the cold air. *Like what? Does he know about Titus?* I dismissed the thought immediately—if Raphael knew the Witch King's spymaster was in his midst, he'd have been tortured and killed long ago. Which meant there were other threats.

It doesn't matter. You're leaving.

"He cares for you, you know," Demos said nonchalantly.

"I'm a stray he picked up and felt sorry for." It was a good thing I didn't have the vampire inability to lie, because the words would never have made it past my lips. *He cares for you*. It was an addictive thought, electrifying.

But one that had no future. Not with what I was about to do.

Demos gave me a look that said as much. "Then why have my best men been ordered to hunt down some careless vampire who got out of hand with a donor?"

My eyes widened. Raphael had said nothing of that. He'd just... let me believe the worst.

And I'd done so. Easily.

"You can go back to the party, Iademos."

I spun around. Raphael was suddenly mere feet away, the mildest twist of irritation on his brow. In his hands, he held two crystal flutes. One was a light amber liquid in a flute, the other clear water.

I suspected I was the only human in history who had a vampire king serving her as if he were a tavern wench.

"I wasn't certain which you would prefer."

Iademos departed per Raphael's instructions while I gave what should have been a simple question far too much thought.

Memories of the last time—the only time—I'd imbibed returned. I probably should stay clear-headed. Or I could use the embrace of liquor to soothe the ever-tightening knot of nerves in my stomach.

"You know I would never let anything happen to you," Raphael said.

I reached for the liquor, not meeting his gaze. I couldn't return the sentiment.

"Is what Demos said true?" I asked.

Raphael grimaced slightly, setting the other flute on the railing. "Demos speaks too easily. I don't boast half-measures."

"What happened to her being a random girl? Unworthy of your attention?" I downed my glass, keen to feel the burn down my throat even as it made me sputter.

"Perhaps things should be different than how I first saw them."

That was as mild an apology as there could be, if it even counted. But the true apology wasn't found in words. It was in the fact he was looking for the killer. I set the glass down next to his and stepped closer. At this distance, his scent wrapped around me, complementing the night air.

"Are you only doing this to please me?"

I wanted him to deny it.

But vampires could not lie.

"Yes."

I turned away. What was I to do with that? Gods, they were monstrous creatures. I'd seen proof over and over again. But could Raphael be better? Could I teach him better? Was such thinking hubris the gods would punish? Or would I kill him as planned, buy my freedom through Titus's plot, only to have a crueler king take his place?

Guilt twisted in my stomach once more. I forced my gaze to the white-topped mountains while reinforcing my mental shield.

"Is it not obvious by now I seek to please you?" he murmured. He reached for my cheek, but I turned away. It was too much to have him this close, in those gentle tones.

"You were going to kill another human tonight if I hadn't volunteered."

How could I look at a man like that as though he was anything but evil?

"I was," he confirmed. "A prisoner was reserved for the occasion, vile even by your standards, I'm sure." I glanced back, uncertain. Was that true? Was it any better? His gaze didn't waver as he continued: "But that does not absolve me, little viper. I would kill a thousand innocents to spare you any pain."

I couldn't be near him. I strode away, my knees shaking as I forced myself to put distance between us.

But Raphael followed me. He cornered me in a small carved-out alcove.

"Don't run, Samara. Not from me."

If I let him catch me, truly hold me the way I'd always craved... it would destroy me.

"You claim you seek to please me, but you planned to take my blood this entire time. You made me your Chosen, and you knew that this was a Chosen's role."

Raphael lifted his hands, bracing them on the top of the alcove as he leaned in. "I have no intention of taking what you do not wish to give. You give, and you give, because you crave acceptance. If you have any flaw, it is that. If you ever wanted my bite, I would give it to you, and we both know you'd like it." He leaned closer. "You haunt my thoughts constantly, yet I fear I am not in yours with anything but contempt. Tell me, Samara. If I took you now, would you hate me? Regret me? Or would you crave me as ruthlessly as I crave you?"

I couldn't answer him with words. Not as I took in his expression, like a barely leashed animal, and felt a hundred conflicting emotions. Not as I remembered my mission, and every cruel thing the vampires had done since I'd been born. Not as he caged me into the alcove, and for once, I didn't feel trapped, but safe.

I surged forward and yanked the metal chain around his neck to pull him to me, and I kissed him.

I had never felt more powerful than the brief second when I felt his lips slack against me. For once, I had shocked the vampire king. Never more intoxicated than when he made a low, masculine sound against my lips and surged into the alcove. I didn't know what I was doing, didn't know how to name the hundreds of sensations sparking through my body. All I knew was him: his scent, his taste, the texture of his skin, the sounds he made against me. And my body answered in kind. I'd never known cedar could have such a dark edge, but I could taste it on his tongue as he took control of the kiss. There was nothing but this moment, this desperate need to stay in my body, wrapped in all he was.

He was an enemy, king of the monsters I despised.

May the ninth hell spare me, he was everything I craved.

Raphael slipped one hand behind my neck, cushioning me from the jagged stone. His thumb just grazed my pulse point, my heart racing. Not with fear, but exhilaration. He groaned slightly and the sound went straight to my core. *Want him. Need him.* His other hand started at my waist and then dipped towards the front. When his hand slid over the sheath with my dagger, I felt his lips curl against mine.

"My little viper with her fangs," he murmured before returning to the kiss.

A venomous, treacherous viper. But the thought was chased away when he caressed my body again.

He knew my body better than I did. Every touch was like a musician's, masterfully stirring the song of my desire. He palmed me through the layers of my skirts, his grip firm and possessive as he moved past the dip in my legs. The sudden pressure made me gasp against his lips. His touch was new and exciting, but it also felt so, so right. Like he knew exactly what I needed. When I'd touched myself before, bare skin to bare skin, I'd only ever felt a fraction of what was muffled between the fabric now. I wrapped my arms around his back, as if to hold him there, but Raphael wasn't going anywhere.

He continued to kiss me, hard, bruising, but I loved the sensation, the need it stirred in me. It was a hunger unlike any other. I'd felt the starts of it at times, watching him, in the kiss we'd shared in anger.

Those were embers compared to the inferno I felt now. He stroked, and I wanted more. My thighs ached and widened for him. His palm was hard against my center, rubbing exactly where I needed more. I was helpless from the contact. I ground my hips against him, desperate for the friction that would bring on more pleasure. It was so close, so tempting, driving every thought away but the hunger I felt for him—

He broke the kiss and stilled his hand.

"What?" Raphael snarled.

I flinched at the tone. But he jerked his head back and glared at something, and I realized it wasn't directed at me. I maneuvered around his broad frame to see Amalthea.

She wore a different shade of red than the bright crimson I and the other humans did, a slightly darker shade with a purple tinge. It was an elegant affair. Her neck was exposed, but the dress was cut high, leaving her more covered than most. Her single eye flickered to me, something unreadable in it.

"It's time, Your Majesty," she said simply.

No.

No, I needed more time. Needed to think through this decision.

You're blinded by lust, a cynical part of me hissed. *You'd put your body's desire over your true kingdom? Knowing what he is, what they are?*

It's more than lust, another part argued. The tender words weren't lies. The way he looked at me, right before I kissed him, half-stunned and then so satisfied against me, so coaxing. *He wasn't just another monster.*

The thought wasn't strong enough to overpower the memories of the bodies. My nightmares since childhood. *But that's their nature. They can't change, they can't help it.*

My internal debate was cut too short as Raphael pulled away. Even though the alcove sheltered me from the worst of the outside chill, it found me immediately, like an aquamancer had formed ice shackles around me. My skirts fell back down, rumpled, and I did my best to smooth them out as though the biggest problem I had was appearing unkempt in front of the court.

Raphael gave me a regretful look. The normally composed king looked, for once, disheveled himself. His cloak was off-center, from me yanking the chain. His lips swollen and slightly darkened from the cosmetics Thea had placed on me. I froze my features to hide my own feelings.

I'd have given anything in that moment to go back to two minutes ago, when nothing had mattered but the pleasure between us.

Pleasure I'd never feel again. Not that way.

"I would take you away right now," he murmured as I slid my palm into his offered hand. "But of all nights, this is our sacred one. For the king not to take blood would be seen as heretical. It would be to spit in Anagenni's face." He composed himself, rolling his shoulders back.

"I understand." There was nothing more to say. My time had run out.

We reentered the ballroom. I wanted to vomit. The scent of copper—blood—tinged the air. There were no goblets of blood, not for the vampires. Instead, a quick scan of the crowd revealed the source. Wrists and necks alike were perforated with bite marks. One man had marks on either side of his neck; a woman's wore twin red bracelets of dried blood. I stopped looking closely after that, my field of view going blurry until there was only Raphael, leading me forward, his broad shoulders covered in black lace and red jewels.

He wore red jewels. I would wear blood.

Blood and blood and blood.

He stopped in the center of the ballroom and addressed the crowd.

"People of Damerel." He didn't need to bellow for his voice to be heard through the ballroom. No one so much as dared whisper while the king was speaking. "The time has come again to honor Anagenni with our most sacred rite, the taking of blood. Tonight, we all drink from the vein, and only the vein. Tonight, we show our power, and honor the goddess-guided hierarchy Anagenni instilled."

He moved behind me. Two words, so soft I wasn't sure I heard them, were breathed against my hair. Then Raphael bent his head. His hair tickled the back of my neck. His fingers held my wrists—my pulse points—at my side. I stiffened in his embrace. Hundreds of eyes on us, on this moment. Somewhere, I was certain, Titus watched with bated breath. Guilt welled in me. I was about to commit the ultimate betrayal. I had justified the logic over and over in my head, but I was nothing more than a scared rat, caught in a trap, waiting for my neck to be snapped.

Two sharp points grazed the column of my throat.

He was going to—

I was going to—

"*No!*"

The room froze at my cry.

"I'm sorry." I wasn't sure who I said it to. "I can't do this."

Chapter 47

I FLED THE BALLROOM as fast as I could. The crowd parted, uncertain.

"Don't follow me," I begged, knowing he'd hear me.

Raphael simply stood there, a stunned look on his face.

I turned away and ran faster. But Iademos was on my tail, and I couldn't have a guard for what I was about to do.

I had to leave. *Now.*

Pardon or no pardon, I couldn't be here any longer.

"Leave me be," I insisted, knowing the general would hear me.

"I'm to guard you," he replied from the shadows. Where my voice shook, winded as I ran quickly, his was even, monotone.

"An hour," I said. "Give me an hour. I'm going to my rooms. I... I need to be alone."

"Raphael would behead me if I did not see you there."

I made a hysterical sound and continued to run. The little rat in me knew only one thing—scurry, escape, *faster*. The stone steps turned to familiar carpet as I reached my chambers. The halls were empty—everybody on this level and below would be at the ballroom.

"Leave, Iademos. I want to be alone. I'll be in my rooms the entire night—and Raphael will behead you for not listening to my wishes," I bluffed.

"As you listened to his?" he snapped.

I flinched at the ire in his normally carefully controlled voice. "Just leave me be," I pleaded, more forcefully.

Demos looked displeased, but he turned on his heel and left. I watched him disappear around the corner, then shut my door. I locked it, even though I would be gone in a matter of minutes.

I need to leave.

Damn Titus and all his bargains. Damn Raphael and his confusing words.

I couldn't cause his death... but I couldn't stay here either. One small bag was packed and stashed within my bed. What was left of the coins from when I'd arrived, some jewelry Amalthea had foisted on me I didn't think she'd miss. I slung it over my shoulder and went for the grimoire. The necromancer—I'd find them. Even if it meant going back to the Witch Kingdom and certain death.

The vampires celebrated Anagenni by taking human blood, but this was the will written in the book. The goddess wanted a witch to rein the vampires in. I would give the witch the tool they needed for that.

I'd had nothing before.

I can do it again. I wished the thought felt less like cleaving my heart in two. Now I had a purpose.

I cast a look around the room, something thick and hot in my throat I couldn't quite swallow. It had been my home for several months. Now that I was leaving, I could admit that to myself. There was no other explanation for the grief that sliced through me. It had been more of a home than I'd had in many years. Raphael, Thea, Demos—not a family, exactly, but I'd had people I was safe with.

Grieve later. Get out now.

The ballgown was cumbersome when it came to escaping. I'd needed Amalthea to get dressed in it. Undoing the lacing would be nearly impossible by myself. A pair of trousers and a tunic would have to suffice for when I had time to change. I bent into the dresser and selected the least conspicuous colors, then quickly set them aside. I'd have to use the dagger on my thigh to cut myself out of the dress.

"Where, precisely, do you think you're going?"

I jerked upright and slammed the drawer shut behind me.

Titus.

His invisible magic slid away, revealing the spymaster. He was only a few feet away, dressed in nondescript gray servant clothing. His dark eyes latched on to my bag with accusation.

"I locked that door." I knew I had.

He smiled, but there was nothing friendly in it. "Doors are nothing when you have cards that let you move through walls, you foolish chit. Now, I'll ask once more: Where do you think you're going?"

"I'm leaving." I willed my hands not to shake. "I know this means no pardon, but I just... I can't do it."

His lips twisted with contempt. I felt echoes of the emotion inside me. What kind of woman would betray her kingdom like this?

Perhaps the Witch Kingdom hadn't been mine since they locked me in Greymere. And I hadn't been theirs since I made a deal with a vampire to break out.

"You must be *joking*," Titus drawled with disbelief.

My heart pounded in my chest. I checked my mental shields—I couldn't let Raphael find out my plans before I left Damerel. If he found out I'd plotted against him... memories of the Monastery floated in my mind, the bodies ripped apart by Raphael's wrathful might.

Titus was eating into my precious time to leave. If this took too long, it would be too late. "I won't tell anyone about you." The words left me in a rush. "I just can't be the one to do it. I can't aid you in this. I know we've been taught they're monsters. But they can be better. Raphael could show them how to be better. Killing him would just have someone worse take his place."

Titus advanced slowly. The wood of the dresser dug into my back. "Worse?" he echoed. "There's no one worse, you stupid girl. He's the strongest of them. If you'd played your role properly, we could have triumphed, cutting the head off the snake. But no. You've told yourself they're not monsters." He smirked, all thin lips and hollow cheeks. "It wasn't enough to see them kill your mother? You need more proof?"

Blood and blood... I swallowed and forced the memory aside. For once, I wouldn't let it trap me. "Just because one vampire did that doesn't mean they all are evil." *Doesn't it?*

Titus actually laughed, throwing his head back. I took the chance to step to the side slightly, trying to shift away from where I was cornered. But his head snapped back, not missing the movement.

"I can't believe this. They've attacked you. Or do you forget those who try to kill you so quickly?"

I flinched at the reminder. "How do you know about that?"

Titus came closer, and I had nowhere to go. "Who do you think told the librarian what you were doing?"

The missing books. I clenched my jaw as realization snapped through me. He'd set me up, playing on their fear of the necromancer. He must have overheard me at some point talking with Amalthea, perhaps some morning over breakfast when we'd thought we were alone.

"And that still wasn't enough for you! You refused me. So I showed you what would happen to humans when vampires rule, and I thought, finally. The stupid girl will see. But now you double-cross me."

My head swam. What would happen... "You? You killed the donor?" I stammered.

"Of course. I needed to show you what vampires are capable of, since you seem to have forgotten what they did to your mother."

"But... you were the one who killed her."

He waved the accusation away. "She sealed her fate the moment she became their blood whore."

Fury slammed into me. I couldn't run, and I didn't want to run.

"You're evil," I snarled. "Worse than them. At least when they kill it's an accident. But you chose to take her life."

"She was a tool, Samara. Just like you. If you'd done your duty, then it would have been a noble sacrifice on her part. Unfortunately, you proved to be useless." Titus's expression went flat. "And I have no need for useless tools."

He surged for me, but I was ready. When I'd realized I couldn't get away, I set another plan in place. I drew the dagger from the harness I'd designed to sit around my thigh. It might be enchanted for vampires, but the blade was sharp enough to draw blood from any creature.

Titus startled slightly, as if not expecting a fight. Then he snorted. "That twig again?"

"I'm stronger than I was before." I lunged forward and swiped at his side, drawing blood.

He knocked me away, and I stumbled into the back of the chair. His face contorted with hideous rage as he drew his own blade. Simple steel, but longer than mine. "You bitch!"

Bitch, traitor, useless tool... perhaps his true talent was finding ways to insult me.

We danced around each other. I *had* grown stronger. My body had put on muscle. The dagger was no longer an extra weight in my hand, but rather an extension of my arm. Unfortunately, the dress made me slow, my footwork sloppy.

We clashed again and again, neither of us managing to land a blow. I caught his blade against mine and threw him back hard enough to stumble. *I can do this.*

"You know your mistake, Samara?" Titus sneered as he recovered from the blow.

I didn't waste my breath answering.

"You can't win against magic."

With a flick of his fingers, he cast a spell. I froze as every part of my body seized. The dagger slipped from my fingers, landing harmlessly against the carpeted floor. Sweat dripped down my back as I tried to force my legs to move. But no matter how I tried, nothing worked.

"I don't normally reveal my magic," he admitted. "Poor form for a spymaster to give up his secrets. But since you're dying, it hardly matters."

"Poi… son…" My tongue was too large in my mouth, the word barely scraping through my teeth.

He strolled over to where I stood, helpless, twirling his blade in his hand. "Yes, Samara. That card was made with my own magic."

He plunged his blade into my chest.

Chapter 48

White pain exploded inside me, blocking out my vision.

A muffled sound as I fell, my ears ringing too loudly to process what was happening.

Dying. I'm dying.

Blood pooled on top of me, the warm liquid soaking my dress. Inside, an inescapable cold bloomed.

There was nothing but the pain. The white turned to black as my eyes shut, unable to focus.

"No!" A roar. Terrifying, vicious, animalistic. It cut through the haze of pain.

I wanted to turn my head and see the source, but any movement was impossible. Because of the poison, or because I was already dead, my spirit slowly detaching from my body...

Numbness coated my senses. Everything was distant

There was a thunderous crash and a shrill scream.

I couldn't move. Couldn't feel my limbs, my torso. My eyelids flickered, lights flashing in my periphery.

"Don't do this!" he snarled. "Don't you dare leave me like this."

The imperious tone... if I could have moved my lips, they might have twitched. As if this had been my choice. Or maybe it was. Somewhere along the way, I'd made a decision and put it all in motion.

"Samara." My name was a plea. I'd gone so many years without hearing my name, and yet he used it over and over. I was grateful for that. The fact the last time I'd hear it wouldn't be from the hate-fueled spymaster.

"I'm... sor... ry..." It took incalculable effort to offer that.

"No, Samara. I'm sorry, because I fear you'll never forgive me for this."

What was he saying?

I thought I could feel nothing anymore, but then...

Pain.

My neck ached sharply, more acute than I should have felt in my state.

Then, at my lips, something hot. Wet.

No. He didn't.

He'd *promised*. The one thing I'd ever asked him to vow.

"Don't... do... this..." I gasped through coated lips.

VASILISA DRAKE

If he responded, I couldn't hear it.
And then it all disappeared.

Epilogue

I WOKE, STARING AT the ceiling.

Only it wasn't the ornate, painted ceiling of my bedroom. Nor was it the bedframe I'd woken to for the past several months.

It was dark, unyielding stone.

I'm in Greymere.

That was my first thought before the events of the evening slammed back to me. Was this the ninth hell, for my treachery? I pushed onto my elbows and looked around. I was surrounded on almost all four sides by solid stone, the same dark granite above and below. It wasn't polished and smooth, but rather a small room carved directly from the mountain.

VASILISA DRAKE

Damerel.

There was no light source. It was completely dark, yet I could see perfectly.

Something was very wrong.

I slapped a palm to my chest, waiting to feel the terrified pounding of my heart.

Nothing.

No, no, no.

It can't be.

I begged him.

I begged him... not to?

The only break in the stone was a small opening blocked with copper bars.

Cursed copper. I roughly shoved myself up, scraping my palms and feet as I stumbled over to the red-hued metal. I grasped them, desperate to deny the truth.

"Ouch!"

I startled at the sound and leaped back. Who had said that? But there was only me. I mumbled something and realized the truth: with my newly changed hearing, I no longer recognized my voice in my ears.

"Damn you," I hissed, blinking rapidly.

Raphael had turned me. I'd begged him not to. Hadn't he promised? Hadn't he given his word he'd never take that choice from me? A taboo, he'd called it. To change someone without permission.

I'd rather die than live like this.

"You're finally awake."

A dark figure stepped forward from the shadows.

Raphael?

I blinked as he stepped out of the shadows.

No.

Demos.

His closest friend. A convenient target for my fury. "How could he do this to me?" I demanded. "Where's Raphael? I need to see him. Now!"

The bark of laughter fell flat off the unyielding stone. "You think you have any right to demand to see the king?" He shook his head. "He's in a coma, recovering from the poison you put in his veins." He gave me a look of disbelief. "The first human he ever agrees to turn, and she poisons him."

I didn't agree to anything.

"A coma?" Why that panic temporarily overpowered the rage I felt at him, I couldn't explain. The fear of Raphael dying was somehow even more primal. Then my rational brain broke through. I felt every single dark, evil emotion I associated with vampires when I hissed, "Good. Let him die from it."

Demos snarled in front of the copper gate. For the first time, I wondered if it was there not to keep me here but to keep the other vampires from the void who had murdered their king.

"King Raphael will wake up," Demos hissed, his usual composure lost.

Gone was Demos who had trained me. In his place was Iademos, general to the Vampire Kingdom of the West. The general wasn't just a strategist; he was a warrior, and he wanted to strike me down for betraying the ruler he'd sworn allegiance to.

"And when he finds out what you've done, he'll make you rue the day you came to Damerel. It won't be a quick death, you gutter rat. Four hundred years I have kept him safe from every threat, but here you slipped into our midst."

No, no, no! The words *I didn't mean to* bubbled up in my throat, but there was no way to vent them. I backed up farther and farther with each accusation landing like an axe on a rotted tree, making me crumble and wilt.

Iademos surged forward, and I flinched, but all he did was push a goblet between the cell bars and set it on the floor. Where it had come from, I didn't know. The smell immediately hit me, and a cavern I'd been unaware of opened up inside my body. Hunger, thirst, an indescribable blend flooded my system.

It smells... good. I dove for the cup, faster than I'd known my body to be able to. It was as though in one second I was across the cell, then the goblet was halfway to my lips before I realized what I was about to do.

Blood. It was blood.

I tossed it across the cell. The blood sprayed across the floor, a glittering crimson beacon. Once, it would have reminded me of my mother's death. Now, all I saw was a cure to this animal hunger, this deep pit of unnatural thirst, inside me.

How dare he do this to me? He'd promised. I'd have chosen to die a thousand deaths before I let myself live as this monster. One who took, and took, and took to survive.

"Don't be petulant." Iademos crossed his arms in front of the gate. "You need to drink. All new vampires do."

"I won't!" I snarled. Did I sound more like an animal that time? *Why did he do this to me*? My chest ached, even though my heart no longer beat.

"You will. If you don't now, you'll be begging for a sip within the next two days." He bent to pick up the goblet. Was he going to bring me more blood?

Could I throw it away a second time if he did? Was my nature so easily changed?

I sprinted forward again and somehow managed to snag the goblet.

Then I hurled it through the slotted bars. It collided with the cavern wall and chipped the stone with terrifying force.

"Get away!" I screamed. "Get away, and don't you dare bring me blood again!"

I expected Iademos to argue.

But instead, while looking at me, he retreated. Five deliberate slow steps. He made no move for the goblet, simply looking at me as if waiting.

There were no rapid heartbeats to accompany the thunderous panic I felt as Iademos obeyed. His eyes were glazed like a human's under thrall.

What?

"Go back to your post and forget what just happened," I stammered. *Is he really going to...*

Demos turned on his heel and went to the other side of the cavern, his spine straight as he assumed the practiced stance of a guard with his hands crossed behind his back. The glazed look left his eyes, but he said nothing.

My mind raced, trying to come up with an explanation, but there was only one possibility. Only one creature had dominion over vampires, only one power could make them obey with the same ease they commanded humans into blind obedience.

The scourge they feared, the way I had feared them ever since my mother died in front on me.

The necromancer.

A feral smile curled over my lips.

I was the necromancer Raphael had been hunting for centuries.

And I was going to tear his kingdom apart, one fanged monster at a time.

Acknowledgements

My favorite thing to write in a book is actually the acknowledgements section. I love getting to reflect on all the ways a book gets made and how many people are involved in bringing a story to life. This one is the first where I'm a little scared, because so many people have been involved in bringing this book together that it's inevitable I'll forget someone. So, if that someone is you, and you helped this book along, please know I'm grateful.

Now, in no particular order...

My critique group, who saw the first chapters and convinced me this wasn't atrocious: Ang, Jen, Jenn, Mel, T.K. (and double thanks to T.K. for nicknaming Daddy Raph because it always makes me smile).

Olivia (OliviaHelpsWriters) for all your developmental work. You really saw this book for what it was, and the book is so much stronger for it.

Lee (Ocean's Edge Editing) for your incredibly thorough copy edit.

Jenny (Owl Eyes Proofs & Edits) for not only proofreading this manuscript, but providing the most educational citations I've ever had for an edit.

Christian (CoversByChristian) for once again, knocking it out of the park with this gorgeous cover. Everyone does, in fact, judge a book by its cover and this is my favorite one you've made yet.

Aaricia (Malice and Mayhem Book Covers) for doing the gorgeous case design—I don't know how you made something as perfect as you did, but just, wow.

The entire FaRoFeb community for your support and input at various points in this process, and for being an all-around wonderful community.

My parents: As ever, I hope you don't actually read this book (but, Mom, I know sometimes you flip to the end to check...) You have always been my biggest supporters, and you're who I'm most excited to tell when good news comes in, and who I can go to with the bad.

My amazing ARC readers and street team members: Thank you for being the first to read this book in its finished form, and for spreading your love of Samara and Raphael to other readers

A BARGAIN SO BLOODY

My readers: Thank you so, so much for picking up this book. Whether this was your first introduction to my books (sorry about the cliff?) or you've been with me since the early days of Forsaken Mate, I'm glad you took a chance on this story.

I hope you enjoyed getting to know Samara, and I look forward to seeing you all at the end of A MAGIC SO DEADLY.

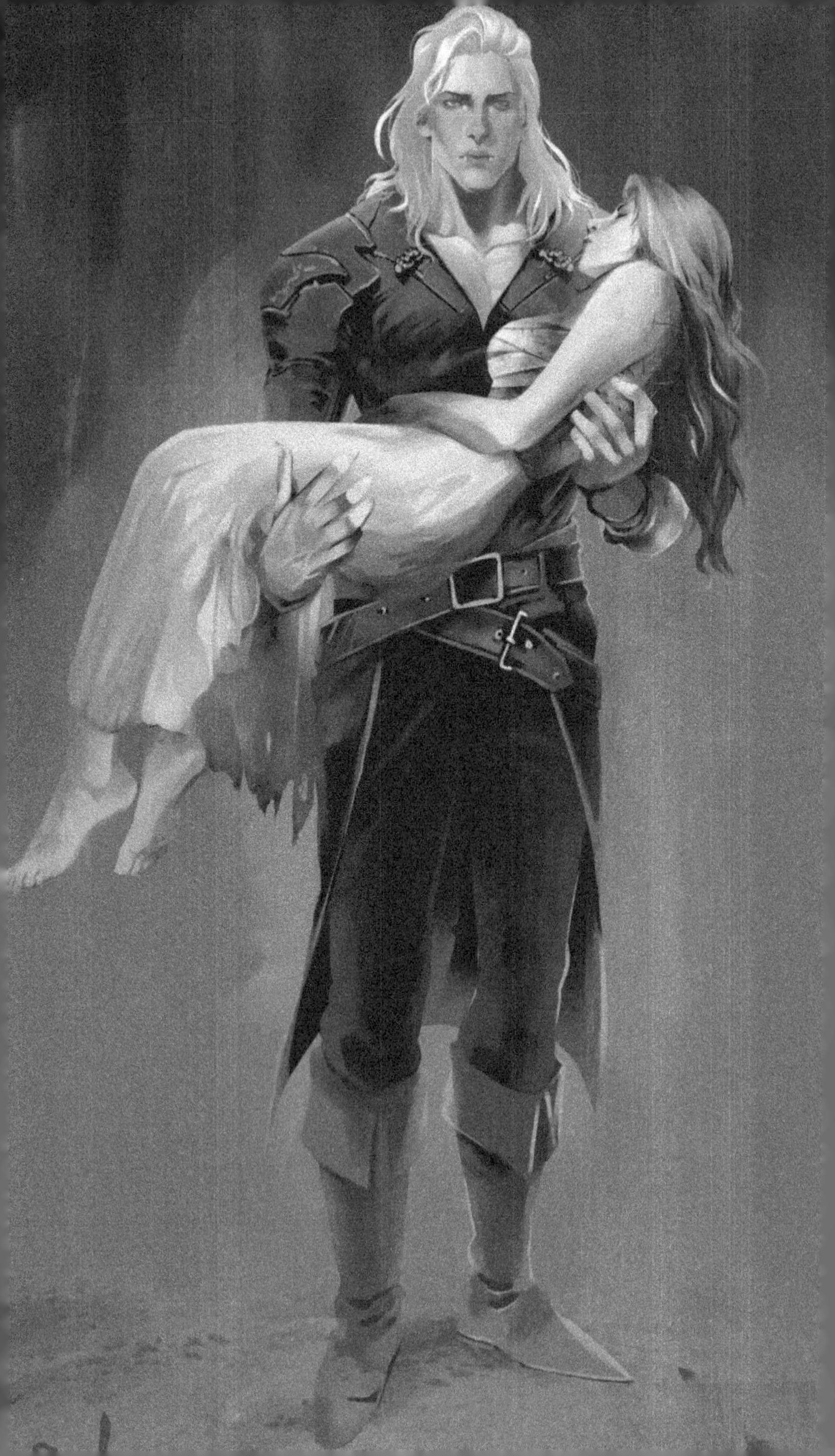

Key Character Guide

Amalthea (u-MAL-thee-uh)—Oracle witch, serves King Rapahel

Iademos (EE-aa-theh-oes)—Vampire general, serves King Raphael

King Raphael (RA-feye-ehl)—King of the Vampire Kingdom of the West, at least 600 years old

King Vaughn the Storm-Blooded (VAWN)—King of the Witch Kingdom, named for the powerful storms and thunder his magic can summon

Marcel the Bountiful (mahr-SEHL)—Firstborn son of King Vaughn and heir to the Witch Kingdom, beloved by the common people, named for the creation magic that allows him to multiply objects in his possession

VASILISA DRAKE

Queen Valentina (vahl-ehn-TEE-nu)—Wife of King Vaughn

Samara Koisemi (su-mahr-U KOY-seh-mee)—Protagonist

Selected Gods & Goddesses

Anagenni—mysterious Goddess of Death, revered by vampires

Askli—God of Healing

Dolor—Thorned God of Suffering

Isolde—Goddess of Night Skies, mother of the three moons (Caria, Phrygia, Lagina)

Lixa—Goddess of Luck

Thiox—God of Spoiled Food

Key Locations

Apante—the City of Answers, home of the Great Library and former capital of the Witch Kingdom

Condemned Cliffs—the mountain range that borders the eastern border of Eurobis; it is said these cliffs are haunted by a monster so neither human nor vampire ventures there

Damerel—capital of the Vampire Kingdom of the West

Eurobis—the name of the continent the Witch Kingdom is on

Great Library—the last remaining bastion containing oracle magic, home to a dedicated order of Librarians that serve the people of Eurobis; vampires are unable to enter

Greymere—prison for dangerous witches; within the gray walls, magic cannot be used, which is said to drive any witch inside its walls insane

Ulryne—new capital of the Witch Kingdom, where the royal family resides

Witch Kingdom—large kingdom in Eurobis where witches and voids reside

Vampire Kingdom(s)—kingdoms that border the Witch Kingdom ruled by vampires; little is known about them

Glossary

Aquamancer—a witch who controls the element of water

Black Grimoire—a mythical grimoire, lost to time

Card—enchanted paper that holds a witch's magic, about the size of one's palm

Caria—the walking moon, one of the three moons above Eurobis

Creation Magic—a specific type of magic that can create anything within certain limits; cannot be used to create enchanted items

Cursed Copper—an anti-vampire metal made by leaving copper out in the sun for 40 days with additional enchantments

Cursed Bronze—an alloy made from cursed copper, but more durable than cursed copper

Disguise Magic—one of the most commonly sought magics, enabling users to change aspects of their appearance; often used to follow fashion trends (i.e. lavender hair) or eliminate perceived imperfections

Grimoire—a book with concentrated magic, often passed between family lines with similar magic; while magic imbued into cards is temporary, magic in grimoires is semi-permanent

Kobold—a crafty, reptilian creature that lives in the woods; about three-fourths the size of a normal human

Lagina—the running moon, one of the three moons above Eurobis

Librarian—servant of the Great Library; known by their blue robes

Marshes—marshland in the north-west region of Eurobis; generally uninhabited by witches and voids

Monastery—sanctuary of witches and voids alike who renounce the use of magic and put their faith solely in the gods; individual branches are spread throughout the Witch Kingdom

Ogre—massive humanoid with tough skin; seen as lesser than witches

Oracle—a witch whose magic allows them to know the future; can be visions, sounds, prophecies, or other manifestations; also see: seer

Phrygia—the dancing moon, one of the three moons above Eurobis

Pilgrimage—the trip a member of the royal family goes on to receive their prophecy from the Great Library

Pyromancer—a witch who controls the element of fire

Seer—a witch whose magic allows them to know the future; can be visions, sounds, prophecies, or other manifestations; also see: oracle

Summoning Bell—enchanted item that, when rung, notifies the individual the bell is tied to

Thrall—vampire ability to compel non-magically protected humans to do their bidding; a human under long-term control would be called "a thrall"

Tithe—magic given in the form of a card every year to the regent of the Witch Kingdom, so they can continue to protect the realm

Vampire—blood-drinking immortal creature, known for their red eyes and white hair; unable to use traditional magic but may have additional abilities depending on their power level

Void—a human who cannot use magic

Witch—a human who can use magic, usually limited to one type; elemental witches are the most common

www.ingramcontent.com/pod-product-compliance
Lightning Source LLC
Chambersburg PA
CBHW031345021125
34857CB00006B/136